The G

Book One

Presto, the Queen's Alley Cat

By the Ghost of Presto

Copyright © 2020 by Presto

All rights reserved.

No part of this book may be reproduced without the permission of the author or the publisher. Cover Design by and Copyrighted by Gary Baloun Designs.

This is a work of fiction. Names, characters, places, events and incidents are either the products of the author's imagination or used in a fictitious manner. Any resemblance to actual persons, living or dead, or actual events is purely coincidental.

G

Dedicated to:

Millie   **Sherry**   **Rose**

Guardian Angel   "The Girl"   Kitty Muse

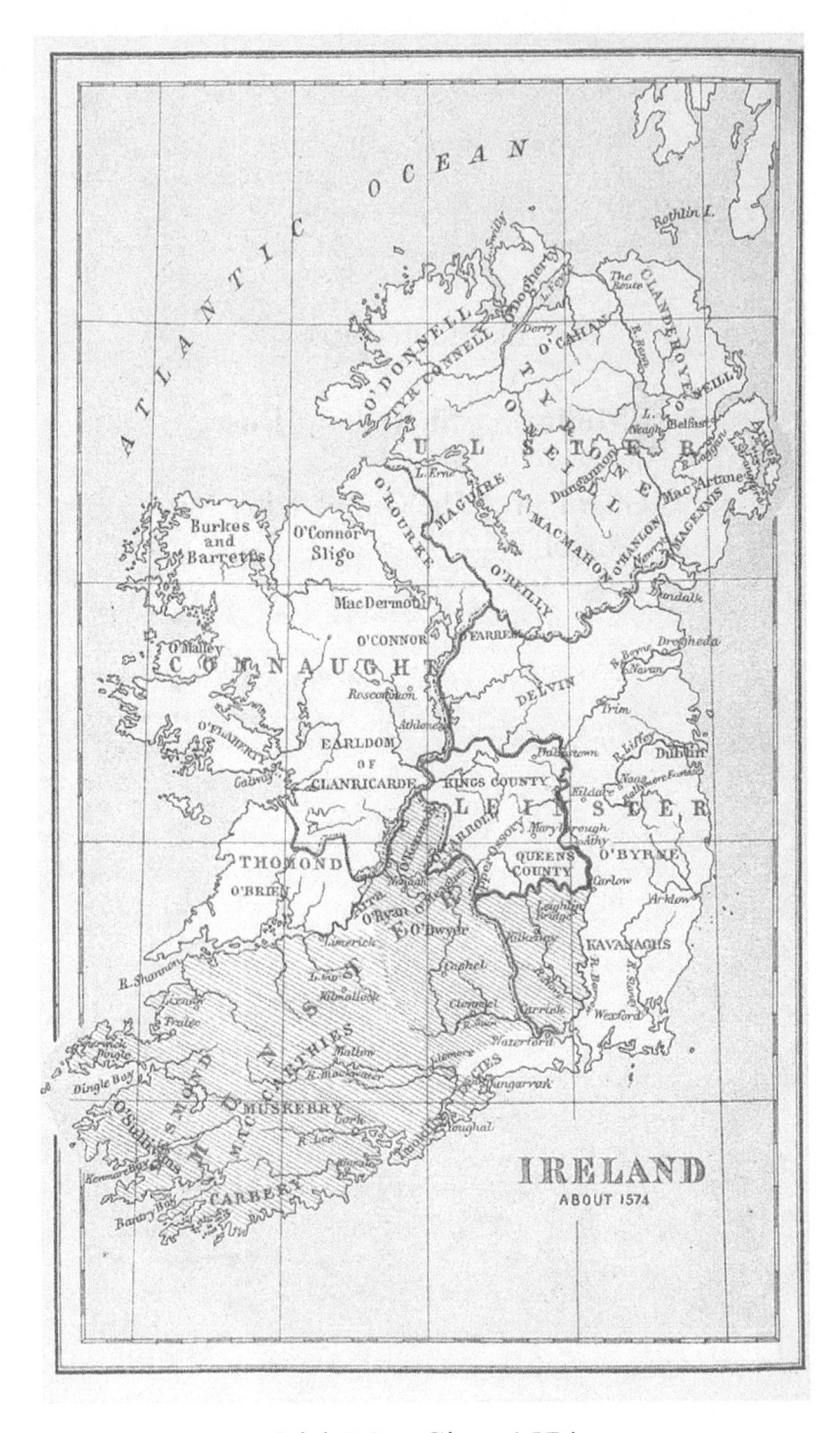

Irish Map Circa 1574

Contents

1	The Orphan	7
2	London	55
3	Fate	95
4	The Queen	127
5	Tea with Her Majesty	183
6	Prelude	239
7	The Armada	285
	Epilogue – Drake is Dead	359

Introduction and Author's Note

The time has come to tell you the tale of an Irish lad trying to survive on the streets of London a long, long, time ago. It is a story of my adventures that Fate laid out before me. As the tale unfolds, you will hopefully see what I saw, feel what I felt and learn what I learned. It is not always an easy story, but there is a bit of Irish humor along the way for mirth and courage.

I have written this tale as if I am reading or performing it for you. I have had to learn a whole new foreign language you still call English to write it. Your grammar is truly different from my time. We loved long sentences, often with repetitions, to make a point. I hope you don't mind if I don't always follow your norms. I will, for instance, always capitalize the word "Queen" out of respect for *my* Queen. I merely ask that you will indulge my diversity as you read my story.

I do hope you enjoy this tale. I hope you share it by telling others that it is a tale worth telling. I also humbly thank you for your kind review. And with that bit complete, it is time for me to begin this story.

You can also hear me perform this tale with the help of Finian Schwarz on your magical Audio Books.

Presto, the Queen's Alley Cat

Chapter 1 – The Orphan

Part 1 – The Library

My name is Presto. I am a ghost. Do not be alarmed or have pity for ghosts have many forms. We might be a guardian angel, a familiar or an imp. We could also be a lost soul or some other form that hasn't even been thought of or recognized yet. We remain ghosts for many reasons, whether for unfinished business, righting a wrong or wronging a right. It might be just to cause some mischief. We could be lost and not knowing the way or just not being ready to … move on. As I said, I am a ghost, well … mostly because I enjoy being a ghost and I've always enjoyed a good tale and mine is not yet finished.

The tale I am about to tell is not a ghost story, but rather one of living, and the adventures that Fate laid out before me. It is not, however, a gentle story. It is a tale of betrayal, soulless cruelty, and all the brutal inhumanity that goes with any era's sovereignties and religions at war. Yet through it all, it is still also a story of a belief in hope, the day-to-day good in humanity, the need for a bit of mirth to get by and the faith and realization that Fate will somehow make it all work out.

I am putting my story to quill and ink, or better now, the modern marvel of a keyboard scribe and a parchment that glows, because words have always been my friend. It is long time past that I tell my own true tale. I have seen another story with a character whose nickname is Presto and is set in my own time. He is brought to a fictitious life with intriguing writing and acting in a wonderful series called Will. Their story is about a young William Shakespeare coming to London for the first time to make his fortune. Will's fictionalized depiction of a historical period is, of course, nothing new. Many well-known poets, such as Shakespeare himself, have been doing it for centuries. The history told, however, may not be the history that was. You would have to be there to know.

One of Will's characters, Presto, was portrayed as a young cunning street rat trying to survive on the streets of London. I, on the other hand, survived these streets as a clever alley cat. In fact, my nickname *is* Alley Cat. Still, I saw much of my own spirit in Lukas Rolfe's talented acting as his Presto. I thought he wove their whole story together quite well. Of course, I would be a bit prejudiced deciding he was my favorite actor. I would, however, observe the differences from his depicted character. Will's Presto was a native of London and he had a sister. I, on the other hand, do not know of any family and only that I came from Ireland.

So I might as well start my tale, complete with taking the Irish liberty of many embellishments, in the beginning. Unfortunately, I don't have a beginning other than clearly, merely, being born. I am an Irish orphan having no idea who my folks were. I do not know exactly where or when I was born. I might be noble or common. I might even be a prince but more likely just another abandoned bastard. All and all it doesn't really matter, except that I couldn't become who I am, if Fate had not delivered me in this state.

I was raised by an elderly retired priest in the borough of Athy, Ireland in County Kildare. His name was Father McNee. He had been a priest during the Reformation, and as he used to put it, "We wouldn't be in this bloody mess if they had just listened to a few things Martin Luther had to say."

Almost forty years earlier, Henry VIII could not get the Pope's permission for a divorce. So he simply took over all the Catholic churches and their lands in England and Ireland to start his own Protestant church. Ultimately these lands were sold to English gentry who became the tenants' new landlords. He would not have dared do this if Luther had not started the Reformation in Europe. The younger Father McNee found himself out of a job, as he would not join this new Church. He had been rather well-to-do and helped his old small Irish parish as best he could. He even helped many with the new English landlords ever increasing rents.

He was able to rent his own old church's cottage where he kept his favorite passion, one of Ireland's finest private libraries. These marvelous books ranged from rare antiquities to contemporary ones fresh off the modern marvel of printing presses. As it was, the new Protestant Vicar Woolsey, like many, was a former Catholic priest who converted. He too was an avid book enthusiast, so they had actually gotten along fine. They both saw the similarities between the faiths rather than divisions and thought their Savior must be more than upset over all the hatred and bloodshed.

And so I found myself about to be raised in an extraordinary library. First, Father McNee, with his ever present sense of humor, gave me the name of Presto, because presto, poof, I had appeared from nowhere. Second, I was given the birthday March 17th, 1574. That was the year I was likely born. He chose the 17th of March because it was the feast day of our patron saint, The Patrick. It was an excellent day to have a birthday in Ireland, as there was always a little celebrating going on even if it wasn't for me. Our church in Rome had yet to recognize him as a Saint, but we Irish all knew better.

Of course, Father McNee couldn't wait to teach me to read. It was no accident he chose a Bible to use. In a twist of Fate's irony, the only way to accomplish this was with the English translated Tyndale Bible, which was strictly banned for Catholics. There was also a 300-year-old Catholic law that basically allowed only the clergy to read the bible in Latin. The clergy were to interpret it for the rest of us. Hmm ... so much for following rules. I enjoyed reading and learning and writing the words. It was never forced upon me. Eventually, I could even choose what books I wanted to read. Stories of knights and noble quests were always my favorite, even though the reality of rebellion and war was happening just a county or so away.

Time went on as Father McNee, now remarkably in his seventies, slowly lost his eyesight. He could no longer read his beloved books. He now had to sell them to pay his own rent and keep us fed. With his eyesight failing, I now read his remaining beloved books to him. This was all I could do to repay him for raising me, for being my only family and my mentor. For his lesson of teaching me to follow what my heart told me was right, rather than what I was told was right. The saddest day of my life was when he passed when I was twelve. He prepared me for this inevitable day by saying when it was time for him to "move on," he still would never be far away.

He said, "You only need look into your heart to see me." His only regret was that he would not have more time to raise me until I was old enough to take care of myself in an adult world. My inheritance was the now, fifty-year-old Tyndale Bible he had used to teach me, and a simple wooden rosary. He had given a family some money to take care of me. So I now found myself having to move out of the cottage and start a new life, somewhere…

Part 2 – Swansea

Somewhere started after laying Father McNee to rest during an otherwise bright October day in the year 1586. He had arranged for the Doyle family, from the parish near Athy, to provide a place for me to live. They also had two young children who, like most poor-Irish-tenant families, were undernourished and frail. I had been relatively well fed growing up, and did not know what hunger really felt like, though I knew of it all around. Father McNee had a few chickens so we always had baked eggs and he could make a good stew, though usually meatless. We also had a sweet kitty, Rose, who would bring a gift of a fresh mouse from time to time. McNee would always thank her and joke about making his next stew with it. No, he never used the mice, at least as far as I know …

Father McNee had given the family money to take care of me, but their landlord quickly demanded most of it for overdue rent. There was far less to eat, and I did not want to jeopardize their younger frail children. The winter was long and wet and in February we learned that Mary Queen of Scots had been executed for treason. This was a blow to the Catholics and would eliminate a rival Queen to Elizabeth should the Spanish ever successfully invade. The war with Spain had started two summers prior, and they were building a great Armada to bring death across the sea. No one knew where they would invade, whether England, Scotland, or even Ireland.

The Spanish would be no treat for the Irish Catholics. They would eventually bring another war to our land after a devastating rebellion had only recently ended. They would merely replace the English landlords with Spanish ones and bring their own tyranny and Inquisition with them. Father McNee feared what would follow and thought we would not be any better off after all the bloodshed that would come first.

The second of two short Irish rebellions in Munster had just ended several years earlier. The first had started and ended before I was born. The second started just as I was beginning to read. The Munster region was outside the "pale." The pale is the region of Ireland under full control of English rule. Well, kind of. It centered in Dublin and the surrounding counties including our own Kildare. Those areas not completely under English control were known as "outside the pale." Munster was outside the pale and is the southwestern area of Ireland only a county or so away.

The second rebellion was more horrific than the first. The Pope had assisted in this one with money, supplies and a small Vatican force to join several hundred from Spain. They were all massacred at D'un an 'Oir after their surrender. The executions, mostly by beheading, took several days. Only the Spanish noble officers had conveniently arranged to be spared. The supplies they brought were used to defeat the rebel Desmond and his army. Ultimately, his head was sent to the Queen in London.

As in any war, it was mostly the civilians who suffered. Many tenants and their families along with their and livestock were slain. Their crops were burned to bring terror, famine and scorched earth. Though most of these atrocities were by the English forces, Desmond's force could be equally cruel. The famine and even plague that followed left thousands upon thousands dead, and the cries of the Banshee filled the land. The English and Loyal Irish armies would pass through our county and we had the ever-present fear that one side or the other would bring scorched earth to us. There had also been many fleeing the terror passing through Kildare trying to find safety.

Spring arrived along with my birthday and I knew the family would not be able to take care of me for much longer. A Catholic merchant offered me an opportunity to learn a trade on the sea. He was a friend of a sea captain. He could get me a position on an English merchant ship out of Dublin as a cabin boy. This was not exactly my first choice as a vocation since I had more of a love and talent for books and words. There could be a danger of being attacked by Spanish warships. I also was not naïve as to what some of the duties might be for a young cabin boy. I especially wanted to avoid being disciplined and its feared "kissing the gunner's daughter."

I had become aware of such things as I always had questions about everything I saw and read around me. I probably drove Father McNee crazy with all my, 'what does this mean?' type of questions but he enjoyed teaching me. He also had a sense of humor and would occasionally set me up to see if I knew when he was kidding. One of his best was when I assisted him at a forbidden Catholic Mass as an altar attendant. Catholic priests were forbidden from holding Masses, eventually, even under threat of being executed as traitors in a most horrific way. This practice was carried out later in England from time to time where the population was now strongly Protestant. Almost everyone was still Catholic in Athy, so he would hold occasional Masses at the cottage, or sometimes the cemetery near the church. The vicar didn't mind.

Part of the Catholic Mass was said in traditional Latin. Fortunately, he had no desire to teach Latin to me. As a reformer, he thought the services should be done in native tongues, and there were far more useful things for me to learn. Just the same he decided to have some fun and teach me a few naughty expressions. One of them, in Latin, roughly translated meant, 'your breath smells like donkey dick.' This expression might have even been considered a compliment. Bathing and hygiene were not a pastime during the Elizabethan era, and people's breath was not always pleasant. At one of the services I was helping in, he inserted this Latin expression into one of the blessings. The entire small congregation responded with the usual, 'Amen.' He just looked at me with a twinkle in his eye to see if I would lose it, which of course I did.

I would eventually have to learn about adult things. I had figured out that babies were not delivered by mythical creatures. I knew they came from ever-bulging-pregnant mothers but had no idea how they managed to get them out. Agriculture was the main way of life in rural Ireland so, of course, there were farm animals. I had noticed the difference between boy and girl goats. One day, probably when I was eight, I simply asked why the girl goats had two assholes and were missing the boy parts. Father McNee almost choked laughing. After he regained his composure, he simply said he'd get back to me on that one. He never did.

The subject would not come up till later during questions about Confession. In the Catholic faith, people go to a priest, confess their sins and receive forgiveness provided they do penance for their remission. Part of main reason for the Reformation was the racket of charging money for the remission of sins and even included paying in advance for sins not yet committed but planned. These were known as indulgences. There were also two types of sins, venial and mortal. A venial sin not yet forgiven upon death would get you time in purgatory. A mortal sin not yet forgiven meant hell. As a child, there wasn't a whole lot to confess. There wasn't really anything I wanted to steal, and I wasn't comfortable telling lies. I found it was easier to leave out important parts of a truth rather than make something up.

There was also the problem of determining just what was sinful. Generally, if it was something that looked good, felt good, tasted good or even smelled good, it was probably sinful. This was true whether you were Catholic or Protestant. Priests listen to all kinds of sins, which is a relief to the penitent, but we often don't consider just what the priest has to go through. On the one hand, much of it is probably quite boring. On the other hand, some of it could be quite racy or so disgusting they probably wished they hadn't heard it. Eventually, it was time for me to ask about the boy-things that had come up and I was hoping it didn't involve those damned mortal sins. Not knowing where this was going to fit in, I finally worked up the nerve to ask questions about adult things.

He mused how fast time was slipping away and it was already time to discuss these things. He did not want to leave me as a naive boy in an adult world because, now in his seventies, he knew his time was long overdue. He explained everything from the proper use of adult pleasures to make babies during marriage, to all the sinful variations men came up with in the meantime. This answered the question of the tale of two assholes. Though he was being quite serious, I knew he also enjoyed a little humor to see if I would catch his tricks. Remembering his donkey dick breath gag, I did ask if he was kidding when he discussed oral activities. I finally understood what a prostitute was and learned that men didn't always prefer women. Worst yet was buggering, and to this he made it clear that young boys especially need be cautious of overly friendly men. He also told me to stay away from goats. That one took a moment to sink in. This was a lot more information than I was expecting and certainly explained a lot of things I did not understand even from the Bible. Sodom and Gomorrah certainly took on new meaning. I now knew what irked our Lord about Sodom, but to this day have never found out what Gomorrah did to piss Him off. Goats maybe?

So now it was time to be off as a cabin boy on a ship to Wales and at least I wasn't naïve as to some of its risks. I cut my hair short so I wouldn't look like a pretty-boy, plus it was a better way to control lice. Fortunately, most merchant ships spent as much time in port as at sea and I was assured my concerns shouldn't be a major fear. I had also read of many a heroic adventure at sea like those of Sir Francis Drake. I might someday even become a captain. Drake had started his career at sea when he was only ten years old. I swallowed my premonitions, and in any event, I knew I had to leave, and this was the only opportunity.

Master Barnett, the name of this merchant, had been paid what little money remained that the Doyle family had received to cover my expenses. He kept just a small portion for his service. We traveled to Dublin, which though only a county over from

Kildare, was the longest journey I had ever made. Dublin was also the largest city I had ever seen. I had read about it along with other great cities, including London. Soon I found myself on a trade ship bound for Swansea, Wales. I pretty much puked my guts out the entire journey and wondered if I ever would get used to the sea.

Swansea was a small Welsh port and was just beginning to develop a trade for coal. Barnett, knowing I had not fared well at sea, said there might be work at the coal dig. I naively joined him to find out there never was any intention for me to be a cabin boy. I was in fact being sold as a slave to work this coalfield along with other indentured-homeless-street urchins he had brought from Ireland over the past years.

Master Powell was the man in charge of the coaling operation. My introduction was short and to the point. I was introduced as a filthy-Catholic thief being indentured here for my crimes. My possessions were searched and they took my precious English Bible, which I was accused of stealing. My wooden rosary was thrown into the fireplace by Master Powell. Then I was turned over to their cruel taskmaster Crowley. I was dragged out to join five other Irish lads who had found themselves facing the same Fate. No one cared about orphaned-homeless boys who would otherwise be on the streets becoming thieves. It was a good way to get rid of us, especially if we were Irish Catholics. The law would not lift a finger to help us. The other lads were all older and some had survived for several years. They were all from the counties of Munster. They must have been around my age or younger when the second rebellion terrorized their homes. Any morality had been beaten out of them. Their only hopes were to get fed if they worked hard enough and not to be singled out for more beatings. The taskmaster Crowley was cruel and brutal. I was the youngest yet. The oldest boy, Robert, shook his head as he told me I wouldn't last a month. I was in shock because of my betrayal. I felt frightened to death and alone. I didn't even know how to think or what to do.

Our work was mostly to break up the coal dug out by the Welsh men who received minimal pay for extracting it. This would make it more marketable for loading and transport. I was still weak from the long winter and sick from the sea crossing, so my first tasks were mostly to bring water and supplies and clean up filth. We didn't get fed unless we worked. I did get as much as the other boys so as to let me recover enough strength. This was so they eventually could get their money's worth from my purchase. The other starving boys were ready to take all my food but a lad, Robert, shrewdly told them I would die within a week and then there wouldn't be any extra food.

He told, or ordered them, as he seemed to be the leader, "Better to only take about a third so he will last longer." He had them rotate each day as to who would get the extra share. He would be first, but only took a quarter. I didn't know if he was being shrewd, kind, or just not good at math.

We were kept in a hut well within the dig next to a ditch where water flowed. We worked every day and were not allowed to leave the grounds. We weren't locked up as there would be no place to go or escape to anyway. We were filthy-Catholic thieves in Protestant Wales. Even the townspeople would help track us down. Two vicious dogs were kept to guard the grounds and further intimidate us.

At least once a week, a drunken Crowley would come to our shed to dish out punishment for the poor lad he thought had underperformed or shown the slightest defiance or disrespect. He would usually drag one of us away to another shed. Sometimes, we would all be forced to watch this abuse and torture so as to try not to be the one chosen the following time. I was told I had been useless and lazy, and it should be my turn. I would be spared for another time only because I was still too weak.

By now I knew the only way to survive was to escape. I would talk to Robert from time to time as to whether anyone had ever escaped or served their time and been released. We all knew, however, we had been indentured illegally and none of us would ever be freed. He said he had heard of some who had tried to escape and all were brought back. He said the only way out he knew of was a grave they dug each time one of us died from illness or accident. He warned that they even had to be careful digging as to not dig into one of us. He laughed and said it was funny how hard they all worked for just another day of hell to avoid the earth that would be our final Fate. He offered to say a few kind words over me when my time came. His offer did not bring me any comfort. I told him I would rather die trying to escape or fighting than just waiting. He only looked at me, though with understanding, and told me never to say that aloud.

I had been there a month now, though it seemed an eternity. I had gained some strength back and it was once again time for a beating for the unlucky one. This time Crowley singled me out and told me he had been savoring this day since I had arrived. I had been in terror this day would finally come and had nowhere to run, let alone fight. I just stood there frozen and trembled.

Robert, who seemed to have gotten most of the worst beatings, stepped up and said, "He's still too sickly and weak." He went on, "Go ahead if you want to kill him, he'll be of no use to your master then."

He knew he had just volunteered for the worst beating ever and I thought him the bravest soul I had ever met. I remembered all the books I read about knights and heroes being brave and noble as I stood there cowering hopelessly. I was ashamed and looked away.

Crowley sneered at Robert and said, "Then you'll take his place!"

Then out of my mouth, I know not from where it came was one soft word, "wait."

"WHAT!" Crowley barked, "Did you mutter something, boy?"

Shaking, I said a little louder, "Wait." And turning to Robert, "I can't let you do this."

Crowley leered, "We'll see, I'm going to whip you so hard you'll beg me to put him back in your place. Then you're going to watch and help hold him." He grabbed my arm and started marching me out to the dreaded shed, signaling Robert to follow. Since I had more or less volunteered for this, I did not put up a struggle.

For far more than a millennium, children were often beaten by adults for discipline. There was a tenant farmer down the road from McNee's cottage whose father beat his children regularly. On some nights with the wind exactly right you could hear the screams. As a young child, hearing this for the first time I feared it was the lament and screams of a banshee coming to take someone. Surprisingly, Father McNee had never taken a belt to me. He had encouraged me to explore everything like a cat. When I crossed the mischievous line, as often I did, he would reel me back. Then he would always have something else up his sleeve to keep my interest. Punishment usually ended up being chores I would have had to do anyway.

So there I was in the hell-shed, where he kept tools along with belts and several whips. I knew my wrists would be tied overhead as I had already witnessed prior scenes in terror. The first taste of the whip across my ass was like a lightning bolt and I shrieked like a banshee. I did not feel a coward for my screams and tears though for the other boys had done the same. The pain was so intense I thought I could see and taste colors. I just kept screaming "NO" over and over. What Crowley really wanted to hear from me was begging him to stop and have Robert take my place.

Funny thing about pain though is that it changes. The expression "numb with pain" is somewhat true for after a while it seemed that I became more aware of its intensity than feeling it. When the pain became more than my mind could handle, I seemed to become completely detached from it. I seemed to drift outward from myself and watch the scene almost from above. I saw my terror and saw my screams but didn't really hear them or anything else Crowley was yelling. I stopped screaming and tried to hold on to that place like a lucid dream. Then I would crash back to reality and keep shrieking.

Years later I would read about these out-of-body experiences induced by pain that had even been written about in ancient Greek and Roman texts. Robert in the meantime was yelling something about, "You're killing him." He tried to step in front of me to stop the lashes. Foolishly, I then swung around trying to block him from the whip, and so we all danced this dance of terror and fury.

I opened my eyes and saw by the dim light I was back in our hut. The moonlight barely shown in through the open shutters, but I could see Robert sitting across the floor staring at me. Somewhere during that dance I had finally passed out.

I said, "I'm sorry he beat you too."

"You only made it worse, you should have just given in and begged," he replied.

Slowly sitting up, I said, "Aye, but we Irish are a stubborn lot. Thanks for your bravery to protect me."

He shook his head, "You were the last one I ever expected would stand up to him." We talked through that night and both knew the only way out was to escape. I ached but the light was to dim for me to see the full extent of my first whipping.

The morning light showed the black and blue welts and bruises he had left. He had been careful not to hit me in my face, probably to hide marks that could be seen too clearly. We went down to bring our dismal breakfast of old bread and some disgusting boiled half rotten turnips back to our shed, before being put to work. Today, no one took part of my portion. The workday was as miserable as any. Crowley gloated at me and just kept saying, "Wait till next time, boy!"

Three days later we were woken up by barking dogs and Crowley dragged us all out onto the grounds. Master Powell was standing waiting there, glaring. He looked like he was counting us but turned and walked away without a word. I didn't see Robert with us, and I was terrified. Then I saw him, lying on the ground, utterly still. I saw that he had been torn apart by the dogs.

Crowley yelled, "This is what I'll do to you if you try to escape, so go ahead and try anytime! I don't need to keep you locked up with a chain or door or gate because this is what will happen to you!" At saying this he released the two ferocious dogs and they tore into Robert's lifeless body again. I wanted to attack and kill him, but all I could do was throw up. He made us bury him, and then get ready for another day of hard work and misery.

Just we lads buried what was left of Robert in the ground where the rest of us would end up. Though unmarked, everyone knew where it was. I offered Catholic prayers just as I had when I helped Father McNee with some funerals and had even spoke at his. I realized it was only a matter of time before I would be joining Robert in this decaying earth. I had to escape not only for myself but now for Robert too.

Robert's murder, for that's what it was, had made escape far more crucial while also making it more possible. First, no one in their right mind would try to escape immediately after such a horrific killing. Second, I knew I had to evade the dogs that would be used to track me. I would need to wait until the next heavy storm night and use the rain to hide my tracks. I had been planning my escape from the first day I recovered from the shock of this cruel betrayal. They would all assume I would head back to port and try to hide on a ship bound back for Ireland. Where else could I possibly go?

… London!

Part 3 – The Storm

Vengeance is a dangerous thing. I had always been taught to seek justice rather than vengeance. We seldom spoke the next couple days, but we all knew we were thinking the same thing. We all wanted to kill Crowley and his cursed dogs. We used tools such as sledgehammers, picks and shovels, but one of us alone wouldn't be able to overpower him and the dogs. I think he realized this as he kept us separated rather than working us in pairs let alone a group.

I thought the best I could do by myself would be to kill one of the dogs. This would be vengeance, but it would result in my own death. In fact, if we did kill Crowley, we'd all hang. Hanging actually did sound better than the inevitable Fate we were living. At least we'd have our brief say in court, though it would do us no good. Vengeance was not the answer, and it would destroy any chance to escape.

Visions of Robert's grave took away our appetites. For the first time, some of the lads couldn't finish what little food we received. Nonetheless, I ate whatever surplus the other boys left. This stunned them, but I said I needed all my strength to survive. And I *was* going to survive. The lad, Thomas, seemed to understand what I meant.

And so I prayed. I prayed for Robert, and I prayed that Fate would bring heavy rains, the courage to escape, and of course, that I would succeed. And I prayed that if I did escape, I would somehow find justice for the other lads and their freedom.

It was now mid-May and I had survived here for just over a month. I prayed the rain would come before the next beating. There was no rain the first day, none the second, and none the third after Robert's murder. The following day, however, started out cloudy. By late morning, the wind had picked up and there was lightning to the west and south toward the bay. I had hoped for a nighttime storm so I would be aided by darkness. This rain might come in too early. The rain did finally come that afternoon and was heavy enough to stop all work. If the rain stopped by early evening, it would probably be an overdue beating night. As I knew I would be the one chosen, I knew I wouldn't have any strength left afterwards to try to escape.

It didn't stop raining. By dusk it was coming in at more than a gale force. I knew it was really time to prepare for my escape. I realized that if I failed, I was spending this day, as my last day alive. I thought how a month earlier I would have never had to consider such terrorizing thoughts. A month earlier I had not been heartlessly betrayed, or beaten, or seen the brutality of a killing, or learned to hate and now even wanted to kill. Had my heart turned that black so quickly? And how much darker would it become?

We were in the darkness of our hut with all the shutters closed to keep the rain out. Lightning still lit up the places through all the cracks. I had three pairs of clothes and a coat. They had not taken them from me since I needed them to work. I put my coat on over all three sets of clothes, with the most worn out one on last. I also still had a cloth bag they hadn't taken with what little else I had. I stowed the pieces of bread I saved in a rag. Thomas had actually given me a piece the day before. When he did, he was going to say something, but then just turned away. So this was all my worldly possessions.

The shed quaked and some of the shutters had come loose. We could also hear water rushing under us down the embankment to the ditch.

"We need to get out of here before this thing gets washed away!" I yelled, with panic in my voice as the shed creaked. The rest of the lads realized this too, and we grabbed our possessions and exited into the blinding cold rain. We headed for the hell-shed to seek shelter and there we found two other men gathering wood planks to take down to the big house.

"Our hut is being washed away!" I yelled over the wind as we entered.

"Grab these planks and start bringing them down to the big house. Be quick about it!" One of the men ordered.

Each of us grabbed a plank piled up alongside the building and worked our way toward the house. The big house, as it was called, was the building that was used to manage the coalfield. It was also the residence of the owner's man in charge, Master Powell. He was the one who paid the merchant Barnett to buy me and my Bible. He had complained that I was way too young and too small to be of any value. He wanted older lads he could get more work from. Barnett was trying to get more for me because he was also selling him the Bible that he claimed I had stolen.

Parts of the path to the house were now treacherous with water rushing across them. Thomas slipped and slid several feet down a slope and lost his plank. I abandoned my board halfway. The scene at the house was pure pandemonium. We had approached from the north and east end, but it was the south and west sides that were being battered. There were windows blown out and a large tree uprooted that had smashed into the building. Several men were trying to board up and secure the damage in the blinding wind and rain. Somewhere, over the howl of the gale, we could hear the crash of our hut giving way and crumbling down into the ditch.

We each arrived separately and were sent back for more planks. I had picked one up that had already been delivered and carried it around to the front. Crowley was there and had seen that we were showing up to help. "Keep getting more planks!" is all he yelled at me. For just a moment, I thought I might be able grab a hammer and sneak up on him in all the confusion.

A voice in my head, or more likely my heart, said, 'Escape. Vengeance will not serve you.' We were all split up now and no one was keeping track of anyone. This couldn't be more perfect for my escape. I perilously trudged my way back to the work shed again, where I had left my bag. I grabbed the whips and belts and threw them into the raging ditch. I worked my way back to the big house. I would have to pass by it to get to the road back toward the town.

The north side, which was not being battered by the full fury of the storm, was also the side with the kitchen. I had occasionally been sent there to haul garbage out, and I sneaked toward its door. No one was inside. I slipped in looking for food and found apples and turnips. I loaded my bag, and as I headed out, I spotted a small pair of polished boots. I recognized them. They belonged to the grandson or nephew of the noble that owned this coaling field. I had heard of this noble, Lord Stevens, and that he owned much land and several farms. He also had an estate where he lived nearby.

I had seen the boy who belonged to these boots dressed all prim and proper like a peacock. He was touring the grounds soon after I arrived. He was about my age. He was with a well-dressed man carrying a riding crop and was no doubt along as a guardian.

The boy saw me and exclaimed, "Oh, there's one of those criminal boys, I want to see it." He walked up to me. "Are you one of the criminals?"

"No," I rebuffed. "I have been enslaved and had all my possessions stolen when I was brought here and sold illegally to your master. The only criminals are the thieves here that robbed me and broke Her Majesty's laws." I retorted without my Irish accent. Father McNee had taught me to speak a proper English gentry language, thinking it would be well to know how to be a gentleman. All the books I had read had also helped.

Stunned by my response, his guardian raised his riding crop. "You insolent-filthy-little rat." I stood my ground as I had felt the anger burn inside me of being referred to as an "it" and now as a "rat".

"Does your Lord know how he is breaking the law? I shall have to call this to our Gracious Majesty the Queen's attention next time we have tea together." I have no idea where these words came from to reach my lips. Of course, it resulted in a good whack with the riding crop. The boy just laughed, and they went on their way.

So I stole his boots. I had been brought here and accused of being a thief, and now had become one. I quickly headed out giving wide birth to the house. I headed toward the wall and hedgerows that led to the entrance's gate. The wind howled like a banshee and I feared she was chasing me. It was unbearable to move headed into the wind and freezing rain. Carrying a bag, and now boots, made it all the more difficult. I made it to the wall and huddled against it to get out of the wind. I took off my shoes and socks and washed the mud and stones out of them with the rain. I then tried on *my* new boots and couldn't believe they fit better than my worn-out shoes.

I decided it would be shorter to follow the wall to the hedgerow rather than to the gate. It was a good choice, because there was an opening or path worn through where they came together. I was now on the route that would take me to the main road that could take me to Swansea to the south, or Gloucester to the north. My route was covered with water in every low spot. In a while, I made it to the main road. The junction was so flooded it looked like a lake. I could barely tell if this was the road where we turned when the merchant had brought me here.

I knew this road went to Gloucester because a traveler had asked us if he was on the right road when I made my first trip here an eternity ago. Father McNee had shown me English maps as well as Irish ones. I remember the strange unpronounceable town of Gloucester because it was just west of the headwaters of the Thames River. I knew if I found the Thames, I could find my way down it through other cities I remembered, like Oxford, all the way to London. He had trained in London and had told me about the grand Cathedrals, Westminster Abbey, the grand palaces like Whitehall, London Bridge and the Tower. He had showed me the geography of the Thames winding through it all.

Before heading north and east to an unknown new life, I needed to head back to Swansea to ensure my escape was complete. Though this was more trudging in the wind and rain in the wrong direction, I decided to stick to my plan despite its risk. I skirted around the edge of the flooded junction and headed south. Swansea seemed to be boarded up and deserted. The smell of the sea from the storm surges filled the town. I was looking for the shop that had served food and sold goods to my abductor when we first arrived off that cursed ship. He had been kind to me there right before he betrayed me.

The shop was boarded up and was being battered by the storm. I broke through a boarded rear window to get in away from the rain and wind. It was dark inside, but some of the boards covering the front windows had come loose and the lightning would give it a ghostly burst of light. I was looking for more supplies and found more apples. I ended up trading turnips for them to fill my bag. I also found a flask of ale and a small knife. I knew that holding onto the bag had been difficult, so I cut two small holes through the bottom corners to run a rope through to tie around me. I also cut some rope to use so I could hang it from my shoulders. I won't claim to have invented the knapsack, but I could now carry it on my back and free up my hands.

As I was quickly going about these tasks, a dazzling lightning strike lit up the room. I jumped out of my skin and knocked over a shelf before the thunderous boom could even shake the shop. I had seen the shadow of the banshee standing right behind me! She had finally caught up with me! But nothing happened since it was just a shadow from goods near the front of the shop. As I stood up and collected myself, I found a hat that must have came from the shelf I had dumped. I might as well grab that too and stuffed it in my bag.

Now it was time to leave a calling card for the dogs. I stripped off my outer worn out pants and left them in a corner. I then peed on them just for the dogs to find if they came hunting for me. I'm not sure that this was necessary, as I'd probably had already wet myself after that last lightning bolt. No way to tell after already being soaked in the rain for the last couple hours. I headed out with one more stop. I went out to the stormy treacherous docks. I left my outer shirt and one of my old shoes by a pier where they could be found, but not blown away by the gale. And now it was time to head north to freedom.

The wind was now at my back and made my treacherous travel less strenuous. I made it to the flooded area where the road split to freedom or back to hell. I stuck my other old shoe in the mud for the dogs to find, and temporarily skirted back around the flooding toward the big house. This fresh trail would hopefully help lead the dogs to Swansea. I then turned back to find one of the many spots where the path was flooded. This is where I would turn into the water and try to wade across the low spot to the side where the road came out to the north, and hopefully Gloucester.

I had no idea how deep the water would get. I had already waded through many places during the night that went up to my knees. I didn't go straight across as it was quickly up to my waist, so I stuck closer to its edge. Fortunately, it had no current to sweep me away. The rain and wind were still relentless. I eventually made it to a neck in the floodwaters that looked like it was the road going out. I was already exhausted when I started walking up the road.

I trudged on and on for what seemed hours, though I had no sense of time. The road was often covered with flowing water, and I had to find higher grounds to pass. It was very slow going and I had no idea how far I was traveling. Occasionally there would be another road connecting and I would have to guess which way to go. I decided to always stay on the larger of the choices. I turned back from one that seemed like it had gotten smaller and rugged. Gloucester was to the north and east, but I had no sense of direction. All I could do is trudge on and offer a few prayers of thanks that I had made it this far. I also asked for strength and guidance to continue.

There were occasional small clusters of buildings along the way, but they couldn't be called boroughs. No one was out, and the rain and wind kept coming. There had been small culverts and bridges along the way that went over rapidly flowing water. These probably all feed a river I felt I must have been following as the flow was always to the right. I finally came to a large bridge over the fierce and angry river. The bridge had an approach on each side with its main structure over the river. Both approaches now had water roaring under them too. I started to cross in awe of the power of these waters raging under my feet. The wind screamed like a banshee behind me.

As I crossed the main part of the bridge, I was horrified to see that the approach on the other side had been washed out. The supports holding it up had been kicked out from under. The top deck had rotated down as it crashed into the river and formed a dam with its planking. The only part that was still above the roaring water was the railing that was now lying horizontal, rather than sticking up vertically. Just below it, many of the planks of the decking were gone, and what was left of the structure was quaking back and forth. The only way to cross would be to climb out onto the railing that now laid flat and crawl across clutching it for dear life. If I couldn't hold on or the entire approach finally ripped free, I would be swept down the river never to be heard of again.

It was one thing to find the courage to try to escape knowing that I would be living my last day if I failed. I was now staring at my last possible minutes. This was a far more frightening reality. If I made it across, I would be free, for there would be no way Crowley and his dogs could follow. If I failed, I fretted how painful and quick it would be to drown, or be dashed against rocks, or impaled by all the debris soaring down the river. If I stayed, I would be trapped on this side of the river with no plan of how to evade Crowley if he tracked me here. As my mind struggled over what I was to do, I was already a quarter of the way across the railing. If the banshee wanted me, I had at least put up a good chase.

I inched across holding on for dear life. I kept my legs wrapped around the rail and crawled like I was climbing a horizontal wooden rope. The surviving planks of the deck under me would occasionally break free and the structure would quake even more. The rain and wind, as always, continued to rip at me. I was about three-fourths of the way now and there never was any way to turn back. Then the railing abruptly ended. The last portion of it had snapped off on the bank and stayed attached, sticking out from the land. There was no way to reach it. I would have to try to drop down to the decking's rotated edge and try to make it across by clutching what was left.

I said a prayer to guide me these last eight or so feet and not let the banshee take me after making it this far. I lowered myself down to the decking that was barely sticking up, and before I could get a good hold, I fell into the furious water. It spun me around like a rag doll and the rampant water slammed me into the shore. I climbed onto the embankment stunned and continuing my prayer and said, "That'll work!" I scrambled up the embankment to the road laughing and crying. I had done it. I was still alive. And I was free. I WAS FREE!

I ran up the road to a grove of trees and ducked in a ways to find the largest one I could. I huddled behind it to get out of the wind and it even gave some cover from the rain. I untied my bag that had somehow survived and laid it next to me. I was exhausted and spent. I started to offer a prayer of thanks and a prayer for Robert, but before I could I was fast asleep.

I woke with a jerk from a booming crash. I was disoriented and didn't know where I was or even who I was. As the haze in my head lifted, I realized that the dying bridge approach had finally broken free and had been swept down the screaming river and smashed to pieces. I wondered how long I had dozed off. The rain and wind were about the same and there was no sign of the dim light of dawn fighting its way through the storm. I had walked for what seemed like hours and had expected the dawn before now. Maybe there wouldn't be another dawn because the Lord had finally had enough of all the butchering in his name and was sending us a biblical storm.

I decided it was probably only ten or fifteen minutes since I had fallen asleep. I thought that if I had arrived here a few minutes later I would have been either trapped on the other side or would have just been swept down the unforgiving river. With that, I finally realized the banshee had not been chasing me, but rather, *Fate had been guiding me.*

I was filled with every possible emotion. I felt the rush from the exhilaration of victory. And I felt the fear of now starting a new life alone with only my bag of apples, a knife, a pair of boots, a flask of ale and a hat, all of which I had stolen this same day. I felt gratitude not only for escaping, but also for all the people that had been kind and helped me during my life. I felt anger at those who imprisoned us and thought our orphaned-Catholic lives were meaningless, as we had less worth than livestock. I felt hatred toward Crowley and tried to banish that emotion. I felt alone but then I remembered what Father McNee had told me. He said that

I only need to look in my heart and I would find him. And then I found the most important emotion of all, *Hope*. With that final emotion I finished those prayers of thanks I had started earlier.

I sat behind that great tree and took off my boots. It was time to eat something and finally sleep. I reached in the bag to find the hat and put it on to stop the rain from beating down on my head. I found the bread in the rag that was nothing more than mush and gobbled it down. Then I treated myself to an apple. I was freezing to the bone from hours of being wet in the cold rain and found the flask of ale. It helped warm my bones.

I still had no concept of how far I had traveled or what time it was. I had started soon after dusk and figured it had to be after midnight by the time I had gotten back from Swansea. I had trudged on and on without any idea of how many hours had passed. It was so slow working my way around the flooding that I doubted I could have gone more than a couple miles each hour. It still wasn't dawn, so I might have gone barely ten miles if I was lucky. I was grateful for the river that lay between me and Swansea. But my brain was as spent as my cold aching body, so it was time to sleep. And so I closed my eyes wondering what the new day would bring. I was asleep in an instant.

Part 4 – Wales

It was a sunlit-beautiful day full of the most enchanting colors. I was riding the most wondrous horse in all the world. She was silvery gray with black tips that seemed to make her shimmer in the light. She was no ordinary horse, for she was magical and could fly. She was magnificent when she unfurled her wings. We floated over the hedgerows as she galloped through the air. Sometimes she would zoom into the clouds which was wondrous, but she knew also scared me, a little. I would dig my nails in hard. She would laugh and tell me I wouldn't fall. Soon we zoomed around her cottage and all the other mythical creatures would come out to play. These were her family and friends. She wasn't my horse or pet, of course, I was more their pet than anything.

I had opened my eyes to a cloudy day with a bellowing breeze. I tried to linger in my dream, but it was rapidly fading away. 'Please stay just a little longer,' I wished. As the world of reality slowly returned, I realized that it had stopped raining and I remembered where I was. The dawn and light had returned, so the Lord had not taken them away. The storm had been epic, but it had not been biblical after all.

My clothes were still wet, and I finally took off my coat and the outer set and shook them out. Aching and cold, I stood up to get my bearings. I was well into the grove of trees and had to figure out which way was back to the road. I was hungry and also thirsty, but as that saying goes, 'Water, water everywhere but none to drink.' Or something like that. As I ate an apple, I tried to remember how many turns I had made coming into the forest and which side of the tree I had sought shelter. I heard the roar of the river, but it seemed to come from the wrong direction.

When I finished calculating the math in my head, I determined which direction would take me to where the forest would be closest to the road crossing the bridge. It was the same direction my gut had told me to go in the first place, without all the bother of figuring it out. I put my wet coat back on and headed through the grove and found clean water to drink along the way. As I got closer to the river, I heard voices. I crept to the edge of the grove undetected for a look. The river had swollen from the night before because I could not see the embankment I had climbed up victorious. The river was still cresting, and no doubt would flood far more. The roar I heard was not the river here, for it came from just up stream, apparently from a waterfall.

There were a couple men on the one side of the bridge talking to those across the water on the shore by the road. Several men and a boy were on this side, probably having come down to cross. I wanted desperately to talk to them and try to learn where I was and which way to go but decided there was just one way to go now anyway. I did not want any word getting back that a lost boy was seen by the bridge. I was still too close to Swansea.

I knew I would have to come up with a new name and identity as an Irish-Catholic orphan was not likely to fare well in this land. I had created many characters in my imagination when I was a child. Yes, I know I still was a child, but Fate had decided I had no time to be one now. In my long trek through the night in the rain, wind and lightning while trying not to be swept away in every flow of water crossing my road, I had time to think. So when I wasn't too busy trying to run away from being killed by the banshee, I decided on a name. After all, it was just an average walk in the park so plenty of time to daydream.

My first name would be Robert in memory of the lad that despite having all his humanity taken from him, still tried to help and protect me. I, myself, had never had a first name before. I was always just, Presto. It wasn't a first name or a last. Most thought it was just my nickname. For my last name, I had made one up that had some humor to it. That name would be quite believable and would be Dumas – pronounced due-moss. It sounded very Dutch. The Dutch were quite popular with the English now as they were their Protestant allies. Her Majesty had signed a treaty with Dutch Rebels fighting Spain. It also could have been French sounding, and that would be okay too. This was the first time in centuries England was not at war with them, now being busy with the Spanish instead.

The humor of the name was how it might be mispronounced. Only a "dumb ass" would make up such a name. So in the morning, still giddy with my escape, I decided to go ahead and use it. I would also have to say where I came from and make up some story as to why I was traveling alone. This story would have to change as I worked my way to Gloucester. Ultimately, I would be from London, the only city in this country I had studied and read about.

I found the road and started out again. There were many parts covered with water. I sighed, 'No dry boots today.' I appreciated more than ever that I would not have made it without these boots. The first people I met on the road were a family with a cart. I excitedly told them that the bridge was washed out and asked if there was another way across to the town. I told them I had been separated from my master who had told me to wait for the storm to end before following. I was dressed properly with decent cloths, a hat, and once again, those life-saving boots. I also spoke carefully without my Irish accent. They would have never dreamed I was an orphan from Ireland that had just escaped slavery!

The ensuing conversation yielded a wealth of information. I soon learned the name of the town on the other side of the river and the one I was headed for by acting a bit dull and confused. I found out the bridge that was washed out went over a different river but joined the river I had been following. The river I was following was the Neath and most of the towns were on the other side. In the storm, I had unknowingly passed a road that went over another bridge to the old Roman town of Neath. I found out I could go up to the next town and cross the river there and then double back. I, of course, didn't need to do any of this, but I had acquired useful information that I could use with the next people I might pass.

The family was kind enough to give me a piece of bread. They decided to continue to assess the damage at the bridge. Armed with all this new knowledge and their kindness, I headed on still not knowing if the road would lead to Gloucester or how many days travel it would be. I'm afraid I don't remember all the names of the boroughs I would end up traveling through on my journey from Swansea. Most who travel aren't likely to remember the names of small towns they pass through after a couple years let alone, several hundred.

I knew I needed to find out which side of the river to follow at the town coming up. I had also developed my cover story. I was going to be an apprentice to a master who made boots in Gloucester. Someday I would make the finest in the land. I pondered what trade I would end up doing. Making boots sounded about as appealing as being a cabin boy. I would say I had come in from London by ship to Swansea, but that I had been separated from the man hired to take me during the storm. I made up a name for this man, but I haven't the slightest what it was, it now being so long ago.

To make up his name I would start with their first. I would roll through names of past kings like Richard, Edward, Henry, much like coming up with passwords for your bedeviled witchcraft devices. I must admit it is an amazement some of them can be used to run a printing press. I also marvel at the spell-checking scribe. However, I digress from my story that I am ghost writing. For a believable English last name just add "ton" to the end of something and it will sound quite proper. So we'll call the imaginary man who was to take me to Gloucester, Richard Somethington.

My road was empty, as word had probably gotten out that the bridge was washed away. I heard only a lone horseman galloping toward me and decided to hide in the trees to let him pass. I had enough information for now and did not want to make up different stories for each person I met. I worked my way to the next borough, crossed its bridge and found a shop similar to the one I broke into in Swansea.

The shop had several people getting supplies and all talking about the storm. This area rarely had any epic storms like this, especially this time of year. I looked around waiting politely to speak. The owner finally asked if he could help me, so I inquired if in the storm he had seen a stranger by the name of Richard. I related my story of being separated in the storm and was looking to find him as he was taking me to Gloucester. I related that he also had all the funds to take me there and I was afraid he might have been washed away at the bridge.

By now they were all interested in my tale and one commented that he may have left me and taken the money. The women with this man gave him a stern look not to frighten this poor boy. I replied, "I would rather a bad man robbed me than a good man drowned." I said it with heart because I didn't want anything bad to happen to him, forgetting for a moment that I had only just made him up.

All in the shop were stricken with sympathy for me like I was a sweet-innocent-lost kitten. I was wet and shivering and had lingered by their hearth. They were kind enough to let me take my coat off to dry near the fire. I told them my only hope was to work my way to Gloucester myself and hope I might find him along the way. They feared I would never be able to make such a journey, especially taking this route that would be mountainous, but I pressed on. I asked if they might have a scrap of parchment that I might write the town's names and junctions and which way to go. At first, they thought I meant that one of them write it down but were even more amazed that I could read and write and do it myself.

They gave me parchment and quill just to watch me write. I doubted that some of them could even read, as it was still rare in rural areas. They then broke into spirited arguments as to the best route in a way that was truly more befitting a group of Irish. I eventually wrote my directions with these variations to please all and to have valuable options. They gave me something to eat and had me stay by the fire to continue warming up. I was finally warm for the first time since the storm started. They asked how I was going to stay warm from the cold at night. The shopkeeper gave me an old flint and said that should help get me through for building a fire. The man who thought I might have been robbed even gave me a pence. So there was still kindness in the world mixed in with the bad I had previously endured. The horrific storm had probably helped remind everyone that there was good in all their hearts.

So I headed out with my map. I had found out that it would be at least a five-day march to Gloucester. I feared how I would survive for *five days* to get there. Then it occurred to me, I would have to survive many more days to get to London. And then what? Every day I would have to find food and shelter. I would have to find work or steal. Some of the work would probably not be wholesome. It occurred to me that I didn't know how to steal or hunt for that matter. Father McNee had not taught me either of these skills that would now, indeed, be handy to know.

As a child, and yes, I know I am still one, we had a cat. She was the sweetest companion and had kittens from time to time. She was my constant playmate and she had taught me like one of her kittens. I missed her and that made me sad to remember Father McNee and the cottage. At least the new tenants that moved into the cottage liked cats, especially since they killed rodents. They said they would take good care of her.

Rose was her name, and she taught me patients and to observe like a cat. I had carefully watched first the family on the road, and then the people in the shop. I tried to figure who might be the kinder, the tougher, the leader or the follower. I did also, however, try to see where they might keep a purse and who would be easier to snatch from. I felt ashamed that I was even thinking ahead of such inevitable things, especially since they had all been kind and helped me. I felt remorse at what I had done at the shop in Swansea and wondered if Crowley was after me.

I had heard the town's church bells and knew it was already after two. Had I been so exhausted I slept till around ten this morning? I now once again had a sense of time and direction and headed out on my new life with a new name. The roads from Swansea started coastal, but I could already see the gentle valleys ahead beyond Neath. I would head north and follow the east side of the river. I would watch for the town that would have the road to take me east around the mountains beyond the river's valley. I figured I would walk until dusk and try to find shelter.

The sun had finally decided to shine, and by eve, there was a magnificent sunset in the mountainous valley. It was a clear sky and the stars were already coming out along with a healthy moon. I had found shelter in an old ruin off the road up a hill to watch it all. The ruin had signs of ageless fires that must have been lit by many other travelers seeking shelter here. I debated whether I should light one too but decided not to draw attention to this spot or myself. I had thrown my blanket over my shoulders during my hike and it had finally dried out. As I laid down, I thought what a difference a day makes. It seemed like a lifetime ago that the last dusk had brought the freezing storm and my freedom. I again wondered if Crowley was hunting me. I doubted it because there would have been far more important tasks repairing damage from the storm. They all knew I was missing though, and I hoped the other boys were not being punished, at least more than usual.

I felt the cold of the night creeping into my bones and drank more of the ale to warm them. I would use the flask later to carry water though there were constant streams along the way for thirst. I would have to sleep like a cat with one eye open unlike the previous night when sheer exhaustion had taken over. There were new dangers now. I might be eaten by some wild animal. Who knows what creatures haunted these valleys and the mountains ahead. I knew there were fay (fairies) in Wales but did not know how numerous or dangerous they were. I did not know if they had wee people in this land, but I did know they had evil witches. Every sound around me made my heart beat harder.

There could also be thieves that might rob or even kill me for what little I had. All of this could make for very unpleasant dreams, but then I remembered two things. First, I had just survived the night before. Second, I remembered our kitty, Rose. She had survived and even raised kittens in the wild. She too had found kindness but knew how to be cautious. There was no sense worrying about what might or might not happen. Fate had guided me this far, and each time I had thought things out to plan as best I could. And the plan now was just to sleep.

I had slept lightly for a couple hours when I heard something approaching. The roofless ruin had several openings and I had positioned myself, so I had several escape routes. I also slept with my boots on just to be ready to run. I held onto the knife in my pocket without brandishing it. A man entered, and being surprised to see me asked, "Who are you, boy?"

"Well, who are you?" I replied. He stared puzzled at my direct response. "I guess we're just a couple of nobodies then seeking a place to rest from our travels. Welcome, Sir." I added during his pause.

He chuckled, "Well, Master Nobody, I think I'll build a fire to help keep us warm and keep mythical beasts from eating us. I understand they prefer young children like you."

"I suppose that depends on which one of us can run the fastest, I might have a slight advantage. But please, I think a fire would be just splendid," as I stood up.

This time he let out a bit more of a laugh and set the large bag down he had on his back. Once again, I realized I had not invented the knapsack, as it was secured about the same way I had improvised mine the night before.

"I'll see if there is any burnable wood left from all the previous visitor's fires." I offered.

"Splendid. I'll go see if I can find some decent branches," he said, while surveying the starlit ruin. "I'll just yell if I run across any big beasts."

After an awkward pause and not thinking of a response, I walked over to one of the previous burnt-out fires. He turned and headed out and I heard him in the underbrush. I listened like a cat to hear which way he had gone and when he would stop. He had left his bag and I thought I had heard him double back. I couldn't help but think he might be trying to watch me. Was he trying to see if I would go into his bag, or was he watching to see if I had anything valuable in mine that I might try to hide? He kept coming back part way and then go out again. I hadn't found any useful burnt wood, so I went out and found where he was piling twigs and small branches and finished hauling them in.

"Oh, I see you brought in what I gathered," he said returning with a large bundle, "very good." He then arranged a portion of the wood and started a fire with a flint rock. "Do you have anything to eat?"

I was hoping he had something, as I wanted to save what little I had for the long journey ahead. "I have a turnip," I said, this being my least favorite food to try to eat raw anyway.

"Well, I could add that to what I have and make a stew for us." He was already digging in his bag for a small pot. "I have some dried meat and some greens."

"Many thanks, as I dug into my bag for a turnip. He busied himself making up the stew. Deep down I just had the feeling he was a probably a thief. He was an older man and he looked about as weathered as his clothes. I felt that he had spent much of his life traveling from place to place. "Where are you headed to?"

"I have some business in Neath, where are you headed?" he answered.

"The bridge is washed out on the west side of the river. You'll have to stay on the east side. I'm headed to Gloucester."

"That's useful to know about the bridge. Why on earth would you be going to Gloucester? That's in bloody England."

"I'm going there to learn a trade, but I was separated from my master, Richard, the man taking me there. I haven't found him since the storm that washed out that bridge. I headed this way hoping to find him since he has all our funds. Some kind town's people gave me directions and fed me too, and even gave me a flint rock to start a fire. I didn't know if it would be safe to light one."

"Are you sure you didn't take it when they weren't looking?" he asked, surprising me with this reply.

"Of course not, I'm no thief!" I answered and then slipped in the question I wanted to ask but wouldn't otherwise dare. "How about you, are you a thief?

"No boy, I'm not a thief, just a traveler like you. Why would you ask?"

"Well, Sir, if I don't find work, I might have to learn to do some thieving to be able to eat. I'm not talking about thieving like the landlords do for profit, no, I'm talking just when there's no other way. I was hoping that if you had ever found yourself in that position, you might have, let's say, some advice."

"Well, well," as he let out a heartier laugh. "So you want to learn to be a thief? I'll admit I've taken a few things in my day, but you best be careful boy. They still cut your hands off if they catch you stealing in England."

"What do they do to you in Wales?"

"Well, they still cut your hands off, but they're more likely to actually do it in Gloucester. You best not be Catholic in that town either. They still hate them after that witch Bloody Queen Mary had their archbishop burned alive at the stake so many years ago. I still can't quite place your tongue, but you sound more English than anything." He was trying to figure me out as I was doing the same about him.

"We are now all united fighting her former husband, King Phillip of Spain." I replied. This answer didn't deny that I was or wasn't Catholic, but clearly indicated that I was loyal to the English crown. "We do not want his cursed Inquisition back in our land."

For those of you who do not follow English history from hundreds of years ago, I might try to give a brief summary of some fun facts. Bloody Queen Mary should not be confused with Mary Queen of Scots, who had only recently had her head lopped off a couple months earlier. There are so many Henrys and Edwards and Marys and even Elizabeths that it's hard to keep track. I'll try to give it a go.

When Henry the VIII died, his nine-year-old son Edward VI became King. During the Reformation, Henry had taken over the Catholic Churches and lands in England and Ireland and started stripping them of their glitter and gold. This also included destruction of Holy Irish Relics of our Saints, including the burning of the most precious of all, our Patrick's Staff, the Bachal Isu. All the Catholic Churches became Protestant Churches and Henry got himself excommunicated. Henry didn't change the religious services all that much, he mostly just plundered what he wanted, became its head, and stopped sending money to the Pope. He could now easily divorce or behead whichever wife he wanted.

His son, Edward, or more those that were his advisors in charge, changed the church's services to a reformed Protestant way of thinking. Edward died at age fifteen but had tried to have a Protestant girl his age, who wasn't even in the line of succession, succeed him. That only lasted nine days and the poor girl had her head lopped off a year later.

Parliament overthrew her because they decided that the blood rights of the order of succession had to be preserved. There were other reasons including powerful lords and the converted clergy who wanted to return to the Catholic faith. There was also the intrigue of replacing Edward's advisers. Henry's next heirs, or daughters, since there was only the one son, were Mary and Elizabeth. Each was from different marriages, but I'm not even going to attempt to describe that cluster fuck. Mary was crowned and she went about the business of restoring the Catholic Church in the most horrific ways. She married Phillip II, who became King of Spain, the very one we are now at war with. She had hundreds of Protestants burned at the stake, creating a hatred and mistrust of Catholics that would haunt English, Irish, and yes, even eventually the Americas' history for hundreds of years.

Mary died after only a few years without an heir. Elizabeth, who was raised Protestant and now imprisoned, would become the next Queen after this horrific reign of Bloody Queen Mary. This is not to say Henry's reign wasn't horrific, it was. It is ironic that Elizabeth would eventually become Queen, since Henry VIII had lopped off her mother's head, Anne Boleyn. This because, basically, there was some adultery, treason, and she didn't give him a son. So now the pendulum would swing back to Protestant rule. The Pope would have none of it, so he declared Elizabeth illegitimate and a heretic and had her excommunicated.

In keeping with the tradition of lopping off the head of the mother of the next monarch, Queen Elizabeth had just succeeded in doing the same with Mary Queen of Scots, her cousin. Elizabeth still had no heir and Mary Queen of Scots would have technically been next in the order of succession. That made Mary's son James, and there will be many James to follow and try to keep track of later, the next heir to the throne. Elizabeth would confirm James as her heir on her death bed. James will have as an incredible reign as Elizabeth, and is, of course, known for the King James Bible. His son, Charles, didn't do as well. He had his head lopped off by Oliver Cromwell.

But I digress, and it will be many printing press ink cartridges from now before we get back to all that. Let us just leave it at Elizabeth has now been Queen for almost thirty years. There had been rebellions in England, Scotland and Ireland to put down. The two Irish rebellions in Munster were only recently ended and she is now at war with Spain. Spain and the Pope want the English and Irish Catholics to overthrow her and there is no heir to her thrown. She is also a Queen, a woman, in a man's world. Everyone is terrified of what war lies ahead and hatreds have been festering for decades. And so I found it was just a lovely time to be a thirteen-year orphan, alone, with only a bag of apples looking to find a new life like so many others.

I think we left off with the making of stew and basically wondering if either of us was likely to rob or slit each other's throat during the night. After eating his attempted stew, I really didn't care. However, it was going to be a long journey and I would stoop to eating things in the months ahead that would make this stew look like it were fit for a king. We spoke more through the night and he did give me some pointers on thieving without being noticed, which is the key to not being caught. He also shook his head and said my sharp tongue was going to get me in a lot of trouble. There are no truer words than those.

The morning came and we were both still quite alive. He went off to throw a line in and caught a fish we had for breakfast. I realized that I needed to procure a hook and line as I had done fishing for our dinner when I was a kid. Yes, once again, I know I'm still only a kid. Instead of robbing me, as I had feared, he gave me a hook and some line to help me on my journey. I was beginning to think that maybe there was still more good than bad in the world despite its appetite for wars. We parted our separate ways and I ventured into the mountains that lay ahead.

The route did not take me directly to Gloucester. It followed the Neath river north through a somewhat mountainous valley until it hit the real mountains. This is where I had spent the previous night. Here I would leave the river and skirt east around the mountain to the first major village. I would score an occasional piece of bread along the way after telling my tale of woe and looking like an adorable kitten.

The stretch ahead was sparsely populated along the foothills of the mountain valley. The going was slow because I had to dedicate time to finding something to eat other than my dwindling supply of apples. The apples had been buffeted around and bruised during my trek through the storm and were starting to spoil. Fishing took an extraordinary amount of time for one had to first find bait, and then wait for the fish. Fortunately, I had stolen that knife earlier and could use it to clean them with. I had the flint to start a fire but cooking them was another matter. The only way was to put them on a stick over the fire and, of course, the stick would burn too.

The first real village I came to was Meythyr Tydfil. The town had been named after some ancient Martyr, hence the Welsh Meythyr part of the name. They asked how I was surviving. I told them I fished along the way, but needed a better way of cooking them. As incredible luck would have it, this village, in the middle of nowhere, had a small iron works. I scored a short metal rod to skewer them with and they gave me a fork. I inquired if my imaginary Master Richard had been through looking for me. Their answer told me that there was no sign of Crowley. I wondered if he had followed my trail back to Swansea and if by now, hopefully just wished I might have drowned.

I remember I found shelter with permission in a barn. It was cold without a fire, but I was safe and had even been fed. I thanked the people and headed out for the next long stretch. I headed for the town of Abergavenny that was on the frontier with England. It was a long-full-day march. The next morning I would cross into England from Wales, though the Welsh were under English rule. Ireland was also under English rule, not that we ever took that very seriously as several hundred more years of rebellions would prove. From here, my road would bow southeast until it finally swung back north to Ros-on-Wye. This was another two-day hike.

Part 5 – Captain Robert

Ros-on-Wye was the crossroad to finally head east on the last leg to Gloucester. My map would run out and I would have to get new directions to find the Thames and head to Oxford and then London. This road to Gloucester had more travelers on it. It not only had come from the south, but also from the west coast of Wales. I assumed that north would lead to Scotland. I continued to avoid men galloping by on horseback just to be on the safe side. Still, I was fairly certain no one was after me. It had actually been a beautiful trek, as the part of Ireland I was from did not have the same impressive valleys and mountains. I still missed Ireland and the way the light made hundreds of shades of green sparkle like emeralds.

After better than half a cloudy day on this road, I heard horses and the rumble of a wagon coming up at more than a casual pace. Once again, I slipped off the road to hide and then watch who passed by.

"COME OUT OF THERE, BOY!" a voice boomed. They had stopped. They had seen me! There were two men on horses and one driving a two-wheel cart drawn by a single horse. They carried swords and pistols and looked like soldiers.

I stepped out to the road holding my puny knife at my side. "You'll find that I have nothing worth stealing, I've already been robbed," I quickly responded.

"We're no thieves, boy. We are soldiers of the Queen," the man retorted.

"Well, we are tax collectors," said the other man on horse with a bit of a grin. "Some would consider us thieves."

The first man glared at him with a 'you're not helping' look.

He then turned to me, "What's your name, boy?"

"Robert, Robert Dumas, Sir." The second man's face lit up with a new grin upon catching the mirth of mispronouncing my name. "I'm trying to get back to London." And I slid my knife noticeably back in my pocket.

"London? You're a long way from London." He replied with a puzzled look. "My name is Captain Robert, and these are my soldiers. What the devil are you doing out here? And try not to cut yourself with that thing."

"Sir, I was going with a friend of my Uncle's to Gloucester to become an apprentice and learn a trade. We were robbed last night just before we got to Gloucester. At first, I thought he knew the thieves, but then he yelled, "Run." I ran, and he ran off another way with everything we had. I went to Gloucester but couldn't find him anywhere. The only thing I could think to do was to go back to London."

"But this isn't the way to London, boy."

"Well I know that now. I asked for directions and was sent this way. It didn't look right, and I knew it must be wrong when I finally saw the sun come out. So now I'm trying to find my way back. Is there nothing but liars and thieves in that cursed town?" I said angrily but quickly added, "Sir."

They all shook their heads and had the what-a-dumbass look on their faces. "If you're from London, why would you have to go to all the way to Gloucester to become an apprentice and of what?" Captain Robert went on.

"My uncle has been raising me with the help of a benefactor. He said my benefactor had died and now he had to move. He made contacts for me to stay in Gloucester to have me live here and learn how to make boots. I would rather learn to be a soldier, Sir, and maybe become a knight someday. A man that had worked for him is the one that was taking me here."

I didn't actually want to become a soldier. I knew well enough of the horrors of the rebellions in Munster. I still had visions of Robert's mutilated body from his only battle. I couldn't fathom what it would be like on a battlefield where there might be hundreds if not thousands of butchered dead and screaming-dying men. Some would be your friends, some would be your enemy but all would have faces. War was close and personal because you saw the person you had to hack to pieces or blow apart with a gun, let alone a cannon. Then there was the worst part of all, the slaughter of the civilians. How could one's mind or soul ever be the same?

"So you want to be a knight, boy? What was the name of this benefactor?" he continued.

"I don't know, I was never told, Sir. I couldn't even go to his funeral."

"He must be some nobles or someone with wealth's bastard son," said Robert's companion.

"I know what a bastard is, Sir," I replied looking down at my feet. I was about to do the sad kitten look but decided that wouldn't do as well with soldiers. I then turned to the Captain, "May I ask you Sir, which way are you headed?" I asked respectfully.

"We are headed to Gloucester and then on to Oxford. Why?"

I decided it was time to make a bold move. "Sir, may I please tag along so I don't get lost or robbed again? I can do work for you. I could feed your horses as long as they don't bite. You also said you were tax collectors and I'm very good at numbers in case you need help there," I implored.

"Horses don't bite," his companion replied.

"I was chased and bit by one when I was a boy, Sir."

"You're still a boy," Captain Robert replied. "And we're not tax collectors. We determine if the taxes collected are all being sent to Her Majesty and not kept by corrupt magistrates. You wouldn't understand the complexity of how we do numbers."

"Try me, Sir," I challenged.

He put his head down with an impatient sigh. "Okay, if someone is to pay a one third tax on 250 pounds, what does he owe, boy?"

"Well, Sir. A third of 210 would be 70, and another third of the 40 left would be another 13 and then what's left is a third of 1, so that would be 83 pounds and some shillings. Sir."

"He's got you on that one," his companion said with a laugh.

They all stared at me with a somewhat bewildered look. "Very well, get on the cart. We'll take you at least to Gloucester. And if my horse doesn't eat you, maybe we'll let you tag along the rest of the way," replied Captain Robert, but this time with a bit of a softer face.

His companion broke in, "My name is John since my Captain hasn't seen fit to introduce us. And that "gentleman" you will be riding with is Craig. He's Scottish and I'd worry more about him eating you than our horses. Don't get between him and a chicken when it's mealtime."

"Nah, he's too scrawny," Craig laughed. "I won't eat you boy, didn't they feed you in London?"

"We also call him Stinky, but you'll figure that out soon enough with his next fart," John added.

Craig, who was rather rotund, responded with a gesture back and proclaimed. "Best in the land!"

I climbed up on the cart with Craig, the man driving its horse. Had I just managed to get a ride to Gloucester and maybe

Oxford? And if I played my cards right, even get fed? Was I that clever or was it just dumb luck? Or maybe it was Fate who had brought me to the right place in the road at the right time to follow wherever she was leading me? In any case, this was now a very risky cat and mouse game I was playing. I would be traveling with the Queen's soldiers, and they were bound to ask me more questions, especially about London.

On my long trek thus far I had time to develop my story that I was now actually implementing. My acting had worked thus far making them believe that I was the bastard son of someone of wealth who had secretly made sure I was taken care of and educated. Strangely, part of it was true. I was probably a bastard, but it never really bothered me for Fate had taken good care of me. Well, except for that bump in the road called Swansea.

It was a short trip riding to Gloucester compared to hiking. I soon discovered what John had warned me about when Craig's body would start to gyrate, and he would let out a bit of a giggle. The aroma that followed was definitely not the best in the land. I heard Captain Robert and John discussing finding a Molly again when they got to town. I also heard John ask what they were going to do with the rug rat after they find her. It soon occurred to me that they were talking about finding a "Lady" to spend the night with. It appears that Gloucester was large enough for not only a Cathedral, but also a brothel. This was getting more interesting by the minute ...

"Sounds like you're going to have some fun with the ladies tonight?" I asked Craig with a grin.

"What would you know about whores, ever had one?" he responded waiting to see how I would react.

"Well of course not, but my uncle would take me along to keep an eye out when he snuck out to see one. I've heard they do rather interesting things with their mouths," I replied.

He started laughing so hard that the other two stopped to turn around. "The boy wants to know if Molly can suck his cock when we find her!" he bellowed.

The other two exploded with laughter and I tried to interrupt by saying, "I never said that! I just said, oh never mind," and started to laugh with them.

"Well, maybe we should let her!" John roared. The thought did give me some rise of excitement, literally, until it occurred to me, I would not be the first in line. This change of heart corresponded directly to another gyration from the driver next to me. So on we road and finally reached Gloucester.

Captain Robert took us to an inn where we all had something to eat. It appeared he was going to feed me along the way. It would be fish again, and I don't want that to sound like a complaint. I remember it was trout, and it is still the best I ever ate. Robert had taken two rooms, one for himself, and one for the rest of us. Our room was also going to be used when it was each of their turns alone with Molly.

Robert was alone in our room when Molly, or whoever the girl really was, arrived. Later, he came back to his room where we were all playing cards and I had my first taste of beer. He said he thought Molly needed company next door. They each went back and forth to the other room. The walls were rather thin, and I heard many sounds that I was unaware people could make. They all laughed at the expressions on my confused face. The girl's sounds were much longer and enthusiastic, but each of the men would also make some robust sounds. I certainly had never heard anything like that back home in the borough of Athy. And no, I did not get a turn. I finally returned to our room with John and Craig. Fortunately, I got to slept on the floor.

We did not get up early the next morning for breakfast to get on the road to Oxford. Molly had stayed over next door and came out to say goodbye to the rest of us. She then asked, "Is this the stray you found along the road? He's adorable! You should have sent him over." I thought I couldn't blush any harder until she reached down and grabbed and squeezed. I had already had a restless night with haunting dreams, and I froze there, rigid. She squeezed a little harder and smiled saying, "This one's going to be trouble ..."

We were on the road again and I sat on the other side of the cart this time, which would be upwind. "Figuring out the wind direction, are yah?" Craig stated with a couple of laughs. "Hope we didn't keep you up last night."

"Time to go," Robert ordered. He had asked me the name of the man who I had come with and made some inquires whether anyone had seen him. He had done this while he made arrangements for their lady of the evening at the inn. I had given him the name Crowley and used his description. Obviously, he didn't find a trace of him. So the four of us set out again and I thanked them for taking me with them and feeding me.

"Next time we might even get you a lady," John said. We would take several more days to get to Oxford. We took a little longer, for they wanted to get in some fishing along the way. John did give me some ledgers to add up, so I did do them some good after all. To avoid more questioning conversations, I started telling stories. I told of legends of ancient Irish knights, and their myths that I made up from books I had read. I even told them a story about an ancient Druid Prince. They enjoyed this unexpected entertainment, as I always was a good storyteller, as I hope I am doing now. They also gave me details of a major victory against Spain that had occurred in April while I was imprisoned. I pretended to know a little about it since I was supposed to have come from London. Sir Francis Drake had destroyed part of the Spanish fleet at Cadiz near the southern tip of Spain. This would set back the planned invasion of England with the Spanish Armada for quite some time.

We arrived in Oxford on a Saturday night and stayed at an inn by a glorious Cathedral. Robert had asked me what church I went to in London, but I told him my uncle wasn't a religious man and we only went occasionally if it involved visiting clients. I had told him my uncle wrote contracts. I did tell him, however, that I had read the old Tyndale Bible. He had decided he and his men would attend church the next morning. He had also decided I would too.

Back home, the Vicar Woolsey would often visit Father McNee at the cottage and, of course, they discussed religion. It was Woolsey who had given McNee the English Bible when I ended up on his doorstep. There were many contentious differences between Protestant and Catholic teachings. Even Holy Communion was in dispute. He asked what the boy, me, was supposed to do if I couldn't receive Communion at a Catholic service. Father McNee finally decided that a Protestant Communion would be better than none, and would say, "I suppose it's the next best thing." It would in fact be heresy for a Catholic to receive this next best thing and be grounds for excommunication.

One could be excommunicated for many things. These ranged from reading the English Bible to expressing loyalty to the Queen. There were an equal number of things one could be convicted for treason too. This basically left Catholics with the choice of eternal damnation and maybe being burned at the stake or being hacked to pieces on the executioner's block for treason. All this nonsense just to be able to walk into a church to hang out with the Lord, offer some prayers of thanks, offer some prayers for forgiveness, and offer some prayers of need.

I had cleaned my clothes during the previous fishing expedition and my decent set was acceptable for church. The Cathedral was magnificent. With its towers and spire, it was the tallest building I had ever seen. The stained-glass windows had survived the Reformation, and though the Church had been stripped of its glitter and gold, it was beautiful. The nobles and the wealthy had their seats toward the front. The peasants like me would stand in the rear. This hierarchy remained the same with the Protestant takeover.

Captain Robert Barrington was somebody. He brought his men and surprisingly me to the somebody section. His men had also brought decent clothes along and we all had laughed how well we had cleaned up from our road trip. We weren't with the nobles who wore clothes so fine that I had never seen the likes of before. I spent more time with my own prayers and looking in awe at the morning sun dancing through the stained-glass, then paying attention to the service. I do remember it did not have any Catholic bashing, as it had apparently been a quiet week.

I did receive Communion and low and behold, the pillars did not shake, and no lightning bolt shattered the stained-glass windows to strike me dead. This was a relief because I wouldn't have wanted such magnificent-glass artwork destroyed on my account. I simply left with a feeling of hope and thanks, which at the end of the day, I believe is the whole point.

Robert had several days' business in Oxford before he would be heading south for his next investigation. He had me stay with them, and I had a couple more days of being fed. It also gave me the opportunity to explore a large city on my own. This could be invaluable knowledge for when I make it to London. *And I was going to make it to London!*

We had all bonded in an unexpected friendship. Robert had arranged for me to travel to the old city gates of London with another soldier who was returning home. I would not be following the Thames after all. It meandered like a snake to the south to Reading and then wiggled its way north and east again to London. I had told him I planned to follow the Thames from Oxford because I didn't know the other roads. Since I couldn't even find my way out of Gloucester without getting lost, he found a man to take me there directly. It would still be several days' travel.

Captain Robert also wrote an official permit allowing passage under his name should I be stopped for any unforeseen reason. Lastly, he supplied me with some dried meat and other food and then gave me a pouch with several shillings and pennies. I had managed to collect several pennies from other kind people along the way, but this was a fortune! Reviewing tax ledgers must have paid very well, although there just might have been some under the table negotiations for those needing a pardon. Her Majesty, however, would always receive what was due to the crown. I again thanked him and hoped there would be a day we might meet again. I was also ashamed that everything I had told him was a lie.

The soldier I was riding with was not overly impressed. He had been paid to take me and he was probably living day to day like me. We had one horse and that meant we had to ride together. Riding the cart earlier with a hard seat had left a few marks. Riding a warhorse where my legs were not designed to stretch wide enough over, was almost unbearable. I could barely walk afterwards. Robert had also given him coins to pay my expenses, so I didn't have to dig into my newfound fortune. We stopped at inns to eat but slept along the road with our blankets.

I had to plan as to what I would do when we finally arrived in London. As we got closer in the last evening's travel, I told him I needed to stop for the night and rest my aching legs. I knew he wanted to get home that night. I told him to go ahead and that I would be just fine. I thanked him for all his help, and he left, glad to be rid of me. We were both glad that he didn't have to deliver me to some imaginary place in London.

I did not want to enter London for the first time at night. I found a hill off the road to bed down. There was far more traffic on this road, and I did not want to be seen. My plan was to enter the city in the early morning. I would then take the day to determine where I might find a safe place to stay and find food. Finding work would come later. I also vowed that I would find some way, some day, to seek justice for the lads I left behind in Wales. First though, I needed to enter the city and survive the first day without getting robbed or discovered that I was an Irish Catholic orphan. I had an anxious night feeling how totally alone I was. The next morning, I would get up with the rising sun. Filled with excitement and fear, I bundled up in the cool air to try to find some sleep and hopefully peaceful dreams.

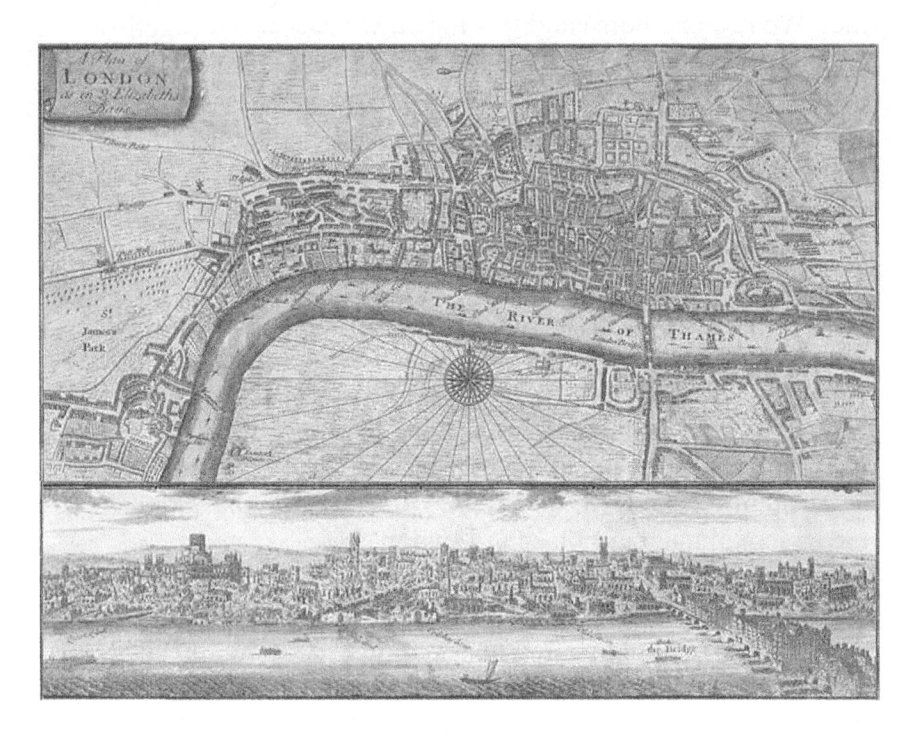

Elizabethan London

Chapter 2 – London

Part 1 – The Dream

I had a restless night and woke with the first rays of light from the sun being reborn for another day. This was the day I would begin a new life. I would be in a land with strangers I did not know in a world I had not seen. I did not know if I would ever return to my home or if I would even survive in this new life. I was being sent away by Aengus mac Nad Froich. He is the mighty King of Munster and has found that the Christian Triune God is indeed the Lord over all the Celtic deities. Unlike the High King Loegaire, who only grudgingly accepted Christianity, our Munster King has embraced this religion with true faith and passion.

I am Prince Enros, son of King Aengus. I am not that important prince who will someday become King. No, I am one of many younger sons, the prince that history would never remember. I am also the son of the Druid Priestess Darenia. She is of an ancient line that is said to have been born of a disobedient angel that broke forbidden laws and lay with a beautiful mortal girl. There is debate as to who indeed seduced who. As with many Irish tales, this one did not end well. Their daughter, however, had many children and seemed to have inherited a lust for life. Some of her daughters, and occasionally some of the daughters of the generations that followed, had inherited a magical sense.

Queen Eithne, whose eldest son will become king someday, claimed that my mother had bewitched the King Aengus into seduction and into also recognizing her as his wife. As I was the result of this seduction, the Queen's eyes burned with hatred every time she saw me. My mother and I stayed with another noble, but eventually she was sent away. She taught me of the Druid ways but did not have time to teach me to memorize many ancient spells that are nothing more than speaking in the tongue of the Celtic gods. How else would they ever understand what you are saying? It takes dozens of years to learn the Druid ways and enchantments as they are passed down only by tongue and memory.

You also had to have the-touch, an inner sense of the world just beyond the mortal veil. Only a very few of Darenia's female ancestors before her ever had this gift. She, however, indeed has this gift. My mother sees things that are yet to be. She had seen that the King would find and accept this Christian Triune God. That also means she had to know that I would be sent away to learn their ways.

I do not know if I will ever see her again, but I do have a sense that she is safe and somehow protecting me. I would visit the King and my many and ever-increasing number of half-brothers and half-sisters several times a year. I enjoyed these visits and had become close to a couple of these brothers, much to Queen Eithne's distain. Many of them had been baptized into this new religion, as had my father. The King had been baptized by their holiest priest, the man they called Patrick. Patrick had stabbed him in the foot with his sacred Bachal Isu during the ritual. I was concerned as I too, was to be baptized soon. I was relieved though, to learn that none of my baptized brothers or sisters endured the same.

And now I am to travel to live with and be taught by this very Patrick. There is that fear that this is the Queen's doing to get rid of me, including the possibility of having me killed along the way. I know, though, that it is the King's wish that sends me because he trusts this Christian God and wants me to share in his faith. I do not know much of this Patrick and just hope he is an honest man that will also be kind. A sense of humor wouldn't hurt either as I intend to ask many questions.

I will have to learn their magical symbols that they use to record the words of the religion of their God. These symbols they then set upon many leaves that make up what they call a book. I am to be able to read and learn this book of their magic and spells, which they call a Bible. I am even to speak it to others. I do not know what path Fate is leading me to. Fate always gives you a choice whether to follow her path. Will you follow bravery or cowardice, justice or vengeance, love or hatred, truth or deception? Sometime maybe foolishness is the correct choice. One's heart knows the answer if you are willing to listen.

The rapid gallop of a horse disturbed my sleep. I wondered who the devil would be in such a hurry at this hour of the morning. The sun had not yet peaked above the horizon, but the eastern sky toward London had that pinkish hazy glow that meant the new day coming was unstoppable. It was strange that of all the restless dreams to have, this one was the one to visit me the night before I started my own new life. I had first dreamed it soon after the very time Father McNee started to teach me to read. Prince Enros had become my favorite childhood hero and fantasy.

He had come to haunt me because, as all orphans, I wondered what my origins were. I seemed to always know I was an orphan but didn't fully realize just what that meant. All that was known of me was that I was left on the old parish's steps when I was just a babe. The vicar didn't know what to do with me. He had been trained as a Catholic priest, but the monastery had become Protestant by the time he was ordained. He had been married, had several grown children, and laid his wife to rest by the time I showed up on his doorstep. So he brought me to Father McNee to see if he had any ideas. He, of course, ended up keeping me just like a stray helpless kitten.

Father McNee did raise me as if his own, but I knew I was not of any of these people of Athy. With the Munster rebellion so close, there were of course, refugees and soldiers and especially many orphans. I was born between the two Munster rebellions and I realized I must be an orphan because no one knew of my parents. The best hope was that they once had time to be a loving family. They had however, vanished. And as I grew a little older, I realized their story would be painful to bear. My father could have been a tenant farmer who perished with his family from the famine that laid most of Munster barren. He could have been a soldier or a rebel. My mother could have been murdered, raped or have been a prostitute. The latter being the best of the choices. There was no happily-ever-after story, and they were gone.

So I was Prince Enros. I was eleven in my fantasy, and I was to be taught about our new Lord and Savior by Saint Patrick himself. I would fight for my King like a knight from the tales of King Arthur that I would read of later. Father McNee, surprisingly, did not dissuade me of these fantasies. He too realized there was no other happily-ever-after story to pursue. If I wanted to be this older, eleven-year-old Druid Prince that was to learn the Christian faith, well, that was just fine.

Father McNee was not only a good teacher, he was also an enchanting storyteller and Ireland had the best stories to tell. He encouraged me to tell him my own stories too. He was puzzled and sometimes concerned that I seemed to know more of the Druid ways and the conversion of this King Aengus of Munster than I possibly could. Sure I knew of Saint Patrick and of his bringing Christianity to Ireland. However, at about five or so, I was barely learning to read and how could I know of some of these things unless he had told me of them himself? Even he didn't know of the King's second wife Darenia, my imagined mother, until he happened to look it up and wondered how on earth I had come up with it.

As to Patrick stabbing the King Aengus in the foot during his baptism, it actually appears that had been accidental. Legend has it that the King thought it was part of the baptism and made no complaint. As he pointed this out to me, it occurred to him that he hadn't told me about the whole incident in the first place and where in heaven, did I know about it.

"Maybe you are this Druid Prince," he would muse, though we'd both have to ignore that it would then make me a 1,000-year-old baby. Eventually we would research the life of this Munster King together and, except for not finding any reference to the existence of my Prince Enros, my story was fairly factual. At least as factual as any Irish history goes ... I had hoped to someday travel to the Rock of Cashel to see where this all began. That pilgrimage would have to wait though, until the wounds of the Munster rebellions had started to heal.

And so I rose stretching like a cat, freshened myself in the cool air by a bubbling brook and started off on my way to London. The outskirts I had stopped at were still a good couple hour walk from London. I was on the road coming from the northwest and decided I would explore the city on the north side of the River Thames first. I could then cross London Bridge and explore the south side. I had acquired old parchment and would draw a map with a writing stick rather than quill and ink as I had none. And so I was off on my way.

Part 2 – The Tourist

I had two goals on my first day. One was to find where to get clean water to drink. I had learned in Oxford that the Thames was too filthy to drink from and that the city had wells and even fountains to find fresher water. As I only had the small stolen flask to carry water in, knowing these locations was crucial. The second task was to try to find a safe place near these sources of water, where I could take refuge and sleep at night. I had to carry and protect all my possessions with me including my bag. I hoped I did not have to travel a couple hours every night back to the safe outskirts to protect what little I had.

I would also have to find food. Captain Robert had given me several shillings, but they would scarcely last a month if I didn't find work. I would not use them to stay at an inn. I would use them strictly for food and for supplies needed to survive or help find work. I wondered if I would have to become a thief. I remembered what the traveler I had first met on the road told me, "Never steal on impulse. Study and follow your prey and make a plan." Just like a cat, I had thought. My hope though, was to find work and avoid thieving. I also realized that I could be that same prey as I had decent dress, a hat and those gentleman's boots which I had stolen what seemed an eternity ago. I at least did not enter the city looking like a hungry orphan from another land.

I wasn't worried about soldiers or men of authority, as I owed my safe arrival to London from such men, even though everything I told them was a lie. I had a paper of passage signed by Captain Robert himself with my Dumas name so that I had proof of who I was. Well, actually wasn't, but that paper could be very helpful. Just what type of work I could find was unknown and I knew that Fate no doubt already had a path in mind.

So I followed this path into London. As a tourist, I would have been awe struck. Oxford, like Dublin, had been the first truly large cities I had been in. This was London though and I was not a tourist. It was the capitol and where the Queen ruled from. Like all large urban centers, it was a walled city with many gates of entrée. Additional walls had developed around the ever-expanding buildup from the original center. With the war with Spain, I did not know how much security there would be at each of the gated entries. The walls were technically obsolete now with the advent of cannon, but they still would control day-to-day entry.

As I passed ever-increasing numbers of buildings and even a church, I realized I would not know when I was in the heart of the city. The first walled gate I passed through had little activity. Further in, I could see the expanse of a larger wall and realized I was finally entering the proper city itself. I could sense this gate had watchful eyes and laid back just a bit to observe other comers and goers. Nothing. They just went about their business. So I simply walked in just as invisible as anyone else.

To make my map, I knew I should find the Thames first but watch for wells or fountains along the way. As I traveled in, I could see the larger buildings and figured the huge Cathedral I saw peering above the rest might be Saint Paul's. Father McNee had told me about this grand Cathedral with the highest spire in Europe. A fire had unfortunately destroyed the spire and roof a couple dozen years ago and it would take decades to restore the Cathedral if ever. I would make my map with this as my central location as it would always be easy to find and return to. From there I worked my way to the Thames.

The city was full of humanity. There were markets, inns, shops, taverns, rent areas and residences. There were also walled estates and palaces though I did not get close to them in the first days. I priced food at the various markets to get a sense how cheaply I could eat on these streets. I would occasionally have short conversations with the venders and would usually begin by asking directions to a common sounding street name that I might have seen in Oxford. Most directions were given based on the location of known places not so much their streets. So I was able to gain names that I could use in the next conversation. This had worked well when I had just escaped from Swansea.

The street beggars would ask me for help, and of course I was in as much a need as they. Fortunately I had enough food for a couple days left over from my journey from Oxford. I also kept careful watch for thieves that might see me as prey. I had distributed my coins and valuables so they couldn't be pickpocketed. I had found several polished colored stones in my travels and put them in the pockets of my coat and britches to see if they disappeared. This would tell me if I was an easy mark.

I worked the London north side of the river back and forth to the cathedral. I wondered if I could even find my way back to the road I had come in on. No, I was going to have to find a new safe place to stay. I had passed the entrance to London Bridge and decided I should cross and explore the south side, or Southwark during the late afternoon. I had not seen any particular area where I could bed down yet on the London side.

London Bridge itself was a medieval, stone-built, many-arched structure. Shops, houses, and a chapel were crammed along its length with archways to pass under or between them. At either end were large entrance gates where heads of traitors were displayed. Across it was a bustling, commercial and sometimes rugged community. As I crossed, I held my bag tighter, even though it was tied around my waste in the usual way. I could tell there were far more orphans on this side looking for their day's way too. If you are an orphan, you just have a sense when you see lads your age and older and know they are just as homeless as you. You also have a sense that you are their prey. Many a stranger asked me if I needed their service and some were almost aggressive in their quest.

This side of the river was far more boisterous and was not as I have indicated, always refined. I saw a bearbaiting pit that was a place of entertainment and betting. Here, dogs were set loose on wild bears for a fight to the death. These arenas were also used as the early playhouses for the presentation of the fledgling art of plays. There were no doubt brothels on these streets too. As I took in all these sights, I also had a sense I was being watched and followed. Yeah, thirteen-year-old reasonably dressed boy alone, can you spell target?

Part 3 – The Graveyard

As the bells tolled six, I headed further south to find the outskirts beyond town. I thought there would be safer places to hide for the night the further away I went. After the last of Southwark thinned out, my street came to a tee at the edge of an old graveyard. Just to the east there was a cluster of buildings, so I decided to get a look that way first. There was an inn at one end and a tavern a bit further. There was a friendlier feel to these streets, possibly out of respect for the dead that were their neighbors.

There were the ruins of a small parish church with a rundown walled gate for an entrance to the cemetery. There was also a building that might still have been for a caretaker. Still I didn't see any place to hide for the night. The church already had one occupant sitting motionless on its crumpled front steps. I continued south to the end of this borough and then further along the side of the graveyard. Then I headed west to walk around its perimeter.

A mix of walls and hedgerows surrounded the graveyard. The graves were marked by anything from modest stones to haunting statues to single above ground vaults to an occasional stone crypt that held the vaults inside. It did not seem well kept. I felt a shiver in my spine as I walked all the way around it. Being raised on Celtic Irish myths of graveyards full of the dead was as scary reality as it got, even in bright sunshine. It would soon be dusk, and I still didn't have a safe place to sleep.

As I walked around the perimeter trying not to be afraid of the graves, I pondered what *was* my greatest fear? Yes, there was the possibility that someone might come along and murder me, but this was not a real likelihood. My first night free in Wales had been with a stranger who was not a murderer. He had ended up being most kind. No, my fear was of being robbed of what little I had. Being robbed at this point would be the same as murdering me. So as I peered into the graveyard, I realized that my greatest fear at the moment was not of the *dead*, but of the *living*.

The dead had never actually bothered me at the small graveyard in Athy, Ireland and in fact the person I loved most rested there. I wondered if the residents amongst these monuments would mind if I found rest here. After all, no thieves would be looking for prey in such a place, as they all feared these gardens of stone. Besides, I didn't really think the dead hung around their markers all the time anyway. I was sure their souls found something better to do. They had either already been judged and moved on, or if that final day was still to come, I'm sure our Lord had something better for them to do.

And so I respectfully walked in through an opening in the hedgerow on the west side and looked for a spot by several nice shade trees. I picked out a place and studied the area so I could find it even in the dark. It was still too early to actually go to sleep. I left the same way I came in, finished my walk around, and returned to the tavern I had passed earlier. I had never been in a tavern before, only inns along the way. I decided to go into the tavern as it sounded a little bit livelier than the rest of this solemn borough.

I waited until another party entered the tavern and simply followed them in. There were tables for those seeking food and ale, and a bar for those who would likely be visiting longer. Sooner or later I would be noticed. Thinking like a cat again, I looked to see who was alone and would be likely to strike up a conversation. There was an older gentleman at the bar who looked like he was well into his ale with no one sitting around him. I had the feeling he was a regular and just liked to talk, mostly due to the absence of any next to him.

I stood near an empty chair next to him and waited for the man tending the bar to see me. "Can I help you, boy?"

"Sir, I was to meet a man here this evening regarding some work. I was wondering if anyone came in looking for me yet?" I replied, starting my tale of lies which shamefully I was getting rather good at.

"No one has inquired about any boy. Did you wish to order something?"

"No, but thank you Sir, I'll have to wait until he gets here, though a cup of water would be most kind. May I wait inside for him? I won't get in the way."

At this point the older gentleman broke in, "Of course you can, lad. Have a seat. What brings you to this area to find work? Want to dig graves?" he asked with a bit of animation. The bartender looked at each of us and seemed to decide his regular needed someone to talk to anyway. He gazed upward with a shake of his head and left to attend another customer that had caught his attention. In no time the old man, who definitely had had a few, and I were deep in a story-telling conversation. I had told him my tale that my only living relation, my uncle who had raised me, had passed. Not wishing to dig myself too deeply into my made-up story, I had innocently asked if he knew of the history of the cemetery. After that it was almost impossible to turn him off.

This conversation did, however, have a chilling effect. It may have been a poor choice to lead him to. He told me about ghosts and ghouls and people, especially children, disappearing. As I slowly started turning white, he continued with fresh tales about Nephilim, angels and demons. The bartender had brought me water and looked at my ever-widening expression with a hidden grin. Neither of them, of course, knew that I was planning on sleeping in the graveyard this very night.

The gentleman noticing my peeked color and said, "Get us a couple bowls of your wicked stew. I better eat something before I go home cause my witch of a wife will certainly not have left anything out for me. This boy looks like he could use some too if he can choke down your usual slop."

The bartender was obviously used to this badgering as he only grinned and brought us the stew. Oh boy! It was my favorite with turnips … I was actually grateful though, turnips or not, as it was the first warm food I had had since being on the road into London. I thanked him, and as the evening was sneaking by, he had to leave to see what he was going to endure from his witch when he got home. The bartender bid him good evening. My imaginary contact, of course, never showed up. So I left quietly a little later, thanking the bartender first. No one asked where I was going or staying at this hour simply because no one really would want to get involved.

I had more than second thoughts about my choice of this night's shelter but told myself, 'they were only stories,' as I stepped outside. It was pitch-black now as I started my walk back around the graveyard's north side. There was at least a gentle comfortable breeze from the south. This breeze, however, only amplified the sounds it made sweeping across the stones to find my ears like a thousand whispers. It also brought the sounds of all the creatures, or whatever, of the night. I had expected the hoots of owls and always found them comforting. What wasn't comforting were the screeches of animals fighting if they were indeed animals and not demons.

I rounded the corner to start my final leg south and started to whistle to try to subdue the scream that was growing in my throat. I found it is a myth that whistling will calm your fears. For one thing, you can't whistle with trembling lips, and it only added to the eerie sounds that were already all around me. I finally arrived at the opening I had previously found in the hedgerow. I stood there looking through it wondering should I go in? There was an overgrown field alongside, but no place to lie and I had foolishly not explored it in daylight. I swallowed hard and with a prayer on my lips, entered.

I found the spot I had picked out. I had chosen it for three reasons. First, it was on a bit of a knoll and I had a clear view all the way across to the borough and could see the care keeper's structure. There was a light in the window, and I assumed it was occupied after all. I didn't think he would walk the grounds overnight but would certainly take a lantern if he did. Second, this was close to my entrance in case I needed to leave in a hurry. I would definitely keep my boots on tonight! Last, it was out of respect for the hallowed grounds I was seeking refuge in. I knew my young bladder was usually good for the entire night. I wasn't going to desecrate anyone's grave in case I had to get up, so I wanted to be close to where I could step out politely.

So I settled in for the night with my coat tight around me, wrapped in my small blanket with my bag as a pillow. It was just like any other night I had been traveling. At least I tried to convince myself, until there was another loud screech to break the night. Fortunately, I was so exhausted as I had risen at dawn and spent the entire day exploring London. Ghosts or not, I quickly fell asleep.

I woke with a start and scrambled back from the gravestone that I lay against. If you thought my ghost story was going to begin here, I'm sorry you'll just have to wait. The sunrise had begun, and its morning rays made the mist and fog all around glow with a pinkish cast. As the fog lifted in my own head, I recalled how I found myself sleeping next to this stone. I peered over it and concluded that I was alone. I had woken with such a start that I did not remember any dreams, as I had not had any time to linger in them. No dreams of a life's past ghost like the night before, which had actually given me courage for the coming day. I looked across the swirling fog to the village on the other side and the odd colors forming on the stones between.

The groundskeeper's light was out, and the town had not yet wakened. Only a couple windows showed a little light. Whether candle or a warm hearth I did not know. I remembered warming myself at the hearth in the cottage back home and wished with all my heart I could be there. But here I was hundreds of miles and an ocean away in a graveyard. I wondered if Fate had led me here to help me or was just messing around. I certainly hoped she had a purpose for all this other than a good laugh. With that thought, I had a bit of a laugh myself remembering the terror I had entering here with the previous night. I offered a prayer of thanks. It ended up that the residents here did not seem to mind my company after all. I just hoped they understood it was temporary, and I wasn't planning on staying.

"Well I best get up and be off to see what this day holds," I said aloud to myself. I occasionally talked to myself out loud on the long treks when I was alone. Everyone talks to themselves from time to time. See what you have to say next time you bash your bare toes into the bedpost. My first stop would be in the little borough to refill my water flask. The bartender had been kind enough to fill it the night before. He was intrigued by its design and I told him I would gladly trade it for a normal poach designed for carrying water. He said he would see what he had, but never got back to me. At least I would have another excuse to return there and maybe mooch another turnip stew. I was hungry so I finished some of my previous travel's supplies.

I headed back to Southwark to spend more time studying and mapping it. Today I could begin looking for some kind of work. I was actually pleased with the previous day's accomplishments. I had gotten a feel for the city, found water and most important, found a safe, though unusual, temporary place to seek refuge. I, of course, wanted to find a less eerie place to sleep and somewhere I could safely leave my coat and blanket behind during the day. It was almost summer, and I did not want to drag around what little I had all day, especially if I found work. I also considered that sleeping next to a stone would not give me cover on a rainy night. I wondered if I would be able to duck inside any of the above ground structures and how they were secured. I decided I did not want or need to think about that and went on.

The markets were just setting up when I arrived. I thought I'd just watch and see where help might be needed and the best way to approach them. I realized that all these people headed this way and that were going to some kind of work. I hoped I could find employment scribing or ciphering, as I really wasn't built for digging graves. I also sensed and observed that others were also watching. Some I recognized from the day before, including an older poorly dressed lad. I wondered how long it would be until I would look the same.

I approached the food vendors first and began by asking prices and then seeing if they needed help. I also asked if they or anyone they knew needed bookkeeping. Most just shooed me away; most thinking I was too young to write. I did the same with other types of venders too. One even sold snakes. I had never seen a snake before because Saint Patrick had driven them all off the isle of Ireland. There are those in your modern times that call this a myth, but riddle me this – why is Ireland the only isle in the world that doesn't have snakes?

I was not making any progress and I kept noticing the lad I mentioned earlier. He would occasionally stop someone and ask if they needed help and also being rejected, would then ask or beg for a coin. He was definitely keeping a watch on me, too. Well, two can play this game and he no doubt is essentially doing what I'm learning to do now. I'll just stalk him a bit and then innocently head toward him to see if he asks me if I need his services. I also checked to see if anyone had pick pocketed those shiny pebbles I had put in each of my pockets. They were still there.

"Sir, Jack at your service here. I can help you find anything you need in all of Southwark or London. All you need do is ask. Are you new to town, Sir?" he greeted as I headed straight toward him.

"No, but I am looking for someone, or some place." I replied. "If you really know these streets well you might be able to help. I'm looking for the brothel around here." I was making this up as I went and even I had no idea where I was headed.

He stared with a blank expression and tried to find the words to respond. "Ah, well ah, what would a fine young gentleman want with the likes of that place?"

"I'm looking for a cousin of mine. Her name is Molly. Maybe you might know of her. You see my only other relation, my uncle, has passed and his solicitors are trying to cheat me out of any inheritance I might receive. The only thing I was able to get was the two pennies over his eyes before they took him away. He died of the plague. Do you want to see them?" I had started reaching for my pouch I had hid two pence in as I answered. The expression on his face was priceless as it went from puzzled to ashen gray.

"Don't worry. I cleaned them and I don't think they carry any curse because, well, I'm still okay," I continued. I didn't think I needed to have any more concerns that he would pick my pockets. "You see, for now I'm as penniless as you. I've been watching you just as you've been watching me. You don't seem to be having much luck, well, begging. I wouldn't either because I only have this decent set of cloths. I have an idea though how we might work together to our advantage."

He was slowly recovering from his shock and went back to the puzzled look. "Go on, just how would we do that?"

"I'll loan you my hat and you find a corner best for begging," I explained. "I'll lay back and wait till several well to do merchants come along and then come up and put a coin in your hat, well my hat, and call upon them to help you too. We'll split the take and you'll get the first coin. I, of course, get my hat back and my black penny too."

"My master may not like me working with someone else. I have to split what I make with him and he has eyes everywhere. He'll know I had to split it with you." he explained. "He takes care of us with shelter and food, but we have to follow his rules."

"It's a cost of doing business and beats not making anything." It hadn't occurred to me that he was actually employed by a handler or whatever he was called. "He might be quite pleased if you bring home a good take. I might even need to see if he needs my services someday."

There was a long pause as he considered and simply said, "All right."

"We must swear that neither one of us will ever try to cheat the other," I said as he nodded. So I gave him my hat out of my bag and then followed behind till he found a spot to set up. At least he didn't run off and steal my, well, stolen hat. I watched for a bit to see his act and then watched patiently for the right crowd approaching and started walking slowly ahead of them.

I started fumbling in my coin pouch stopping for a moment. "Another poor orphan, I'm so grateful that it's not me sitting there. Scripture says we should feed the hungry and take care of the poor." I started by saying this to no one but looked at the well dressed, probably merchants. I continued, "Everyone keeps walking by trying not to look, but I'm going to find one orphan and give a pence every day as long as I'm able." With that I dropped a coin in the hat. "Surely we could all help," I said looking directly at the one I perceived as their leader.

"Let him work for it, like all the rest of us righteous men," he rebuffed.

"Excellent then. Do you have some work for him to do? Soon, like me, he will be of age when we can fight the Spanish and it will be of no good if he starves before then." I calmly replied squarely looking him in the eye. Other passersby had now stopped and were listening.

"Hear, hear," one of them agreed but did not reach into his pocket.

"Very well," the merchant replied with some degree of disgust and finally reached into his pocket and threw in what looked like a pence. Those with him followed suit along with some on lookers while others just slinked away. It seemed that a little religion mixed with patriotism had done the job.

"Gramercy kind Sir, gramercy." Jack kept repeating using the English expression for thank you. "Gramercy." After the original crowd had all moved on, I thought it best we not repeat the same performance there. I declared that I would take this beggar to find some bread. Now I would see if he would make a run for it. He didn't and I started splitting the take. I had a rough idea how many donations were made, and it seemed the hat was a little light. It appears maybe his fingers had got into the hat first.

I subdued a grin and said, "That's strange, I don't see my cursed penny. Could someone who appeared to be giving you a coin in fact have pinched one?" I saw his face tense up confirming my suspicion. "Oh wait, here it is," I corrected. And with that he had a sigh of relief. I guess I didn't mind he pinched extra because he was going to have to split his share anyway. We walked and shared a bit of a laugh. He was impressed how I had done some really good acting. Maybe I should try to find work at the playhouse, I thought. He showed me where the brothel was, and I said I would see if I could spot my imaginary cousin sometime in the evening. We parted indicating we would see each other around and see if his master was okay with us occasionally working together.

Wow, I had made three pence for a morning's work. Not actually all that good. I spent the rest of the day looking for better work ideas and even went to one of the bearbaiting playhouses to look for opportunities. There was going to be dogfight and that wasn't the type of acting I was thinking of. As the afternoon slipped away, I decided I better start heading back to the tavern and, unfortunately, the graveyard, as I hadn't found a safer place. It looked like rain, so I again pondered whether one of the above ground enclosed crypts were open. I shuddered at the thought of going in one. I best check during daylight because I certainly wouldn't have the nerve after dark.

I went to the crypts first then, while there was still light. I remembered there were a couple of the gated ones near where I had slept. The first one was chained tight with a lock and had a double set of small ancient ornate doors. I went to another nearby one that was smaller. "Reynolds," I read. This one's entrance was blocked from the view of the caretaker's window. That would be a better choice. It too had a chained gate with an old-rusted lock. I noticed, however, the iron eyelet that held the chain to the stone was neither vertical nor horizontal. I doubted a stonemason would design it that way for these monuments were to be seen by the living, not their occupant. Without thinking, I reached for it to straighten it and it moved. In fact it was loose enough to pull right out.

The gate could now swing open freely with its chain hanging. It must not have been opened for years. There was a single less ornate weathered door with a bar that one apparently lifted to open its latch. I lifted it and pushed. It seemed to be jammed so I pushed a little harder and jiggled the bar. It moved but it was binding at the bottom. I had the horrifying thought of what would happen if I got trapped inside and stopped and shuttered. I pushed the door further and light streamed inside slowly lighting more of its details. There was a single crypt and what appeared to be bird nest material scattered about. I now noticed that the door was not the only source of light as there were vents alongside the inner edge of the roof that was also letting in light, and also birds.

"Well, it certainly needs tidying up, I hope you don't mind?" I said to no one. I worked the door back and forth and whatever was binding it loosened to my relief. I read the inscription on the crypt and concluded it dated back to the War of the Roses. This was a lengthy war between the House of York and the House of Lancaster as they fought for the monarchy. Their standard's each included a different colored rose. York had a white rose and Lancaster a red one, hence the War of the Roses. The monarchy changed houses repeatedly, and finally ended when York's Richard III was defeated about a hundred years ago. Henry, from still another House, the House of Tudor, defeated him. He is the father of Henry VIII and the grandfather of Queen Elizabeth.

This crypt's occupant may have been on the losing side and why it seemed to have had no visitors other than the birds. I went to find something to sweep and tidy up the inside. There were broken pine branches nearby that covered cloven hoof imprints. I hoped they were from deer and not demons. I swept out all the bird nest debris and every edge and corner. I decided I was far more afraid of creepy spiders than the crypt's long forgotten soul. 'There, that's better,' I tried to convince myself.

I re-secured the gate and headed to the tavern. The elder ale-loving gentleman was already there, and no surprise, had open seats around him. He waved me on, and I had a seat. He inquired if the man that was to offer me work had ever showed up, and I told him I had not found him. It wasn't long before he was once again engaging me with ghost stories, some the same as the day before. I changed the direction of these tales, wondering if there were any interesting older stories from the time of the War of the Roses.

He lit up and exclaimed, "Of course! There are two of the most important ghosts here from all times! It's said that Edward IV's sons, both the young Prince Edward and his brother Richard, were secretly buried here. They were both murdered by their uncle, King Richard III!"

I did find this a more interesting tale, and in fact to this day, no one really knows just what happened to the two boys. Others claim it was Lord Buckingham who had it done to turn the people against Richard III. He led a rebellion against Richard III and would have two less heirs in his way for his own designs on the crown. He lost his head when biblical rains crushed his rebellion. It is said the boys' mother, the former Queen Elizabeth Woodville, had sent the storms using witchcraft. That would be somewhat ironic, since she was part of Buckingham's rebellion before her sons were murdered in the Tower. It all sounds like it would make a grand play for some clever poet to sort out. Soon I found myself with another warm bowl of stew. I also worked out a trade with the bartender for a water pouch in exchange for my flask.

As it darkened and as I was again exhausted, I left politely. I told them that someone was allowing me to stay with them, but I had to wait till they were home. A storm was on its way. I headed back to Sir Reynolds and found I could still get in just as it started to rain. I pulled the gate shut but left the door cracked open quite a bit. It was deathly dark inside, but at least the outdoor sounds helped liven it up. I now had to figure out where to lie in the crypt. Which was creepier, on top or alongside the stone vault? I opted for on top, as I was far more afraid of there being even a single spider. I then wondered if the ghosts of the two boys had been hidden inside.

I laid on my blanket and bag, but this was uncomfortable compared to sleeping outside where I could find ground to match the contour of my body. This was a far more restless night. I was worried as to what I was to do if I couldn't find work. I had inquired at the tavern and asked the bartender if he knew anyone who needed scribing or ciphering or even be taught reading. He said he would check, as did my ale-loving gentleman.

Part 4 – Topcliffe

And so my days began surviving the streets of London. Each day I would go out but made no serious progress. Occasionally I would team up with the lad Jack. His Master had no concern as long as he came back with something. He even started teaching me sleight of hand, or in short, pick pocketing. I didn't know if I had the nerve. I know that might seem strange coming from someone who's sleeping in a graveyard. I also thought I'd try telling stories on the corners near the playhouses on the London side, but most people just walked away.

I decided I needed an acting prop. I needed a book to make it appear I was reading a story. Didn't matter what the book was about, I was going to make the story up anyway. There were shops that had sprung up around the partial ruins of St. Paul's Cathedral. Some sold books. I had frequented one hoping to find work. The proprietor of course thought I couldn't read and that I was just another thieving street urchin. He was impressed though when I read aloud, but he still didn't have any work.

I thought to steal a book as they were expensive, and I had so little funds. But I knew he would know, and it might jinx using it. I struggled to make enough to barely eat during the week. I decided I would get a warm meal once a week at the tavern with the coins from Captain Robert before I ended up sick.

The weeks passed into a month and into a very warm summer. I finally decided to buy a book and would try to get one that I could actually enjoy reading. It was of course about a fighting prince. I used it to tell stories near the book vendor which helped his business but added no coins to my hat.

I had a little more success by the "Theatre," which was actually its name up on the north side outside the city limits. It was run by the Burbage's and was the first playhouse built that was not for bearbaiting. My best night was when they had a play, for those who could not afford admission, would listen to my stories. Of course they weren't keen on paying me anything either, since it only cost a penny to stand and watch the play. Occasionally the Theatre would have something decent enough that there wasn't room to cram everyone else inside, and they would be more generous. I used the story of my young Druid Prince Enros but initially changed it to a Scottish tale. I could mumble my Irish accent to sound like a Scott. I eventually changed it back to my original Irish story because it was missing something without Saint Patrick.

I continued learning and doing a few tricks with the lad Jack and one day he told me with much excitement that today I was going to steal! "What are you talking about?" I asked.

"There's going to be an execution of a traitor today at Tyburn! Topcliffe himself is going to preside over it. The entire town will be out to watch. It's a pickpocket's delight!" he exclaimed. Sir Richard Topcliffe is the Queen's chief torturer for interrogations, especially of Catholics. There is no one feared more in the land. The expression "give him the third degree" is based on his torture techniques.

"Everyone will bring rotten food to throw at the traitor. Some of it still good enough to eat if you steal it from the wealthy watching the spectacle. You can pick their pockets like I showed you and get something to eat at the same time!" he added excitedly.

He led me across to the north side of the river to Tyburn Gallows where it was to take place. As we crossed the bridge, I looked up at the heads on pikes adorning the arched gate. I shuttered as I realized there would be a fresh one added today. Sure enough, you could hear the din of the crowd that had formed, some having come out hours early to get a good view. A traitor's execution is not for the faint of heart. It starts with dragging the convicted to the execution platform while the crowd hurls their insults and rotten food. Then he is slowly pulled up and hung, not to kill him, but to begin his public torture. The crowd again will bombard him. Then he is tied down on a block for the executioner and his sharp instruments to begin their bloody business. The first part to be cut away is the traitor's manhood, much to the crowd's wild cheers. Then he is disemboweled and afterwards, quartered, so that his limbs and head can be sent throughout the Kingdom as a warning to all would-be traitors.

I had helped Jack with some of his thieving by watching for potential marks or creating some kind of distraction. I hadn't actually stolen anything yet and was still terrified of the thought. Never mind that it was wrong, I was afraid to get caught. This scene did create an excellent opportunity to watch, pick my prey, follow, and then make a move. I started by pinching some of the food brought to be hurled. I behaved like a mischievous child, or cat, with a "catch me if you can" or "I can throw better than you" as I grabbed things. Since I was small and still looked very much like a child, I could slide through the crowd more rudely than would be allowed to an older spectator. In fact, occasional small fights did break out over claimed spots. Queen's soldiers were meant to maintain order, but they were fairly passive in letting the crowd go wild.

So I scored something still reasonable enough to eat and got some things out of pockets. I had no idea what I had stolen. You never look until afterwards and you usually don't even know what you're trying to take. Just grab and go and find out later. I had managed to work my way up to the actual execution stand but was now to close to see where the man would be strapped down. I didn't know what I actually wanted to see, for I had never seen anyone killed.

They brought the traitor out to the jeers of the crowd like a great sporting event. I suppose the sport in the bearbaiting pits had the same effect. The man couldn't have been out of his twenties. Somehow I just expected he would be someone older. The hanging started up and down and up and down as the crowd hurled everything they had. The front row was maybe not the best place to be because much of it landed all around. I would have to clean my clothes tonight. Then he was tied down and Topcliffe, who had stayed clear of the barrage, stepped up. He gave the most loathing speech about Catholic traitors I had ever heard and held up some abnormal looking knives to the roar of the crowd.

I will spare you the details of what followed. I stayed with a growing feel of revulsion as Topcliffe completed the first task. The continued roar and cheers of the crowd drowned any of the poor man's screams. Fortunately I could not actually see what Topcliffe was doing, but I clearly knew. Then as Topcliffe looked down at the crowd our eyes met, and he smiled at me. He had such a look of glee and lust in his eyes that my heart sunk with terror. I had to get out of there and wanted to throw up. The crowd laughed at me as my sickness showed, but they cleared back just in case I hurled. I worked my way out of the crowd and ran. Ran as fast as I could away from there, back across the bridge with no idea of where I wanted to go.

Part 5 – Employment

The first month had passed and now the second. The sultry summer was now moderating. I was still staying with Sir Reynold's, which gave me a safe place to leave my almost non-existent valuables. When I had finally looked at my first thieving after that execution day, I hadn't even scored a coin. I wasn't doing any better now. I could no longer afford my weekly warm meal at the tavern, as Captain Robert's coins were all but gone. I had hoped to find him someday but would be ashamed to meet his eyes. I still looked for work and did my story telling on corners on the London side of the Thames. I did my thieving in Southwark on the south side. I actually was able to pick some pockets but rarely ended up with coins. I would give the objects to Jack who would give them to his employer. He would at least bring back some food the next day. I still had not met his man, as he apparently did not need any more orphans.

One cooler day I was doing my usual stalking in Southwark when I saw Jack running down the street with terror in his eyes. Men were after him, but he had managed to get well ahead of them. He flew by me and ducked down an alleyway as the passersby shifted out of the way. Without thinking, I moved forward toward the men who were chasing and looking for which way he went.

"He went that way!" I yelled pointing straight down the street. "Is it a street boy you're chasing? He ran down to the next corner. What did he do, what did he do?" I exclaimed with excitement as my heart pounded.

"Which way did he turn, which way, where did you see him go?" the first man barked as he grabbed me and shook me.

"He went straight down the street and disappeared around the corner past the inn. There were people in the way, so I didn't see him turn. When they cleared he was gone. I think I would have seen him run to the right, so he must have gone that way," as I pointed left. "What did he do?"

"Never you mind" and they all ran off in the direction I had pointed. I slowly melted back into the alley and found Jack hiding under some garbage, so I stopped to take a pee.

"Stay here. I've led them away. I'll keep an out eye out and let you know when it's clear. Put my coat on," which I took off. "Leave yours behind so they don't recognize you."

The men had spread out but did not seem to be heading back. I waited till the excitement had died down and told Jack which way I thought was clear. I didn't see him in the days that followed and feared he might have been caught. I also figured or hoped he was just laying low. In any event my good deed had cost me my coat. I had retrieved his tattered one that was too big for me, and it indeed made me look like a beggar. I would not be able to wear it for my storytelling. I also had to do my thieving on my own now but was too afraid after I had seen him almost get caught.

A little over a week had passed and having had another unsuccessful day, I started my solemn walk back to Sir Reynolds' place. Today had warmed up, and I kept Jack's coat in my now equally tattered bag. I would put it on in the evening as the temperature would drop after dark. It was early September now. The old man at the tavern had finally fallen when stumbling back home and had not returned for over a month. The tavern was getting busier now with cooler evenings. The bartender would leave stale bread and any left-over stew or broth out for me, but since business had picked up, little or none was left. I also now looked like a beggar and knew I would be asked to leave if I continued to wander in. I was like a stray cat looking for food at the back door.

So I had started my trek back when a Viking of a man came up behind me and grabbed my arm. "That's a good lad, come along and you'll be alright." He paused for a moment and added, "Assuming you want to live," and pressed a knife to my throat. "This way!" he motioned and let my arm go and put his knife back in his pocket. I followed his directions in terror. Where was he taking me and why? He certainly wasn't the law. I suspected that he must be a thief or part of a thieves' gang or worse. His humming didn't help.

He took me to a rear of a two-level building in an area that had many businesses on the south side of the river. I knew this area and that there was an inn and a tavern nearby. He ushered me in and told another man inside, "Got him." The man left and quickly returned to lead us upstairs. It occurred to me that I might finally be meeting Jack's employer and considered how I should act. We went through a doorway and into a room with a well-dressed man sitting at a table. "I have brought you the boy, dumb ass," and he bowed with me standing in front him.

In a flash I responded, "That's Dumas, Master Robert Dumas," and I shocked him by pointing his very own knife at his throat that I had just picked out of his pocket as we entered. He was stunned. I could see he was thinking of making a grab for me. "Back off!" and I hurled the knife to the floor away from both of us. "You can pick that up later." My heart felt like it would burst out of my chest as I turned around and faced my host wondering how he would respond. "I apologize if I was rude, Sir. How may I be of service? I am afraid you have the advantage of knowing my name, and I'm sorry but I don't know yours," and then quickly added another, "Sir."

"Well, well, Jack is right, you are a very pretty boy," the man behind the desk said nonchalantly as if nothing had just happened. I stared blankly as this was not exactly the response I was expecting. "Pretty boy" was far from what I wanted to be called. He had said, "Jack," so I was right as to him being his master or ringleader.

"I should introduce myself though I only do that with those I decide to keep." He paused letting me get the drift of those words. "My name is Master Brian Wilson, and just who are you master of?"

"Myself," I replied. "Consider me like a cat. I like to roam, Sir."

"Not doing very well roaming are you? Even a clever cat knows when to come in out of the cold."

"Yes, as long as that cat knows the way back out, Sir. Is Jack all right? He didn't get caught?" I asked with concern.

"No, thanks to you he got away. I must admit you are a clever and brave lad."

"Many thanks Sir. I'm glad he made it. I was hoping to return his coat and get mine back. I'm sure it doesn't fit him very well, but hopefully helped his escape."

"Sit," he motioned, and then looked at his Viking with a mocking grin. "You may go, and it appears you dropped something."

I could hear the man picking his knife up and leaving. I couldn't see him, but I could feel his eyes burning a hole in the back of my head.

"You're probably hungry. You may start with this." He pointed to some bread and cheese on a tray on his table. Then he picked up a small silver bell and jingled it. A servant soon walked in.

"Get this boy something decent to eat."

"Gramercy Sir. May I ask you why you've brought me here, Sir?" I asked politely.

"Well I suppose I finally wanted to see you for myself, ever since Jack started telling me all about you. Pennies off the eyes of a man who died from the plague. I think he must almost have pissed himself," he chuckled. "Do you still have them? I would love to buy them. How did you ever come up with such a clever lie?"

I grinned. "Well it would keep him from picking my pockets, Sir"

"Now to business," he said as the food arrived. I could feel my stomach weep with joy. "I brought you here, I suppose, to thank you for keeping Jack out of the hands of the law. I might have some use for you, and I'd hate to see you starve to death with that long cold winter coming just around the corner. You see, I give the lads shelter and food and they go out and bring back what they can. I keep my share for the expense of taking care of them and give them what I think they deserve. I then occasionally have more lucrative business for them to do depending on each of their talents."

I had already realized this was an interview for work. What type I wasn't sure. I was getting desperate for any work, as I knew I could not survive winter without warm shelter and food. The mortality rate for orphans over winter was merciless. I also knew what happened to the orphans, the poor and the victims of the plague. They did not find rest in quiet graveyards like the one I now resided in. I had seen where they were dumped and covered with lye on my journey just out of Oxford. They dig long ditches and just roll the dead in until it's time to dig another trench. Then they cover the old one with the dirt from the new. I knew there were such places at the outskirts of London and Southwark.

"I'm not sure what I can do with you," he continued. "You are younger than what I usually employ, simply because those your age always get caught. You don't seem to be that good at taking and I don't know if I have a market for clever or brave. But you are a pretty boy and there is always a market for that." He watched me to see how I would respond. I knew exactly where he was going with this. It didn't take an alchemist to figure it out.

I measured my response carefully, knowing that neither path that Fate was having me choose had any mercy. I was already deeply ashamed that I had turned out to be a liar and a thief to survive. I thought of Father McNee and finally my words.

"If you can determine ways to market what you call pretty from time to time, Sir, I would be interested in seeing what you can find. I do have to make it clear though that there are some things I will not do. My ass is not for sale, and I am not going to be touched by or touch anyone else, Sir." I hopelessly stated, thereby probably putting a nail in my own winter's coffin.

"Well, aren't we the prim and proper one? You honestly think you can survive without help? My help? I guess I need to add stubborn to your bravery and foolish to your cleverness. You leave me with little to sell. What else am I to do with a virgin, assuming you're still one?"

"A virgin isn't worth as much after they're no longer a virgin, Sir," I offered. Though I'm not proud of what followed, as you will soon learn, I did somehow manage to avoid becoming a prostitute.

He thought for a while as I hurriedly finished the meal he had given me, not knowing if I was soon to be thrown out or worse, taken away and locked up.

"I suppose I could show you off as a pretty virgin though you are a lot younger than I like. Do you like to bathe? Or are you like a cat and can't stand the sight of water?" he asked bluntly.

"Actually, I think most cats do like water, Sir. You wouldn't be talking about a bath in a tub with clean warm water?" I asked. I would actually do almost anything for a real bath without freezing water. I had done little more but wash myself using my clothes as a rag after I washed them first. The bartender had been kind once again and left a bucket out for me to go to the well with. It was understood I would leave it full after I was done borrowing it. I didn't wait for his response. I simply asked, "How much would I be paid, Sir?"

He looked at me with amusement. "A pence, and you'll also have to get the water and make it whatever way you like."

"Four pence. After all, I need to eat, Sir."

"Two pence and you'll get something to eat."

"Three pence and I keep any tip I might be offered, Sir."

"Very well, three pence, but you'll have to undress first, you know, do a bit of a bashful show, maybe even be wearing a dress."

"What!" What indeed? What had I just negotiated into, well, never mind. I thought about what I had just done and then tried not to. "Where would I be doing this and when, Sir?"

"Here and when I find those refined gentlemen that are looking for more "artful" things. You'll have to be available when I say. In the meantime, you go out on the street and find things to take. Then, maybe I'll let you stay like the rest of the lads," he answered.

"Do they stay here, Sir?"

"Of course not, this is a business. I have places that are under my protection along the docks for shelter. That's where you'll report with your take."

"I will be available for what you schedule as long as I know in advance, Sir. I still have other work that I am pursuing, but I will come each time we agree on a time," I shamefully offered.

"Boy, you are pushy. Best not let the other lads know or I'll have a rebellion. Now I have to see if you're worth selling and I can rely on you." This was clearly more than a challenge but an order. "Now means now, boy."

"Three pence then, Sir." I breathed out loud as I was led to another room.

So I took a warm bath after I heated the water with hot irons left in the fire of the hearth. The tub was brass and shaped so you could sit in it. Only the very wealthiest had one. The water came from a public well a couple streets over and it took many tiresome trips to fill it. The servant who had brought me the food showed me what to do. It was actually a lot of work. He then went to get Wilson.

He walked in and let out an "Ehh," not overly complementary sound and added, "Skinnier than I would like. I should have stuck to two pence. Don't tie your hair back, leave it long." And he simply left. I think I had just been insulted. His servant returned and waited for me to finish, completely ignoring me. He also showed me how to empty the tub afterwards but told me to leave it this time. Fortunately, he was not very talkative.

"Master Wilson said you will return here at noon Friday for instructions. You may go." And he showed me out the rear door where I had come in. I felt dirtier after this bath than before I took it, but I couldn't see how else I was going to survive the winter that was coming.

Wilson quickly found several of those secret-refined gentlemen seeking to see finer art. It wasn't as bad compared to what else was going on throughout this or any city with young boys or worse young girls. I started to feel more ashamed of not what I was doing but, what I didn't have to do compared to the plight of others. I also remembered about the lads in Swansea and my vow to help them and cried that I could do nothing.

I had no idea what I was supposed to do other than take a bath, so I decided it might be less creepy if I offered to tell a story. This seemed to work as I told the tale of a fighting prince and would dance about with an imaginary sword. This cut down on otherwise having to have an awkward conversation. Ironically, I had finally found a way to earn income by telling stories.

I stayed at the business on those sporadic nights when I took a bath during the next couple weeks. I also got my coat back and was able to return to the tavern on my nights off. I could have my weekly warm meal again. "You must have found work. You've cleaned up quite nice," the bartender observed. Oh, the irony of those words I thought. I hid what coins I was earning at Sir Reynolds' since I was otherwise still staying there.

I saw Jack and we were glad to see each other, but he looked more tattered than ever. We would still do some teamwork seeking out pockets and would have a good laugh now and then. What else could we do? Might as well try to make the best of what we had been dealt. He showed me where he stayed, and I met some of the other lads and men that worked the area under Wilson's protection. They tended to insult and taunt me with "pretty boy." I dreaded knowing that I would have to stay there soon, as the weather would get colder.

When I went to Master Wilson's business to do his business, I would bring my street-take there. It was usually the servant that collected them, told me when I would be needed, and paid me afterwards. He would also feed me. The Viking, as I referred to him, was also often there and would occasionally do the servant's assignment. When he did, I simply assumed he spit in my food as I don't think he liked me.

It was now late September and I was told Master Wilson wanted to see me. This summon had a built-in dread as I knew he probably had some new plan for me. Refuse and I might be out. I was led to the office where we had first met, and he already had set food out for me. Well, at least that might be a sign that I hadn't done something wrong.

"Sit, eat." He greeted and waved to the food. Sitting, I acknowledged with thanks and wondered if this would be my last meal.

"I have a special task for you. I have a powerful client that I really can't refuse. He's quite generous, too." My heart was sinking fast. "It's not all that bad and not what you might be thinking."

"And what exactly is it that he is interested in me doing, Sir?" I asked while taking a deep breath and waiting for his reply.

"Spanking," is all he said. Just as when we had first met, his words were not what I was expecting him to say.

"*Spanking?*" I responded, completely taken aback.

"Yes, spanking. And you will get half a shilling for it."

I recalled Crowley had whipped me to unconsciousness and had not even left a tip. "He wants to hurt me, Sir?" I exclaimed.

"Well, of course, it will hurt a bit, but he won't harm you. I'm afraid I have no one else as he requested you. He heard of you from one of *your* other clients."

"And when is this supposed to happen?" I asked, this time without the usual "sir" at the end.

"Friday evening be here at six. I have some special clothes for you to wear. Don't worry, you'll be fine. You can have some wine and that will make it easier." With that he simply got up and left without allowing me to say yes or no. "Enjoy your dinner," were his only parting words

When I was first brought to Wilson, he had offered that even a roaming cat knew when to come in out of the cold. I had replied,

"As long as that cat knows the way back out." I had been able to explore the room where I was employed when alone while bringing up the water. It had windowed doors with a simple latch behind a drape that opened onto a small balcony. I thought I would be able to climb over the rail and lower myself to the street below if I needed a quick escape. I studied the drop from the outside more closely as I left this evening. I had also been bringing my knife and had been hiding it in the room just in case I needed some protection.

I arrived on time that Friday with a foreboding feeling. I was shown in as usual by the servant and he left some things out for me to change into. Oddly, the clothes were worn out and looked like those of a pickpocket or street urchin. Well, at least they weren't a girls. I was still dreading the day one of Wilson's clients would make that request. The tub had already been filled, which was a first. I also had to smear a little dirt on my face and arms, so I looked like a fresh catch off the street. Looks like I'll at least get another bath out of it I thought. The servant left a decanter of wine out and told me to drink a glass while I was getting ready.

Well, it was a bit weird, nothing compared to Crowley of course, and I got more than my half a shilling. He was punishing me for being a pickpocket and common thief. I had to clean myself first of the street dirt I had just put on. I apparently put on a decent enough show with the right amount of howling and squirming from his spanking because he also tipped me another whole shilling! He was no doubt a noble and younger than the rest of my previous clients.

It occurred to me that I had been paid far more than most of the lady prostitutes were getting. I could get a warmer used coat and a better blanket. Maybe a pair of shoes too, so I didn't have to wear my boots all the time. I had a very sore bottom, but nothing more. The worst was where I had a pimple. I, of course, had some acne here and there, though a lot of it had cleared up from all the excessive bathing. Whacking that one spot definitely brought tears to my eyes and almost brought on those out-of-body experiences.

The wine had a very strange effect. I had drunk ale before, and even had a full cup of it from the elder gentleman at the tavern. It didn't take much to make me drunk and dizzy. This was more than a dizzy though. This was different. It seemed to make me lose my sense of perception and made me edgy. I was, of course, already edgy so I didn't pay that much mind. The effects continued to last long after I left. I found I was confused and had to wander about to reorient myself. I suspected there might have been something else that had been put into the wine and started panicking that I was poisoned. I finally got a grip on myself. I knew everything was fine. I had made a shilling and a half and had left safely and still a virgin!

I went back to the tavern where I could now gingerly sit at the bar since I was a now a paying customer. I surprised the bartender and ordered an ale to steady my nerves, which were still not cooperating.

"Rough day at work was it?" he grinned. I had told them that I had found work teaching a total monster of a brat how to read. This, of course, made perfect sense since that was the type of work I had asked the bartender to be on the lookout for. My head pounded that night almost worse than the spanking. I was glad that it was a nice evening and I could sleep outside under the trees and stars. Oddly, I felt as frightened as the first night I had slept in the graveyard. I had gotten over that feeling after the first week, so I again wondered if it was the drink. I finally fell asleep wondering what else would lie ahead.

Part 6 – The Devil

I woke bewildered from the previous night's events. I was still baffled by my new client's obsession. I had an easier time understanding Crowley's, since he was simply evil and filled with hate. In any event, I was going to have a "me" day, as you put it in your modern times. I didn't have to return to Wilson's till Monday, and I didn't feel like thieving this weekend. Besides, I was doing far better doing whatever this was that I was doing. I know, that's a bit of a tongue twister, but these days were a bit of a mind twister.

Today I was going to find the warmest used coat and blanket I could for the coming winter. So I headed to one of the Southwark markets where I knew prices were lower. I found a used coat I could afford and would fit me. There wasn't a great demand for my size. It seems children had a difficult time making it to fourteen as I was already learning. The seller promised it had been washed thoroughly and was lice free along with a blanket I picked. I deferred getting shoes, as it would be my boots I would need for the winter. I did get some warm socks though.

Monday, I went to Wilson's and the servant told me I had a very important assignment on Friday. There would be no baths this week and I shouldn't do any thieving either. I would be paid well he said, along with what was due from other items I had taken. We didn't get paid for our takes until after they were sold, and of course, only got a small portion. I asked what this assignment was, and he simply replied, "Like the last time." Another spanking then, it appeared. He said I should just wear plain clothes and nothing special would be supplied this time.

I was good at math and had tried to determine how much I needed to make to survive the winter and how often I would have to endure these activities. I didn't think there could be that many clients willing to pay a shilling or more for this. I also wasn't sure my bottom would want to endure this more than once a week. However, the math was not in my favor and I knew I would have to ride this storm through winter.

I also nonchalantly mentioned that the wine had made me a little sick and he quickly apologized and said they had discovered it was spoiled. He said that the noble I would see this time would be bringing a finer wine than I would ever taste in my lifetime. This very important client would expect me to share in it and I should be obedient. So I now knew he was a noble and not the same one from last time. I didn't buy the spoiled wine explanation, so I knew there must have been something extra put in it. I did not press the question. Besides it hadn't killed me. I was fed and he gave me some bread, cheese and dried salted meat to take with. That was a first as there were in fact many unusual aspects of this week's instructions.

In your modern times, you have these wonderful moving paintings with stories of adventure, not unlike mine. There are comedies, dramas, music and all the likes, just as are evolving in the fledgling playhouses of my time. You also have horror stories that are also sometimes not unlike mine. In your horror stories there is always that scene where the audience yells "Don't open the door!" or "Don't go in!" I, of course, had to decide whether I should show up on that rainy Friday that was coming. Every bone in my body, like in your horror moving paintings said, "Don't go in." *I went in.*

It was indeed a very stormy Friday night. The door opened. The Viking had a triumphant grin on his face as he led a man in. I had already been there long enough to have a sip of, I must admit, very fine wine and saw how the room was set up. The tub had been removed. It had been replaced by a cabinet with a cloth covering its flat top. There had been lamps hanging from the ceiling by chains. They had all been removed leaving only the chains hanging just above my reach. Only candles lighted the room, but there was still enough light to read.

I would like to describe the horror I felt as that door opened. Assume for a moment that you are afraid of spiders. Assume that you just sat in a nest of very-fast-moving spiders that are crawling all around and on you, but you don't know how many. Now multiply that by, oh about 100, and then double that again as the effects of poisoned wine started to kick in. What followed, happened very quickly.

The door had opened, and the most horrifying spider of all time entered. Topcliffe!

"Where is this treasonous-filthy Catholic!" he shrieked, as he advanced on me. "I will have no mercy until you tell me where every other Catholic traitor in London is."

I wilted back. How could he know I was Catholic? Was this his game or was he really going to torture me? I had seen what he was capable of and I remember the longing in his eyes when they met mine at the execution. Besides, I didn't know any fellow Catholics, let alone traitors, anywhere.

"Please Sir, I only agreed to a spanking, Sir," I pleaded.

"Silence you filthy traitor!" he yelled as he struck me hard and then ripped my shirt open. "We'll see how many degrees your tender flesh will survive." He turned to the Viking and ordered, "Leave us, we are not to be disturbed."

The door closed loudly behind him and I was alone with Topcliffe. He then said in an almost a consoling voice. "Now, now, just cooperate and do exactly as I say. Get rid of those filthy rags so I can decide where I will begin."

I hesitated because I was frozen to the spot and couldn't speak.

"NOW!" he screamed and then opened one of the cabinet drawers and took out some short lengths of rope. "I said, NOW!" he yelled again.

I took off my torn shirt and let my trousers drop as I tried to think and plan an escape. He grabbed my arm and pulled me toward the cabinet, almost tripping me over my dragging pants. I kicked them off over my boots, as I knew I wouldn't be able to run with them around my ankles.

"Please Sir, this has gone far enough. This isn't what I agreed to," I started to plead. He was still holding my arm and started to try to tie the rope around my wrist.

He again struck me and shrieked. "I'll show you what you agreed to!" and with that threw the lid open on top of the chest and again grabbed my arm. "Stand Still!" I peered into the top and my heart sank in absolute terror. I think I pissed. It was filled with sharp steel objects many of which I had never seen or imagined. I did recognize one, a double-edged knife whose blade wiggled back and forth like a snake from its tip. He had held it up to the crowd at the execution.

"Hold your arm out like a good boy and maybe I'll go easy."

I had already figured out he intended to tie my wrists to the lamp chains hanging above us. I would be completely helpless once he succeeded. I started pleading and crying as loud as I could.

"Please Sir, don't hurt me. Please, I'll do whatever you want ... Please Sir. Sir!" I was screaming and whimpering over and over, but at the same time I held my one arm out so he could tie it.

As he tied my surrendered wrist, I raised it up higher toward one of the chains as if to help. I still continued begging and screaming. He looked up and raised my arm to secure it to the chain as I swooped my free hand to the cabinet and grabbed that snaky knife. As he tried to pull me back toward him, I took all my might and plunged it around into the back of his side. I struck deep between his ribs and hip. He shrieked and let me go as he tried to reach behind to grab the knife protruding from him. He looked at me with shock and absolute burning hatred, and then crumbled.

I kept screaming and begging as if he still had me and ran to the drapes covering the glassed door to the balcony. I tore it open and pulled the door wide and flung myself over the top of the balcony like a cat on fire. I grabbed onto the rail so I could drop myself from its bottom rod. I dropped hard, picked myself up, and ran as fast as I could in the now heavy rain and lightning.

I ran one direction and then another down the streets and alleyways. I must have looked like a ghostly white apparition swooping by in my boots to anyone peering out their stormy windows. I had no idea which way I was going or where I was going. The only thing I could think was that *I just killed Topcliffe*. I kept looking behind me to see if I was being chased. Then I saw him. It was the black-demon ghost of Topcliffe with burning red eyes! He was coming to take my soul to hell with his! I cried and prayed to God to forgive me and help me escape.

I prayed to let Topcliffe live. I ran and ran crying, "Please Lord, please Lord."

Without thinking it, I knew I had to head back to the graveyard. There was no place else for me to go. I knew it was south, but just like my escape from Swansea in the blinding rain, I had no concept of direction or time. I kept seeing Topcliffe's demon, but then it would vanish. I didn't know if I was running away from him or to him. I finally understood with dread that I had to find my graveyard and meet my Fate. I remembered there was a knoll overlooking the north side of it, so I looked for a hill in the lightning. I recognized it and headed toward it to get my bearings. I got to the top and could see the forest of gravestones as the lightning flashed across them.

I ran, absolutely frozen from the rain and cold, to the hedgerow and worked my way around to my opening. I ran inside and stopped with horror. There he was, Topcliffe, standing, waiting for me. I stood there in the blinding rain and just surrendered. There was nothing I could do and resigned myself to my Fate. I had escaped Topcliffe in life, only so he could torment me for eternity in death. I had murdered a man while committing shameful sins to make money. I had sold my soul for what? Merely a couple of shillings. There was no just way to expect forgiveness. And then a giant burst of lightning flashed. I stared with a blank expression and saw that I had surrendered to a statue! Topcliffe had not found me.

I ran to Reynolds' tomb. I tried to pull the iron eyelet out of the stone, but it would not budge. I had been locked out. The whole graveyard was murmuring and must know I had murdered. I ran around the tomb's side and collapsed on my knees, weeping. The icy water was cascading like a waterfall from the roof onto my bareback. I sank down to the ground as everything started to spin into blackness.

Chapter 3 – Fate

Part 1 – Beyond the Veil

The first sense to return is hearing. I heard a gentle breeze wrestling across the leaves above and the grass alongside me. The second sense was that I could feel this gentle breeze across my face and hair. The third sense was to see the gold glow of light through my closed eyelids. I opened them slowly. I could see a sunset sky surrounded with the most beautiful blue background filled with clouds of pink and orange of infinite hues. I looked up further and saw that the leaves of the trees were lit up from underneath by a low sun that made them glow like thousands of emeralds and rubies.

I moved my eyes downward and peered into two green eyes of a cat lying on my chest. Her eyes were the very same I had been peering out of earlier, but I couldn't quite remember when or why or how. Slowly thought and hence memory started to return. I remembered being this cat and running with all urgency to this place. I couldn't recall from where or why.

'Not the boy, you promised,' I remembered. And through this cat's eyes, I saw what I had witnessed. There were three soldiers dressed in strange uniforms, the likes of which I had never seen before. They looked like they were made of brown leather with high collars.

'Not the boy,' I cried again, for they were hanging him from a tree just off the ground. They were taunting him and telling him that he was going to hell. I could hear his soul screaming in terror though he could make no sound with the rope around his neck. I flew to him to hold him and protect him and comfort him. As I did, I found I was not alone.

Father McNee was there and he also clung to him along with my friend The Patrick. "You're safe now, it's okay," they were saying, and the boy's soul was no longer in terror. "We've got you. We're with you. You can let go." And with that a mist of the most magnificent light of colors more beautiful than a perfect sunset engulfed us.

And then I remembered hearing that breeze and feeling its touch. I remembered I had just opened my eyes and was no longer seeing through the eyes of this cat. She was purring now with understanding as she gazed back into my eyes. I didn't understand and yet I did. I didn't know who I was, and yet I did. I could see the tree I had been hanging from and feel the abrasions on my throat. The cat rose, stretched and hopped off my chest. She walked slowly to the tall grass that was whispering in the breeze. I said aloud, "Don't go yet," waking the voice within me. But she simply strode off and disappeared into the brush.

I was drowning in a cascade of water. I must have been washed down the river when the bridge collapsed. I tried to burst out of the freezing water, and I grabbed at a stone wall. I kneeled there a moment thinking I was escaping Swansea but realized I was in a graveyard. I was freezing and scrambled around the corner to try to get inside where I had clothes and coat and blanket, but the iron gate still wouldn't let me in. Then I realized I was at the wrong tomb. I spun around looking and ran to another one. "Reynolds." I had found it. "Please let me in," I prayed aloud. The chain opened as usual and I pulled the gate wide and pushed the door in. I found my bag and shaking, pulled everything out. I dried off and put on everything I had in no particular order to stop the freezing cold. Then I just sat there shivering.

I had killed Topcliffe. All the Queen's horses and all the Queen's men would be out looking for me. They would know my name, Robert Dumb Ass. I would be executed, and then I would have no defense to ever find heaven. I would be sent to where Topcliffe was. NO. I was going to live. I would escape. I would do something that would atone for these sins. I cried in shame and asked Father McNee's forgiveness. I also prayed that I had not killed Topcliffe and to let him live.

I somehow fell asleep until the morning's light started to filter in. It had long stopped raining. I did not have any more dreams but I remembered the earlier one clearly. Was it a sign of what was to come? Was I going to be hanged? It couldn't be though because I knew that dream had happened in Ireland. I recognized the place where it would happen. But I didn't have time to consider it further. Now I had to make a plan. Robert Dumas was dead. I would bury him in this tomb. I redressed myself properly and packed my bag. I left the letter of passage from Captain Robert in the tomb. It would be a death warrant if it were found on me. I dared not wear my hat either as many might recognize it. I tied my hair back and wanted to cut it off, but I had hid and lost my knife at Wilson's.

Now where was I to go? I hadn't been paid so I had little to live on. I had lost my old coat and my better set of clothes. Thank God I still had the boots and my new heavier coat. I considered going to Oxford, but I still had the wee problem of surviving winter. No. I would stay in London. I would hide in plain sight. I would be Presto again. I would be Irish again and speak with my native accent. After all, they would be looking for an English boy. I would cross the Thames and try to make an honest living on the north side. I had not needed to use my Dumas name on that side when I was trying to find honest work. I decided this was my best chance.

First I had to get across the river. No way was I going to cross at London Bridge. It would be watched and was always busy. I would take one of the many water taxis, called wherries, all along the river. I would find one to observe and see if there were soldiers on either side. There were private wherries for the nobles and the well to do. They would take them wherever they wanted to go. Then there were the taxies for us riffraff commoners like me. I observed them. They would load passengers until the boat was filled, and then row across. Then they would repeat the process from that side. I did not see any soldiers.

I decided to cross upriver to the west beyond the city center's main walls. I decided to go to the "Liberties" on the northeast side of London. There was no reason to enter through a major gate into the main part of the city only to exit through the northern most wall. I could skirt around the more protected older section and head to the north, out of the city limits. I found a busier crossing where I wouldn't stand out alone. The remains of a smaller wall were far beyond the river's shore on the other side. Its openings seemed to be unwatched. It cost one precious penny and I gave the boatman one of the two I kept in my little pouch. These were the same two that I had shown, the lad, Jack when we first met. I had kept them as good luck charms as that's the type of thing we Irish do. They had also come from Captain Robert.

I stood near a family with younger children so it looked like I might be with them. I didn't start any stories, as I was tired of lying. I did, however, have a new name, Edmond Reynolds, in case I needed one. I still spoke without my Irish accent so as not have anyone remember my passage. As we waited to fill the boat, another small group arrived, and I could see there would not be room for all of us. Someone would be asked to leave, and the boatman knew I was alone. He politely asked me to wait for the next one. He gave me my penny back and said if he had an extra seat on the next crossing, he wouldn't charge me.

So I went back to waiting. As he rowed across, I made myself invisible by the nearby buildings. I was hungry, but that would have to wait, for how long I didn't know. Fortunately, I had found a place to fill my water pouch. As he once again returned across the river, I went down to join the few that arrived to wait. I simply smiled and said, "Good morning," and waited. The boat unloaded and we only needed a couple more and I would finally be off.

Soldiers! My heart held tight, but they only seemed to be there to cross. "Good morning," I said and then asked, "I heard that Sir Francis Drake has attacked the Spanish fleet again and done great damage! Have you heard anything?"

"No lad, I haven't heard anything. Where did you hear this?" one of them asked.

"My grandfather," I said, now having an imaginary family. "I want to enlist and fight alongside Sir Francis, but I don't know where to go to join. Do you know where I can join to fight the Spaniards, Sir?"

"Well, you're a little too small for fighting yet. We're landlubber soldiers. If you want to fight, we always need boys to carry water or beat the drums," the same one answered.

We proceeded to chat on the trip across and I gave them all the details of Sir Francis' attack at Cadiz the previous April. When we left the boat I simply walked and talked with them as we entered the city hidden in plain view. There had been no mention of Topcliffe either. So we parted our separate ways.

As I worked my way around the city to the northern outskirts I wondered if Topcliffe might have survived as I had prayed. It occurred to me that he couldn't very well say that a small boy he was trying to bugger had stabbed him. This would not make him a hero. He would not have access to the Queen's soldiers to track me down. The blessed rain would have once again covered my tracks from any dogs. He would only have his own resources to hunt me. And oh yes, *he would hunt me down the rest of his life*. Still it would give me a better chance than if all the Queen's soldiers were looking.

I traveled to the northern outskirts near Burbage's Theatre. It was actually about as rough as the parts of Southwark where I had been doing my thieving. I was now the Irish-lad Presto. I was glad to finally be myself. No worry, all I had to do now is find a way to not starve or freeze to death while not being caught and butchered by Topcliffe. Just another typical day for me. This time I was more street-smart than book-smart, as when I had arrived in London. This time I would seek cover at night in alleyways just like a stray cat and do a little begging. But where would be a safe place? Alleyways were exposed to other riffraff like me, so again thinking like a cat, I looked up. Some buildings had small balconies like the one I had escaped from the night before. That already seemed like an eternity ago.

The lad, Jack, had taught me that it was best to be high above the humanity to seek prey below. During the heat of summer, the balconies were left wide open to let fresh air in. They were not a wise place to expose oneself to being caught. Now that the weather was cold at night they were shut tight. I would seek out one that could be easily climbed, and more important, escaped from. If I was quiet and nimble like a cat, I could sneak up, find some sleep, and be off before the occupants even knew I had graced their abode.

I resolved to give up thieving, though I had stolen a knife as I worked my way through the city. Knives are actually easier to steal as the Viking had found out. They usually hang in a sheath that already has some weight to it. It's so exposed that the owner will not notice its absence until you've already disappeared. I quickly cut off my ponytail with it and whatever I could hack off without seeing what I was doing. I must have looked like the cat dragged me through the alley.

I stopped at a market to sell my hat, which was of decent quality. I bargained for enough to buy a heavier one for cold weather and one that would better cover my reddish-blond hair. I put it on and thus finished my metamorphosis. I had morphed from a butterfly to a caterpillar. No one would call me a "pretty boy."

When I tried to ask if anyone needed my honest services, I finally heard word of Topcliffe. It was said that three armed traitors had attacked him, but that he had fought them off. He was gravely wounded. Catholic or Protestant, no one seemed to have much sympathy for him because he was the most feared and hated man in London. I was so relieved. I was not guilty of the sin of murder, even if it was Topcliffe. He would have to try to hunt me down on his own after he recovered. I had a chance, though this would be the most dangerous cat and mouse game yet. Later I heard it was five men that had attacked him. I laughed for the first time in days.

Part 2 – Hopeless

London had become a far more relaxed town. With autumn's arrival the entire nation felt relief that there would be no Spanish invasion this year. Wars and offenses were rarely started as winter approached. Often warring nations would even withdraw forces to try again the following spring. People had become more giving. I went back to telling stories from my book. I did this near Burbage's Theatre.

They performed a play by the popular poet, Christopher Marlow. It was very well received. There wasn't even enough standing room, so I had an audience left over that was turned away. They actually threw coins to listen to my tale. Though I didn't know it at the time, Master Burbage had walked by, casually glancing at me. However, he did not throw in a pence. I continued my story of Prince Enros, but now, he had become a man. It was a story of fighting a war with his King Aengus against another Celtic clan trying to claim his King's throne. Once again, I changed the story to a Scottish one but told it with my Irish accent. There was beginning to be a little hope.

October arrived and it was getting colder. Then the Theatre had a terrible play, a comedy. Comedies, with good acting, are my favorite, especially if there is a moral. But this play, well, it was just supposedly vulgar and crude. No audience, so it was back to begging and scrounging. It started raining on and off every day. My clothes and coat had gotten wet and they just wouldn't dry. I had nothing left to buy food. I was so desperate, I had completely forgotten about whether Topcliffe would find me and really didn't care.

As October slowly moved on, I hadn't eaten in four days. I was miserable. As another damp night came, I ducked under a porch by one of the buildings on the Theatre's grounds. I had been hungry enough to eat food from a bowl Mistress Burrbage left out for a stray cat. I had waited till the cat finished. I suppose due to respect for honor among orphans. The cat even let me pet her and she didn't seem to mind sharing.

I had done the math. I wouldn't be able to hold on for more than a couple weeks – maybe not even a few days. I had failed. With all that Father McNee had taught me, I had failed. When I escaped Swansea, I wasn't really afraid to die. Well, I didn't want to, and I was afraid I might. But I knew that Father McNee would be there to welcome me and be proud that I had tried.

Now, I was ashamed. How could I ever feel his joy in seeing me after I had become a liar, a thief, well on the way to being a whore, and almost murdered a man? I cried and prayed for his forgiveness.

As I sat there in desperation knowing my miserable end was nearing, I asked myself the final question. The question was not *why did I have to die,* but rather, *why had I lived?* I had no answer and I would be forgotten here, and in the life after. I sat shivering and crying and praying under my blanket, alone. And then an equally cold and shivering cat appeared out of nowhere and hopped up on my lap. I opened my blanket around me, and she cuddled in.

"Poor kitty, I know what it's like." Then she started to purr. I wondered what she had to purr about for she was a lot like me, homeless. She was living day to day just like me. Or was I living like her?

It occurred to me that she could survive and had done so. She also did good and had worth. She killed rats. Though it wasn't known at the time, rats probably brought the plague. I had already learned that wherever rats were, disease was sure to follow. She also found people with kind hearts to occasionally help. I had so wanted to do some good, to be like a knight and use all the wisdom Father McNee had given me. No, I can't just give up.

'Fate, if you've got a path, this would be a real good time to show me,' I prayed. And exhausted, I fell asleep.

I woke when a lady called from the door, "Hey, what are you doing here? What do you want?"

"I'm sorry ma'am, I was just taking shelter from the cold," I answered shivering. "I'm a friend of your cat. We were keeping each other warm."

"Where is she off to?" she replied.

"She got up early, probably looking for something to eat."

"Well off with you then. I have much to do."

"My Lady," I said with pleading eyes. "May I just ask you one favor before I go? May I just have a cup of clean water and a moment to warm by your hearth?" This was all I actually wanted. It was not a trick or a lie.

She looked with pity at me. "Just for a minute, but you better be off before my husband comes down," and she motioned me in.

She gave me water and I stood by the fire. "Ma'am, may I repay you for your kindness. I know you have a fine playhouse here and no doubt need to have copies made of the words your players need to practice. I want to just do something useful to say many thanks. I could copy a page for you." I had actually planned on seeking that type of work here, scribing. "I just want someone to see that I can do something of worth."

She looked at me oddly like she didn't quite understand what I meant. "You mean write? You can write?" she questioned.

"Yes, ma'am."

Part 3 – Presto

A moment later master Burbage walked in. "What is that doing in here?" he asked with indignation. Well, at least I wasn't an "it" this time.

"I gave him water and he is going to repay us by copying a page of the player's words."

"What?" he exclaimed. "You think this lad can write, let alone even read? Silly woman!"

"Veni, Vidi, Vici," I said. "It's Latin for "I saw, I conquered, I came." The words, the words you're standing under, Sir." And I pointed to words that were painted over the hallway passage he had just entered through.

He stood puzzled for a moment. "You're going to write or copy a page for us for whatever it is she gave you? That's impossible, I'm not going to waste a piece of valuable parchment for some street urchin's tricks," he said incredulously.

"Then a wager, Sir. I will bet you that I can copy a page and do it, so it is of use to you. I want to repay the kindness. I just want to do something to show that I am of value before I go." And I fought back a real tear.

"And what could you possibly bet that I would want?" he asked.

"I have a book. I read from it to tell stories near the playhouse to earn money to eat."

"I think I've seen you begging on the corner. Where did you steal the book?"

I shrugged and shook my head. "Yes, I've had to steal to eat, but I bought this book with a shilling I was paid by a Queen's Soldier at Oxford, Sir. I worked for him on a journey from Gloucester. It is the only thing I have to try to do honest work." I pulled it out of my bag as I spoke.

He let out a laugh. "I'm beginning to think you're just putting on an act."

"Well, this is a playhouse, and then at least I hope it's a good act, Sir.

"I don't need any more actors."

"Oh just let him try. Let the boy warm up and do his copy. What harm could there be?" his wife now broke in.

"Waste of paper. And what am I to wager against this book of yours?" he inquired.

"Nothing, she's already paid, Sir. But, if it is of use, I ask to copy another for a piece of bread or anything you have to offer to eat."

It finally occurred to him the desperate state I was in, something his wife had long figured out. He closed his eyes with a sigh and softly said, "All right ... Bloody waste of parchment ... Oh, have you a name, something to call you by?"

"I'm sorry, I should have introduced myself. My name is Presto."

There was a long pause apparently waiting for me to add something. "Presto what?" he asked.

"Just Presto," I replied. "There was no name tag on me when the vicar in Athy, Ireland found me on his doorstep. They needed a name for me when I was baptized, so they made me Presto." I did not go into the rest of details with them, as I feared what they might think if they knew a priest had raised me.

I suppose it is time I relate to you how I happened to become named Presto. Father McNee had told me the story of how the rather distraught Vicar Woolsey came knocking at his cottage door one January night with a bundle in his arms.

"What on earth do you have there?" McNee had asked.

"It's a baby, someone left a baby on the church steps! Did any of your folk have a child recently?" the vicar replied.

"No, and I would certainly know. Let me see," and I was handed to him. "He's nothing but skin and bones, but he's too long to be newborn. Must be getting on maybe almost a year. Poor thing."

"What should we do with him?"

"Well, feed him for one. We should also be attending to his soul by the looks of him," McNee replied with concern. "I wonder if he's been baptized."

The vicar and the priest found themselves at a defining moment. What faith was I to be baptized? It is a testament to their own faith and friendship of how they proceeded.

"Is he Catholic or Protestant then?" the vicar mused. "How do we decide?" They both looked at each other and then me. Then they realized that really wasn't the point.

"I suppose we could shoot dice to decide," McNee offered with a bit of a grin.

"Neither of our religions allow dice. Do you really have some?"

"Aye."

"We should play sometime. Why don't we let the child decide?" Woolsey asked.

"How is he supposed to know the difference? He's just a babe," McNee answered. "We should just baptize him together."

The vicar nodded his head in agreement. "We'll let our Lord decide then, if he thinks it matters. I'll get some water to bless. It's too cold to take him back outside to the church."

"No wait!" McNee interrupted. "We need to have a name to enter him by. Any ideas? You found him." They both stared at each other. "The parents always come with the baby's name. All we have to do is to try not to drown them," McNee added with a chuckle.

"I should have never told you of the one that slipped out of my hands at the first baptism I performed. I was so nervous," the vicar said scowling. "It wasn't as bad as when Patrick stabbed the King in the foot, and everyone thought it was part of the ritual. We could name him Patrick."

"No, not in this time. It's too political just like Henry or Elizabeth would be." McNee replied. "But we need a date of birth too. Let's use the Patrick Day Feast for it.

"Seems appropriate enough," the vicar answered. "But we still need a name. I suppose since he was in a makeshift basket, we could name him Moses. After all they found Moses in one on the Nile."

"That's way too Jewish. He'll have enough trouble trying to survive as a Christian in these times," McNee replied.

They both looked at each other dumbfounded. It was difficult to name someone. "Presto!" Father McNee exclaimed.

"Presto? You have an idea?"

"No, I mean Presto, for a name. He's suddenly here." As he snapped his fingers chuckling, "Presto, just like that. If he wants to come up with his own name later, he can."

About then I started crying. "He either doesn't like the name or we better feed him. What are we going to do with him? I can't take him. My wife's been gone almost three years. Now ... well, I just can't," Woolsey choked out.

"I think I'm up to saving one more soul before it's my time," McNee said looking at me. "Let's get it done. Let's baptize Presto," he proclaimed.

And so they did together. One in Latin, one in English, both essentially the same words. Afterwards, aside from feeding me some milk and a mashed up baked egg, the vicar went back to the church. He returned shortly afterwards. "Here. I want you to have this for your library. It's an English Bible. Maybe by the time he's old enough it will be all right to teach him with this." And so I was Presto.

The confused Burbages then introduced themselves as James and Ellen. I was allowed to hang my coat near the fire to dry. James brought a stack of papers that he had gone through and cleaned up for the beginning of the latest play. Its author was supposed to write and bring the rest of it that afternoon. It was another comedy and Ellen hoped it would not be another bad one as she made breakfast. Somehow I suspected she was making a little extra.

"Why don't you just do Marlow's play again? You know it brings them in," she said.

"No, I had to give out too many free tokens from the last disaster. I don't want them to use them on a play we can make money on."

He brought me a writing board along with quill and ink and hesitated as he handed them to me. I laid down on the floor near the fire and waited for the last shiver from the cold to leave me. First, I took a practice run with a dry quill without ink to make sure my hand was steady. I then inked up and started to write very slowly.

He looked down at me and shook his head. "At that rate it will be noon before you finish the first line."

"I always copy the first line slowly so it's straight on the page, then I gauge the rest to follow, Sir. It's also been about six months since I held a quill. It always takes some getting used to how heavy the ink will flow from each one." The second line went much faster and soon I had the feel back.

"Let me see," he said, and I handed what I had copied to Ellen Burbage who looked at it, smiled, and handed it to him. He looked at it and handed it back without comment. As they talked more about the plans for the play and how they were ever going to pull it off, I finished the first page. Breakfast was ready and she offered me some.

I handed up the completed page and thanked her for the offer but then insisted, "Let me copy another page, Ma`am." Master Burbage scowled as he took the page from her and then read through what I had copied. His face softened with approval of what I had done. Talking under his breath, he said, "I guess you can write."

"You're going to need someone to help copy all this before we can start rehearsing. You know you won't have enough time." She triumphantly replied.

"Humph, I've got work to do," and he gulped down his breakfast and went back upstairs.

"Don't mind him. He's a bit stubborn, but I think he can really use you." My heart and soul leaped with joy and I knew Father McNee was back in both. My stomach also leaped with joy as she gave me a baked egg and some bread and cheese and some milk.

Part 4 – The Play

I kept copying the pages of the play. I figured the more I did, the greater chance I could make arrangements to be fed in the days ahead. I had never read or seen a play. It is mostly dialogue. Each player needs to connect to the next to tell the tale. There is rarely narration to set up or explain each part like in a book. A book story uses both. I had probably read a hundred books by then. Now, centuries later, I find you have other marvels that will even let the book read itself to you.

I discovered your magical audio book tapes. They must have a thousand feet of words hidden on a brown ribbon. Now, though they are still called the same, they come in many other forms. They can come on round shiny disks that spin. You even have little doodads that are called thumb drives, though they have no resemblance to a thumb and they certainly don't drive. They even can be "streamed" on some of your bedeviled devices. All of these marvels would have gotten you burned at the stake in a flash in my day, a Fate I strongly advise you avoid …

The audio performer narrates these tales and must create all the characters with his voice. You can recognize each one just by the tone and reflection of the voices he gives them. It is always amazing to read a great tale, but then to have the opportunity to hear it played … well, now maybe you begin to understand why

I've stuck around all this time. One of the finest tales you have from your era is the Harry Potter series by J. K. Rowling performed by Jim Dale.

My era became known as the Renaissance of Theater, even though non-religious plays had been largely outlawed. The Renaissance was changing that and many ways of thinking. Many great poets or writers of my era are still known in your time. Christopher Marlow for instance, whose recent play had filled Burbage's Theatre and thus helped me eat for a week, is one. William Shakespeare is, of course, another you have all heard of. He is still taught to your children in school when you can pry them free from their bedeviled cell devices.

So getting back to the point, plays are much harder to write. A book is mostly a narration that you add the right amount of dialogue to enrich and color it with. Writing dialogue is the most difficult if you ever decide to take on the task. So I as I copied the play, this one being all dialogue, I was amazed by this contrast. I finished copying the whole stack during the course of the day. Master Burbage had gone out to attend to many other varied preparations.

When he returned and opened the door, he saw me sitting at the kitchen table asleep. "What the devil?" he bellowed which woke me with a start. I realized I must have been a bit of a site as I was now wearing a monk's set of robes.

"Oh, hello Sir. I finished copying all the pages," and pointed to the papers stacked up, with the last still drying. "Your wife was kind enough to loan me this robe so I could clean and dry my clothes. I hope you don't mind."

"She would. She probably thinks you're another one of her blasted stray cats she keeps feeding," James scowled. Then his eyes opened wide and he exclaimed, "Oh, shite! Ellen? Ellen! Where are you? You're not going to keep him. Ellen!" he called out as he started off to find her. But then he stopped, turned around and took the pile of papers stacked in front of me.

Well, they did decide to keep me. I had written so many pages that James knew he owed me several days' food. "Where do you stay, and how did you come from Ireland?" he eventually asked while waiting for his poet with the rest of the play to arrive.

"That is a sad tale probably worthy of a book, but I don't think it would work for a play, Sir. I was betrayed and tricked to go to Wales for work, but was sold as a slave instead," I said in a sad bashful way, as it was uncomfortable to speak of it for the first time, along with remembering Robert. "I escaped and worked my way toward London. I joined some of her Queen's soldiers at Gloucester and they helped me find my way here in exchange for use of my quill. Well, their quill. We even went to the great cathedral in Oxford, the first I had ever seen." I included that little bit in hopes they would not question me as to my religion, as that would probably end any hope of employment. I hadn't decided if I would lie when that question would inevitably come up.

"When I got to London I didn't have any place safe to stay, so, well, I ended up hiding in a graveyard at night because I decided I was more afraid of the living than the dead. It was okay in summer when it was warmer," I continued.

Shocked by my reply, Ellen exclaimed. "Where are you staying *now*!"

"I was hoping you would let me stay outside under the overhang out of the weather where you first found me. I could guard your property and keep your kitty company."

"It's getting too cold," she said.

"I have a heavy coat and two blankets to keep me warm. I do have a problem finding a safe place to leave my bag and blankets during the day to find work. I won't survive if I get robbed."

I could see James Burbage thinking how strange it was that this probable thief had more to fear of being robbed than he did. "You can stay outside the back door, but don't ever let me find you stealing anything. I'd give you such a third degree, you'd never forget," he surprisingly broke in, even to the amazement of his wife. "I will probably have a lot more for you to copy once that bloody poet gets here. If you're up for it, there will be a lot more to do tonight. I can't pay you much and nothing now. We'll have to reach some kind of arrangement."

"There is nothing you have that I want to steal. The only thing I need coins for is so that I don't starve or freeze. This is the first time I ate in four days. You're right. I am a stray cat, and all you need to offer me is food and warmth. I will gladly work all through the night just to stay warm inside."

"And what happened to your head or rather your hair? Lice?" he then asked.

"No, there are some evil men who wanted me to do some horrible things. They do not take kindly to being refused. It was down to my shoulders, so I cut it off, so I wasn't easily recognizable. Is it that bad? I don't see many mirrors on the streets."

"I can trim it up if you like," Ellen offered. "I do our players' hair quite often."

He frowned as he no doubt thought he shouldn't have brought it up. Of course this would be his wife's response. At that, the poet arrived, and all attention turned away from me. James immediately took the poet upstairs and his wife left for other errands. Not knowing what I should do next I simply sat there. From the loud voices I heard later, I was actually glad I wasn't that poet.

Shortly afterwards, a man walked in, saw me sitting at the table, nodded as if it was perfectly natural to see a boy sitting at the table in a monk's robe, and went upstairs. Once again I sat there alone and waited for, I wasn't sure what.

A while after that, Ellen returned and asked, "Did Richard come in yet?"

I didn't know who Richard was, but assumed he must have been the man who had recently come in. I pointed to the hallway opening that led upstairs with the words "Veni, Vidi, Vici" over it, and she went upstairs. 'Strange household,' I thought to myself, and then looked down at the monk's robe I was wearing. 'Strange household indeed.'

Still another bit later, Mistress Burbage came back downstairs to go out and simply said, "You're needed." Two simple words. It didn't matter if they had been whispered or shouted across the streets of all of London.

'You're needed,' my mind repeated. They were the sweetest words I had yearned to hear since I had left Ireland. I grabbed the writing supplies in front of me and dashed upstairs.

I entered the upper level and waited to be addressed, as the men were deep in discussion. Part of the room had a large table with papers spread all over where they were working. There were haphazard shelves filled with papers and books. Half of the floor had a balcony above it also filled with more shelves and open spaces stacked up like an unorganized attic. A taller man would have to duck to access what was below it. There was short set of steps with a platform midway where the steps doubled back to the top. This was basically Burbage's office. The downstairs had the kitchen and apparently some living quarters.

"Good. You said you could do some copying. Now's the time," James began as he addressed me. He simply introduced me as Presto without any need for further explanation. He then introduced me to the other two men. One was the poet or author of the play. The other was his son, Richard, who was an actor. He also mostly directed the other players and worked out the actions and flow of the play on the stage. The senior Burbage, James, mostly took care of all the logistics of getting the play put together. The copies of the plays for the players were done by whoever was available. Sometimes the players copied them when there was more time before rehearsals. They were a bit scarce right now having not being paid for the previous disaster. The

Burbages also did copies, especially as the final version was rewritten and finalized.

"We start rehearsal tomorrow and I need enough copies to get my players started," Richard began. "We have the first bit completed but still have to finish working through the ending parts. James said you are a very good scribe, and I'm sure there's a very good story as to why you're dressed as a monk, later. There won't be time to copy the whole play over for each player, so I'd like you to copy just the lines for each one separately. Do you understand?"

"I want one full completed copy first, so we have two sets to work from. That way you can see how you have to break out each player," James interrupted.

"Aye, Sir. If the players are going to read this through while trying to act and memorize it, how large a print do you want me to use and how do you want it spaced out? Also, Sirs, should I write the last line of the previous player's words just before, so they know when they're supposed to jump in?"

"That would be helpful as they won't have their own complete set," Richard said with somewhat of an impressed look. "You're an Irish Monk, then?" he added with a now puzzled expression. These were the first words he heard me speak and I had my Irish accent.

"It's complicated," his father, James, answered. Here is the first part to copy, and here is an example of how large to space it out," he continued while digging out an old script from a previous play.

I had looked around for a clear place to work and then suggested, "I could set up on the stairway landing to copy, Sir. There is good light there and I won't be in the way, unless you want me to bring it down to the kitchen. Also, I need more ink and possible another quill and I see you have quite a few lying about."

"Yes, that will be fine, take what you need," James said.

So I set up and copied all night. The men kept going over lines, sometimes arguing and sometimes laughing. Laughing was good since it was to be a comedy. Ellen brought up food and smiled when she gave me mine. I did step out occasionally to do my business, as I knew where it was and thank God was not where all the patrons would go. I brought my bag and clothes back up with me and placed them under the stairs. Occasionally James would ask how I was advancing and during those times I was able to ask for clarification on some of the wording. He was relieved at my progress.

"There are some lines that just seem like there might be something missing," I started to explain. "I made a list of the line and even a couple possible suggestions as to what to include. I left those lines blank on the copies until I was sure what to fill in."

"Oh, a poet now too, and a scribe, and a monk and Irish!" Richard interjected with a grin.

James went over my questions with a tiresome look as he probably hoped for no additional changes.

"Hmm, oh yes, I knew about that one and forgot to scratch it out and fix it. I don't remember now how I was going to, but yours will do." Richard let out a bit of a laugh and James proceeded to make the other corrections so I could continue.

The bells had easily rung three in the morning and Richard and the poet had long left. James had also finally fallen asleep at the table, even though Ellen had told him to go to bed several times earlier. I had finished each player's script and, exhausted, curled up under the steps with my blanket and was fast asleep. I had changed back into my own worn clothes. I was warm and dry for the first time in as long as I could remember. I had barely fallen asleep when I was nudged by a foot.

"Wake up, we've work to do," James yawned. I realized it was actually morning, so I had at least gotten several hours sleep. "How much did you finish copying?"

I yawned deeper. "Morning Sir. I finished all the player's parts. They're on the table. The last couple pages I left out to dry."

"Well, let's get breakfast. We still have to finish the last parts," and we headed downstairs where Ellen already was making some eggs.

"Morning. Did you let the boy get any sleep? I'll have breakfast ready in a few."

"We got enough," though our bloodshot eyes said otherwise. "Richard is supposed to have the players rounded up by noon to start rehearsing. We still have to copy the rest of the parts."

"Not until we eat and I'm going to trim the boy's hair this morning."

"Many thanks, ma`am," I started to say.

"We don't have time to fool with his hair."

"Of course we do. You didn't even have him for any of this yesterday at this hour. Imagine if he hadn't found shelter with *our* cat the previous night. You'd be in a real pickle without him. Besides, I'll cut it while you eat."

I saw that they liked to do this back and forth type of bantering between them. I suppose it was like their form of trying to out act each other. I wondered if this is what it was like to have parents. Still, I had no regrets having been raised by Father McNee. It made me who I am, and I felt a tinge of pride.

I did get my hair trimmed and we finished the copies in time. Ellen also found a decent pair of pants that fit me from their costumes. We went to the Theatre to meet Richard and the other players. It was an octagon-shaped building. The Burbages and others had built it here outside London's jurisdiction sometimes called the Liberties, in an area referred to as the marsh. A little over a decade later they tore it down for material to build the new Globe playhouse just over London Bridge in Southwark. Years later the Globe burned down in its famous fire, and no, I had nothing to do with it. At least as far as I know …

I was going to be able to watch the rehearsal! Funny how Fate is. In one day, she had changed my life from its likely final days, to being needed. I, of course, had offered prayers of thanks to our Lord and Father McNee and thought how strange Fate was. I had all but given up. It appears she was looking out for me after all. That is, except when she wasn't trying to scare the blazes out of me or kill me. Still, I thanked her just the same.

It was a sunny day as we entered the playhouse where Richard had already assembled the players. "What? No monk today?" as he greeted us. I had never seen a playhouse before, in fact few had back then. The stage was already full of props that had been chosen from ones that were previously used and stored in other shed like buildings on the grounds.

There was a brief introduction by James.

"Look here everyone, this is Presto. He's a scribe and has made copies of your scripts. If you have any problem reading them, talk to him."

"Can't be any worse than your writing," one of them answered. And then they all started asking various questions about the play, when it was to open, and when they might expect some pay. Enough questions were answered, and directions given to finally get the rehearsal started.

"Where the devil is Sessions? We don't have time to rehearse without him and I don't have time to fill in," James grumbled loudly. "He's always late."

"I could read his lines until he gets here," I offered.

"You don't just read lines. You have to present them so the next player can act on them." James rebuffed.

"I just copied them along with the whole play, so I know the flow well enough to try to present them."

"Let him try, he can't do any worse than Sessions. Besides his Irish accent might make the lines funnier. Could always pretend he's Scottish," one of the players jumped in and said.

James looked at me and took a page from the script he was holding.

"Here, I'll present these lines to you and you try to read this bit back to me. Let's see how you do." At that he read, or presented, his lines and I followed. There was a little chuckling and I thought I hadn't done that well. He read his next lines and I again followed. This time they all broke out in laughter.

"See, I told you he could do better than Sessions!" one of them howled. They weren't laughing *at* me; they were laughing *for* me.

"Well, well. First a scribe and an Irish monk, then a poet, and now even a player! What are we to expect next? I like what you've done with your hair, by the way. And where did your lovely Irish accent go?" Richard humorously interjected.

Before I could answer, James raised his hand.

"Calm down, we have work to do. Presto, go ahead and cover Session's part till he gets here." And with that, he looked at me and shook his head with an approving grin.

And so we rehearsed and got to know each other. It was a grand bunch, even including Sessions when he finally arrived. Though rushed to produce, the play worked out well enough to recover from the previous disaster. I basically moved in under the stairs to the balcony and had plenty of work. They gave me decent clothes to wear from their costume wardrobes. Mistress Burbage was a good cook and surprisingly, I ate with them. I always kept a little for the kitty who had now also moved in with me, much to Ellen's delight, and James's annoyance. This was especially true when the kitty would lie down on all his papers, just the way you would expect any cat to do. I named her Hope.

You can also imagine Hope's fascination with feathered quills and the effect on my efforts at scribing. It was far more entertaining than a kitty today on your bedeviled keyboards and mouse. It appears that my guardian angel muse, Millie is about to try to prove me wrong. She is sitting on my lap with mischief in her eyes and, as my muse, knows what I have just written. ccccccaaaaaa Could I have the keyboard back now, Millie? aaaattttttt I think we're only allowed one ghost writer at a time. ccccaaaaatt I think someone wants to play so I best give in. I'll be back in a bit to continue my tale.

The end of October had become pretty decent, especially since I had expected to be dead. I had found work, honest work, and you cannot imagine how grateful I felt. I enjoyed this work and was glad when James found new tasks for me. The next play was a bit of a frolic for All Hallow's Eve. It was actually more of a traditional Irish folk play performed by amateur actors we called mummers and guisers. The rehearsal was complete mayhem and didn't have a normal script that was followed. It had mock combat scenes mixed in with some paganism along with the recognition of the changing of the Celtic season. I even got to glide across the stage as a ghost. I felt right at home.

November and December quickly passed. Business was down after an unfortunate fatal accident at one of the playhouses in November. A woman and her baby had been killed. There was again an attempt to close all playhouses by the lord mayor. It was only due to the influence of a group of nobles called the Admiral's Men with her Majesty that prevented them from being shut down. This only added more stress to putting plays on that would make ends meet. James was not paying me any coins, but I was more than happy to survive by staying with them. I would go out on decent days when James didn't need me, and do my story telling on the corners in the older, busier parts of London.

One day he walked by and watched my performance. He gave me a pence, and then hustled others to do the same. It was funny because it was basically the same bit I had done with Jack the day we met. It was my best haul ever! I thanked him later that night and he indicated he wanted his pence back. I grinned as I handed it back to him.

He asked me what I was going to do with my newfound fortune, and I told him I would save it. I told him I had bought a pence worth of bread for a little girl that was begging. I knew too well what it was like.

"You can't afford that," he said.

"I don't think I can afford not to," I replied. He gave me the pence back.

A disturbing event occurred during one of these jaunts into London. As I was walking, I recognized one of my "clients" from my Wilson days. It seemed so long ago. Unfortunately, he also recognized me and was more terrorized than I was. He seemed to signal me not to acknowledge him, but I knew he wanted to talk out of sight. I waited for him to pass, and then turned and followed after waiting a bit. He turned down an alleyway and I followed casually. He was waiting, ducked out of sight.

"Topcliffe's been looking for you, boy," he whispered from his hiding place. "He questioned all of us. Wilson told him of everyone you had been with."

"Why?"

"Wilson didn't say and then he disappeared."

"What about Wilson's other lads?" I asked, hoping nothing had happened to Jack.

"He interrogated all of us at Gatehouse Prison. I didn't know if I was going to be released. He's probably having me watched and them too. You best not be seen with any of us," he pleaded.

"I won't. I hoped he had forgotten about me. I've made arrangements to get out of the city. Are you going to tell him you saw me?"

"No. I hope to never see him again. Now get away from me and never ever acknowledge seeing me."

With that I continued down the alley and disappeared into a crowd. I circled the city aimlessly and found places where I could watch to see if I recognized anyone I might have seen earlier. It did not appear I was being followed. As I walked, I considered whether I should leave London. No, I had no place to go and I would then be back to starving and freezing.

Topcliffe would logically conclude that I had run away from London. He was also looking for the English boy, Robert Dumas. Jack was the only one I had talked that much to, and I never told him of the cemetery or tavern or where I went at night. I hadn't even told him I could read and write very well, or what type of employment I was looking for. I didn't tell him of my north side London adventures, fearing that he might be caught some day.

He hadn't told me much about himself either. All I knew was that he had a sister that worked at the brothel and they had been orphaned. His sister, of course, had never heard of my imaginary cousin, Molly. I prayed he was all right. I thought how I missed the tavern keeper but didn't dare go back to visit. I hoped Topcliffe had not tracked me to there. I didn't want others to be harmed and the tavern knew what type of work I sought. I would just have to wait and let Fate play out her hand.

In December, one of the plays needed an additional girl. Women and girls were not allowed to perform on stage, so men and boys had to fill the roles. I was pressed into service to play a very small part. I had hoped to play a role someday, but as a boy. I had tried to forget about Topcliffe, but how could I? I had only heard that he was back at the Gatehouse prison, obviously enjoying torturing poor hapless beings. I did not want to be seen on stage and be recognized with long light-colored hair. Fortunately, I was able to choose a dark-brown wig without raising any questions. It was another comedy and I did nervously enjoy doing it.

The end of December neared, and it would soon be Christmas. Though Christmas was considered a Catholic holiday, England's Protestants still loved it. That is, except for the Puritans that pretty much banned it. The Theatre had a Christmas Eve performance during the day of mostly caroling. My voice had not quite changed, and I sang a tenor-Celtic-Irish-Hallelujah song that was well received. And I even did it as a boy! Since the performance was during the day, we all went to the local parish for church services that evening. The Burbages attended church occasionally and I would go with them. I was happy and content. To this day it was one of the happiest Christmas Eves I can remember just sleeping under the stairs of the balcony with Hope. I offered many prayers that night. Prayers of thanks, prayers for the Burbages who had saved me, prayers for the lads at Swansea that I could still do nothing for, prayers for Robert and Father McNee. And then prayers for all the orphans like Jack who had no stairs to seek shelter under or food to eat that eve.

Part 5 – Shakespeare

The winter months of January and February were not exactly the playhouse season in London, and crowds were sparse. I did not have as much work, but I still stayed and ate with the Burbages. Ellen had joked with her husband that it cost nothing to feed me since she was making the same amount of food. The only difference now was that she had put him on a diet that freed up the food I was eating. I'm not sure that exactly endeared me to him.

The quest for plays to get through winter and especially have some exceptional ones for spring brought many a poet to the Theatre. Christopher Marlowe's first plays had been performed just the previous season. His most famous play, Doctor Faustus, was yet to be written. This play would have the devil on stage buying the soul of Faustus and showing that the devil could be just as evil as man. There would be many famous playwrights in this era. Most had one thing in common, they were all university educated. That meant they were from wealthy families and likely noble. The crass comedies could be written by anyone. A serious piece that could be considered literature had to be written by those of this elite-educated group. Burbage had tended to view his poets accordingly and would not give much consideration for a serious play from someone more common in their education.

This view might have softened when he considered that his scribe, me, had no formal education. Yet here I was, not only copying various works, but also helping to correct them. Poets were coming and going pitching their ideas to James. One slow morning, I was sitting at the kitchen table writing my own piece of literature. I had decided to write down the story of my Druid Prince Enros. I thought I might do better performing it on street corners if I had taken the time to write it down.

Another unknown poet, who came from Stratford, was to stop by with a play. He was not from the university crowd. He was actually a player; however, Burbage wasn't looking for any more actors. He would only hire him as an actor if the play was useable. The young man from Stratford introduced himself as William Shakespeare and I was eventually introduced as Burbage's scribe, Presto. Shakespeare looked up at the words over the hallway passage and read, "Veni, Vidi, Vici."

I responded, "That's Latin for 'I saw, I conquered, I came'."

James laughed and said, "No boy, you've got that wrong again. It's 'I came, I saw, I conquered'." Where did you ever learn that anyway?"

"The soldiers I was traveling with at Gloucester had used it. They had, well, been enjoying the company of a lady and kept repeating it. I thought it rather strange over your hallway."

Burbage started laughing uproariously while Shakespeare stood trying to look amused since he had no idea what we were talking about. "You mean these past months you thought ..." and continued laughing harder. "Oh, wait until I tell Ellen what her little stray has been thinking."

As I blushed and realized the soldiers had changed the order of the words I pleaded, "Don't you dare!"

"Ellen, oh Ellen, I have something to tell you!" he taunted.

"But who are you going to tell her I thought conquered who?" I then slyly grinned.

At that he stopped laughing for a moment, as if realizing he was going to be checkmated in two moves, but then he grinned. "All right, we'll keep this between the two of us," and then continued laughing. "Come along Shakespeare, let's see what you've got," and motioned him on under the Latin words.

Shakespeare, still trying to look amused, passed under the words and no doubt thought, 'Strange household, strange household indeed.' As it was, he did have a rather good play. It was about a brooding ghost, but I don't remember the name. I've never heard of it since. I always hoped a copy of it might turn up some day, and, of course, would be very proud if it was one I had scribed.

I enjoyed working with this new poet and actor. He seemed more down to earth than those who were from the universities. He had an amazing wit and a way with words, and we shared a few laughs. I purposely walked with him to the playhouse the day we were to do the first rehearsal. I had hoped to someday do some acting myself and decided to pitch an idea.

"Sir, have you ever considered writing a play with a prince that is still a boy?"

"Sounds like someone wants me to write a part he can play, possibly your Prince Enros?" he answered smiling.

"Doesn't have to be my prince. All of our past Kings were boys at some time. There's got to be a haunting story somewhere."

"Yes, there were a few that would make a good tragedy," he pondered aloud.

I grinned and tried some childish wit, "To pee, or not to pee? That is the question. I think tis nobler that I do so before we begin our rehearsal. I'll see you inside in a bit." And then, hoping I had planted seed for some ideas for future plays, we parted paths. The play was a success and I just had a feeling that this young man in his twenties was going to do more with the Burbages.

Queen Elizabeth, The Pelican Portrait by Nicholas Hilliard

Chapter 4 – The Queen

Part 1 – Her Majesty's Visit

March brought many new beginnings. It soon would be spring and was always a welcome relief from winter. Spring would be a double-edged sword though because it also meant Catholic Spain would again be preparing for their invasion. No one knew where their Armada would land, but regardless, *they would be coming to London.* There was no way to escape the simple reality the city would eventually be under siege.

Many people in London had become my friends. I did not want to see them harmed. The Spanish Inquisition would have zero tolerance for Protestants, let alone playhouses for that matter. There was fear that another Saint Bartholomew Day type massacre of Protestants, as had happened in Paris a little over a dozen years previous, would happen in London. And the Spanish would certainly burn Burbage's Theatre down. Even though I had to hide being Catholic, I could not support these Spaniards. Their interference in the second Munster rebellion ultimately led to the deaths of thousands of Irish by the English.

Setting that unpleasant thought behind, figuring Topcliffe would probably murder me long before I would have to worry about the Spanish anyway, I looked forward to my coming birthday. I was going to be fourteen! I had beaten the childhood mortality odds. This simply meant that if you survived to fourteen, you would then probably make it to twenty-five! When you're thirteen, that is almost a half a lifetime.

Now I had to decide which March 17th I would use to celebrate my Saint Patrick's Day birthday. Father McNee had decided to have some fun confusing me on my eighth birthday. It seems our Julian calendar had a slight miscalculation. This miscalculation had actually made our old calendar off by being ten days behind. This was well known, but it was Pope Gregory XIII that decided to finally fix it with a new calendar. Ten days were magically jumped ahead in October 1582. An occasional leap century day would be added in the future to prevent further errors.

None of the Protestant countries would accept this. Imagine the ensuing chaos, Catholic Europe calendar-wise was ten days ahead of the rest. England and Ireland were still ten days behind. Can you imagine how annoying it would be to plan a battle and show up on the wrong day? There were also problems with every contract written since they had dates based on the Julian calendar. Landlords could cheat their tenants out of ten days' rent since that October month now ended ten days earlier. And you thought the year 2000 and the start of the second millennium was going to bring an end to the world! It would be over a 150 years later that England and Ireland (which was still under English rule) and the Northern-Americas corrected their calendars. By then they were off by eleven days!

Father McNee had given me a choice as to which day I would celebrate. I decided to stick with the old English 17th since Ireland was not changing their calendar either. That, plus we really didn't know what day I was born anyway. To add just little more fun to the month of March, the calendar year did not change until near the end of March. New Year's Day on January 1st was still the old year.

It was up to the Queen and her advisors to make a plan for England to prevent a siege this coming year. The two most powerful men in England were her two chief advisors. Sir William Cecil, 1st Baron of Burghley, was her Lord High Treasurer, and Sir Francis Walsingham was her Principle Secretary, often referred to as her Spy Master. The two of them had kept careful watch on Mary, Queen of Scots. They were the ones that found proof Mary had accepted a Catholic plan to assassinate Elizabeth. She was Elizabeth's only true rival to the throne that Pope Sixtus V and the Spanish could replace her with. It was Cecil who made sure the execution order for treason was carried out. Elizabeth had signed the death warrant but had left instructions that only she could give the final order.

It was rumored William Cecil had fallen out of favor with Elizabeth after the execution. It was not unusual to fall out of favor with her Majesty. Some even ended up in London Tower. Most would return to her favor if they still had their head attached. In the meantime, this could leave a serious power void. Cecil's son, Robert, was being groomed by both Walsingham and his father, as the heir apparent. This was assuming that he too, had not fallen into disfavor. That could mean other ambitious and ruthless men like Topcliffe could and would try to step in. Maybe I should have twisted that knife …

The Queen felt it was her duty to be seen by her subjects much to the fear of Walsingham and either of the Cecils. Spain could throw their enemy into complete chaos with the Queen's assassination since she had no heir. The Pope had declared her a heretic, which meant any fanatical Catholic could consider it their duty to kill her.

In her famous Tilbury speech that you'll hear more of later, she spoke her immortalized words.

"I know I have the body of a weak, feeble woman; but I have the heart and stomach of a King, and a King of England too."

She was not weak and feeble. She could ride a horse as well as any man. She was an avid game hunter and was good with a bow and arrow. She did her own killings even finishing with a knife. She was known to a have temper, and you didn't want to be on the wrong side of it. She was clever and cunning. She also had a sense of humor and enjoyed pulling both practical and impractical jokes. She had nicknames for everyone, and they weren't always complimentary.

So one crisp-sunlit day in the beginning of March, she decided to walk to Westminster Abbey for some kind of recognition ceremony. I had gone into the central part of London to buy parchment for the Theatre that day. There seemed to be some excitement and I heard it was rumored the Queen might be seen going to the Abbey. It had not been officially announced, but word seemed to have gotten out.

I had never seen a Queen before, so of course, I thought I might not ever have another opportunity. I had only gone to the west side of the Thames Westminster area once. This is where Parliament met. I had no idea where to go other than basically follow where small groups were forming and guessing her route. I decided it was time to play cat again, and if I was on the correct street, I should try to find a place up high like a balcony to watch from.

I left it to Fate to guide me to the most likely street and chose the largest one going to the Abbey. No one actually knew where she was coming from or when. When several soldiers rode through on horses, I figured I was on the right path. Though it wasn't even spring, the earthen streets had dried fairly well. The scarce balconies along the way were mostly occupied, but I did see one that was empty. There was a bit of a puddle under this one so there was only one man standing near it. Despite having a fear of heights, I had enjoyed climbing small trees when I was growing up. I had used that skill to scale balconies for shelter when I finally stayed on this side of the river.

The lone man waiting there didn't try to stop me when I found a way to climb up. I was wearing my only heavy coat. It had impeded my climb and was now a bit too warm. I took it off and hung it over my shoulders. I had a very good view. Then I just stood and waited. More people gathered up and down the street and eventually more guards rode by. Eventually I could hear cheering and I could see the enclave coming. I was going to see the Queen! There would likely be extremely important lords and nobles along enjoying this casual walk with her Majesty. I considered for a moment Topcliffe might possibly be one and stood ready to hide if Fate had tried to trick me.

As she passed, I waved with more excitement than I had expected, though I don't think she noticed me. She was magnificent, the most elegant lady I had ever seen. Her face glowed the purest white in the sun as if she were a mythical goddess. As I waved and she passed, the man I had seen under the balcony stepped out toward the street holding his coat closed. Then I saw he had a gun he was just starting to pull out from under his coat!

Time seemed to stand still. I did not have time to think consciously, but without even realizing it, I acted. I screamed as loud as I could and hurled myself over the top of the balcony at the assassin below. I wasn't just dropping down on him. I had leaped upward and launching myself away from the balcony. There was no way to adjust my flight. I was a ninety-pound boy on a collision course with the ground below or the man with the gun.

I hit hard but I had found my mark. The man crashed to the ground just has he raised his gun. It went off with an explosion as we both hit the earth and he rolled on top of me. I was dazed for a moment until I saw he had pulled out a knife and had already pressed its point into the hollow of my throat. I grabbed his hand but knew it would be over in seconds. He was easily two and half times my size and there was no way I could stop his thrust. In that moment, our eyes met, both filled with terror. In that split moment though, I had enough time for my mind to race at the speed of a dream. I remembered a time before when in my worst moment, I had asked myself the final question *"why had I lived?"* This time I was at peace with the answer.

And as our eyes remained locked, he hesitated. His hand on the knife went limp and he whispered, "Have mercy, kill me," and then pleaded, "Please." He had let the knife loose in my hands. I knew why he asked since I had seen what Topcliffe did to traitors. The Queen's guards were rushing us. I took the knife and tried stabbing him in the chest. That only got a slight ouch out of him, and a look of dismay. I then took the knife and thrust it into his throat. I pulled it out to strike again but it had found its mark. I did not know blood was so hot. Like a horse's pant in winter, it steamed in the cool air as it gushed over me. He rolled over as I pushed myself away shocked, trying to stand holding the knife. The blood that covered me also steamed its eerie white mist.

Everyone had seen what had happened including the Queen. My scream had alerted them all and they had turned to see. The guards were rushing upon us and I staggered, dropping the knife. I just stood there.

One of the guards had reached the assassin on the ground and simply announced, "DEAD."

The Queen was also now approaching, though the lords and nobles with her were trying to stop her. At the same time her guards were clearing her path.

I bowed, and without thinking said in my sweetest Irish brogue, "Your Majesty, I pray you are not harmed." The blood on my shirt was still steaming.

"Thanks to you I am safe, but are you hurt?" her Majesty replied with concern.

"No, Ma'Lady, me thinks it 'tis is all his blood, not mine," I answered as I became more aware of the sight I must have been.

By now the crowd was attempting to kick the lifeless traitor and even dip their fingers in his blood. They were starting to shout. "Death. Death to all Catholics!"

One of the lords with her tried to silence the crowd and then the Queen asked me, "Are you Irish?"

"Aye, Your Majesty, I am Irish, I am your most loyal subject, and I AM CATHOLIC." I declared the last loudly, more to the crowd then the Queen. The crowd that heard me went silent.

"Why did you save me then if you're Catholic?" she asked puzzled.

"Well, first Your Majesty, you are the most lovely Lady I have ever had the pleasure to lay my eyes upon, and, well, as a Catholic I was brought up to prevent harm to others. Besides, you are my Queen. Why wouldn't I protect you, Your Majesty?" I answered.

"You will be rewarded greatly for your loyalty and bravery. All you need to do is ask," she declared. "What is your name, boy?"

"My name is Presto, Your Majesty. I would be honored to have tea with Your Majesty someday, though I'm afraid I won't be able clean all these stains out," I replied as I looked down at what was left of the clothes the Theatre had loaned me.

I did not dive over the balcony seeking a reward. On the other hand, I thought for a second what I might ask for. She certainly had a lot of gold and silver! I would never fear going hungry again. But I already knew what I would really ask for. Justice. Justice and help for the enslaved Irish lads at Swansea. That still remained the one hope above all others that drove me. That, and just surviving.

"Lord Walsingham, make sure this boy has the finest clothes made and arrange to bring him to Whitehall Palace so I can reward him properly," she declared.

"Many thanks Ma'am, I mean Your Majesty. You don't need to have my clothes made too fine, just something sturdy I can wear to make a proper living."

Lord Walsingham then broke in, "Your Majesty, I think we need to protect this boy and also have him questioned about anything he might know about the attempt upon your life. It is imperative we learn if there are more traitors and conspirators."

"My Lord, I'm afraid I wouldn't know. I was just watching from the balcony when I saw the man step out with a gun below me," I stated, not having a good feeling about being "protected" or "questioned."

"You need to see if the boy has been hurt," the Queen in effect ordered him.

"Captain Lovett take this boy to the Gatehouse and have a physician attend to any of his needs. He is to be treated well. Give him one of the guest rooms and keep him secure until we have an opportunity to talk to him," Lord Walsingham now commanded.

"But My Lord, I am not harmed. Please do not send me to the Gatehouse Prison to be tortured! Catholics go in, but they never come out the same, if they come out at all," I desperately pleaded. The terror of being taken to the Gatehouse where Topcliffe does his three degrees of interrogation hit me like a bullet. He would recognize me and butcher me.

"My sweet boy," her Majesty interrupted. "No harm will come to you. That is my direct order. You will be taken care of and I will have you brought to me in a few days when Sir Francis and I return. Sir Francis, you are to insure nothing happens to this boy."

"But, but …" I started to say without being able to finish as Lord Walsingham was ushering her away as he still feared danger to his Queen.

"I have a carriage ordered up. We must leave here immediately. Please, Your Majesty. I will make sure the boy is safe. Now please, we must go," Lord Walsingham pleaded, but in a way that the Queen accepted stubbornly, almost as if an order.

"But My Lord," I began again.

"Go with the captain. I must protect the Queen. You don't want to interfere with Her safety, do you? You have done Her a great service today, boy, now serve Her again. You'll be fine. You have my word."

Part 2 – The Gatehouse

'Right,' I thought, until Topcliffe gets his hands on me. I had no choice but to go with the captain. I rode with him on his warhorse that was, as before, a bit of a stretch to fit on. Fortunately, it was a short ride. Why had I opened my big mouth and declared I was a Catholic to the crowd, let alone to the Queen and Lord

Walsingham? I could have just been adorable and went my way proudly. But no, this time it wasn't my mouth that got in the way, it was my mind. The crowd had turned ugly shouting for vengeance and violence. They were undoubtedly correct. It was likely a Catholic who had tried to murder the Queen. Catholics and eventually Protestants would be killed if the mob spread and rioted. But it was also a Catholic that killed the assassin, and that was the reason the fateful words fell from my mouth. They were declared to stop the killing before it would take root. However, Lord Walsingham probably thought I was some kind of fanatical Catholic bent on martyrdom.

I considered my options. I could try to escape; how difficult could that be? Only a big man with a bigger horse to chase me ... I could try throwing myself in the river to drown and get it over quickly, but we weren't going to be crossing the Thames. Funny how Fate is. I had always wanted to have an opportunity to do some knightly deed. I had also hoped I would have time to do some deed to redeem myself from that horrid night I had stabbed Topcliffe. Now that I had seemingly done both, was it time my debt had finely come due?

I had also killed a man, as the blood drying on me attested. I had killed him because I didn't want him to have second thoughts and again thrust the blade into my throat. I had also done it for mercy. I was going to be questioned as to how I managed to kill him.

"Oh, he just asked me, so I figured why not," probably would not be a good answer.

And who was going to question me? That brought me back to the question I wanted to block from my mind. Topcliffe. Topcliffe was all I could think of. And then I could see the Gatehouse and prison. I wondered how many others had been brought here with the hopeless terror I felt. My mind was numb. Captain Lovett turned me over to another captain and gave him Lord Francis and the Queen's orders along with a brief description of the earlier events. I was locked in a comfortable room and given a basin of water to wash with. The room must have been for holding more important people, but it did have bars over the window. There was a real bed and adequate blankets, but no fire in the fireplace.

I was left alone for hours in what seemed like an eternity each time I heard noises. My flying and landing had left me surprisingly uninjured. I had a sore ankle and bit of a limp. I knew there would be some bruises, but nothing broken. I washed as best I could, but the basin's water barely cleansed me and would do little to clean my bloody shirt. It hadn't even occurred to me that my coat was still up on the balcony. The only contact I had was another guard bringing me food and lighting the hearth. He had no answers to my many questions which included inquiring about my coat.

The coat had my pouch with coins in it from Burbage for parchment. They would wonder what happened to me when I didn't return. I didn't know how to get a message to them, or if I should. I wondered how they would react to finding out I am Catholic, and I had killed an assassin. Would I still be able to work and find shelter with them? I would just have to wait, and I would know what would happen when it happened.

My temperament went from sobbing to anger and pounding on the door screaming. I decided that wasn't a good idea in case Topcliffe was creeping about and heard me. I was truly alone. I had to make a plan if I was going to survive to my fourteenth birthday in just a few days. Wouldn't it be funny to die on my birthday, Saint Patrick's Day, the same day the saint died? Well, not really, unless you're into all that Irish irony stuff which, of course, I am.

So there were three paths Fate might place before me. One, Topcliffe is not here. If that is the case, I would be fine because after all, I had saved the Queen. Two, Topcliffe is here and immediately recognizes me. In that case, probably watch for some way to end it quickly, like dive out a window. Three, Topcliffe is here but doesn't recognize me. That is a possibility… He only saw me briefly as he prepared to do, well, whatever. I have grown and am taller. My hair is short now where it had covered my face somewhat, when he had me before. My voice is deeper and, in fact, is a little hoarse now. Finally, I'm Irish, not English.

If the third path is the case, how should I play it? Should I show my education and behave more nobly, or should I be an ignorant meaningless street urchin? I knew enough about Topcliffe to know he lives to be the one who has the power. It would be best to be ignorant and meaningless and not appear to be clever. I also knew about his three degrees of interrogation. Everyone did. Funny, Crowley might have even done me a favor by preparing me. And so I waited.

I had a sleepless night. I had no idea when they would come for me. The guard brought breakfast but again knew nothing. Finally, the Captain returned and said he had received word. The Queen and Lord Walsingham were to be back by the end of the week. Topcliffe would return tomorrow and he would likely have a few questions for me. The first bit of news had made my heart soar. The second bit nearly stopped it.

So that was it, Topcliffe would be interrogating me tomorrow. It appeared everything in my life had been led by Fate to the coming day. Fate, which started by teaching me to read, which then helped me escape after being sold as a slave. That Fate had brought me to London, taught me to survive and led me to being on a balcony just a few days before my birthday. Well, let's see how Fate has treated me during the most critical past days of my life. Usually she scares the hell out of me, maybe beats the crap out of me, almost kills me and then at the end, surprise! Only kidding! Tomorrow is going to be a bad day to be a Catholic.

I again went about making a plan. I tried to recall everything I had done, every word, plea, scream and mannerism from our brief encounter at Wilson's. I could not duplicate any. I replaced them with rehearsed pleas and even low screams to try to make my voice deeper. I also decided to leave my boots behind. Topcliffe might recognize them. They were the last thing he saw of me as I streaked, literally, to the balcony window to escape. One of my ankles was slightly swollen from my earlier leap of Fate, so it would not seem unusual to leave them.

I had to decide what I would tell him about my past. Being brought up by a priest would not fare well. I'll tell him that I came to London to learn to be a servant, but the contacts never happened, and I was abandoned. I'll tell him I work at the Theatre doing handiwork for food and shelter and hope to learn a trade. I will not tell him I read and write and that, in fact, I'm a scribe.

And so I waited for what seemed the longest day and then eternal night of my life. I was numb with terror and tried not to think of what might happen. Morning again came after another sleepless night, though I remember dreaming some of the dreams I had had before. I also did a lot of praying. Praying about everything from giving thanks, to asking that I might survive a bit longer. The guard again brought breakfast and I was too afraid even to ask if he knew what was to happen next and when. Finally, close to noon, the captain came in and brought me downstairs. He told me Topcliffe would arrive soon and they had caught the man who had stabbed him some months back.

'The man who had stabbed him some months back,' my mind repeated in shock. I'm the one who stabbed him! Is this some game they're playing with me and bloody well know I'm the one? Or is Fate the one playing a game, and is she going to help me or, well … My mind was so numb I just went with him and was seated at a table in a room with a fireplace that was at least warm. I could see this room opened into a larger room. It had chains hanging from the wall along with other apparatus. No Topcliffe, so it was back to waiting.

A while later, another guard brought in some papers and piled them on the other end of the table.

"You might not want to sit there," was all he said.

I could hear noises of more men coming and stood up and moved to the side of the table. The door opened and the most horrifying spider of all time entered, Topcliffe! A man was shoved in by the guards who followed. He was bound like a spider's prey and had already been beaten. The man was quiet with, not a look of terror, but one of resolve. The guards shoved him past Topcliffe and me to the other room. Topcliffe followed, stopped and stared at me.

"What is that doing here?" he exclaimed. The guard who had brought me in then mumbled something to him. Topcliffe then looked into my down-turned eyes and said, "So you're that filthy-Catholic boy."

"I'm sorry, Your Lordship, I have not been able to clean my clothes and the new ones Lord Walsingham is sending have not yet arrived," I answered with my heaviest Irish tongue. My tongue had decided to take filthy literally before my brain could intervene.

'Great move!' I thought. 'Go ahead and piss him off with your first words.'

"Silence! You ignorant-Irish peasant. I'll deal with you later. First, I have a little business to attend to. Watch. Learn. And get rid of that filthy rag," he ordered.

"Yes, My Lord." I bowed and then took off my blood-stained shirt as he walked to the other room. I folded it and laid it on the floor under the table. I stood there with my heart pounding. Had he not recognized me? The cat and mouse, or rat, game had begun. I was going to have to be the cat of a lifetime if I was going to survive.

The man had been shackled and the guards sent away. It was just the three of us now. I will spare you the details of what occurred next to the poor human being in the adjacent room. I have placed that memory in a chamber in my mind with locks and chains never to be opened again these past near 500 years. Topcliffe was interrogating him, not about being the one who stabbed him, but rather about the papers that lay upon the table before me. He was slowly destroying them, in fact, burning the man with them in hideous ways. Topcliffe was interrogating him to learn where the authors of these writings were so he could catch them, and also destroy all other copies.

As I tried to block out what was going on in that room, I started to look at the papers. One stack, which was turned sideways from me, had a letter that appeared to be addressed to the Queen.

Topcliffe returned to gather more papers to burn the man with. "What are you looking at?"

"I, I was just looking at some of the symbols, Sir. I can recognize some of them, Sir," I said cowardly as I picked up the letter upside down. "I see an aR, Sir."

"Put that down," he ordered. "Your kind will never be able to read and shouldn't be allowed to. Only us nobles are intelligent enough and ordained by our birth and God to have that right," he said as he scowled with contempt.

As he spoke, I held and read the upside-down letter. I realized it was a proposal to negotiate returning rights for English Catholics in exchange for asking the Pope to lift a papal bull against the Queen. This order had excommunicated Queen Elizabeth and declared her a heretic. That papal bull also forbade Catholics from acknowledging her as their Queen. I stared blankly. Why would he want to destroy such a proposal and keep it from the Queen? Was he an idiot? Such an agreement would eliminate the fear that English and Irish Catholics might rebel and aid Spain. I laid the letter back down bowing my head.

"Ignorant," is all he said as he walked back to the man to continue his business with him.

If the Queen's Catholics rebelled, it would be English and Irish blood spilled instead of Spanish blood. The poorly-armed Catholics wouldn't have a chance. Spain could simply wait and march in to fight the Queen's weakened and dispersed army. Spain would win, and the Protestants would likely be burned at the stake again. There wouldn't be any Catholics left to free after the fighting. Why should the English and Irish do the dirty work?

Spain was supposed to help the Irish Munster Rebellions, but only sent a token few hundred men. Thousands and thousands of Irish died, and they lost. Munster is bare, there is no one left there to save let alone free now. The only hope for Catholics to have their freedoms returned is through negotiations as proposed in this letter.

My Irish blood started to boil. The terror in my heart changed to anger. I stood there thinking I was going to do something really, really, stupid. I didn't know what it would be as I was already doing it. I grabbed the Queen's letter while Topcliffe was walking back to that poor man. I folded the letter into quarters behind my back and stuffed it down my pants.

'Brilliant.' I thought. 'Now what?' I knew he would notice it missing but I was now committed.

As he went back to his tortures that were getting even viler, I sat down on the floor by the table. I remembered noticing the beams going across under it had gaps when I laid my shirt down. I retrieved the folded letter and slid it in between them for a hiding place. At least it wouldn't be on me when he noticed it missing. I stood up as the horrifying screams were once again echoing louder. It was sickening and I again acted without consciously thinking. The last thing I wanted to do was to draw attention to myself away from the hapless being shrieking in the next room. I grabbed a stack of the papers on the table and violently vomited on them. From what I had already witnessed, this was not a difficult task. He heard me and turned. As he did, I threw the first stack of papers into the fire and grabbed more to wipe the table with.

I started apologizing in a begging tone, "I'm sorry, My Lord, I'll clean it up, I'm sorry, I'm sorry!"

"STOP, STOP!" he yelled and rushed toward me knocking over a table as he grabbed a whip from it. "You fucking-useless-ignorant-stupid boy! I'll teach you to interrupt me."

He was livid! I backed away from between the table and fireplace as he stopped at the head of the table. "Come here boy, NOW!"

I had no choice but to obey. He grabbed my arm and started dragging me into the other room cursing and beating me with the whip.

"Please, I'm sorry Sir, I didn't want to make a mess. I thought I could help you burn some of them. The Queen said I wasn't to be hurt! She wants to see me and reward me for killing her assassin." I pleaded and cried.

He continued his cursing and threw me on the floor in front of the man who had mercifully passed out, "You dare mention the Queen! No filthy Catholic is ever going to receive a reward from her. She will only believe what I tell her."

"You can have my reward, Sir, please stop, please!" I begged as he started slashing me with the whip again. I curled up on the floor trying to protect myself.

"You won't receive any reward if you hurt me. She will reward you if you teach me to be a proper Protestant. Please Sir, I'm only a boy that wants to be good," I cried.

With the idea of being honored by the Queen, he stopped whipping me. He thought for a moment, panting.

"Stand up," he ordered. I rose up on my hands and knees not sure what was next. He landed another lash on me and repeated, "I said stand up!" I tried to stand staggering. "Now you know what will happen to you if you don't do exactly what I tell you. I will teach you exactly what I want you to say when you are allowed to address Her Majesty. Do you understand, you worthless-sniveling vermin?"

"Yes Sir, gramercy Sir," I choked out thanking him while biting my tongue. I wanted to attack him. "I'm sorry, My Lord."

He walked back toward the table and yelled, "Guards!" Two quickly came in. "Get that out of here," pointing to the man hanging by his bloody wrists. I didn't know if he was still alive, I didn't know if I should hope he was or wasn't. "Get me some roasted meat and wine, I've worked up an appetite," he gloated.

"Come boy," he ordered. "What are you called other than a useless piece of shite?" he asked as he beckoned me to follow him back to the table.

"Presto, Sir."

"Stupid name. Let's see how stupid you are and if I can teach you to remember my words," he said and shoved the rest of the papers out his way almost unto the floor. I feared if they did, the Queen's letter hidden under the table so close, might be discovered.

"Clean the table first and get rid of the rest of these. Clean yourself up, too," he ordered.

I obeyed and placed the pages into the fire while quickly glancing at them. The guards brought a bowl of water and towels for him to wash up with which I used afterwards. His food quickly came, as it must have already been prepared. I figured the guards and servants knew his routine and feared him.

He pointed to a chair. "Sit."

As he ate, he started questioning me as to how an Irish Catholic boy ended up in London. I told him politely about coming for work. He was disgusted because so many English Protestants needed work. When I told him where I worked, he said he found the playhouses equally disgusting and vile and that they should all be shut down. At least he thought it was better that I worked there, where the righteous shouldn't.

I watched him eat and realized how thirsty I was. Somehow, I was hungry despite what I had seen and endured. After starving at Swansea and on London streets, I was accustomed to wanting to eat whenever there was an opportunity, no matter how horrid the day had been.

"I suppose I'm supposed to feed you now. Guards, get this gutter boy something suitable for his likes," he ordered.

Was I about to dine with Topcliffe? It was a vile thought but beat hanging from chains from the wall in the next room. They eventually brought some kind of turnip stew with some kind of fatty chewy meat in it. I had eaten worse, but why does it always have to be those damned turnips?

"Take him back to his room and get him cleaned up. I will let you know when to bring him to me for cleansing his mind," he finally ordered.

They took me to a room with a barrel of water in it to bathe in. It looked like a wine barrel and reminded me of the story that King Richard III had supposedly drowned his brother, or some relative, in one a century ago. This was the first real bath I had taken since Wilson's. The water was cold, but it helped sooth the welts I could see from Topcliffe's beating. There were clean common clothes waiting in my chamber along with shoes. Apparently, the new promised clothes had finally been sent. I couldn't believe I had made it through the day alive. Well, at least so far.

I also couldn't believe he hadn't recognized me. I had somehow managed to jump out of the fire, but now was in the frying pan. The Queen's letter was under the table. How was I going to get it out of there? If I did, how was I going to get it to the Queen? If I did, I would be openly declaring war on the most dangerous man in England. A man that still hasn't figured out I'm the one who stabbed him. I was too exhausted to do anymore thinking and closed my eyes to try to sleep it out of my mind for a while.

Early that evening, the guards came to take me back to Topcliffe. We were back at the same table and he spent quite some time telling me all about the evils and corruptions of the Catholic Church. Most of them had been pointed out by Martin Luther and had led to the Reformation. He also told me about Bloody Queen

Mary's reign, the Paris Saint Bartholomew Massacre, and especially of the Spanish Inquisition. I, of course, knew of all these things, and would have little defense for many of them. But neither was there any defense for the way innocent Catholics were being treated now who had nothing to do with those evils.

He then had a few lines for me to practice denouncing the Pope and his church. I rationalized I could learn these lines like an actor on the stage at the Theatre. I would be acting, but this performance would be for Topcliffe only. I would have to make my own lines to learn when it came time to speak to the Queen, if I would, indeed, be allowed. A commoner doesn't just strike up a conversation with the Queen, even if you happen to be her guest. I pretended to struggle to learn his few lines and managed without being slapped too many times. I suggested he make the lines shorter.

I did not see any opportunity to snatch the letter from under the table and he again had me sent away. I don't remember much about that night other than still being numb with fear. I said a lot of prayers, including for the man I had seen butchered. I eventually did sleep. It wasn't until the next afternoon I was brought back to Topcliffe in the same room with the table.

There was another set of very fine clothes waiting for me. These were the ones Lord Walsingham had actually sent. I have no idea where the ones I now was wearing came from. Topcliffe explained these were the ones I was to wear the next day when he would bring me to present to the Queen. He had me change into them to see if I could be presented properly. As I stripped, I placed the clothes I had been wearing under the table. I put the new ones on, and they were, indeed, fit for a noble. He then had me practice a short speech I would present to the Queen. He also explained what would happen if I failed, pointing to the wall in the next room.

I was noticeably nervous and sweating as I rehearsed his words. This was because *I had to get that letter under the table*. I had considered it might be a trap to catch me, but if he already knew it was there, well, my life would matter little. He would know I was the one. When the lesson ended, I asked if we could toast her Majesty. He had put away a good part of a decanter of what must be very fine wine, and no doubt didn't want to waste it on a peasant like me. He seemed to be in a good mood, so he relented, surprised at my request. I recognized it as the same excellent wine that had been left out for me at Wilson's. That is, except for the drug or poison that was missing.

As he sent for the guards to take me back, I kneeled down to gather up my other set of clothes. As I got back up, I purposely banged my head on the table bottom while I grabbed the letter and slipped it into the folded clothes.

"Ouch," I exclaimed.

"You are a dumb ass, aren't you?" he mocked, as I froze at those words and turned red as a beat. When the guards closed me back in my room I almost fainted. He had called me by my "dumb ass" name. The one that Wilson would have given him when he was questioned as to just who the hell had stabbed him!

I started to laugh and thought, "Oh Fate, My Lady, you have a wicked sense of humor!" I laughed and cried, *and I had the Queen's letter!*

It would be another sleepless night for I now had work to do. First, I read the letter over and over and memorized as much as I could. It was indeed a letter proposing negotiations to lift the well-known papal bull, "Regnans in Excelsis" against the Queen, in exchange for certain Catholic rights to be restored. The other papers that had been burned were apparently the specifics that might be the basis of negotiations. It was written with elegance and perfect English, as one would expect for a Queen.

The plays I copied were written to tell a tale, and just like writing a novel, take many liberties with grammar. Even as I write this tale, the bedeviled scribe within this keyboard is constantly bitching at me with little red and green lines. "That's a sentence fragment," and "That's a dangling participle," what ever the hell that is. Well maybe that's the way I need to present it. You don't tell a story using perfect grammar. But the Queen's letter had to be perfect. Surprisingly, there's only one exception my keyboard tormenter scribe has found wrong with this paragraph. See if you can find it, or not.

A hunted priest by the name of John Boste had written this hopeful letter to the Queen. I only knew of his name by accident. The Theatre needed a lot of paper for its scripts. I was occasionally sent out on errands, much like the one that led me to the balcony, to buy paper. I also scrounged for used parchment. The backside of any paper that was blank, such as posted bulletins, was still useable. In one group of used papers I had found, there was something Father Boste had written and distributed. James Burbage panicked when he saw it. He said it could be treason to be found with it. Boste was being hunted by the Privy Council and anyone with his writings would be sent to Gatehouse or worse, the Tower, for interrogation. He promptly burned it.

Now I have to make my own fateful perfect speech for the Queen. Topcliffe had made a serious mistake. I knew I was going to be able address her. It would not, however, be his speech. I had to compose a short damning paragraph I could start with before he could stop me. I had to accuse him of treachery and somehow interrogate him to lie and trap him. This would be a declaration of war on a trusted noble by a foolish-stubborn-Irish orphan. Was I out of my mind? I had just barely survived Topcliffe playing a meek and frightened child. That wasn't hard to do since I was in utter terror.

I could just be happy with some meager reward and disappear. That wouldn't work though. Topcliffe had said I wouldn't be able to work at that disgusting Theatre after I became a proper Protestant. He said he would teach me how to become a servant while working at the Gatehouse. No, I don't think so, already tried the slave thing, didn't work out. I knew what I must do. It is my duty to the Queen. It was also my duty to my fellow Catholics, though actually I didn't know any, and the Protestants too. It was also my duty to myself. After all, hadn't I always asked that Fate grant me some task worthy of a noble knight?

And then have the courage to succeed? So I prepared my speech for the Queen carefully rehearsing and memorizing it.

I also had to decide where to hide and protect the Queen's letter. It would be far too dangerous to have it on me. It would be my death warrant if it were found by Topcliffe. I decided my life-saving boots that I had stolen less than a year ago was the best hope. They were now well worn. I had cut heavy parchment out to make soles or pads inside them. With a trembling heart, I carefully tore the letter in half to fold up and place under the parchment in each boot. I felt like I was desecrating her Majesty's letter, but it was my secret weapon and was my only hope if I was to be believed. I finally finished my preparations, prayed for courage, and tried to get a little sleep. Tomorrow would be another fateful day.

Part 3 – Whitehall

The sun's morning rays ended the night. The captain and a guard came in early to make sure I dressed properly with the clothes Walsingham had sent the day before. These clothes were, indeed, very finely embroidered, truly fit for any noble. They were not clothes I would ever otherwise be able to use. The Theatre would have better use for them than I, though maybe I could wear them to play a prince on stage if Shakespeare got busy. That, or a peacock.

I asked the captain if there was any word on my coat as it also had money in it that belonged to the Theatre. He had not heard anything and doubted anyone would inquire with Sir Walsingham on such a trivial matter. I had neatly folded my old clothes with the new set and placed them with my boots. I wanted to know how I should carry them. He informed me they were to be left in the room and they could be sent for if I didn't return. "Didn't return" was a double-edged sword. I didn't want to return, but I might not be returning anywhere, after today.

I also had to brush my short, tangled hair. The captain and I decided I was not quite as ignorant as Topcliffe thought, and I could manage that myself. There was also perfumed oil. I had not yet mentioned that London, like any city of the era, had a stench about it. Garbage and sewage were pretty much dumped on the streets. I think I previously alluded to people's overall hygiene. Perfume wasn't invented to make one smell good. It was made to help mask all the odors from within and around. The wealthiest carried scented hankies they could hold to their noise when the going got tough.

So there I was. I was dressed as a knight going into battle perfumed like a Spartan Warrior. I rode with Topcliffe in an open carriage escorted with four of his private soldiers on horses. I had no idea where we were even going. The handful of people along the way stared at us, but generally shrunk back, not wanting to be in the way of Topcliffe. I grinned as I thought if they wondered who the young peacock was sitting across from him.

The horse's pant steamed in the cool sunlit morning. It reminded me that I had killed a man. That made me realize Topcliffe had also freshly killed. I had killed for my own preservation and mercy. Topcliffe had killed, because, well, I didn't really comprehend. We were mortal enemies. I knew it, he knew it too, but he had no clue to what extent yet. He would probably kill me some day, maybe even today. The ride was short and Topcliffe had me practice my speech again. I didn't think he'd hit me along the way, so I repeated it with slight errors and hesitations, which exasperated him. I did it right by the time we arrived. We were at Whitehall Palace.

I had seen the immense building complexes of the Westminster area when I had come once just to have a look see. The nearby Westminster Palace was where Parliament met. Whitehall Palace had been expanded by Henry VIII at incredible expense. It had hundreds of rooms and many courtyards and stables. Words cannot describe the awe a fourteen-year old boy, who had recently been living in a cemetery, felt being escorted through the magnificent palace. Yes, I was finally fourteen today if I was using the Gregorian calendar. I thought I'd better count my birthday today in case I didn't make it to the Julian calendar one.

Topcliffe and I were finally brought to a door with guards and I assume a secretary in charge. The secretary escorted us into a comfortable sized hall, bowed, and we were announced. "Sir Richard Topcliffe and the boy Presto, Your Majesty."

There she was, her Majesty, Queen Elizabeth! She looked more magnificent than when I had first seen her, what seemed an eternity four days earlier. She was seated by the side of a table surrounded by several other gentry. Most had those frilly collars that indicated nobility or high rank. One of them I recognized as Sir Francis Walsingham. I felt some degree of hope when I saw him because he had seen what I had done and knew the Queen wanted me treated well. That hope was dashed when I considered he might consider Topcliffe a friend.

They seemed to be having some kind of meeting or discussion that must have been informal since we were simply brought in and announced. They all looked toward us, and I felt butterflies as I started to freeze remembering the speech I had prepared.

I followed Topcliffe's bow as he spoke the first words. "Your Majesty, I am delighted and humbled to see you. I believe you will be most happy the boy I present to you today, has decided to please Your Majesty by becoming a Protestant. I have already begun in his teachings." He again bowed.

The Queen addressed us both. "Gramercy, Sir Richard. And I am happy to again meet the brave boy who stopped the assassin."

Feeling it was now my turn, I spoke with my sweetest Irish brogue, "Your Majesty, I am humbled not only seeing you to serve you again, but also by your beauty that is even greater than when I first set my eyes upon you." This was not part of Topcliffe's script, but he seemed pleased, though surprised, that I had suddenly developed charm.

She had stood up and smiled at my compliment. She had noticed I had walked in with a limp that I had, in fact, exaggerated.

"I hope you are not injured from your bravery and you have been treated well," she replied.

I took a deep breath and began, now in a gentleman's English. "Your Majesty, my injuries are not from diving off a balcony to protect you. I will always be ready to serve and protect you, My Queen. My injuries are from being whipped and tortured by Sir Richard Topcliffe as I witnessed him butcher a man who had letters addressed to Your Majesty. Topcliffe was destroying these letters that proposed negotiating the lifting of the Pope's Regnans in Excelsis against Your Gracious Majesty." By now Topcliffe's face had turned to shock and then rage and he started to try to break in.

He started, "The boy has deceived me! He is speaking Catholic lies!!!" and he reached to grab me.

"I am only alive because I led him to believe I would become a Protestant so Your Majesty would reward him!" I exclaimed. I turned to him and shouted over his protests and grip, "Do you deny that you burned letters addressed to the Queen from the Priest John Boste?" Everyone looked stunned and the room was dead silent.

I repeated. "Do you deny that you burned letters addressed to the Her Majesty from the Priest John Boste?"

"Of course not. This boy is making up lies. He must be a Catholic traitor and spy," Topcliffe shouted.

"THEN YOU ARE A LIAR! And you deceive My Queen!" I screamed back.

"I'll teach you to call me a liar!" and he tried to tear at me.

"SILENCE!" both the Queen and Walsingham shouted at the same time. "No one will speak unless they are addressed," Walsingham demanded.

Ignoring Walsingham's order, Topcliffe blurted out with rage, "The boy is the one who lies. He is a spy sent here to trick us."

Also ignoring Walsingham and the Queen's order I quickly replied, "I am here to again serve My Queen, I am not a spy, which would be a bad reflection on you as a spymaster if I was!" I yelled as I glared at Topcliffe.

One of the other stunned gentry, who was finely dressed but without the fluffy collar, let out, "This fearless lad is bent on getting himself killed, must be a martyr, but I am impressed."

"SILENCE!" Walsingham again demanded.

The Queen now spoke. "No one is to speak. I will ask the questions. Let go of the boy. What is the boy talking about Richard?"

"I do not know, Your Majesty. I was interrogating the traitor who stabbed me when they brought the boy in for me to question. I was told he was a Catholic that might have been part of the conspiracy to assassinate you."

"But he saved me, Richard, I saw it. What is this about a letter written to me from this priest, Boste? He isn't in London, is he? He causes enough trouble in the North."

"The boy lies and is making stories up, probably to discredit me, Your Majesty. This makes me believe he was in on the conspiracy to murder you. I will take him back to the Gatehouse to question him and have him recant these false and malicious lies against me. I will hunt down this priest if he is in London. The boy is nothing more than a peasant, an Irish peasant, and has no right to accuse any noble without proof."

"Do you have any proof, boy?" she now asked me.

"Your Majesty, I saw the papers on the table at the Gatehouse. He was interrogating the man, not about being stabbed, but about whether there were other copies. He wanted to destroy all of them and keep them from your eyes. He used some of them to burn and torture the man with," I replied.

"Liar!" Topcliffe broke in. The Queen shot him a look that indicated she was the one speaking.

"How do you know what these letters were about?" she then asked me.

"Your Majesty, I know because Topcliffe said what they were to the man he was butchering in my sight. The man pleaded with him to deliver the letters to you because they were meant to bring peace, not more bloodshed."

"Your Majesty, I have endured these lies upon me long enough. I ask you to grant me permission to return to the Gatehouse and get a full confession from him. It is my right," Topcliffe broke in.

"Your Majesty, may I continue answering your question?" I asked.

She was studying both of us and nodded. "You are to refer to your superior as Sir Topcliffe."

"Yes, Your Majesty, if Topcl, Sir Topcliffe takes me back to the Gatehouse, he will torture anything he wants out of me and kill me. I have proof of his previous torture by the marks already upon me. You will never know the truth. I am not here to try to die as some fool martyr. I am here because of my duty to you, My Queen, with the truth. Your servant, Sir Topcliffe, has taken it upon himself to take away your right to read your own important letters. It is my duty to you to report this treachery to you even if it costs me my short life. I would be Your Knight, Your Majesty, not a martyr." Topcliffe was seething waiting to break in and refute all I had said.

The Queen spoke, "You have surprising eloquence, my dear boy, Presto. I brought you here to reward you for your service to me, not to have you killed. If you apologize to Sir Richard, we can get on to rewarding you for your courage. Otherwise as a noble, he has the right to have you recant, since it appears it is only your word against his." She watched me closely to see how I would respond.

I now had to make a decision, was the letter safe? Could I get the letter to the Queen? If I told them about it and it was gone, it would be over. No one would believe me. If Topcliffe couldn't kill me now, he certainly would later. No, I had to press on and convince them all that I was telling the truth even without the letter. I knew I had only one very bad feared option.

"Your Majesty, one of us is lying to you. Both of our honors are at stake. If I apologize, I by default, recant the truth. This would be a betrayal to you. You asked what reward I seek for stopping the assassin. Let it be this, Your Majesty. Let Sir Topcliffe try to make me recant the truth here and now in your presence. That is the only way you will know that the truth is in me. You will not know the truth if I return to the Gatehouse."

"Maybe he is a knight?" proclaimed the same man who had earlier commented that I must be a martyr. "I'm more impressed."

This broke the silence and Topcliffe saw his chance and spoke, "Your Majesty, I can clear this whole matter up in just minutes. The boy has asked for his reward and I have the right to have him recant. He will stop his lies to you, and you will see he is trying to deceive us all, Your Majesty,"

The Queen looked at Walsingham who shrugged and said, "None of this I expected. If you are willing, Your Majesty, we might as well let the hand play out."

"But how?" she asked.

"Lashes, I suppose, Your Majesty, but he is to be careful not to bring permanent harm," Walsingham answered.

She looked at Topcliffe and back to Walsingham. "Who decides when it is over if he doesn't recant?"

"I will, Your Majesty. I will know if the boy is lying," Walsingham replied.

The Queen looked at both of us. Topcliffe had a look of menacing triumph on his face. I had a look of fearful defiance and pride. "Very well," she said and shrugged.

Now the logistics of this insanity had to be worked out. While the other gentry started talking with much animation and discussed various wagers, a servant was called and sent out to find a whip. It appears Topcliffe wasn't carrying this morning.

The wagering as to how many lashes it would take to make me recant reached my ears and I calmly interrupted. "I should win all your wagers when I show you that I stand firm on my word." They all looked thoroughly amused at my challenge.

"Maybe I'll bet on the boy," stepped in the one who had been making the comments earlier.

In the meantime, I had thanked her Majesty for the magnificent clothes she had sent and took the jacket off. The whip quickly arrived. The palace complex had hundreds of rooms and no doubt had its own prison and dungeon. Topcliffe wanted to tie me, but I insisted that I just stand at a column close to the door.

He ripped at my shirt, tearing it, at which I exclaimed, "You owe me a shirt! You just ruined the one Her Majesty gave me!" I took my shirt off, slowly examined it, and carefully folded it. Everyone could see my welts and knew I had told the truth that Topcliffe had beat me. I walked up to the post bravely, though I was trembling inside. "Is this good?" and I leaned against it to hold on tight.

Topcliffe looked at the Queen. Walsingham nodded and calmly uttered the frightening word, "Begin."

Topcliffe swung his first lash and it felt like it would break bones almost tearing me off the post. I let out an escaping low scream.

The explosion ripped through me and my fear turned to complete and hopeless terror. This was nothing like Crowley or Topcliffe had done before. I had thought that I could just withstand this, as I had before, and it would all be over quickly. The second lash cruelly hit the exact same flesh as the first. I again could not hold my escaping scream. I felt something warm running down my back. I buckled and, as I tried to escape with an out of body moment, I felt totally alone and hopeless. I realized I had failed.

But as I drifted a moment as if watching what was unfolding, I felt something else. I remembered that I was the Knight Prince Enros fighting for truth. It wasn't much of a truth and it probably wouldn't make any difference. Fate had led me here. Everything had led me here. And it occurred to me that, though this wasn't my best scenario, this was going rather well. I had made my accusation. My words had been heard and were being listened to. In that moment, a little spark ignited inside me. Hope started to return. That hope grew and as it did brought back courage. And then as I realized I was still standing, I felt what I felt when I escaped Swansea. I felt Victory!

I turned to Topcliffe and screamed, "LIAR!"

He responded by slashing again and caught me by the side and sent me sprawling.

I picked myself up and declared, "While you tortured the man that stabbed you, I picked up and read the letter addressed to Her Majesty from Boste."

Everyone was stunned.

"You can't read, you lying peasant!" he exclaimed.

"I can read better than you can," I retorted as I moved back to the post, but he struck me again before I could grab it. "The post! Wait until I am back at the post," and I grabbed the column smearing a little red that had found its way onto my hands. "You never asked the man once that you were torturing about stabbing you. You only used that as cover to butcher him about the Queen's papers!"

He struck me hard, tearing me from the post again as he shouted, "He was the traitor that tried to kill me!"

"That's not what I've heard on the streets. I heard it was a terrified little boy you were trying to bugger that grabbed a knife and stabbed you! Do you deny it?" I shouted out for all to hear and understand. In that moment, Topcliffe not only understood, *but he recognized me.*

He attacked me with the whip as I lay on the floor, "I just killed the man that stabbed me which is my right, you lying piece of shite!" he screamed as I rolled and slid away from his seething whip. Walsingham and the Queen both yelled, "STOP."

He stopped and tried to regain his composure.

"If you swear to Her Majesty and all here that the man you were interrogating was the one who stabbed you, then I owe you an apology for speaking from rumors," I said, amazingly calm as I stood up. The hatred in his eyes was as when I had plunged the knife into him.

"It was that Catholic traitor!" he shrieked, as everyone looked on baffled as this new twist sank in.

"Then I apologize for I misspoke. But you are still a LIAR and deceive the Queen about Her letters!"

With that he attacked me with the whip and physically kicked and punched me as I crawled away on the floor begging to stop. It was finally the gentries who restrained him as Walsingham demanded order. I could hardly breathe and felt broken.

"Your Majesty, Your Majesty, please, I want to confess, please, please," I gasped on the floor.

Everyone went silent. They let go of Topcliffe who had a triumphant grimace.

"Your Majesty," I gasped as I tried to lift up on a knee and then slowly rose to stand. I took a deep breath and with all the will that was left in me loudly declared, "I Am Not A Liar… But I Am A Thief! I took your letter from the table as Topcliffe tortured that man."

I turned to Topcliffe and said, "Don't you remember when I became ill on the papers and then threw them in the fire? That's when I took it!"

"Then you're the one who took the papers and burned them before I could determine they were for the Queen!" Topcliffe roared without thinking.

"What papers? You said there weren't any papers. You said there weren't any papers burned." I triumphantly gasped, as I was barely able to remain standing. But I regained my breath and went on. "Do you now expect Her Majesty to believe that you had valuable papers for her in front of you and didn't know it? That I'm the one who destroyed them? That either makes you the stupidest spymaster in the history of England, or a Liar, or Both!" I shouted.

I wasn't surprised he again attacked me and sent me sprawling on the floor toward the table where the Queen was standing aghast. There was a lot of yelling and calling for guards and silence and it took a while for order to be restored. Walsingham stood over me and demanded where the letter was now. I think I had done it! I think they all believed me.

"I hid the letter in my boots back in the room I have at the Gatehouse," I whispered as I tried to breath. I was helped to a chair brought out from the table. Topcliffe had continued calling me a liar but had been ordered by the Queen to be silent.

"I apologize Your Majesty, but I tore it in half to hide it."

"I will send our most trusted guards to collect it, Your Majesty," and Walsingham then gave orders. A physician was also sent for. It wouldn't take long. The Gatehouse was not that far away.

"Your Majesty, may I ask your permission to prove one other truth that I told you? May I be allowed to prove I can read, possibly from a Bible?" I asked in barely more than a whisper.

"I don't think we have any Latin Bibles here," she replied.

"I meant an English one, Your Majesty. I had a Tyndale Bible once, but it was stolen from me."

"Are you Catholic or Protestant then?" she asked puzzled.

"Catholic, Your Majesty."

"But isn't it heresy for you to read an English Bible?"

"Your Majesty, you no doubt have already noticed we Irish are not much on following rules. I was taught to read with an English Bible by the Irish priest, Father McNee, who raised me. I am an orphan. He taught me how our faiths are the same, not their differences."

With that, all the stunned faces remained stunned a bit longer. She sent for a vicar to bring a Bible and in the meantime her physician arrived. I knew I had some serious wounds but was doing a good job ignoring them until he came and started fiddling with them.

The vicar soon arrived and had Henry VIII's Bible translation. This was mostly known as the "Grand Bible" because it was really big. I had no idea how it was laid out, so I asked the vicar to find a certain passage from Matthew. It was always my favorite. It is the bit where our Savior tells us that our faith must remain as pure and innocent as that of a child's.

The first three verses were the very ones that I started to learn how to read from. I think you can understand why Father McNee chose them to begin my education when I was about five. The more eloquent King James Version of the Bible, to be written decades later, includes them too. They are still favorite verses in many a sermon. I steadied my voice and read the words as eloquently as I could with all the strength I had left:

"And Jesus called a little child unto him, and set him in the midst of them,"

"And said, Verily I say unto you, Except ye be converted, and become as little children, ye shall not enter into the kingdom of heaven."

"Whosoever therefore shall humble himself as this little child, the same is greatest in the kingdom of heaven."

And with a pause, I continued.

"And whoso shall receive one such little child in my name receiveth me."

"But whoso shall offend one of these little ones which believe in me, it were better for him that a millstone were hanged about his neck, and that he were drowned in the depth of the sea."

I then moved on several passages to another set of verses from Matthew.

"Then little children were brought to Him that He might put His hands on them and pray, but the disciples rebuked them."

"But Jesus said, "Let the little children come to Me, and do not forbid them; for of such is the kingdom of heaven."

They all stared with amazement that I, a Catholic commoner, was really reading to them in English. Topcliffe was beside himself with anger. He realized I had made him look a fool, and the Queen had no doubt I had been true. He stopped his protests and attempts to wiggle his way back out of the lie I had trapped him with at the beginning.

The guard arrived soon after I finished reading. He had my boots and was holding two pieces of parchment. I said a prayer out loud. He handed them to Sir Walsingham who studied and then started reading from one of them. As he did, I started reciting the beginning of the letter from memory. It began with addressing her Majesty as the Queen, which was already a concession. I continued about a paragraph as Sir Walsingham read the letter to himself.

He stopped and simple declared, "It is as the boy, Presto says, your Majesty," and handed her the halves of the letter.

Topcliffe tried to start a protest with a new lie but stopped as the Queen looked at the letter and at each of us. With fury in her face, her voice boomed throughout the hall at Topcliffe, "Get Out! I do not want to see you in my presence. Get OUT!"

Topcliffe quickly bowed, not daring to say another word, and backed away and out with guards following.

"You still owe me a shirt!" I blurted out the best I could has my voice was fading fast. I turned back to the Queen and tried to steady my voice. "I apologize Your Majesty for my lack of manners before you. I hope you now know my words are true, and I held fast to them, in your service."

"It is we who need to apologize to you, Presto, my loyal boy. I should not have allowed this to happen to you. I am now indebted to you for risking your life twice for me. I will do anything I can for you. You only need ask when you are able," she replied with a look of appreciation and concern.

I knew I had few words left as I felt my strength vanishing. So I best make every word count, "I do not seek gold or silver, Your Majesty, as I do not know if my wounds will allow me anything more than a stone above my head. I would therefore first ask, well, your help to stop an injustice. I was betrayed and sold as a slave to a coal dig in Swansea, Wales. There are other Irish lads who were also sold illegally as slaves. They remain there being tortured and abused. One of them was murdered while I was with them, and there is a grave that holds the bones of many others. I seek freedom, help and justice for them. This was my vow when I made my escape. This is how I came to be in London."

I went on, "Your Majesty, for myself I only ask one thing. I ask for opportunity. Opportunity to first live, and not be hunted down and butchered by a vengeful Topcliffe. An opportunity to earn my own living by the work of my own hands, as your subject, and as a Catholic. Opportunity, like any of your subjects, that I can find pride in my work, and maybe even raise a family some day in peace. And lastly, when my bones are laid to rest that I will have earned a simple stone with my name: "Presto, A Good and Decent Man" and maybe some bit about not being an arshole, begging your pardon, Your Majesty."

They all looked at me with surprising respect. The same gentry that had praised me for my courage hastily declared, "Your Majesty, may I ask your permission to take the boy in, to be his mentor and make sure he has this opportunity he seeks?"

"I think he's had enough exploits already, I'm not sure he would need your type of adventures," she mused.

"May I ask who this fine gentleman is that has made such a kind offer? I am very grateful, but please know, I am a bit of an alley cat. I like my freedom to roam the streets of London where I have finally found honest work."

"I'm sorry, *Alley Cat* Presto. I should have introduced myself. My name is Sir Francis Drake."

"Sir Francis Drake!" I exclaimed. "Thee Sir Francis Drake? The Captain of the Golden Hind and the Cadiz raid? Suddenly I had regained a touch of strength in my voice.

"You've heard of me?" Drake replied with a bit of pride.

"Every boy has heard of you!" I exclaimed. But my strength was all but gone.

They all laughed. The Queen shook her head and said, "I think he's happier to have met you than myself."

"I think we need to attend to the boy's wounds, Your Majesty," Walsingham broke in with mounting concern.

I did need to escape from myself. I didn't have to be told the pain in my side was broken ribs. "Gramercy, many thanks, thank..." I now could barely whisper as the room seemed to be twisting around. "And now, if Your Majesty would please excuse me, I must take your leave." With that I drifted into a fog that wasn't darkness or light ...

Part 4 – The Interrogation

I was sitting on a carved Celtic cross gravestone. I knew this stone. It was Father McNees's. I had seen it new less than a year ago, but now it was old and weathered with the long passage of time. The inscriptions were worn, now barely legible. Other old stones had joined the site since I had said my goodbyes before leaving this land on a ship bound by Fate. I hopped down to see if I recognized the other inscriptions.

"Looking for someone?" a voice behind me gently asked.

I knew that voice immediately. It was Father McNee. I turned with joy and hopped back up on the stone. "I'm so happy to see you!"

He started rubbing my ears and I started to purr. "My sweet Presto, you've had to grow up so fast," he said.

"I think no more than any orphan through the millennia. I was so ashamed of some of the things I did and that you would turn away from me."

"Presto, I would never turn away from you. I knew what was in your heart, and that is what really matters. Sometimes there are only bad choices to choose from in life. You never gave up, though."

"Close, there were times I didn't know what purpose I had. I thought Fate had brought me to an end until a cat reminded me not to quit. And then Fate lead me to safety, and then to purpose. But then she seems to enjoy having me knocked about. What's with that? How many lives does she think I have left?"

"You're the one who wanted to have deeds worthy of a knight to be part of your life, your purpose."

"Yeah, and who gave me that bright idea?" I asked with sarcasm.

"You had that idea in you long before you graced my threshold," he beamed. "I don't think you would have survived that first winter night otherwise." I turned around and looked down at the other stones. "Wondering if any of those are yours?" Father McNee continued.

"No, I best not. Well, I suppose I should get back before they decide I'm a ghost and start covering me up with dirt."

"*You* know you can't bury a ghost. There's no rush, I think it's safe to stay a little longer. Or you can just stay…"

"Well, maybe a nice booty rub before I go, but we both know I must go." And with that I got a heavenly rub from my shoulders to my tail.

I woke up shrieking, gasping for breath. I was in another room somewhere in Whitehall. The Queen's physician was stitching my wounds feverously. I was astonished to see Lord Walsingham there also and helping hold me up.

"Easy, easy, drink this. It will stop your pain," the physician said, looking gravely at Walsingham as he shook his head.

Gritting my teeth, I tried to speak. "I'm not done fighting the battle yet. I didn't come this far to lose now. Don't give up on me just because of my wee bit of whining. Just keep me breathing." I knew if I took his potion, which was probably made from poppies, that my next dream would be my last.

"Sir Walsingham, my coat, did you find my coat on the balcony?" I gasped, trying to talk. "It had money in it for me to buy paper for the Theatre where I work as a scribe. They won't know what happened to me. Please let the Burbages know and return their purse, please. I don't know if I'll be able to work for them once they learn I'm Catholic."

"We did find a coat when we studied where you leaped from. I must apologize for putting you through all this. I should have attended to you myself," he answered solemnly.

"It was your duty to protect the Queen. Besides, it was Fate that led you to put me at the Gatehouse to further serve her. But please let them know. They gave me shelter and work at their playhouse, Burbage's Theatre, the one just to the north of London."

I did make it through the night. I ended up with somewhere around twenty-seven stitches and three cracked ribs. I was eventually able to breath without gasping for breath, so I could have the poppies' potion. I don't remember much of the next two or three days. I finally found myself in another one of the palace's rooms that by any standard was more than grand. I then came to realize it not only had several sleeping quarters, but also a study with a library, a huge meeting room, servant quarters, and even a room that served as a water closet. There were two servants assigned to me, which I found quite amusing, not to mention, a bit awkward. The elder one was very formal and clearly used to dealing with the highest nobles and lords. He was the one in charge. The second one was a lad who stayed and worked out of the servant's quarter.

I was grateful though, as there was no way my ribs would allow me to bend to even be able to put my shoes on. I was finally able to hobble around carefully in my chambers and it felt good to be able to move about. I learned this wing of the palace had many other sets of rooms assigned to other visiting lords, diplomats and special guests. My chambers were some of the largest ones, and I heard the Queen is the one that had ordered me brought to them. The food was also unbelievable, and the best I ever had.

I was informed Sir Francis Drake was going to see to my continued education. He also had rooms assigned to him in the same wing of the palace when he stayed at Whitehall. He was now away from London. There was no indication as to when or if I was to leave, or where I was to eventually go. The only thing I knew for sure was that I was indeed going to have tea with her Majesty, after I had sufficiently recovered. I now had several sets of very fine clothes worthy of any peacock.

After a few days, I was strong enough to be taken outside for fresh air and to see the magnificent grounds. I was closely eyed by the ravens, and the various baffled nobles and lords. Since I didn't know any of them, I didn't know the proper way to greet any. The elder servant, Alexander, coached me and introduced me, should we pass any. I practiced with some of the ravens too, but Alexander did not seem to be very amused.

My coat from the balcony had been found and brought to me. The coin pouch was not with it though. I asked for quill and paper to write to the Burbages to let them know I was all right. I also spent time composing a written complaint against those that were involved in the slavery at Swansea, and my account as a witness. I hoped the other lads would finally be rescued and taken care of. I would somehow get this letter to Lord Walsingham. That would not be difficult, as I found out that I was to be taken to him soon.

The week had now passed, and it was the Ides of March. This date was not known as being a particularly great hair day for Julius Caesar. I was hoping for a far better day. I was dressed in another set of very fine clothes. I was brought to another part of the palace where the elder William Cecil, Lord Burghley, had an office. Lord Francis Walsingham and another man were seated at a large desk to see me. The other man was introduced as the junior Cecil, Sir Robert. I was simply introduced as Master Presto.

"My Lords," I greeted. "I am humbled and honored to have tea with the most powerful men in England. We are going to have tea, aren't we?"

Sir Francis raised his eyes with a bit of a grin while Cecil stared somewhat taken back by my informal airs. "I think I could use a spot of tea," Sir Francis replied. "I'll send for some and maybe some cheese and biscuits too,"

I was beckoned to be seated in front of them, and gently sat down. I grimaced as one of the stitches caught the elegant clothing, and I opened a button to adjust.

"Sorry. Please thank Her Majesty for these very fine clothes, her hospitality in this very fine palace, and the physician for saving me. I would like to say many thanks for you staying with me also, Lord Walsingham."

"I again must apologize for putting you through all this," Walsingham answered.

Then Cecil spoke, "You could have avoided all this by simply giving Sir Francis the Queen's letter. You're lucky you didn't get yourself killed by your foolish actions. Were you trying to make a martyr of yourself?"

"Lord Cecil, since I came to your land a year ago, I have done nothing but fight to stay alive. I'll have no part of being called a martyr. I did it to serve Her Majesty, as is my duty. I didn't know if the letter was safe or still existed. Without it, a commoner's word against a noble's would not be believed by anyone, or by the law. Yes, my plan was foolish, but the only one that Fate offered. I had to catch Topcliffe in a lie, and then somehow interrogate him to prove his deception to Her Majesty."

"Interrogate, interrogate?" Cecil retorted incredulously, "You interrogated Sir Richard Topcliffe while he was lashing you? And you will address him by his title."

"Of course I was interrogating him. Lord Walsingham, you were there. Did I not ask questions with 'Do you deny'? Everything I asked I had planned in advance. Sure, I was hoping it would not be under those circumstances, but I had to prove his deceit even without the letter. And his title represents respect on my part. After what I endured from him at the Gatehouse? No, I apologize, but I will never show him respect."

"Now that you mention it, I do see you were interrogating him," Sir Francis realized out loud with this new perspective.

"But I understand you went out of your way to antagonize and bring on his rage. It was like you were baiting him to kill you!" Cecil rebuked.

"Sir, a man in rage doesn't have time to think clearly. I had seen his rage when he butchered the man he was interrogating. I felt his rage because I was a filthy Catholic and how dare I protect the Queen rather than a Protestant noble. I used his own weakness against him."

About then the tea and cheese arrived and there was a well-needed pause in our discussion. I thanked them as the formalities of pouring the tea and being bid to indulge passed.

"Lords, I assume you have some questions about how I happened to be on that balcony and what else I might know. A task that Topcli, or, you know who, failed to do at the Gatehouse. I might suggest I simply tell you my story of how I happened to come from Ireland, and the road Fate laid out for, well, us, to be here in this elegant room. I see it is filled with many fine books. Is this a library of some sort?" I asked.

"This is Lord Burghley's office, Sir Robert's father. And yes, he has collected many fine books," Sir Francis replied. "And yes, I think it would be best we simply let the boy tell his story. But first, we don't actually know your name other than Presto"

"Well, My Lords, it's not that long of a tale and I'll avoid embellishing it too much. First as to my name, it is only Presto. I suppose I should begin my story with the Priest, Father McNee. He raised me as an orphan in Athy, Ireland. That's near Kildare. No one knows where I came from. I was found in winter on the steps of the old church by the vicar. He brought me to Father McNee. They didn't know if I had been baptized so they decided to do it together. They couldn't come up with a name, so they decided to simply call me Presto. They also gave me a birthday of the seventeenth of March. I will be fourteen in a couple days."

"You mean you were baptized as a Catholic and a Protestant? I've never heard of such," Sir Francis asked now already puzzled.

"I was just being baptized. I am not aware of there being any difference. I was being given to our Lord not a church. Father McNee kept me to raise me. He also collected books. He had as fine a library as you could find. It would easily rival this. As I already indicated, he taught me to read using the Tyndale English translation of the Bible. The vicar had given it to him. Father McNee thought he'd get two birds with one stone. To learn to read and to know of our Savior." I had stood as I spoke and walked to the bookshelves.

"May I?" and pointed to a book. Sir Francis nodded. I carefully slid it out and held it to my chest. "I see you have a copy of the Tyndale Bible," and returned with it to my chair and continued.

"As I grew, I literally wanted to read everything in his library. He had books of adventure, math, science, history, maps, everything. He was my family and my mentor. He didn't hide any truths. I even read translations of Martin Luther's ninety-four complaints. He taught me that our faiths are fundamentally the same. But I also learned of both their shortcomings, and how easy it is to lose sight of that pure and innocent faith we start with as a child. I was a child. And yes, I hope I still am and always will be in that respect."

I continued with my story. "And then he passed. He was seventy-five. That was almost a year and a half ago and the saddest day of my life. He had left me the Bible he had taught me from. I spent a few months with a kind family that could ill afford to keep me. Then I had an opportunity to learn a trade on the sea. It was a brutal betrayal though. I was being sold into slavery, just like other Irish lads, to a cursed coal dig in Wales. They took my Bible, the only thing I had left of Father McNee." With that, I held their Tyndale Bible dearly. Tears filled my eyes that I could not hold back.

"They claimed we were convicted criminals, common thieves. They beat us and treated us like vermin. One of the boys tried to escape, but they set their dogs out to find him. They tore him apart. We had to bury what was left with the rest the lads who had already perished. So I escaped a few days later during an epic storm. I knew they would look for me at the docks trying to return to Ireland like the other boy. But I went to London. I have written this account as a legal complaint listing those who committed these horrific crimes. There are also the names of the four lads who were there when I escaped and might still survive." I laid the paper in front of them.

Cecil, somewhat skeptically, asked how I could make it to London from Wales, a mere boy, obviously with nothing.

"Well, first I became the thief that they had already accused me of being. As I escaped during the storm, I took food, supplies, and a pair of life-saving boots. Ironically, they ended up being the ones I hid the Queen's letter in. I worked my way toward Gloucester through the valleys. I made up a name and pretended I was from London. I spoke with a proper gentleman's English that Father McNee had taught me. He had done his studies in London before the Reformation and lived there for some time. He told me much of the city and how grand it is."

Walsingham was paying close attention to the details of my story. He had also picked up my written complaint. "Please continue but tell us the name you decided to use."

"For my first name I chose Robert, after the boy who had been murdered where we were enslaved. For my last name I chose Dumas, D U M A S, Dumas," I spelled out.

"Dumas? That's a strange name, how did you come up with it?" Cecil asked, almost mispronouncing it properly. Walsingham looked on, beginning to catch it.

"Well it does sound very Flemish, and the Dutch are quite popular now. Also it is rather fun to mispronounce as you almost have. Try it again, My Lord, you'll get the idea," I said with a whimsical smirk.

"You can't possibly mean you meant to be called "Dumb ass"?" Walsingham asked with a bewildered look.

"Well, no one would ever think anyone would make up such a name. There would be no fear of someone inquiring about a 'dumb ass' relation they might know. And it is a great funny distraction if you don't want too many questions."

They both stared in disbelief as I again continued. "When I got near Gloucester, I was questioned by soldiers. I told them a good story and they allowed me to go with them to Oxford. They saved my life. The Captain's name is Robert Barrington. I think it was the humor of my name more than anything that helped him decide to let me tag along. He even took me with his men to the cathedral in Oxford. We all received Communion, the first time since Ireland for me. I owe him my life and am ashamed that so much of what I told him was a lie. I didn't dare tell him that I was an escaping Irish-Catholic orphan. Someday I would like to thank him and tell him the truth. He made arrangements for me to get to London safely, from Oxford."

Walsingham now spoke, though with a bit of a continued astonished expression, "I know Captain Robert. He is a fine soldier."

Cecil interrupted, "But you're Catholic, you couldn't possibly receive Communion in *our* church."

"Father McNee said it was the next best thing," I said with a bit of a grin.

"Next best thing?" Cecil said in disbelief, while Walsingham looked on speechless.

There were no further comments, so I continued. "Captain Barrington even gave me several shillings to help me survive. London is an immense town. But I couldn't find work. I spent several months seeking shelter in a graveyard on the south side of the river. I found one of those fancy tombs that has a stone hut to hold the crypt. I was too afraid to be on the streets where I might be robbed of what little I had. To survive, well, yes, I did do some petty thieving and feared I might have to become a whore. There are few choices for an orphan on the streets alone. I wasn't a very good thief, sometimes I went almost a week without eating."

Now their looks had turned to back to stunned, probably due to my saying I lived in a graveyard. I continued.

"There were men that wanted me to do things that I refused. I ran away to the far north side and became who I really am, the Irish boy, Presto. But I was still desperate, the cold weather was coming and now I was living on the streets. Finally, when I thought I was done for Fate took me to Burbage's Theatre. I finally found honest work there scribing their plays for the actors along with other work, even a bit of acting. I would not have survived winter without their shelter. They don't know what happened to me. They don't know I'm Catholic and I pray I can still work for them. I was on an errand for them when I heard the Queen was coming. So I followed the crowd to have a look see. I snuck up that balcony to get the best view. I think you know the rest since you were there, Lord Walsingham."

They both stared as I finished my story. Cecil was the first to respond. "Well that's a fine tale, but how do we know it's true or you're not just acting. Living in a cemetery, seriously? You said you had planned everything you said when you "interrogated" Sir Richard. How do we know you haven't planned all this knowing you would finally be questioned?"

"To what end?" I replied. "Lord Walsingham, and indeed your father are known as *the* spymasters. You are the masters, the most powerful men in England. I would be a fool to try to lie to any of you. Everything I have told you can be verified. And my actions speak for themselves."

"You did the same acting to Sir Richard and see how you tricked him," he replied.

"Topcliffe is not a master. He is your attack dog. Besides, a child could outwit him!" I knew I probably went a bit too far with that bit.

"You need to know your place! It is not your business to decide or judge the role of a noble. Topcliffe is a noble and your superior. It is up to us to determine his role." Cecil now emphatically stated as a command.

Dumb Irish me had to furiously respond, "I apologize, Lord Cecil, you're right, I am only a lowly commoner, a peasant, an orphan, yes, even a child. *But I'm making it my business.* You weren't there at the Gatehouse. You didn't see him butcher the man he claimed stabbed him while telling me it was my turn next. I was terrified, but there I was standing alone at the table trying to hide my mind from the screams in the next room. I started to read the papers he was burning. He said my kind was too ignorant to read and shouldn't be allowed. So I hid Her Majesty's letter under the table. I threw up on the other papers to throw them in the fire so he wouldn't notice the one I hid was gone. Do you have any idea what he did to me next?"

Sir Francis was looking back and forth between us during our exchange. "I think it's understandable the boy has strong emotions which are, in fact, justified, considering all that has occurred. You have told us things that are, as you said, all verifiable. I think you are clever enough not to lie to us, and you have even told us things most would not confess."

"Too clever," Cecil spat. "He says he is an alley cat. How do we know he won't scratch Her Majesty's eyes out?"

"I am now bound to always protect Her Majesty. That's more of an Irish Druid thing than being Catholic. And yes, I'm proud to be like a cat. A cat decides who he will be loyal to and that bond becomes unbreakable. Besides, if we are going to defeat the Spanish, you need clever people, not dumb ones on your side." I argued these points more calmly and again stood to take a stretch and look at the books on the shelves.

Walsingham also stood, gestured to the cheese that was quite good and started to ask me questions. "I would like to know more about what you know of the assassin. I know what I saw, but I don't know what you saw. Had you seen or known the man before?"

"And how could a mere boy manage to kill him?" Cecil added, interrupting before I could respond.

"I had seen the man standing under the balcony when I decided to climb up on it. I didn't know him or recognize him. That doesn't mean I never saw him in a crowd, but I don't recall him. I was concerned he might stop me from climbing to the empty balcony, but he surprisingly ignored me. I suppose he was trying to avoid me, as much as I, him. I didn't see him after that below me. I slid my heavy coat off and draped it over my shoulders and then just waited from above. After Her Majesty passed, I saw him step out and pull a gun out from under his coat. I didn't have time to think consciously, but I clearly thought at the speed of a dream to respond."

"Speed of a dream?" Walsingham inquired, "I don't know what you mean?"

"Do you dream? Especially in the morning? You can sometimes remember a bit of them. When you wake up, and then fall back asleep for only a few minutes, can you remember the brief dream you had in between? If you do, you might realize that it spanned a lot longer time. It might have been hours, even days. Yet only a few minutes passed. That's how fast our sub mind works. In that split second, I screamed to alert everyone, then calculated how I had to launch myself over the balcony to land on him moving away and decide to do it in the first place. I'd still be up there thinking about it if I hadn't thought at the speed of a dream."

"But how did you kill him?" Cecil again asked.

"Fortunately, either my calculation was true, or it was just blind luck. I hit him square. The gun went off and we hit the ground hard. He rolled on top of me and had his knife out and its tip pressing into the hollow of my throat." I pointed where his blade was. "I grabbed his hand, but I knew I was done. There was no way I could stop his size or strength. In the speed of a dream, I saw my entire life pass, and somehow felt ready, no regrets. Terrified, of course. But when our eyes locked, he suddenly stopped, he let the knife loose in my struggling hands. Then he cried, "Have mercy, kill me… Please." So I did, I stabbed him in the throat." I paused, as this was the first time I had recalled the event out loud. "I don't even know his name."

I really needed to take that moment, but Cecil already pressed on. "We needed to question him. You should have waited. The guards would have been upon him in an instant."

"I'm sure that's what I'll do next time someone is about to kill me and says, "Why don't you kill me instead before I change my mind." I didn't have an instant to wait for the guards to save me. I didn't even know who had seen what and whether they might kill both of us," I replied, now drained.

"Why did you declare you were a Catholic to the Queen? You seem to indicate you told no one until then. I have to confess I thought your words were from one seeking martyrdom." Walsingham now asked, thoughtfully.

"No, it was to stop a riot. You heard what the crowd was shouting. They wanted to kill all the Catholics. At the speed of a dream again, I declared I was a Catholic. A Catholic who had just stopped an assassination. And you responded, demanded and got their silence. That again must have been why Fate chose me. A Catholic had to stop a Catholic to save Catholics and Protestants."

"Understand our position. We are at war with the Catholics. You are a Catholic. How do we know what side you're really on? Yes, you have done great deeds for Her Majesty these past days. But you have also been betrayed, and you've been tortured, I'll admit unfairly. How do we know where your heart really is and where it will stay? How do we determine if we can trust you?" Cecil now decisively asked.

"I thought we were at war with Spain, but I will answer your question, My Lord. Fate," I replied. "Fate. You're not used to considering Fate. You've likely been brought up not to trust anyone. You study what someone has done in the past and all that's happened to them. Then you try to determine what you think they hold in their heart and will do in the future. I know I am still only a child and admittedly you have little of my short past to figure out my true heart. But you have overlooked Fate. It is Fate that has put the three of us in *this* room at *this* point in time. Fate. Just as she put me on the balcony, or in the Gatehouse, or all the roads I have described that brought me here, starting with Father McNee teaching me to read."

"May I?" I said hopefully as I carefully picked a book from the shelves. My face lit up in awe at Lady Fate, and I almost started to laugh. "Do you know what *this* is? It's probably the rarest book you have on these shelves, or any shelves. It's over 200-years old and handwritten. It is copied from Laghamon's Brut, the earliest known English translation of the Welsh poem of King Arthur and his Knights of the Roundtable. It is of chivalry, and of willing to pay the price to do what is right. This is the book I read with the help of Father McNee as my seventh birthday present. This is the book that made me pray that someday Fate would give me a task to help others, to have the courage to try regardless of risk to myself, and with all hope, succeed. This is what burned in my heart to dive over a balcony, or to declare I was Catholic to a mob, or to challenge Topcliffe."

"So you read a book, how does it show me this Fate you speak of?" Cecil asked puzzled.

"Because this *is* the book I read when I was seven. This *is* Father McNee's book that he sold over two years ago to keep us fed. Fate has brought it here to *this* room just as she has brought *us* here. She and Father McNee are dancing to an Irish song on top of your desk and I can hear them having a good laugh." And I started to dance around with a bit of a clumsy one of my own. They both looked at me as if I'd gone mad.

Cecil started to laugh sarcastically, "Are you trying to say this book came from your priest in Ireland and its words are what led you here? Now that's good acting boy! You really think you're clever enough to make us believe it? You went too far with this. Now you've said something you can't back out of or prove."

"Lord Cecil, that sounds like a challenge for a wager. I can prove Fate has brought *this* book here to show what I say is true in my heart."

"And what would you wager, you don't have any gold," Cecil retorted.

"Oh, my bet is far more valuable than gold. I will bet … my life against what you value most. Trust. My life for your trust, My Lord."

They both now looked beyond stunned. Now Walsingham spoke. "We do not make wagers on people's lives. Despite what powers you think we might have we do have laws."

"But, My Lord, this wager has already been made. It was made the moment I walked through that door. If you do not trust me, I am as good as dead. You know Topcliffe is a vengeful cruel man and he will kill me unless I have your protection. Fate has placed this book in this room to settle that wager."

I had stopped my dance and placed the book on the desk before Walsingham. I had opened it to a certain page. "Could you read "Ode to a Knight," My Lord? Please."

He looked at me, then Cecil, and then the book. He shrugged and then began: *"Ode to a Knight. Many a poet has tried to put to words the virtues of a Knight. I hope my humble attempt will be of worth to all who honor reading my words and hopes. There are many a brave Knight who daily do righteous deeds. A true Knight seeks..."* Then he stopped mid-sentence and stared at the page and then with his eyes wide, looked at me.

"Pray, please continue, possibly again from the start, My Lord." I calmly asked with a proud grin.

Shaking, Lord Francis Walsingham, the Queen's Principle Secretary and known as her Spy Master, started again. *"Ode to a Knight. Many a poet has tried to put to words the virtues of a Knight. I hope my humble attempt will be of worth to all who honor reading my words and hopes. There are many a brave Knight who daily do righteous deeds. A true Knight seeks to protect and help those of innocence from harm's way or who are in need. They do not seek glory from battle, but rather fight to bring peace. Hundreds of these brave Knights across all lands do daily good whether recognized or not. True Knights may be Noble or they may be Common, for their deeds do not need title. I pray that Fate will someday grant me three wishes to allow me to be a true Knight. First, I ask for a deed that brings help to those in need. Next, I ask for the courage and strength to do this deed regardless of any grave peril it places upon me. Last, I ask that I succeed no matter what cost I may have to pay. I pray our Lord leads the paths of Fate to grant me these three wishes. I ask these that my life may have worth, and that my heart may then rest in peace when my bones are laid to earth.*

*Signed this Seventeenth Day of March, My Birthday,
In the Year of our Lord, 1581. Presto"*

Walsingham again repeated in hushed astonishment, "Presto… This was written by Presto seven years ago."

"Yes, I wrote that half a lifetime ago. And Fate answered my prayer," I beamed.

"What? What are you talking about, this can't be possible?" Cecil now exclaimed as Sir Francis slid the book toward him. "It's got to be some kind of clever trick."

"It is no trick. It is all in the boy's hand," Sir Francis said as he had looked at the statement I had given him about the injustice in Swansea.

I was once again dancing with imaginary partners and bowing gracefully for I knew Father McNee and Lady Fate were doing the same with me. I finally stopped. "Sir Francis, do you trust me?"

With a pause, he answered, "Yes Presto, I believe I do."

"Many thanks, gramercy My Lord, that means a lot to me. It also means that this day, at least one Protestant trusts one Catholic. I can only hope that someday we can all live in peace trusting each other." I said this with a great deal of pride and continued.

"I also think it is safe to agree there be no more need of talk of me wanting to be a martyr. Lord Cecil, I believe you aren't quite ready to trust this alley cat yet, but in time, I believe you will. I would like to apologize to both of you for my often-strong statements, and the informal candor I have spoken to both of you. I mean no disrespect for your position or titles. But I felt it necessary to dispense with formalities and simply show you who I am with my words. I do know my place. Those who have been tending me in my magnificent rooms have taught me how I should behave to show respect to Her Majesty, should we again meet. I hope we do as I wish to thank her for all the kindness she has shown me."

"Yes," Sir Francis said as he nodded, "She has been worried about you, and wants to see you as soon as you are strong enough. I think you are ready, and I will be accompanying you."

Cecil was still staring with a baffled expression but finally shrugged, "I have to admit I had to be skeptical. I've never had to deal with a cat before. You're not what I expected. I don't think you're what anyone expected."

"Do either of you have further questions of me?" I asked.

"Yes, and I hope you understand why I ask them," Walsingham answered and then continued. "Do you know anything else about the priest John Boste or the writings you saw at the Gatehouse? Though they are probably a trick to divert our attention from rebellions being plotted, our Queen is interested in finding them."

"I do not, nor do I have a clue how to find them." I simply answered and then added, "But I don't think Fate is done with me yet. If anything, the papers are more likely to find me."

"And what would you do with them?" Walsingham asked.

"My Lord, I would bring them to you and trust your determination of their worth." I paused, and surprisingly, there seemed to be no further inquiries.

"May I then ask a question, Sir?" Walsingham nodded while Cecil still sat contemplating everything that had just occurred. "Staying at Whitehall is indeed an honor, but I know eventually I will need to find my own opportunities back in this great city. Richard Topcliffe is a vengeful man and he made it quite clear what he would do to me if I crossed him. Am I to be protected from him? I have some possible suggestions that might help."

"Why am I not surprised you have a plan," Walsingham replied. "And yes, the Queen has made it clear you are to be protected. Anyone who tries to harm you would be treated as committing treason the same as if they had assaulted Her Majesty. There might be fanatical Catholics who pose a grave risk to you. We are keeping discussions of this attempt on the Queen's life from spreading. Sir Richard knows he is not to harm you."

"My Lord, he may know he is not to harm me, but I fear he will spend the rest my life plotting his vengeance. I think he will want to do it himself, so I don't fear him finding an assassin, not even a fanatical Catholic. I fear he might try to produce false evidence and accuse me of treason, so he can have me back at the Gatehouse to himself. I also fear he might try to harm others that give me work, like those at the Theatre, which he already expressed his disdain for. I fear for the protection of others, as well as myself. But I do have a thought of what might prevent him."

I paused and Walsingham responded. "I would hear your idea."

"First, I would ask you point out to him it would be a personal displeasure if anything happens to me, especially since Her Majesty has ordered my protection. I must apologize to you since you're now responsible for me. Next, I would tell him you will be having me watched, and you will know of anyone I come in contact with. Finally, I would ask you tell him that *he* will also be watched, and you will know of any contacts he makes involving me. I know I'm not worth having your resources fighting the Spanish keeping an eye on me or Topcliffe, but he only has to think you're doing it. Just let him see someone who is clearly watching him from time to time."

"I'm beginning to think you would make a good spy as you're able to think like one," Walsingham laughed. "But I am already going to do what you suggest. I am going to have a strict discussion with Sir Richard and make certain things are very, very, clear. And yes, I am going to keep an eye on both of you. You will be staying at Whitehall until your wounds are healed and then other arrangements will probably be made with Sir Francis Drake. You will be safe. You have my word. And this time, you can trust it."

"Gramercy, many thanks, My Lord. Will I be able to leave Whitehall to visit the Theatre or others I know?"

"Not until after you have met with Her Majesty. This will be in two days, which I believe is your birthday. It seems Fate does follow you about. Afterwards, when you are strong enough, I will arrange for someone to accompany you." He replied with a kind smile.

"Gramercy My Lords, and I am humbled that I will see Her Majesty. I won't let you down. Many thanks." I was absolutely beaming.

Cecil's face had also softened, and he gave me a nod of approval, though his eyes could not hide a bit of concern. I was escorted back to my rooms still glowing. Later I heard it was said that Cecil had asked Sir Francis, "Are you sure you know what you're unleashing?"

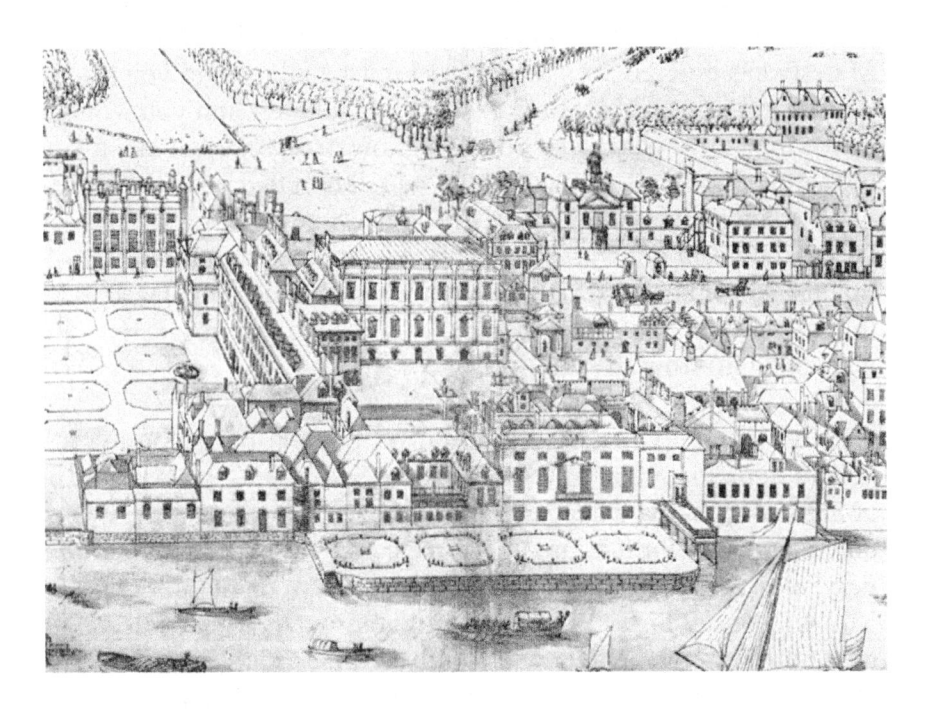

Whitehall Palace.

Chapter 5 – Tea with Her Majesty

Part 1 – Warm Soft Pillow

I couldn't believe my luck, my Fate. I was going to see her Majesty, the Queen, in two days! It would be on my birthday, no less! I had returned triumphantly from being questioned by the most powerful lords in her Majesty's Court. I think I even earned the respect of Sir Francis Walsingham. Even the head servant, Alexander, seemed to show more genuine warm respect rather than that due to duty. He had probably wondered if I was going to even return, after he escorted me to Lord Burghley's private office. That evening, Alexander arranged a very fine dinner for me.

When I first arrived in these chambers a week earlier, Alexander had no idea who, or what I was. He only knew he had to treat me as if I were nobility. He had been used to serving the most important nobles, lords and royalty, before finding a beat-up commoner under his care. I had been taken to what was referred to as the "Royal Chambers." He was used to showing the utmost respect and being strictly formal with every mannerism, word and service. He always accepted that the guest in his charge was his superior. He was the most trusted and senior servant who was assigned the Queen's most prestige guests. Her Majesty herself had placed me under his care, and he knew I was to see her.

This was awkward for both of us. I wasn't used to being attended to and having servants hovering about me. The first couple days had been rough, and the poppy potion had left me mostly in a daze. I appreciated any help, just trying to get comfortable. Once I gained some strength and weaned off the poppies though, I became aware of my surroundings and went back to being my mischievous self. My Irish brogue and informality left Alexander somewhat bewildered. My drifting in and out of my Irish accent and gentleman's English probably didn't help either.

It was on the fourth night at Whitehall that I was able to have a real dinner. I was brought to a very lavish table set with the finest china trimmed with gold leaf. The silverware appeared to have more gold than silver in them. I was nervous just touching them. I'm not sure if Alexander wondered whether I knew how to use them or if he would have to count them after my stay. One spoon would bring enough money to feed me, and the street boy, Jack, for weeks. Alexander and the lad assigned to me, Michael, served the dinner and stood there at attention. I asked them to join me as there was far more food and courses than I could possibly eat. Alexander was aghast at the thought of joining his guest at dinner. That just wasn't done. They would eat later, separately.

I finally had to tell them to please sit down, as it would be easier for me to see them if I needed anything. Once I had them seated, I eventually was able to get them to "please" try some of the dishes and tell me what they were. It was the first time I actually had beef. Alexander couldn't fathom someone who had never had beef.

Cows were kept mostly for dairy in my Irish village and only the wealthy would actually have roast beef for dinner. Father McNee had some wealth but saw no need for such luxury. We had the fish we caught and wild game, including venison that usually came from members of the congregation. We had an occasional chicken and whatever our kitty, Rose, brought us for stew. Once a year we had a goose. Father McNee would buy the goose and then give it to the Doyle family for their Christmas dinner. They couldn't afford one, so they would prepare it and we would join them in a Christmas feast. We didn't have one the Christmas after he passed.

I had told them about our more simple foods where I was from but did not go into details of how I was raised. I thought it best to see what they knew about me first. I at least got a little laugh from the lad, Michael, when I told him about our kitty's help with making stew. That got him a stern look from Alexander. What, didn't they ever laugh at what the lords said?

The next day was the first time I was able to visit the grounds and meet some of the nobles or lords, and a number of the ravens. I was simply introduced as Master Presto. Alexander had coached me how to properly meet them, the nobles that is, not the ravens.

That evening, I was in an exuberant mood with my recovery. Alexander now seemed to be more relaxed having me under his charge. We were able to have easier conversations. I had asked with those pleading kitten eyes that had worked so well in the past, for him and Michael to join me for dinner. Alexander relented and they both finally ate with me.

We had not discussed why the Queen was being so kind to me. The only thing I learned, is that it was said I was in some kind of service for her. Michael finally innocently tried to ask, "Master Presto, may I ask what happened to you?"

This got an immediate stern look from Alexander who told the lad, "You know it is not your place to ask such questions."

"I think Michael has the right to ask me that," I replied. "After all, both of you have been tending to my wounds and I am very grateful to both of you. It is rather obvious *what* happened to me, the real question is *who* happened to me." With that statement, Alexander's look went from stern to grave.

"I see from the look on your face, that you know *that* answer." He tried to glance away, but I continued. "I have been meaning to ask you what is actually known about me, shall we say, outside these rooms. This is something I need you to coach me on, for I don't know if others know what happened to me. I am hoping it is not a subject of discussion among your other nobler guests. They must wonder who the lad is at the end of the hall."

"They know little of you other than you have done some great mission for the Queen and were injured in the process. Some think it had something to do with work for Sir Francis Drake. It is not proper for me to tell them anything about you, your ancestry, your status, or your actual deeds."

"I appreciate this, for I have no idea what I should say myself. I'm not, shall we say, looking for fame out of this. But I will be asked. My only plan is to simply shyly say that I'm not up to discussing it yet. I assume you know the events of why I'm here?"

He paused and then answered, "Yes, Master Presto, I do." Then he added, "And I offer you gratitude on behalf of all of our Queen's loyal subjects."

I still couldn't get over being called Master Presto. I went on, "I assume you both know that I am Irish, that I am not high born, and that I am not likely Protestant?"

They both nodded as I looked at each.

"Are the nobles down the hall aware of the same?" I asked.

Alexander nodded.

"Are you aware I have pledged my loyalty to Her Majesty, despite the Spanish influence on my own religion to do otherwise?"

Alexander paused again and answered honestly, "I have had no doubt to your loyalty, but I must confess it is puzzling, especially considering what happened to you afterwards."

"Let's just say Topcliffe and I had a little misunderstanding on loyalties, but we straightened it all out with the help of Her Majesty," I said now with a bit of a grin. "Does Topcliffe have rooms set aside for him at Whitehall?"

"No. he does not," Alexander replied, this time with more of look of respect.

"Hmm," I responded, I suppose with a bit of glee before continuing. "Do the other guests know the source of my injuries?"

"I don't believe they do as the story regarding Sir Francis Drake seems to be the most popular." Alexander had stated this in a way that confirmed my belief he knew everything that was going on and being said, in this section of the palace. I also assumed he was reporting everything I said and did to Walsingham. I wondered, though, how the Drake story had started, unless it was Walsingham himself.

I then turned to the lad, "Michael, I assume that you have the same discretion as Master Alexander. I would ask you do not repeat this discussion, especially regarding Topcliffe."

"Yes, Master Presto. I would never repeat anything that goes on with any of those I serve. I apologize for my asking you; it was not my place." He answered bashfully.

"I'm glad you did, we, I, needed to have this conversation for I too, must learn my place." I now said with humility because, after all, I wasn't anyone's superior.

Each day I was able to eat a little more and couldn't believe the menus. The food was rich and there were sweet unending desserts. The water was clear and sweet to drink too. I could get used to this, though I knew this was only temporary. I was a feral cat that had found the softest warmest pillow in all of Kitty Dom. I thought of what it would be like to sleep under the balcony stairs once again back at the Burbage's if they would still have me.

As the week passed, I could move around without wincing, and my ribs were far more forgiving. The worst was when I laughed or, well, farted. I did laugh a lot more these days because, really, this was all just too funny that I was here. The rich food was also creating surprising results. When you're basically starving, there isn't much in you to create such an effect. Not even the garbage I picked off the alleys to eat in my worst days reacted like this rich food. This created a double-edged sword, as this event would also make me laugh which only doubled the pain. All young lads tend to find such gaseous events humorous. Some never grow out of this cause to giggle. Simply recall the rotund Scott Craig on the road to Oxford, and you'll see what I mean. He even spoke of lighting his with a candle, a vision I have desperately blocked from my mind these many years.

I learned the history of where I was staying. Whitehall had been a major palace for centuries. Henry VIII had rebuilt this palace at enormous expense. It had well over 1,000 rooms and mine were possibly the finest for visiting royalty. The Queen had her own privy section of chambers for her and her personal court. There were various chambers that were permanently rented to the finest noble families of earls and dukes. Others were rented to those lords and nobles seeking favor with her Majesty. The many other rooms were used for visiting dignitaries, diplomats, and her Majesty's special guests.

I found out my chambers were the very same rooms Phillip of Spain stayed in during a visit to England when he married "Bloody" Queen Mary decades earlier. He is now Phillip II, the very King of Spain we are at war with. And I'm sleeping in the same bed! Still, I missed cuddling up under the stairs of the balcony at the Theatre, and the kitty that gave me hope to go on.

During the remaining week, I spent more time going outside. The weather was exceptional as spring felt like it was coming early. I never had expected to survive winter and hoped the lads at Swansea had somehow managed to. I also wondered what had happen to the lad, Jack, somewhere on the streets of London. I could go outside directly from my rooms but preferred going down the hallway to see the phenomenal artwork, tapestries, architecture and furniture along the way. There were also ornate meeting rooms where the nobles held private dining parties. I learned there was always competition as to who would be the guests at these opulent events. I, of course, hadn't been invited to any. No one really knew exactly what my status was going to be. Neither did I, for that matter.

It was on the day before seeing Walsingham and Cecil that I again ventured down the hallway to go outside. As I did, I saw a young girl about my age coming back down the hall with her servant. I was glad to see someone my own age, as I had wondered if I might be the youngest guest here. As she approached, I suddenly lit up with a glow of butterflies. She had long, blonde hair and a sweet, adorable face. As we got closer, I saw she had the most beautiful eyes I had ever seen. They were filled with kindness.

I thought to myself, 'Fate, if you ever lead me to someone to share my life with, let her be the soul behind those beautiful eyes. If not in this lifetime, then another, even if it takes all nine.'

"Morning, My Lady," I had said without thinking before Alexander could do a more proper introduction.

"Good afternoon, kind Sir," she replied with a smile.

It was, in fact, midafternoon, but I was happy I could just spend a moment gazing into her eyes. Alexander then interrupted with those proper introductions and we continued our journeys in our opposite ways. I asked Alexander who she was, and he told me she was from one of the oldest and most respected noble families in the kingdom. He also added she was well protected. He had said this in a diplomatic way, but it made me remember a low-born like me would not likely even have an opportunity to speak, let alone develop a friendship, with someone as enchanting as her.

I hadn't really thought about what it would be like to have a girlfriend. In Ireland I was too young, and the last year there, I mostly was taking care of Father McNee. And then I, needless to say, had no time for such things after I arrived in Wales. While just trying to survive, there were rare chances to find someone my age to speak to. I suddenly realized this as she walked away and disappeared, possibly forever. I would try to casually get a little more information about her from Michael later.

That night I had to prepare my thoughts for the day ahead when I knew I would be taken to Walsingham. He would be questioning me, and I had to decide just what of my short life I should tell him. I knew he really didn't know anything about me other than being raised by a priest and being as defiant as any rebel he had ever met. I knew I had to show him I was not some fanatic that couldn't be trusted, if I was going to get any protection from being harmed or killed by Topcliffe.

But my mind was distracted by thinking of "The Girl." I mostly just wanted to have an opportunity to become a friend. I didn't know anything about romance or falling in love. What was love?

Of course, I loved Father McNee, just as if he were my parent. Loving someone new, well, what was that all about? The only thing I could think of was our kitty. There was no reason for me to go out of my way to start petting her and try to make her happy and purr. Yet that made me happy myself because I wanted to bring joy into her heart. She, of course, returned the favor. Was that what love was all about? Was it feeling joy at making someone else happy and longing to be with her?

Then, of course, there was the physical attraction or lustful part. I was still too young to partake in such activities. I was old enough to be wondering what that would be like though. Frightening for one. But this was not what I was thinking about in regard to the sweet lass I had just seen. After all, she was only a young girl, and I still a boy. All these questions distracted my mind from deciding what I was finally going to tell Walsingham the next day. I decided there was no sense telling any lies to the Queen's Spymaster. I would just tell him how I ended up and survived in London. Fortunately, Fate surprised us all with a bit of help when my "Ode" showed up the next day, in Lord Burghley's book collection. That day went very well indeed, I thought. Now it was just two more days until I would see her Majesty.

That first day before meeting the Queen again was another incredible one. It began when Alexander brought me a small ornate box with a note from Sir Francis Drake. The note simply read, "I made us all pay up, for you won the wager. I hope this will ease your pain." When I opened the box, I was stunned. It was filled with gold coins! There was twenty-five pounds inside! It was a fortune. I had never seen so much money. They had each bet five pounds as to which lash would break me. This was little more than the cost of respectable aged wine for most nobles.

I asked Alexander if I could get a pound broken into shillings, so I could send the two shillings I owed to Burbage. I had already written a note letting them know I was all right, that I was in the service of the Queen at Whitehall, and I would return his two shillings. I had no idea how I was going to pay him back until now.

It also occurred to me, I would have to pay someone to take the note and coins to Burbage. How much should I pay? I had run errands and goods for Wilson, so I knew what I had been paid. I was happy to get a pence. This would probably involve a servant who would take a horse or even a carriage. How much was that going to cost? Ah, money problems already and I hadn't had any a few moments earlier. I also thought I should send something to the Doyles.

The next event was having my stitches out by the Queen's physician. This wasn't particularly pleasant, but there was no sign of infection. I had made it clear to the physician that he was not to be using pagan Greek medications made out of goat crap or trying to balance my four "humors." Bleeding was one of the treatments used even on the Queen to cure illnesses caused by imbalances in the humors.

"Just keep my wounds clean with salt water or strong spirits, preferably while I'm out cold from the poppies," I had pleaded. I learned these theories of treatments from Father McNee and his many different books on so many subjects. I'm not sure, but I think it was based on more successful Islamic medical treatments from the Crusades.

The next event was a warm bath. The water closet, which was actually a large room, had a magnificent ornate tub. It was larger than the one at Wilson's. You still sat in it, but there was more room to stretch out. It appeared to be made out of gold and silver with a porcelain interior. It was delicious and felt heavenly to submerge in the perfect temperate water that had been prepared by the servant Michael. This was the very tub King Phillip II would have used. Even my aching ribs felt good in the warm water. That is until I released a couple bubbles and started giggling at the thought Phillip II probably had done the same. Michael and Alexander, of course, stayed in attendance, so I still had an audience. This was just as awkward as when I took a bath at Wilson's. Again Fate, are you just sitting there laughing?

Alexander did finally leave, so I had an opportunity to ask Michael about the girl. I told him it was nice to see someone more our age and that Alexander had said she was from a very esteemed family. He told me her family was Welsh, going back to the time of King Alfred the Great. This was long before Strongbow and King Edward II started getting an English stranglehold on Ireland. It was also said the family had Viking or Norwegian blood in their heritage.

We had a very late lunch, after I had again been dressed in clothes worthy of a peacock. I looked out the windows at the bare gardens below. There were at least some bushes with buds coming to life. It was a beautiful day and I was looking forward to going outside and try to figure out what I would do when I met the Queen tomorrow. And then I saw her! The girl. The girl was walking with her servant!

"We're going outside, now!" I said to Michael who looked bewildered. Alexander was the one who normally escorted me. Michael was hesitant and confused as I headed to the doorway to the veranda that led outside.

He grabbed a coat for me and expressed concerns that we should wait for Alexander. I was studying the girl's route like a cat calculating which way I should go to intercept her. I also had to decide what to say, what to talk about. We could talk about the beautiful weather. Seriously, think, I can do better than that, I thought. Probably shouldn't mention I recently was living in a graveyard. No, that won't do either. What am I supposed to say when I catch up with her?

As I casually circled around in a direction that would approach her, she stopped with her servant and sat down on a bench near the sundial. This was perfect as the warm sun was in her face on the path I had calculated to take. As I approached, I continued to strain to think of what to say. I had nothing and now I was closing with inevitability. I was now only seconds away from where she was sitting, and still nothing. Then a tabby cat sauntered out from the bushes near her bench. She walked up to me with a "Meow." Then she flopped down and rolled over a couple times.

"Pretty kitty! Where did you come from?" I said as I kneeled on one knee to give her a pet. "Is she your kitty?" I asked looking up at the girl and gazing into her eyes.

"No, I've not seen her before," she replied as she got up and then kneeled down to give the kitty a rub. The kitty rolled, got up, and flopped back and forth between us as I shifted to kneel on both knees. "I've heard you're the boy from Ireland?"

"Aye, My Lady, that I am, and at your service," I answered now letting a little of my Irish accent out. "And I've heard you're from Wales?"

"Yes, I'm from Aberystwyth, on the west coast. Possibly you traveled my way when you came over from your Ireland?"

"No, unfortunately, I missed the route that would have taken me by your home. I came up from the south through Swansea. I took the valley and mountain route toward Gloucester. Your Wales is absolutely beautiful."

"I've heard Ireland is also mountainous but can be rough. Is it pretty too?

"Oh yes, My Lady. Our mountains are not as grand or high as yours. But there is something in Ireland's air that does something to the sunlight. It makes all the colors glow like emeralds and sapphires, almost as beautiful as the way the sun now sparkles in your eyes." And I continued to gaze into them as much as I dare.

She grinned and blushed slightly which was the effect I was hoping for. "You are most kind, Sir. Are all the Irish filled with such charm?

"Well, some of us might be better at it than others," I said with a beaming smile.

We continued talking about nothing in particular, just as any boy and girl should. We continued petting the affectionate kitty and our hands would occasionally touch. She eventually asked me, "Do cats always come out to greet you?"

"Aye, quite often. You see, it is said that I am part cat that was once a Druid Prince a long time ago," I replied with a bit of a mischievous smile. She laughed the most wonderful laugh.

In the meantime, Michael looked on nervously, while her older servant looked on with disdain at our lack of formality. She did not know we had been introduced, as she was not the one with her when we first met in the hall. This just wasn't the way it was supposed to be done. Fortunately, she just sat on the bench trying to decide what, if anything, she was supposed to do. I heard footsteps coming and didn't have to turn to look, as I recognized them as being Alexander's.

"Morning," I greeted, though it was midafternoon with the sun getting a little lower. "I saw this beautiful kitty and had to come out to see who she belongs to. You, no doubt, know everyone here. Do you know where this sweet one belongs?"

He hesitated as he always does when I stump him with an unexpected question or answer. "Ah, no, Master Presto, I do not. I was concerned when I did not see you. We still have to prepare for your visit with Her Majesty tomorrow."

By now the kitty had raised her tail and marched proudly off to the bushes. The girl and I both rose, and I said more to her than Alexander, "Oh yes, many thanks. I'm honored to have tea with Her Majesty tomorrow on my birthday."

In the meantime her servant had gotten up and indicated they should be going.

"Maybe we can see where our kitty is off to sometime and give her a name," I said to the girl, in an effort to stare one more time into her eyes before I knew we would part.

"Many birthday wishes, but sadly I am to leave tomorrow to go back home. My father wants to be back in Wales for the coming of spring and the change of the year in just over a week." She said this in a way that made me feel she would have liked to visit again.

"Well then, until Fate has us meet again. May the Lord bid you safe travels, may the sun always shine upon your enchanting face, and may the wind stay mild upon your back." And I bowed a gentleman's bow as she reached out her hand so I could kiss it as I finished with "My Lady."

We then both laughed, and she turned to walk away with her servant. I stood and stared with my heart pounding. I had never felt this way before. Somewhere, somehow, we would meet again. I fancied for a moment, that someday, we would be together with the sweet kitty Fate had sent us. In the meantime, the kitty had sauntered off and disappeared like a ghost.

I finally turned to both Alexander and Michael whose expressions varied from stern, to still anxious, and said, "Do you mind if we walk a bit before returning?"

As we strolled, the sun started its low golden descent. I treasured its warmth and the memory of every moment spent with "The Girl." I finally relented to Alexander's hints and we returned to my rooms. As the night fell, I continued being distracted by the thought of her when I should have been concentrating on how to behave meeting her Majesty. As to the name of the girl who now haunted me, well, I think I'll just hold that close to my heart for now.

Part 2 – A Tale of Two Knives

The day had finally come. I was to have tea with her Majesty! Alexander made sure I was dressed as respectably as any distinguished lord. He had coached me as to the proper way to speak to the Queen and generally not to speak unless spoken to first. He escorted me to Walsingham's office late that morning before the teatime, which would be around one. Walsingham's office was as impressive as the elder Cecil's, but you could tell the difference in their characters from the subtle ways it was organized. There was also a padlocked door down a short inner hallway that, no doubt, led to the secrets of the kingdom.

"Good morning, Lord Walsingham," I greeted.

"Welcome, Presto, please come in and please sit. I see Alexander has prepared you properly. Gramercy, Alexander," and he bid him to be excused. "I'm afraid I don't have quite the collection of books as Lord Burghley. I thought we would talk a bit before you visit with Her Majesty. I have been keeping her informed as to your healing and she is looking forward to seeing you. This is quite an honor. How are you feeling?"

"Quite well, My Lord. I had the stitches out yesterday. I also had a warm bath in a golden tub I understand Phillip II used when he visited England before I was born. You can imagine how I think this is all a just a dream after having lived in a graveyard this past summer. I am really humbled and grateful for all the kindness Her Majesty has bestowed upon me. And I am again thankful for all your help, and for believing in me."

"Well, you have done us a great service. You also told me a great number of things. I wanted to talk to you about some things you need not bring up with Her Majesty. You probably don't need to go into details about living in a cemetery, for instance."

"No My Lord, I didn't think that would be appropriate either. I don't know what you've told her about me. I am hoping you have not told her about some of the regrettable things I had to do, well, like thieving. I told my story plain and true, so you knew what I did to survive. I don't think it suitable for discussing during tea with Her Majesty. I also was not going to bring up Topcliffe, as I am trusting my protection is in your hands."

"I am not surprised at your perception. And I think you understand this meeting will be more formal and respectful. Your last two meetings with the Queen were, shall we say, a bit intense. Today, we're just having tea. I also have some things for you." With that he opened his desk drawer and placed a pouch in front of me. "Your coin pouch from your coat had been misplaced. The shillings from Burbage are in it and I will arrange to send the note I believe you have written to him."

"Many thanks, Sir. I have so wanted to get word to them."

"I also have your knife that was in your coat, which, of course, you haven't had need of while at Whitehall." With that he reached into the drawer and placed a knife on the desk before me. The knife, however, wasn't the stolen knife that had been in my coat. Rather, it was the other knife I had stolen in Swansea, the one that I had left at Wilson's the night I stabbed Topcliffe. Are we playing a game of chess, and to what end?

"Uh, that's not my knife, My Lord," I said truthfully with a puzzled look that lacked the shock I really felt.

"Oh, wrong knife," he replied as he was placing the sheath from my knife in front of me and then retrieved a longer knife from the drawer. "At first I was confused as to why you still had a knife in your coat since you had stabbed the assassin. You cleared it up when you said you used his knife. I believe this one is yours."

"Yes, that is the one I had in my coat."

"I notice the sheath has been modified, like it was made longer. It looks like it would have originally fit a shorter knife," he now quizzed.

"Yes, I stole more than one knife. As I said, I wasn't a very good thief, but knives are easier to steal than pickpocketing. I made the sheath longer when I acquired this one. I had a shorter one I would leave at the tomb I stayed at. I would prefer a shorter one like that first one as it is easier to carry. Is that another lost knife?" I finally asked casually, adding "My Lord."

"That is the one was used to stab Sir Richard Topcliffe," he said, now watching me closely. I, of course, knew this was not the knife I had used to stab him. I had used Topcliffe's own snaky knife.

I looked at it somewhat bewildered and reached toward it. "May I? It seems such a small knife. I would have expected something, grander." He nodded and I picked it up. "Not very sharp either. I guess Topcliffe was right. My Lord, a Viking of a man would have to be the one to use this one. A mere boy wouldn't be able to wound him enough to get away."

Walsingham's expression became perplexed. It now occurred to him that an assassin wouldn't have used such a lackluster, worn knife.

He then spoke. "I still don't understand why you brought up a boy had stabbed him, almost making it sound like it was you? He almost killed you."

"Well, there were several reasons, My Lord. As I said, I was trying to rattle him so he would make a mistake. But I had also heard he had rounded up some of the lads I knew and had interrogated and tortured them about his attack. That was around the time I left working the south side of the river. There are laws, after all. You can't just grab boys off the street and get away abusing them. I thought this would bring more scrutiny to his unlawful activities. I hoped to have them stopped, just as I am seeking justice for the lads in Swansea."

He looked at me, now with a serious look. "I did not pursue this question earlier when we were with Sir Robert, but you know I do need to ask. Did you stab Topcliffe?"

"Topcliffe swore to Her Majesty and all those present, including yourself, that it was the man he had tortured before my eyes that stabbed him. I would have no proof to challenge him otherwise, and, of course, it would be foolish to confess to such a crime. I believe there would be a very harsh punishment for a commoner attacking a noble, even if it were in self-defense, My Lord."

"Yes, but the question is, did *you* stab him?"

"My Lord, let us for a moment consider this alternative, that a boy did stab him. First, there would be the why? What could possibly be the reason for such an attack? No lad would willingly go to meet him privately for pay unless he was tricked or likely drugged. Imagine if he had seen Topcliffe at an execution at Tyburn and knew what he is capable of. Of course, he would panic, and do whatever he had to do to get away."

I continued, "You wonder if that boy could have been me. Well, just think of the terror I would have been in when you sent me to the Gatehouse. How could he possibly not recognize me? Wouldn't I want to be as invisible as possible while he butchered a man and told me I would be next? Would I dare to steal Her Majesty's letter right out from his very nose? Twice, as a matter of fact. How could I have left the Gatehouse alive, My Lord?"

"All very good points as to how it couldn't possibly have been you, and I again apologize for the terror I put you through. But you still have not answered me straight," he replied.

"I think I have answered your question straight, My Lord. I think it is plain enough. Sir Topcliffe has settled this matter," I answered with the hope we might have an understanding.

"My Lord, I have a favor to ask, based on the events that Fate placed upon me when you sent me to the Gatehouse. May we accept Sir Topcliffe's sworn denial I forced from him, that it was not a boy?"

Walsingham paused and looked at me with consideration, "Very well, I think we do have an understanding. My main concern is to what degree he wishes to harm you. I will protect you, but understand, my time is limited. You will eventually have to rely on Sir Robert Cecil, and you best stay on the good side of him."

"Many thanks, My Lord, and Topcliffe can only kill me once for whatever number of reasons. As to my knife, I would like to keep one in case I should find I have to protect myself alone. It probably wouldn't do me that much good, but at least I'd try to put up a good fight. I was wondering if you have any further intentions with the smaller of the two knives. I would prefer having that one rather than the larger one that I, well, stole. It would be easier to carry and keep concealed. I would, of course, have to sharpen it."

"You would rather have the knife used to stabbed Topcliffe?" he answered incredulously.

"Yes, though I have serious doubts that *is* the actual knife," I replied, and I think he knew my eyes did not lie.

He stared with a somewhat perplexed look, but this was more from him deciding to agree while he was shaking his head no. "Very well, since you seem to be the one who knows. Needless to say you won't need it now. I will send these items to you later."

"Gramercy, My Lord. I also need to know what I am to tell others that inquire why Her Majesty has made me her guest at Whitehall? I do not know if I'm to discuss the attack upon her."

"We are keeping the assassination attempt hushed up. We have generally let out more of a controlled story of our awareness of a deranged fanatic and were watching for him. We indicated we trapped him and there was a boy who had stepped in and tried to help. We have not stated you were the boy. I do not mean to steal your glory, but we wish to protect the Queen by downplaying this attempt. As to your being here, we have indicated you are in Sir Drake's charge, and were injured in Her Majesty's service. I hope you understand."

"I do, Sir. As my 'Ode' I wrote says, I did not do my deeds for glory. It appears that Fate has decided I will continue play-acting different roles from time to time. Will I actually meet Sir Drake again? Is he going to see to my further education? After all, he has a war to fight, and it will be this year the Spanish are coming in their ships. In short, what is to become of me?"

"First you're going to meet with Her Majesty and have tea. It is time to celebrate your bravery and service to her. Then Her

Majesty is the one who will decide what is to become of you. Be of good cheer because you have found her favor. I am proud to be the one to present you." As he spoke, he finished with a kind, sincere smile. It was time for us to go, and with that he sent for Alexander, and we were off to see her Majesty.

Part 3 – Tea and Chocolate

I was escorted through more of the magnificent hallways of Whitehall. The finest one had crystal windows overlooking the Thames along with incredibly colorful tapestries on the opposite walls. They were immense and went from floor to ceiling. We entered a graceful sitting room. It had a friendly warmth to it, despite its unbelievable elegance. Her Majesty was seated at a table that already had teacups, biscuits, cheese, fruits, and most important, sweets. She was reading correspondence and happily set them aside as we entered. Once again, her face was pure white. I wondered if all Queens wore such makeup, though I never recalled reading about it.

Alexander introduced us, and I could tell he was an old hand at introducing guests to the Queen. "Welcome, Sir Francis, and welcome, my dear boy Presto. How are you feeling?" She greeted.

"Quite well, Your Majesty. I am very much on the mend thanks to your kindness and that of Lord Walsingham and Master Alexander. They have been so gracious to me these past days. You have gone out of your way to spoil me and I am most humbled." I bowed as I thanked her for all these considerations.

"Well, since you didn't ask for anything I could hand to you, I thought I could at least spoil you a little," she replied as she smiled. "I also understand it is your birthday and I am happy to share it with you."

"Gramercy ever so much Your Majesty, I think you've done more than spoil me a little," I beamed.

She motioned for us to sit and sent for tea. Alexander knew when he was to leave and bowed gracefully away as another servant poured tea. She then spoke, "Sir Francis has told me more details of some of your adventures. I am sorry about Swansea and the situation will be handled. He has told me more of the depth of your education and you fancy yourself a knight."

"I am thankful Your Majesty, I mean about Swansea. When I escaped, I swore I would try to help them. I hope the other lads can be saved and compensated for their unjust misery. As to being a knight, it is more that I always prayed I would someday be able to do deeds worthy of a knight. I wrote my own poem about what I thought it would take to be a true knight after I read an early translation of King Arthur and the Knights of the Round Table."

"Yes, Sir Francis told me of your words and how they showed him what was really in your heart. I would like to hear your 'Ode' sometime."

"I would be happy to recite my words to you, Ma'Lady, as they are still written on my heart."

"Yes, Presto, I would very much like to hear them."

"If it pleases you then," I said as I stood and gracefully began.

"Ode to a Knight. Many a poet has tried to put to words the virtues of a Knight. I hope my humble attempt will be of worth to all who honor reading my words and hopes. There are many a brave Knight who daily do righteous deeds. A true Knight seeks to protect and help those of innocence from harm's way or who are in need. They do not seek glory from battle, but rather fight to bring peace. Hundreds of these brave Knights across all lands do daily good whether recognized or not. True Knights may be Noble or they may be Common, for their deeds do not need title. I pray that Fate will someday grant me three wishes to allow me to be a true Knight. First, I ask for a deed that brings help to those in need. Next, I ask for the courage and strength to do this deed regardless of any grave peril it places upon me. Last, I ask that I

succeed no matter what cost I may have to pay. I pray our Lord leads the paths of Fate to grant me these three wishes. I ask these that my life may have worth, and that my heart may then rest in peace when my bones are laid to earth."

As I finished, I again did a graceful bow. Her Majesty beamed as she seemed to be taken by my words. She gestured that I again may be seated and bid me to have tea and sweets. She pointed to a dark brown colored cake. "You must try this. It is made from cocoa from the Americas of the South. It is heavenly, but not as much as the words you have just spoken. The priest who raised you must have been a remarkable man to have filled your heart with such truth."

"Gramercy, Your Majesty. You are again most kind," and I tried a piece of the cocoa cake. I thought I was in heaven. Today you would indulge in this treat called chocolate. But back then, it was something new and since it was from the lands controlled by Spain, few would be able to taste it in England. Its wonder made me think of "The Girl," and I suddenly found myself longing to spend all my gold to acquire some of this chocolate. I would then dash off to Wales so I could be the first to present her tongue with this delightful temptation. I had to snap out of this fantasy as I remembered I was having tea with the Queen.

We had a casual conversation. She inquired about my name and I told her the story of how it came about when I was baptized by both a priest and a vicar. I told her of the Theatre and the writing of plays. There were many that had tried to convince her to ban them, but she had no look of disdain when I had finished. We also spoke of the elegant rooms I was staying in. She laughed and said that only royalty had used these rooms and they sat empty since the war had largely curtailed such visits. She said no doubt just a few lords and nobles would be jealous that her stray "Alley Cat" was now using them. She said this in a kind way and added, "I hope you don't mind if I've given you the nickname of Alley Cat."

Queen Elizabeth was known for coming up with nicknames. Some were not exactly kind, while others were quite an honor.

She called the younger Robert Cecil I had recently been interrogated by as, "Pygmy." His father, Lord Burghley, was "Spirit."

"I would be honored, Your Majesty. I've never had a nickname. Everyone just assumes that my name, Presto, is one."

I thanked her for allowing me to stay at this magnificent palace. I told her how I was amazed at the fine furniture, antiques and book collection that filled the large study or meeting hall that one entered to access the rest of the royal chambers she had me residing in. It was larger than the separate halls that were available for other lords and nobles to reserve to throw their dinner parties. I told her the room felt lonely and she might consider opening it up for her other guests to just come in and visit casually with friends. The suggestion astonished her as well as Sir Francis.

Then she said, "I suppose it is a shame not to use it more often. Alexander will have a fit though." And she laughed.

As we finished our visit, she smiled and spoke, "I am delighted we finally were able to have a cozy visit. You are a clever and an intelligent stray cat. I would like to show you off. Are you up to having dinner with just a few of my lords and a knight this evening? It is your birthday. Drake will be there."

I sat there stunned, as did Walsingham, no doubt. "Of course, Your Majesty," I replied with delight. "Will there be more cocoa cake?" She laughed as did Walsingham.

Walsingham's laugh did not hide the expression on his face of remembering Robert Cecil's words after they had finished questioning me, "Are you sure you know what you're unleashing?"

Part 4 – Dinner and Religion

I was escorted back to my rooms by Alexander. He was quite nervous as now I would have to change to another fine set of peacock cloths and be prepared for a formal dinner. He knew who the guests were and told me of them. Now I was even more nervous, as if I wasn't enough already. Walsingham and Drake would be there and that thought gave me some confidence.

Lord Charles Howard of Effingham, 1st Earl of Nottingham, would also be there. He is the Lord High Admiral in charge of the whole bloody war to defeat Spain. He is Francis Drake's commander. He is also the leader of the Admiral's Men. This is an influential group that supports the growth of London's playhouses. He was against the London Mayor and many others attempts to shut them down. It is his influence with her Majesty that has allowed them to remain open. He would undoubtedly have to know James Burbage.

The remaining guest was the Archbishop of Canterbury, John Whitgift, the head of the Anglican Church of England. He is probably not a big fan of Catholics, especially with Catholic Spain about to invade us. He also has the task of reigning in all the Protestant splinter groups, like the Puritans, to conform to her Majesty's official Anglican Church.

These men, more than any others, would give counsel to her Majesty to determine the Fate and survival of England in the coming year. Most are a part of the Privy Council and I was about to become privy to their dinner discussions with the Queen. They really didn't need a street boy listening in, and I was baffled by her Majesty's invitation. Alexander further stunned me by telling me that I was not the first orphan boy she had brought into the Royal Court.

Alexander brought me to the private dining room in the Queen's quarters. I was to be brought in last, introduced and seated. Her Majesty was already seated at the head, along with the rest on either side. I had half humorously expected there would be a kid's table set up off to the side for me. But no, there was an empty seat right next to her Majesty! I saw Drake was sitting next to that spot, while Walsingham was across with the other two next to him. There were also several servants all standing formally in their assigned spots.

"Your Majesty, I have brought you Master Presto," Alexander proclaimed as he bowed, and I followed his lead and also bowed.

All waited for the Queen to speak. "This is the boy I've been telling you about. She looked at Walsingham. "Sir Francis, you, of course, already know our Presto quite well by now."

I again bowed and said, "I am again glad to see you, My Lord," and he nodded with approval.

"This is Lord Charles Howard of Effingham, our Lord High Admiral who will defeat the Spaniards," was her next introduction.

I again bowed and said, "My Lord, I hope with all my heart you succeed."

"We will. And I give you thanks for the service you have done for Our Majesty. I have heard you have found work at Burbage's Theatre," he replied. "I am quite familiar with his work and support his efforts to grow the playhouses."

"Yes, My Lord, I have been helping make copies of the plays for the actors and hope I might write a grand one some day, myself."

Her Majesty continued her introductions, "This is John Whitgift, the Archbishop of Canterbury. Walsingham says you have many unusual ideas about our churches, and I look forward to your conversations with my Archbishop." I thought I had detected a slight twinkle in her eye as she said this. Had she just invited me to speak and have conversations with these powerful dinner guests? Alexander's advice was to only speak when spoken to. Walsingham probably already knew that was hopeless.

"I am honored and humbled to meet you, My Lord. I was raised to first know and love our Savior and where our religions are the same. I have lived with Protestants for a year now and find them as fine a folk as mine back home." I was speaking with only a slight Irish brogue and assumed he already knew I was Catholic and from Ireland.

"I have heard many interesting puzzling things about you," he answered as he nodded with a curious, but cold expression.

Her Majesty continued, "And you have also met our other Sir Francis," as she gestured toward Sir Francis Drake.

"I am honored to meet you again, and also thank you for the surprise box I received from you, Sir Drake.

"I thought it was the least I could do and am looking forward to what conversations we will have this evening," Drake replied with a whimsical grin.

With that I was beckoned to be seated but not before I thanked her Majesty for her invitation and kindness. Walsingham then proposed a toast to her Majesty and to the defeat of Spain. We all rose for this toast and drank from fine crystal goblets. It was a very fine wine, whatever it was. The archbishop offered grace and again included the defeat of Spain and added the defeat of their unholy Inquisition. When he finished, I added an amen, but that was not apparently the custom as the rest did not follow. We were seated and Drake just smiled at me with an encouraging wink.

Short light conversations of social natures circulated the table as the first course was served. It was a selection of finely seasoned fowl in pies and some heavenly tasting broth. This would have been more than a complete meal for me, but I already knew from Alexander's dinners that we were just getting started. The conversations were all very informal unless her Majesty initiated or joined in on a subject. Then the conversation was continued until it met some form of conclusion. One subject they all had enthusiasm for was hunting and that they all had their favorite horses. Drake finally asked me if I had any experience with horses. I told him that I mostly was still just learning the art of falling off them. They all laughed.

The next courses were served with more fowl, venison, rabbit and various vegetables. Happily, there were no turnips. All the dishes were highly decorated to make them more appealing. There was also another new food from the Americas that was called a "potato." I was impressed that the dinners Alexander had been bringing me were as fine as this one.

Finally, the inevitability of being asked a question came from Lord Howard. "How is James Burbage getting along? Does he have any plays that are going to be decent? You said you have been making copies, so you must have an opinion of what is quality and what is not."

"Yes, My Lord, I believe he does have some quality ones coming up. He has a new poet that writes very well. He is not university educated, but his writing I thought was as good as Sir Christopher Marlow's."

"That's quite a compliment for a new poet. What is his name, and have you met Marlow?" Lord Howard replied.

"The new poet's name is William Shakespeare, and no, I have not met Sir Marlow yet, but we did do one of his plays."

"Are you university educated?" the archbishop casually asked.

"No, My Lord, but I think I have been luckier than that. I was raised in a fine private library with books on so many subjects. The priest that raised me skipped teaching ancient languages like Latin when I could simply read their English translations. He thought I could learn so much more that way and I devoured every book I could once I learned to read."

This put a very perplexed gaze on the archbishop's face and a bit of a look of amusement on the rest. "Is it true you have read our English Bible?" he inquired.

"Yes, My Lord, Father McNee, the priest that raised me, started teaching me to read by using the Tyndale Bible when I was about five. He started with a passage from Mathew about the innocent belief of children."

"Isn't it heresy for a Catholic to touch, let alone read from this Bible?" he asked incredulously.

"Aye, but I haven't been burned at the stake yet, My Lord," I said with a whimsical grin.

They all laughed, and her Majesty added, "I told you he sees things in the oddest ways. But I might not be here if his priest hadn't taught him the way he did."

"You seem to have a remarkable start on an education," Lord Howard began. "What do you want to do with your life when you grow up? You could make a very good page."

"Well, My Lord, I am grateful for your kindness. A page is indeed well sought-after work. But I would much rather be a book. Her Majesty has been most kind to give me the nickname of Alley Cat and indeed I like to roam. I don't think I could be trapped on a single page and never know what's on the next. I am good at reading and writing. I am also very good at math and ciphering, and I can read a map. I would seek work that would use these talents. Secretary of State would be very grand!" I said with enthusiasm and a whimsical grin.

They all broke into laughter with astonished expressions including her Majesty. They knew, or hoped I wasn't serious. I continued. "For now I do enjoy the Theatre where I might someday write my own words or even be one of the players. I have had brief moments on stage already." I then became a little more serious and went on. "But we have to get through this year first and I fear the math of the coming Spanish invasion. I tend to see things from the mathematical outcome of events, and I fear if we don't stop the Spanish on the sea, well, I probably will be burned at the stake along with the playhouses. The math is not in our favor if they land and hold a port."

Their expressions turned far more serious and I added before any could speak. "I'm sorry if I have spoken out of turn, My Lords and Your Majesty, for I've not told you anything you don't already know. My intent is more to be of use in preventing their landing, before worrying about what work I would pursue during peace. I don't know what I can do, but I stand ready to take a rowboat out and throw rocks at them if need be."

Lord Howard then spoke, "I don't think that will be necessary. And just how does this math of yours work, Master Presto?"

"Well, if I may, My Lord." I gulped, realizing what I had just marched into. "The math is in the blood and gold. If Spain has an army of say 30,000 men, and I, of course, do not have any real numbers to use, other than we will need much larger armies to stop them. We don't know where they are going to land since we have thousands of miles of coast. We do know they will need to lay siege to London, so we almost have to have an army to match their strength here. Then we will need additional armies strategically placed throughout the kingdom. An army that can destroy their landing before it is secure. Where do we place these armies? How large will they be and how quickly can they be trained, supplied and placed? That is the blood math and it is of limited supply."

I continued, as no one had interrupted. "Then there is the gold math. Where are the funds going to come from? Again we have a disadvantage to Spain. They are harvesting wealth from the Americas and likely will receive funds from the Vatican. We are likely to run out of gold before they do, especially if they can successfully land."

I went on, "Spain will also try to get my Catholic brethren to rebel so as to replace their Spanish blood with English blood to do their fighting. If they do land successfully, there is a greater chance that could occur. That's why the math says they have to be stopped at sea. Our ships don't have to have armies on them, just cannon and gunpowder. The cost of fitted ships is far more efficient than fitting land armies. This is the way I see the math. Forgive me if I have expressed my fears. I'm sure, however, I have not spoke of anything different from the weight that rests upon all your shoulders."

Her Majesty now spoke, "How can a mere lad understand and summarize what we've been arguing about for months. Is our plight so obvious? Presto, do those on the street fear the same?

"Your Majesty, I have not been in a position to talk politics on the streets, but I do know the people are afraid of London being under siege. My fear is that Spain sees the same math," I replied nervously fearing that what I had spoken was way out of line. But no sense stopping now as the next question was asked.

"I don't understand," the archbishop began, "why a Catholic would be against Spain?"

"Archbishop," as I started my reply, "I have many reasons why I do not support the Spanish, but I will answer the Catholic part first. The only way to save the Catholic Church is for Her Majesty to defeat Spain."

All of their faces stared in disbelief at my words and Walsingham almost struggled to say, "That's not exactly our intent!"

"My Lords, it may not be your intent, but it will be the effect. As long as Spain's monarchy and the Spanish cardinals control the influence over the papacy, the Catholic Church will never get back to its own Counter Reformation. The Spanish Inquisition is a blight upon *my* religion and I just pray that the Protestants do not follow suit with their own. We must defeat Spain so the cardinals from other lands and city states can try to get the church back to serving our Lord and not making orphans with war." My words even surprised me, and I was shaking with emotion.

They all remained speechless until her Majesty spoke, "Well Presto, I had not considered that perspective before, too bad more Catholics could not be convinced to feel the same. I expected you would have interesting things to say, and you have far exceeded my expectations." Then she smiled and added, "And we have a way to go until the sweet cocoa cake."

They all let out a little chuckle and I was relieved that I had not offended. Walsingham looked at me and directed another question to me. "You said you had other reasons why you oppose Spain; you've gone this far, so you might as well go the rest."

"Well, My Lord, everything I have read about war ends up with the men, women and children from all over the land suffering the most, even long after the armies have finished their battles. And then there are the orphans. They have no one and no place. They are abandoned; they might as well seek refuge in a graveyard, as that is where they will likely end. If we have a land war, well, there will be nothing but orphans."

Sir Francis Drake then asserted, "There will be no land war. I will stop them at sea."

"Many thanks, Sir Drake, I pray you do. Otherwise, I fear the Spaniards will probably burn me at the stake. Granted, mine would probably only be a twig compared to the grander stakes that would await so many others."

"Why would they burn you at the stake?" the archbishop asked.

"Oh, well, I think there are a few things they just might consider heresy. Let me ponder, My Lord. There's the bit about supporting Her Majesty against the papal bull's edict. Then there's reading the English Tyndale Bible; they did burn him at the stake, after all. And then, since I cannot receive Holy Communion at a Catholic Church, I have done the next best thing by thankfully receiving the Eucharist in an Anglican Church."

"The next best thing!" Archbishop Whitgift exclaimed incredulously as Walsingham cupped the palm of his hand to his forehead. "The next best thing!" the archbishop repeated. "Your Catholic priests would have us believe they are performing a miracle changing bread and wine into our Savior. This cannot be.

It is still bread and wine we have blessed to honor and remember his sacrifice for us. Your Catholic way is not superior because of a belief in a false miracle!"

"I apologize, for that is not the point I'm trying to make. I was hoping that the English Anglican view would be that the Catholic Communion would be their 'next best thing.' Remember your Protestant brothers that follow Luther; they believe as do the Catholics. But my point is that it's not what it is if I may explain."

Her Majesty looked at me with a serious look, "Go on, as this has been a point of major argument and has often led to violence."

"Gramercy, Your Majesty. When I was a child, and yes, I know I still am one, Father McNee and the Vicar Woolsey discussed what I was to do if I was unable to receive the Holy Eucharist in a Catholic Church. We ultimately reasoned the following. We saw that there were three roles that made up this honoring of our Savior with Communion. One is the role of the church, whether priest or vicar. They do the preparations. Then there is the role of the congregation, or more specifically, the individual. He, or she, must make reparation. They, we, have to prepare our hearts and soul first by reflecting on our sins and seeking forgiveness. And no, that forgiveness is not based on any amount of coins offered for the remission of sins through indulgences. Even the Catholic Church changed that with the Counter Reformation some twenty years ago. We actually have to realize our failings and want, not expect, forgiveness. And then there is the part of our Lord. If we are true, He will still be true and want us as part of his family. I would then ask a question about these three roles."

"Continue," her Majesty said slowly with a thoughtful look.

"First, which is the most important role? The role of our Lord, the role of the people, or the role of the church? I think we will all agree on that answer."

"The Lord, obviously," the archbishop replied.

"Then of the remaining two, the role of the church or the role of the people, which is the *least* important?"

"Well, we know how your Pope would answer that question," the archbishop retorted.

"Yes, no doubt. But I am asking what the Anglican's answer is, or better yet, may I rephrase the question. This is ultimately the question of the Reformation and probably the century. Does the church serve the people or do the people serve the church?"

The Queen's face softened to me and she looked almost triumphantly at the archbishop and asked, "Yes, Archbishop, which way is it? Does our church serve the people, or do the people serve the church?"

"Well Your Majesty," he nervously began, "You are the head of the church and your subjects serve you."

As he briefly paused, I interjected, "True, Her Majesty's subjects are to serve her, but there is no one in the kingdom that serves her people more than the Queen herself. She leads and guides us. She protects us and has the ultimate responsibility to save us from Spain."

She looked at me with pride and then to her archbishop, "Best not play chess with this lad! Which way is it, who serves who?" Then she looked at me, "Since it was your question, do I even need to ask your answer, my Presto?"

"I think not, for you know my answer is that the church should serve its people. I do not receive Communion for the church. I do it to thank our Lord and seek forgiveness and his blessing. I accept Communion either way a priest or vicar offers it." With that, they all gave a conciliatory acknowledgement.

"But the church still has to guide its people, and your church's guidance has you worshipping idols and praying more to saints and our Savior's mother as a goddess, than to our Lord." Whitgift rebuked.

"Doesn't our Queen delegate authority to many others? Our Lord probably wouldn't mind a little help with all the millions of prayers he hears every day. I do pray to our Lord, but I see no reason not to pray to Saint Patrick or Saint Bridget for a little help to put in a good word for me. Saint Bridget is from my county of Kildare. She is the only woman I know that was ordained as a priest. Maybe your Anglican Church will have lady vicars too some day. As to prayers to Mother Mary, I consider them giving her a bouquet of flowers to thank her for being our Lord's mother. I don't think our Lord minds."

"But you still have to do everything through your priests who demand absolute obedience to the Pope. How can such a church serve rather than be served?" Whitgift questioned.

"By continuing its own Reformation, but that can only occur after there is peace and the Spanish cardinals no longer control the papacy. That is one reason I would take a rowboat out to sea to fight their Armada even if I have only the help of my guardian angel."

"And now you have a guardian angel to pray to. Who do think is your guardian angel?" the archbishop replied.

"I'm not sure. I suppose a guardian angel could take many forms. We Irish believe in a lot more mystical things than even my church would like. I don't know if she is in spirit form like a real angel, or if she takes on physical forms. I don't know that a guardian angel couldn't be your horse that guides you safely on your journeys, or a raven watching from above, or all the childhood kitties that have shown me many things. Who knows, mine might even be our pet chicken when I was growing up."

"Well, I'm sure you'll let us know when you figure it out," Whitgift sarcastically replied.

"No, I think not, My Lord. I think the only way you finally meet your guardian angel is after you die." With that I picked up the remains of what looked like a chicken leg from my plate and spoke directly to it with mirth, "So you were my guardian angel! I'm sorry I ate you, but you really weren't all that good of a guardian angel, were you?"

They all erupted in laughter. The Queen laughed so hard she almost choked. It took a while for her to stop and even the archbishop laughed as he shook his head. Finally Drake, who was laughing as hard as her Majesty, gave me a healthy slap on the back. I gasped in pain and gritted my teeth as he realized what he had done, and the rest went silent.

"Oh, I'm so sorry," Drake pleaded. Then I just burst out laughing again and the rest followed. I probably had tears in my eyes, but I think they were more from the laughter than the slap.

Finally, her Majesty said, "I think it's time we got this lad some of the cake with cocoa and wish him birthday hopes."

The sweets were served, and I again tasted the marvel of this new delight, chocolate. Archbishop Whitgift continued our conversation. "You are the strangest Catholic. You believe more as Her Majesty's church than your own, so I am baffled as to why you don't convert. You go against so many of your religion's rules I'm surprised you haven't been excommunicated."

"I will always be an Irish Catholic first out of love and respect for the priest that raised me. He taught me to follow the truth in my heart. I could never betray his memory. I also cannot be a part of my own church's true Reformation if I am not a member of her."

"But what if they excommunicate you?" he asked. "You won't be able to partake in any of their services or sacraments."

"Nothing. I will still be a true Catholic. If a visit to the Gatehouse didn't beat it out of me, you don't think a Spanish cardinal murmuring some words over a candle is going to change anything?" This time their stares were of total shock, as they had probably never heard an answer like that before. The Queen herself had been excommunicated, and for most it was something that would tear at their heart.

"Besides, it's not like I can exactly attend any of their services anyway. Maybe someday when there is peace," I added.

Interestingly, the conversation then slowly changed to concerns about the Protestant Puritans. They believed they followed the only true religion. They wanted a purer Protestant Church, void of all older Catholic traditions that the Anglican Church still used. All Catholics were certainly destined for hell, and their rituals should not be followed. Puritan theologians were also openly questioning the Book of Prayers and other changes that Queen Elizabeth had brought about. They further believed our Lord had already chosen the only ones who would ever enter heaven, and that they only belonged to *their* true religion. Whitgift saw this as a growing disobedience and threat to her Majesty's church.

Of course, the Catholics claimed all Protestants, along with all Jews, were predestined to go to hell too, but surprisingly, that wasn't brought up. Sadly, the Jews were condemned by everyone. I had little to say during these conversations other than agreeing with concerns over these divisions and my fear of Puritans. After the Saint Bartholomew Massacre, Walsingham himself believed as many of the Puritans did. However, he also had to protect the Queen from their fanaticism that was growing in strength fueled by hatred of Catholics, Spain, and the papacy. It was odd to hear the most powerful leaders in the kingdom having as many concerns about other Protestants as they did Catholics.

As it was, the concerns were justified. In the coming century, the Puritan Commander Oliver Cromwell would seize control of the Monarchy. He would lop off the head of King Charles I who was actually Mary Queen of Scots' grandson. The Puritan rule would surpass Spanish tyranny. Oliver Cromwell would slaughter a third of the Irish with his "Roundhead" or "Leather Neck's" army dressed in brown. They murdered Catholic and non-puritan Protestants alike. The Scots did not fare any better.

The Puritans would even ban celebrating Christmas after Cromwell seized control. A small group of them had done the same several decades before Cromwell's rule, when they first stepped off a tiny ship called the Mayflower. They had gone to start the "New England" of the Americas as a religious and business venture. Catholics dared not step foot in this New England for the coming century and a half. Not until a commander by the name of George Washington had to unify a Continental Army to overthrow English rule. Ironically, it was the New England Puritans that fueled this rebellion for freedom. Now Puritans, Protestants, Catholics and even Jews had to unite to bring about their independence. But I digress again, as I am only fourteen this day. I will have to survive this mortal life into my sixties and seventies to see the coming curse of Cromwell.

So back to the chocolate cake. The evening's conversations finally returned to horses, especially as Archbishop Whitgift sometimes loved traveling with a parade of hundreds of them. I also sensed Lord Howard would like to discuss matters of state privately, but the Queen did not seem to be in a hurry to excuse me. She did finally inquire if the healing of my wounds needed any attention. They all knew how I had received them, but Topcliffe's name was never brought up.

"They are healing amazingly well with all the care I have received," I replied. "I was wondering if I could take some of this wonderful cake with me for Master Alexander and the lad, Michael, as they have been so good to me, Your Majesty?"

"Of course you may and I think it quite thoughtful of you," she said as she smiled warmly.

I then continued, thinking it would be wise to gracefully offer a way to leave while I seemed to be in their favor. "I thank you for this grand dinner and allowing me to join you on my birthday. I hope I haven't spoken out of turn during the many conversations of this evening, an evening I will always remember and treasure. I know all that has been said is private. I suspect, however, there are matters of state that need to be discussed more privately."

"Yes, I suppose we have to get to the arguing part and you probably need to rest up to regain your strength. I look forward to seeing you again as you are quite a rascal, my Alley Cat," she beamed. With that, Alexander was summoned. I hoped he didn't have to sit in the hallway the whole time waiting. Before he entered, Sir Drake spoke.

"Presto, I'm staying at Whitehall part of this week and will be getting together with some friends in a couple nights before I return to Plymouth. I would be honored if you would join us. It would be an excellent time to talk. After all, I am supposed to see to your future. I know enough about you and that it will have to be of your own choosing."

"I would be proud to join you!" I said exuberantly. "I will be looking forward to it."

"Presto says we should be using the grand meeting room in the royal chambers I have him staying in. You should use it, but don't be getting the boy in trouble," her Majesty said with a grin.

Walsingham quickly commented, "No, I think it will be Sir Francis who will need to be on his toes. And don't break anything or you'll be answering to Alexander." They all laughed. I blushed with pride. I still thought this was just a dream and I would wake up at any moment. But I didn't, and I returned with Alexander and he seemed quite proud. He must have figured, since I had spent such a better part of the evening without being thrown out the window, that I must have behaved. Oh, if he only knew...

Part 5 – Reunions

The chocolate cake did follow us back to my quarters and Alexander and Michael did partake. This was the grandest birthday I had ever had. I told Alexander that Sir Drake had invited me to a get together in a couple days and he might be using the royal meeting rooms in my quarters. Needless to say, he had a bit of a befuddled look. I finally went to bed in the huge king's chamber that Alexander continued to prepare for me, despite my request to use one of the smaller more informal ones. Oh well, it was my birthday.

With the excitement of meeting the Queen passed, the new morning seemed empty. True, there was a party coming up with Drake, but just what was I supposed to do? The meeting room had a library attached and I had spent time going through its imposing collection. There were more Greek, Latin, French, Spanish, and so on books, than those in English. Still there were plenty of English ones including more recent essays from the writers of the day to keep me occupied. I still had no idea how long I was going to stay here and, in short, what would be next.

I found out early that afternoon when Alexander informed me Walsingham wanted to see me. Uh oh, was I in trouble? Her Majesty had been so kind to me, and I hoped I hadn't offended her by speaking so freely. At least I had twenty-five pounds to live on and hopefully would still have work at Burbage's Theatre when I left. I also hoped I had not disappointed Walsingham.

I was escorted to Walsingham's office and beckoned in. Much to my surprise and delight, there sat Captain Robert who rose with a grin on his face as I entered.

"I believe you two know each other, but I think I'll introduce you anyway," Walsingham said with a smile. "Captain Barrington, this is Master Presto."

"Captain Robert, I am so happy to see you and hoped we would meet again! You saved my life and I will always be indebted to you. I must also apologize for I was not truthful to you as to who I am. I am so ashamed I lied to you."

"Lord Walsingham has already told me all about your not being the Dumb Ass as you had introduced yourself. And it is I who must apologize to you for had you told me who you were, I would have likely sent you back. I am glad to see you too and wondered how you were doing. I must say I am impressed, and so very thankful for the service you rendered to Her Majesty. I knew you were a brave lad."

"Many thanks, but I wouldn't have been there to help if it were not for you. How are masters John and Craig?"

"They have finally escaped me and are in the Queen's army preparing to fight the Spanish. I so want to be on the field with them but was not able to escape my present duties."

Walsingham had interrogated Captain Robert about me earlier that day. Though Walsingham did no doubt trust me, it was still his job to verify my story. Robert was in London and he had been summoned. Their meeting was related to me later. An unexpected summons by Lord Walsingham was always a matter of concern. Captain Robert's response would have been the same "uh oh" as mine. I do not know how to spell "uh oh" as my keyboard scribe is clueless. The closest my scribe can come up with is "ahoy" which just doesn't have the same effect. Oh well.

When Robert arrived, he was beckoned to be seated in front of Walsingham's desk. Walsingham was finishing some correspondence and greeted him.

"Captain Barrington, I appreciate your coming on short notice. I will be with you in a moment. I have some questions for you, so please pardon me while I finish this dispatch. There is never enough time in the day to take care of all Her Majesty's duties."

"I will be happy to assist you in any way I can, Lord Walsingham," Robert had replied, not having any idea what questions he was about to be asked.

Walsingham finished his letter, sealed it and gave it to the attendant that had brought Robert in, dismissing him. "There, that's done. Captain Robert, I wanted to ask you about something from almost a year ago when you were returning from duties in West Wales. You were ensuring the honesty of the magistrates handling Her Majesty's taxes. You might recall there had been quite a storm coming up from the south."

"Yes, I believe I then went to Oxford before going down to Reading and then returned to London," Robert replied, now more weary than before.

"Yes, that was the journey. Anything interesting happen along the way?"

Robert thought nervously for a moment, trying to think of anything he or his men had done that was improper. He couldn't imagine their visit with Molly could be of any interest. "No, My Lord, it was just a typical trip as far as I can recall."

"Did you meet anyone interesting?"

Anxiously thinking of an answer, he responded, "There was a lost boy we picked up around Gloucester who joined us for a while, but otherwise, not really."

"A boy you say. Interesting. What was his name? Why would he join you?"

"Well, he was hopelessly lost and had already been robbed. He was trying to return to London, and I thought he didn't have a chance on his own. He had a funny name. It was Robert Dumas, and, well, his last name wasn't going to help him much in his travels. He was well educated and was probably the illegitimate son of someone of means."

"Was he now? Are you in the habit of picking up strays?"

"Well no, but he seemed an alright lad. Why do you ask, My Lord?"

"Do you know what land he was from or anything else about him, even religion?

"I assumed he was English as he said he was from London. He didn't sound like he went to church often, so I don't know if he was a good Anglican. We did go to the Cathedral in Oxford."

"When he was at the cathedral, how did he behave? Was he attentive, nervous, apprehensive, or?" Walsingham asked.

"No, he seemed perfectly content and in awe of the stained-glass. Why, My Lord? He didn't steal anything did he? He was with us the whole time." As he spoke, he remembered I had spent time on my own in Oxford before we all parted.

"Did he take Communion?" Walsingham continued.

"Well yes, we all did, My Lord," Robert answered, now more confused and nervous than ever.

Finally, Walsingham showed his hand like a game of cards. "Did you have any sense the boy you were bringing to London might be Irish and a Catholic? That he had recently escaped from being indentured?"

"Of course not, My Lord! I would have sent him back in an instant. I can't believe he could have deceived me. Please tell me I didn't bring him to London to commit crimes."

"I thought so. As to crimes, I now tell you this in the strictest confidence. There was an attempt on Her Majesty's life."

"No, My Lord!" Robert gasped. "He was such a decent lad. I would never have …"

But before he could finish, Walsingham finally let him off the hook. "Your lad bounded over the top of a balcony and knocked over an assassin with a pistol. He then killed the traitor with a knife. He saved Her Majesty's life."

Robert sat stunned and speechless.

"So you see, by saving this boy, you saved Her Majesty. Funny how Fate is, one little change in its path and, well…" Walsingham pondered while pausing.

"He killed the assassin and saved her?" Robert asked in disbelief.

"Yes, and you're about to meet him. By the way, his name is not Dumb Ass. His wit made it up. His name isn't Robert for that matter either. It is simply, Presto. Strangely appropriate."

Walsingham also gave him the details of my betrayal and being sold into slavery in Swansea. He told him of my "disagreement" with Topcliffe too. That was, for the most part, the conversation they had before I arrived. So getting back to our conversation after he mentioned wanting to join John and Craig in the coming fight.

"I too hope to do something to help stop the Spanish. I might even be joining Sir Francis Drake," I said.

"Let's not get too far ahead of ourselves, Presto," Walsingham replied. "The Queen has left strict instructions I am to see to your protection."

"Yes, but I was thinking, My Lord. I don't know if I will still have work at the Theatre. If there is something useful I can do with Sir Drake, I would be safe from the clutches of Topcliffe or any other fanatics. Let's face it if Drake doesn't return, well, I won't need protecting. I haven't spoken to Sir Drake yet, but we are supposedly saying that I am working with him. We've already set the stage, or maybe it's again Fate moving us all along." I spoke this with some degree of animation, while at the same time, remembering I didn't really fair all that well at sea. "I would at least like to see what he has to say tomorrow."

Captain Robert then interrupted, "It will be up to Her Majesty and Lord Walsingham as to your part and he has already made some plans."

"Yes, I have. I've assigned Captain Robert for your well-being and protection."

With a surprised look, I responded. "That is very kind of, well both of you. I enjoyed your company and you did save my life, Captain Robert. Even those shillings made all the difference in the world. I owe you everything and I don't want to put you in danger with Topcliffe if he tries to pull anything. He travels with his own guards and he's merciless. I'm more afraid of what he might do to my friends than what I know he'd do to me."

"I'm a soldier and believe me, I can take care of myself and you," Robert declared firmly.

"I don't think you need to worry about Sir Richard for now," Walsingham replied. "You are under the protection of the Queen. He knows it is treason if he tries to touch you."

"Yes, but I don't want to hurt your career either, watching over a stray boy," I said looking at Robert.

"Actually, it is quite a promotion," Walsingham said. "He is now part of Her Majesty's Personal Guard. Not every soldier is known by Her Majesty and it is quite an honor."

"And I am finally free of those bloody taxes. I might still be able to fight the Spaniards," Robert said cheerfully.

"Well, I hope you can swim," I smirked. "Can we at least see if Sir Drake has any use of me, My Lord?"

"I suppose, it seems your Mistress Fate is always up to something with you. In the meantime while I decide, I believe you wanted to visit the Burbages. If the Queen's physician says you're fit to travel, Captain Robert will take you there in a couple days. In the meantime, Robert will join you here at Whitehall starting tomorrow. I'm sure you'll have some catching up to do. Robert, you might as well meet Drake too."

"Many thanks, My Lord, and many thanks, Captain Robert. I'll try to behave," I said with a smile.

"You won't," is all Walsingham answered.

With that our meeting was pretty much over and we soon departed. I gave Captain Robert an awkward hug and looked forward to seeing him the next day. Alexander escorted me back to my rooms, and already knew he would have the Captain to look after too. I finally put my foot down and said I was too uncomfortable to sleep in the king's room and wanted the one next to the library. I wanted to grab that one before Captain Robert had his assigned, as there were several bedchambers for guests in these royal quarters. Alexander threatened to put me in the one for a queen, but fortunately was joking.

That evening I found I was to have another guest. Drake felt quite pleased to be able to use the royal hall for his guests and had to make arrangements with Alexander. He also thought we could dine late and talk casually. This was ending up being another spectacular day! I was nervous though as to what plans he might have for me. I knew nothing about the sea other than what I had read about from the adventures of others. I knew of these stories because Father McNee kept up with the news of the day. Granted, it might take several months to hear of it. Some of those stories I had read about were of Drake's adventures soon after I had read of the exploits of King Arthur.

Sir Francis Drake had been knighted by her Majesty in 1581 after he was the first Englishman to circumvent the globe with his handful of ships. He captured Spanish ships and their treasures along the way. He had transversed the Straits of Magellan and raided Spanish ports, even along the America's California coast. He returned around the African Cape of Good Hope with his ship, the Golden Hind. That ship was now on display on the Thames at Greenwich. I looked forward to seeing her some day.

But what use could I be with such an adventurer that was soon to be the Vice Admiral? He and Lord Howard had to stop the Armada that was making preparations even as I sat soaking my ribs in the very tub the king we were fighting had used decades ago. I now wanted to be part of the action but knew I would be back to trying to be a cabin boy. Granted, some of the more famous captains and adventurers that would be part of the defense against King Phillip had started as cabin boys, including Drake. But what could I learn to be of any use in what might be only a couple months?

I had gotten sick on my first seafaring adventure almost as soon as I stepped on board. Between the stench of the ship and the constant rocking, I never stopped heaving my guts out. Fortunately, my constitution was a lot stronger now. I had, after all, spent several months eating garbage off the streets to survive. I had also gotten used to the constant stench of the city. Now if I could just get used to the swaying and rocking back and forth, up and down and ... urp. I had one other wee problem too. I could barely swim. I was more afraid of being an embarrassment to myself, and Sir Drake, than that of going into battle.

Alexander was, by no surprise, a good diplomat. He suggested that I might show Drake around these royal suites first and then he would join to work out the details of the party he would be arranging for Drake's guests. He had made similar arrangements with him in the past. There would be food, lots of drink, cards, gambling and, hopefully, not too many things broken from when a bunch of sailors get together. Poor Alexander, now I understood why they kept this hall locked up.

Drake arrived and was happy to see me. He almost gave me another slap on the back until he remembered just in time not to. I was proud as a peacock just to have met him, let alone possibly join him in the adventure that would determine history. I gave him the tour and he and Alexander went about the business of making the arrangements. I assumed that Drake, and any other guests at Whitehall, probably paid their own way, including dinner parties. I was glad her Majesty was footing my bill as I doubted my fortune of twenty-five pounds might not cover a day.

We then had dinner and Sir Drake said he wanted to take me with him on an inspection tour of the fleet just to get my feet wet. He grinned when he used the expression "Get your feet wet."

"I would be proud to join you and hope I can learn to be of some service, Sir Drake," I said, beaming.

"You can use Francis. As to use, oh, I don't know ... Have you ever fired a cannon?" he replied.

"Uh, can't say that I have."

"Well you're never too old to learn. What experience have you had at sea? I hear you were supposed to begin as a cabin boy before you were betrayed," he asked. Walsingham had apparently told him some of the events that ultimately brought me to London.

"I must confess that I mostly puked my guts out on the trip over here. How long does it take to get one's sea legs?"

"I wouldn't worry. Everyone goes through it, and everyone gets over it. Just don't puke into the wind."

"I also have a bit of a problem swimming. I'm not that strong at it."

"I wouldn't worry much about swimming either. You'd be surprised how many seamen, especially transcripts, can't swim. Besides, no matter how good of a swimmer you are, if the ship goes down, you're going to drown anyway."

Well that certainly sounds encouraging, I thought. "I was thinking though, and this might seem a bit odd. I thought that if I could make a tight-fitting shirt with pockets or bands of sawdust sewn in, that I might be able to stay afloat. The bands would go around me above my waist and over my shoulders. The sawdust might hold me upright. That way I could at least be of use to even help someone else, rather than having to be saved. Have you ever heard of such an idea?" I asked.

He looked at me perplexed. "Some have tried different ideas to keep a seaman afloat, but they haven't been successful. A seaman is always too heavy, especially if he is wearing gear. That's the advantage we have when we sink the Spanish transports, their soldiers will all drown like rats. But you're smaller and lighter. It might just work on you. Try it. We can test it by throwing you overboard. If you don't bob back up to the top, we'll know it didn't work.

"Many thanks, I think. Maybe I can talk Alexander into having something made up. Her Gracious Majesty keeps having these fine clothes made up for me, which I have no idea what I'm going to do with them. Maybe he can have it done. I also have one other concern. I don't want to be an embarrassment to you when you bring me on board with your crew. I'm a bit afraid of heights and I can be a bit clumsy. I'm not as afraid to climb up to the crow's nest, but I'm not sure I could do the rigging on the sails."

Drake started laughing, "Let me get this straight. The boy who lived in a cemetery, dove over a balcony to save the Queen and stood up to Topcliffe, no less, is afraid of getting killed from heights?"

"I'm not afraid of getting killed. I'm getting rather used to that. No, I'm simply afraid of falling. It would be rather embarrassing."

Drake continued to laugh, "Don't worry, I'll keep you off the rigging, but I know you'll love being up in the crow's nest, I can tell. Any other concerns?"

"Well, I've heard the captain always goes down with the ship, and I think that quite brave. Not that I would expect that to ever happen to your ship, but I have noticed there is only one small boat on deck that can't possibly holds the entire crew. I was told the cabin boy is always one chosen to go on it for luck. Is that true?" I asked, somewhat awkwardly.

"Of course, the cabin boy always goes. The surviving crew brings him along for a snack in case they are out to sea too long," Drake answered trying to hold a straight face.

My eyes opened wide and then we both started to laugh. He had managed to eliminate all my fears by simply replacing them with far worse ones. With that, we talked through the evening and he told me of many of his adventures. He also told me I would have to learn to play cards, provided it wasn't against my religion, remembering I was Catholic. I told him the priest who raised me had a set, and the vicar and I all played from time to time. The cards Drake played, of course, were for gambling. I told him I only had the twenty-five pounds he had sent me and couldn't afford to gamble. He said some day I would have more, especially if we raided a fat Spanish ship.

So another magnificent day had passed, and Drake's party would be the next. Captain Robert joined me the following morning and I showed him around after Alexander settled him in to his room. He would be joining me at Drake's party. I told him of my adventures, and he was shocked when I told him I had stayed in a cemetery. I told him of the horrors of the enslavement in Swansea, and that I wanted to go there and free the other lads. I told him I felt guilty living in all this luxury, while they suffered, and I didn't even know if any had survived. He told me of his many adventures, and of the battles he had fought in during the rebellions in the North.

Alexander had additional help along with Michael to serve Drake's guests. It was a small and interesting gathering. There were two other captains, one of them was John Hawkins. Hawkins had many accomplishments to his credit that rivaled even Sir Drake. He had foiled the Spanish and Vatican's Ridolfi plot to assassinate her Majesty by being a double agent. He had built his own and England's navy to be of the strongest in the world. He had also redesigned ships that were now the fastest and most maneuverable on the sea. Oh, and did I mention he and Drake sailed many an adventure? History has largely forgotten Hawkins, but let me say this, the better-known Sir Walter Raleigh, couldn't fill a piss pot compared to him.

There was a full assortment of other seamen from officers to gunners to those that had been through it all. These were the real men, low and high that I had read about who had now come to life before my eyes. Captain Robert fell right in with them all, even though he was a landlubber. I was glad he had a good time, as I owed him so much.

There were two other especially interesting guests. The first was Robert Devereux, 2nd Earl of Essex. Barely in his twenties, he had already fought admirably in the conflicts in the Netherlands. He had gained the favor of the Queen in her Majesty's court through his wit and charm. I guess I was doing the same. He was already a Knight of the Garter and the Queen's Master of the Horse. The Earl was overly ambitious. Whereas I hated war, most nobles relished it. War was how they made their name, favor and fortune. The Earl wanted to join Drake in the coming historic battle and was rapidly befriending him.

The final noteworthy guest was Sir Francis Bacon, who was a friend of the Earl, and basically becoming his lawyer. Now in his late twenties, he too was trying to gain the favor of the Queen. His livelihood was being a barrister and he was a Member of Parliament. His main interests were philosophy and science. He had started his education at the age of twelve at Cambridge Trinity College under the supervision of Dr. John Whitgift, who would become the Archbishop of Canterbury. Yes, the very same I had just dined with two nights previous. Bacon would become known as the "Father of Empiricism Theory," or the use of empirical evidence. He believed science and philosophy should be based on what can be observed with by the senses and scientific experiment. This was a contrast to the Greek theories of Aristotle and Plato whom he dearly loved. Their theories, however, involved more tradition and myth, as to explaining the mysteries of life and the universe.

The funny thing was that I knew him, for we had already met. In fact, he had for all empirical reasons, saved my life. Though it was obvious he hadn't recognized me yet, I recognized him. Granted, it was a few months ago and I had grown a bit. My face had lost its adolescent look and I had more chiseled features. My hair was also much shorter and, of course, I was now dressed as a peacock. We had met when I had done a bit of acting for him. I was playing a dirty street urchin thief, and he was going to punish me after I cleaned myself up in the bath. He had tipped me the shilling that I bought a life-saving coat and blanket with.

Most had heard of what they considered my heroic acts including standing up to Topcliffe. So much for Walsingham's trying to keep it all hushed up. To be considered heroic by these men was more than an honor. Granted, the next time they will be seeing me, I'll probably be puking my guts out over their ship's rail. The Earl had heard of me from the Queen herself and introduced me as clever and highly educated to Sir Bacon.

"Oh, you are university educated then?" Bacon inquired. "I started when I was a little younger than you are now. Which school and who is your tutor?"

It seems I had been asked that just the other day. "No, Sir Bacon, I was taught how to read by the priest that raised me. He had one of the finest libraries in all of Ireland. His books taught me math, science, even philosophy. I have even read some of Aristotle's theories, which I understand you have an interest in." Bacon had mentioned Aristotle during our acting bit, though I don't remember why. He seemed to be very into Greek things. He was already beginning to be known for his own theories, and I had heard of him before.

He stared at me blankly, not because he recognized me, but because you just had to be university educated to even speak of such things. "Oh, you've learned Greek and Latin already? How else could you read Aristotle?"

"Oh no," I answered with a bit of a smirk. "My priest thought it was a waste of time for me to learn ancient languages. He said there are so many fine university gentlemen that spend years learning them, and then translate it all to English. That has saved years in my education. In fact, I learned to read from an English Bible."

The Earl turned away to hide his amused expression as Bacon looked dumbfounded. I went on, "I would love to see the libraries at universities like Cambridge some-day though. This library is also phenomenal. There are many foreign books here which I'm sure you would enjoy touring," I continued as I pointed toward the open hallway that led to the library.

"Her Majesty has been letting me stay here, and I've enjoyed getting caught up on my reading. Sometimes I even sneak a book in to read when I take a bath." I paused, to let the word "bath" sink in. "Did you know King Phillip of Spain stayed here? I wonder if he sneaked any books in to read when he bathed in the same tub."

With that last bit, Bacon's face exploded with recognition. He was speechless. "Cat got your tongue?" the Earl inquired after the lack of a response. "It's unusual for you to not have a witty return. Maybe this lad can teach you," he mused turning to me. "Presto, do you play chess?"

"Yes, My Lord, but not very recently and I'm really only fair at it. They have a magnificent set in the library if you'd like to see it."

We wandered into the library while Bacon remained nervously speechless. We looked at the craftsmanship of the chess pieces that were inlaid with gold and silver, and gems for the eyes of even the pawns. Bacon regained his composure and we talked about some of the books. After a short bit, Drake walked in and declared, "Now don't make a book worm out of the lad, I have to make a mariner of him. It's time we eat and drink and see who can tell the most lies about their adventures."

He turned and left with the Earl following. Bacon laid back and asked me where the Aristotle books were. I took him to the Greek and Latin books, where I remembered seeing Aristotle's name.

He then grabbed my shoulder and pointed his finger in my face. "I don't know what your game is, boy, but one word of our previous meeting and I'll destroy you and have you back on the street so fast your head will spin!"

I grabbed his finger and bent it away from my face as I replied, "I was going to tell you the same thing, except without the drama and the threat. Besides, I found our bit of acting as intriguing as you did." I let go of his finger with a grin and he softened his hold.

"Well, I just wanted to make sure you understood," as he lowered his hand. "How on earth did you end up here?" He had not apparently heard of my adventures yet.

"Well, a bit of Fate, I suppose," I replied. "Sometimes she has a sense of humor, sometimes she likes to play rough, kind of like you. Sometimes she's kind. That shilling you gave me for instance, it probably saved my life. I owe you thanks for what was probably insignificant to you. But with it, I bought a heavy coat and blanket that I might not have survived without, until I found some work at Burbage's Theatre. I work as a scribe copying and sometimes fixing lines in the plays he puts on."

"But how did you end up here?" he again asked still baffled.

There were some loud laughs echoing out of the hallway and I said, "We best be joining the party, so you'll just have to wait for my turn to embellish my tales of adventure."

"You're a strange lad," he said as we returned.

"I'm the strange one?" I answered incredulously. But then, I suppose sleeping in a crypt would qualify.

We had an excellent dinner and the stories of adventures were better than any books I had ever read. They even told *my* story. There were card games and gambling that went on all night, and some of us finally fell asleep in the various soft armchairs. Alexander finally rounded each of us up and found sleeping quarters for all, using this royal suite and Drake's down the main hall. I don't even remember being put to bed. The morning came and my head hurt as I had been challenged to drink a bit during the night. The rest looked about the same as I felt, as Alexander served breakfast. He looked exhausted too.

Everyone slowly parted and I thanked Drake for inviting me. He said he would send word when it was time for Captain Robert to deliver me to Plymouth. Captain Hawkins seemed to like me too. The Earl indicated he would no doubt see me in Court. Lastly,

Bacon said we should get together sometime and he'd show me his library and maybe play chess.

It was a rainy morning, so Captain Robert decided we would wait a day before venturing out on the streets of London to visit the Theatre and the Burbages. This was all subject to Walsingham's approval. I didn't even know if Walsingham was going to let me join Sir Drake for sure. I was so looking forward to getting out and I hoped I might even find Jack and help him with at least a shilling or two. I didn't know if he was on his own now or working with someone else since Wilson seemed to have vanished. I spent the rest of the day reading, and we played cards that night with Alexander and Michael.

The next day was gorgeous, so I was finally going to get back out into the city. We walked down to the Thames and around the long way, so I could see Westminster Abby. Someday I would like to see it from the inside. We also went by the Westminster Palace where Parliament met, and even past the Gatehouse. I wondered if Topcliffe was there. We took a water taxi down the Thames to a landing by London Bridge. Ah, that wonderful stench of the city. Westminster could get a little ripe too, but it was generally upwind of the rest of the city. From the bridge, we walked up through town toward the Theatre. No one really paid us any mind. I was dressed well but had put on the plainer set of clothes I had been given. We were just another couple of faces in the morning din of people going to work and attending to their business.

I could feel my heartbeat as we arrived at the Burbage's. I didn't know if I would still be welcome if they knew I was Catholic, not that I had actually outright deceived them. They didn't seem to be overly political. I just hoped they would be as happy to see me just as I was happy to see them. I had not gone into many details in my letter, as to why I was in service to her Majesty.

Having a Captain of the Queen's Guard knocking on your door would be an initial cause for concern. Ellen Burbage opened the door cautiously, and then immediately hugged me. "I was so worried about you. Are you all right? Let me get James," as she ushered us inside and I introduced Captain Barrington to her, and then James as he came down.

"You're looking fit and must be doing rather well, judging from your clothes. What on earth are you doing for the Queen? She must be paying you well too," James Burbage said.

Captain Robert then delivered an explanation. "What I am about to tell you is confidential and will not leave this room." Both the James and Ellen acknowledged his instruction with questioning concern.

"Earlier this month an attempt was made on Her Majesty's life by a fanatical Catholic, possibly an agent of Spain."

"Those filthy-Catholic vermin!" Ellen exclaimed.

James quickly added, "They hide in our midst waiting to strike. We should round them all up and get rid of them once and for all!"

Captain Robert held up his hand and said, "Presto saved her life at his own peril and killed the assassin." They both stared at me dumbfounded.

Robert went on. "Presto *is* a Catholic."

Ellen gasped and looked at me with shame, "Oh Presto, I didn't mean … I'm, I'm so sorry, you know I didn't …" as she drifted off unable to complete her sentence while James just looked away embarrassed.

"Oh, I've been called far worse. Now, now, remember you saved my life just like Captain Robert here. He was the one who brought me from Gloucester," I said, nodding to him as I tried to soothe Ellen who was almost in tears. "That's why I don't go out of my way to mention my faith. I'm sorry if I deceived you. Besides, the priest that raised me taught me how we are all the same, not our differences."

"And there is more," Robert continued. "Because he announced he is Catholic, Presto was sent to Gatehouse for questioning by Richard Topcliffe. He was tortured by him and is still recovering. Her Majesty is livid with Topcliffe. She has assigned me to protect Presto from any vengeance he might plot, or any fanatical Catholics that might also wish to harm him. I am also to ensure the safety of any of his friends."

This was a lot more information than the Burbages were expecting on this bright beautiful day. It took a while to marinate or sink in. It was also strange for me to hear, almost forgetting that he was talking about me. "I have missed both of you and working for you, and hope I am still welcome. I don't want to jeopardize anyone though."

"Presto, you'll always be welcome here. We've missed you and were scared something bad had happened to you. Our kitty has been wondering around lost without you," Ellen Burbage replied.

"And I've needed your quill. You don't know how difficult its been trying to get it all done without you. I didn't realize what a difference you really made. And that cat won't let me alone either. So I hope you can come back," James added.

And almost on cue, Hope started banging and meowing at the door. Robert turned and opened it, and I instantly had a cat all over me. Ellen made hot cider and brought out some biscuits, and we had a nice reunion. I told them I had no idea when I would be able to return, and that Sir Francis Drake himself might be taking me to sea. I found out Shakespeare was working on another play and I was hoping I could work on it too. In the meantime, they had a rehearsal of a comedy at noon and the players were already assembling with their son, Richard. They were happy to see me too, and we stayed a bit to watch them get set up.

I knew our visit had put James behind in his frantic schedule to put a play on that evening. We left and were invited to return later to watch it. James indicated not to expect much though, as this was not what he would consider the finest. We went back to London Bridge to cross it so I could see Southwark again. This was the first time I had come across since running away after stabbing Topcliffe. I had been afraid that I might be recognized as Robert Dumas. But now, I didn't need to hide. I could dance naked in front of Topcliffe, and he couldn't touch me. I suppose that is a bit of a bad choice of words, but you may have noticed I do like a twist of irony.

We walked by Wilson's building and there was a new business in it. I watched for Jack but didn't see him. There was also a nice inn on this side that served excellent food. I knew this because I had picked some mighty fine meals out of their garbage. You had to move fast to get it, as I wasn't the only alley cat scrounging. I thought it would be nice to have a real meal from the inside. This time I could have the honor of buying Captain Robert dinner, as I told him his money was no good. We had a great meal. He ordered roast beef, I trout. We then returned to watch the play at the Theatre. Burbage was right. It did kind of suck, but it was fun to be part of the audience.

We returned late by water taxi to Whitehall. I had not seen the Thames lit up all along the way by the evening's activities. I had usually been hiding at night either in a cemetery or finding some other place to take cover. Alexander had to stay up to make sure we didn't need anything. I thanked him and Michael and we all had a little nightcap. Alexander had gotten used to my lack of formality and think he did really enjoy having me as the guest in his charge.

Chapter 6 – Prelude

Part 1 – Winds of War

March has been another life changing month. In fact, the last years' worth of months have all been life changing. In several days it would officially be 1588, as the calendar year didn't change until March 25th. It is also already April in Spain. You'll remember they are ten days ahead because of using a different calendar. Your modern world gets confused trying to figure out what time it is in a city in another time zone. We only had to figure out what the date and the year were. Also every city was probably off fifteen minutes or more from each other if they couldn't hear each other's church bells. The coming month was no doubt going to be another month of Fate's changes. For one, I knew the day would soon be coming when I would depart these royal chambers, and I had no idea where I was going, or even be allowed to go.

These rooms were supposed to be kept for royalty, but now they were humorously referred to as the peasant's rooms. This was okay though because now they were needed to move the Queen's guests out of her main residence, the Palace of Placentia in Greenwich. Henry VIII, Bloody Queen Mary, and Queen Elizabeth were all born there. The problem was its indefensible position to the east of London. If the Spanish decided to go for the throat and land their armies to attack London, Greenwich would be their first prize.

The Thames empties into the North Sea just a bit above Dover, which is near the end of English Channel. As you start to head a bit up the Thames on the north side, you will come to Greenwich Palace and Drake's Golden Hind. This is just east of London. Up a short bit more would be The Tower of London and the beginning of the old walled city. Next is London Bridge. A bit more and then the river makes a bend south at Westminster which puts it on the west side of the river. Westminster has the Abbey and a cathedral, Westminster Palace where parliament meets, Whitehall Palace, and also my favorite vacation spot, the Gatehouse.

I had theorized her Majesty would need to keep a sizable army close to protect London. It didn't take an alchemist to figure that one out. However, we didn't know where the Armada was really going to land. This was in fact true of the previous year before Drake's Cadiz raid. King Phillip was planning a diversionary raid in Scotland to split the English forces before attacking London. Now the plan was simpler. He would use the Armada to pick up a force of 30,000 Spanish soldiers in the Netherlands under the command of the Duke of Parma. This army was being used to subdue a rebellion by the Dutch. It was comprised of a multinational force which even included 1,000 Irish soldiers. The Armada would pick them up from Duinkerke (Dunkirk) in the low country of the Netherlands.

The Armada would be carrying an additional 20,000 soldiers from Spain. These men were primarily for fighting at sea. The Spanish strategy for sea warfare was to use their cannons to cripple their enemy's ship, grapple it and send their soldiers aboard to capture it. They could also be used as an additional land force. The Armada would cross just north of the English Channel and likely land on the north side of the Thames River. They could also land on the south side or even do both. From there they would march west and crush London. It didn't take much spying by Walsingham to notice Parma's army. Elizabeth would be lucky to raise a force of 15,000 to stop them.

The English Channel, or "Narrow Sea" as it was called then, was the site of many a sea battle and invasion throughout history. It begins at the southern tip of England with Plymouth being the first major port. It follows the French coast to Calais across from Dover where it is a mere twenty-one miles across. Great for an afternoon swim. Here the Narrow Sea joins the North Sea just below the inlet to the Thames. And just across that bit is Duinkerke where Parma's army is assembling

The reason France and England were traditionally at war is because they were across from each other and parts of France were often under English rule. The Normandy portion of France was under the English crown because William the Conqueror had invaded England from there when his "Normans" conquered the "Saxons." The English considered it theirs, so they battled with the French back and forth for it, making for many a fine play for Shakespeare and others to write. Calais was English just before the beginning of Elizabeth's reign.

You might wonder then, what the Spanish would be doing with 30,000 soldiers in the Netherlands on the border of France. That would necessitate explaining why this bloody conflict was about to occur in the first place. You might remember Henry VIII's first marriage didn't work out. He had married Catherine of Aragon who happened to be the daughter of the King of Spain, Ferdinand II. Actually, his older brother, Arthur, had married her first, but he died at age fifteen just a year older than me. She claimed she was still a virgin, so there was no problem Henry was getting sloppy seconds, at least till later when he needed a reason to dump her. Henry and Catherine had one surviving child, Mary, who would become Bloody Queen Mary. Catherine was unable to produce a male heir to the throne.

The marriage was designed to check the power of France by having an English - Spanish alliance. France and Spain were not exactly buddy-buddy at the time. Henry VIII tried to get the Pope to let him divorce or annul the marriage to Catherine partially on the grounds that his older brother had gotten in her after all. The papacy was basically under control of the Spanish Monarchy, so they'd have no part of it. Henry then simply took over all the Catholic Churches in England, became the Church's head and granted himself a divorce. While he was at it, he might as well grab all the Church's land and wealth. Spain and the Pope were understandably, not impressed.

Fast-forward a bit and you might remember that after Henry died, eventually Catherine's daughter, Mary I, became the Bloody Queen and married Phillip II. All was a happy dance again with Spain and the Pope as England was again Catholic. Phillip was now actually King of England and then he also ascended to the throne in Spain. Then Bloody Mary died, and the imprisoned-illegitimate-Protestant-bastard Elizabeth became Queen. The papacy did not want to recognize this and eventually excommunicated her and put out a papal bull renouncing her claim to the throne.

Now it's time to stir in America. So once again we need to back up a bit. Christopher Columbus visited America in 1492. The Spanish King Ferdinand II and his Queen Isabella I, Catherine of Aragon's parents, had chartered him to find a new route to India. You may have also heard of Ferdinand and Isabella. They had something to do with starting the Spanish Inquisition that was initially brought against Jews and Muslims who had claimed to convert to Christianity. Anyway, Columbus found the America's continents were in the way, so he was a bit confused when he discovered them.

Well actually Columbus wasn't the first to discover them. Leif Erickson already had in the year 999. However there is one more contender, the Irish Saint Brendan, who went on a seven-year voyage around the year 520. This has always been claimed as just another fanciful Irish myth like Saint Patrick driving the snakes out of Ireland. By the way, why are the snakes missing? As to this Irish claim, there are some mysterious ancient Celtic relics in South Carolina and Georgia in the Americas of the North. There are also Spanish reports *written* in 1521 of red-haired Indians. There was a copy of this report at Whitehall. Hmm …

There is also chocolate. Cocoa traces have supposedly been found in ancient Egyptian tombs, which would mean the Egyptians visited the Americas of the South. Or maybe vice versa? So, as a ghost, I'll take the liberty of just leaving it at the Irish discovered the Americas of the North, and the Egyptians that of the South. In any event, Columbus had given Spain whole new continents to plunder and colonize while slaughtering and spreading smallpox to the natural inhabitants. The Indians, named after a land another ocean away, refused to become their slaves. So Columbus and the Spanish simply replaced them with the brutal slave trade they developed from West Africa. Spain had now been at this for almost a hundred years.

England was also discovering the New World and had tried a little colonizing of her own. There were also many "Privateer" companies formed with investors to outfit ships to explore this New World and plunder the Spanish owned American ports and their ships laden with, especially gold. Queen Elizabeth was one of these investors and of course the Crown's treasury got a healthy percentage.

We can finally get back to the Netherlands. The Netherlands were part of the Holy Roman Empire and its provinces came under the rule of, you guessed it, King Phillip II in 1555. The Netherlands was having their own spats between Protestants and Catholics. Phillip, of course, had to help a bit with the Spanish Inquisition against the Protestants and even Catholics who were against all his new taxes. This led to the Dutch Rebellion in 1568. This was the beginning of an eighty-year war in the Netherlands with Spain. England and France were opposing Spain at every juncture, so of course, they supported the Dutch in a proxy war. The rebellion ground on with each side winning and losing ground.

The Spanish laid siege to the Dutch rebel capital Antwerp and built a platoon bridge of ships across the inlet to cut it off from relief. The Dutch, with the aid of England, launched "fire ships" into it to stop the blockade but failed. Antwerp fell in August, 1585 to Parma. The same month England signed the Treaty of Nonsuch with the Dutch and sent a force of about 6,000 men to aid them. The then-teenage Earl of Essex I had just met, was one of them. This was the beginning of the undeclared war between England and Spain that had started three summers ago. Declared or not, it made no difference to the soldiers killed or wounded, the civilians slaughtered on either side, or the famine, disease and orphans that followed.

So Phillip went to work building an Armada to crush the English-Protestant-heretic-bastard Queen Elizabeth and replace her with Mary Queen of Scots. Mary Queen of Scots had been executed just over a year ago in February, just before my journey began many ink cartridges ago. Now it is time to find out where you acquire this ink and if you even still have quills.

Whew, glad the history and geography lessons are over. I didn't mention France in all this, as that will get more interesting in a bit. If you're going to get a feel of what it is like to be in London in 1588, you need to know what they knew and feared. And what I knew and feared for that matter. These things were known on the street. The English even put on pageants of Spanish soldiers marching through the streets raping the women and killing the children. I didn't know if I was going to be in this fight. A month ago I would want no part of it, but again, Fate seems to have other plans. Now I realized there are people I want to fight for, including the Burbages, who I didn't even know a half a year ago.

I kept busy in the coming weeks waiting for word from Drake. Captain Robert was sent out to find lodging for us in the old walled city on its north side. He would find a second-floor set of rooms in a safe area. This was also close enough to the Theatre should I return to work there. It was also equally close to Whitehall should my presence be wanted. I didn't know who was footing the bill, but it would be a lower expense than living in the royal chambers. It would be another week until we moved.

In the meantime, I had become of more intrigue to the other noble guests. I seemed to have free reign wondering about the immense palace now, even without Alexander in tow. Some were starting to greet me and be introduced by their servants. We would even have small talk. Word had spread about me, which I found very amusing. They knew I was in her Majesty's favor, so even though I was common, it didn't hurt to be friendly. I went with the innocent kitten look.

I found where the young Earl, Robert Devereux, the one I met at Drake's party, had his rooms when he sent an invitation for me to visit. We ate and had a good talk. He told me he occasionally visited her Majesty in her private chambers in the evening with other of her "after-hours favorites." He indicated I shouldn't be surprised if I was called for a late-night visit after all the official business and dinning was done. He indicated she enjoyed my company. "You'll see," he added.

He also introduced me to other nobles and guests. Most knew and respected him. They all knew he was in the Queen's favor and already Master of Horse. It never hurt for them to go out of their way to be on good terms with him. They all had long titles and names, so I think he found it amusing to introduce someone with a one-word name. Originally, he jokingly said I really needed to get a longer fancy name. He soon decided mine was far more fun just the way it was. There was one guest he introduced that is certainly worth remembering.

"Presto," he began, as he liked introducing me first. "I'd like to introduce you to someone you might have heard of. This is Sir Walter Raleigh."

I froze with fear and revulsion. Everyone in Ireland knew who he was. When the second Munster Rebellion began, the Vatican and Spain sent several hundred men and a stash of supplies to aid the Desmond rebels. They had surrendered after they were trapped and besieged at Smerwick by a far superior force soon after they landed. The Viceroy of Ireland ordered their execution. It was Captain Raleigh that carried out this massacre at D'un an 'Oir mostly by beheading.

He then received grants for large tracts of land in Munster to colonize. This "plantation" concept was to bring Protestant Welsh and English settlers to replace the Irish Catholic inhabitants who had mostly starved from famine. He never was successful and eventually gave up his holdings. He was in and out of favor with the Queen and ended up in the Tower of London more than once. Finally he was charged with treason against the new King James. Ironically, he was ultimately beheaded. I often wondered if the final vision that rolled around in his head as the ax fell to take it off, was that of the hundreds of heads that rolled on the fields of D'un an 'Oir.

"All in Ireland know your name, Captain Raleigh," I replied courteously with my strongest Irish brogue and a slight phony respectful bow.

"Ah, you must be the stray Irish orphan I've heard the Queen has taken in. You must be overwhelmed by Her Majesty's Court," Raleigh said with superior disdain.

"Oh not at all, not at all, it is quite nice. There are many a fine library here just like in my Ireland, so I've had time to catch up with me reading. Her Majesty has been most gracious too, along with so many others," I said quite proudly with a smirk.

"Where are you from in Ireland?" he asked, now somewhat puzzled.

"No clue, I was left on the doorsteps of me Irish church in Kildare when I was about one. The vicar gave me to the retired priest to raise. He had as fine a library as I've seen here, even in the royal chambers. Some of his books have even found their way into Lord William Cecil's private library, here in Whitehall. I assume you'll be off to sea again soon."

"That is a matter between me and Lord Howard," he answered indignantly.

"Yes, I just met Lord Howard when Her Majesty invited me for dinner. Great man, great man. I'm hoping to join Sir Drake soon myself along with Earl Robert here." The Earl was definitely relishing our exchange. The Queen did not allow the young Earl to go with Drake, however.

The effect was what I was going for, Raleigh stood stunned as I went back to my innocent kitten look.

"Well, it's been interesting meeting you …" Raleigh said with a pause.

"Presto, just Presto, Sir Raleigh. Then until our paths meet again," and I did another slight bow and we were on our way. The Earl of Essex had a bemused expression as we wandered on.

The young Earl was correct about Queen Elizabeth summoning me late one night to her chambers. This time it was not

Alexander escorting me but her page. I wanted to change, as I was dressed casually. "Come as you are," is all he said. As I was shown in through her privy chamber door, the page simply bowed, turned and left. Her Majesty was sitting at a small table with her back to me being attended by one of her personal ladies-in-waiting. I could see her red wig was removed and she was wearing very elegant bedclothes.

Nervously I said, "Your Majesty, I understand you wanted to see me. If this is a bad time, I can wait, Your Majesty."

"No Presto, come in, sit," as she pointed to a chair at the table across from her and she turned. "I wanted to see you."

With that I bowed and went to politely take a seat. I realized she was not wearing her white makeup. As I came closer in the candlelight and sat, I realized her face was covered with long faded scars from smallpox. I had seen this before and easily recognized it.

"Do you still think I'm the most lovely lady you've ever seen, my Alley Cat?" she asked with a straightforward look, watching what she would see in my face and eyes.

"Yes, Ma`Lady, more than ever," I said with truth in my eyes.

"Presto, I know you can be sweet and charming, but you said you would never lie to me," she said disappointed.

"Your Majesty, I do not lie now. When you are Queen you must be Queen. You must be like a Knight dressed in shining armor that commands the recognition and respect that makes you *The Queen*. I had never seen a Queen before, so I thought the magnificent white on your face was part of showing you are *the Queen*, and I still do. But you are also flesh and blood, and I am overwhelmed you have shared the beauty of the scars of your life, and the sacrifices you have made for all of us. I see the beauty of your strength in your eyes, and the honesty of your fears."

"You are quite kind, and I see now the words you speak are, as usual, from your heart. That is why I felt I could trust having you here without having to hide behind my mask. Gramercy, or many thanks as you Irish say."

I could see she had a tear in her eye, as did I. We spoke honestly through the night. She told me of some of her stories, including when she was my age. She had a far rougher time growing up than most. Her mother had been executed when she was an infant, so she never knew her. She had been imprisoned, and even feared being executed for treason by her stepsister, Bloody Queen Mary. By feeling her fears I was able to pull the mask off my own fears. It was okay to be afraid for yourself and not just others. She understood my fears and I even told her of how I was so afraid I had stayed in a graveyard. She understood enough that she wasn't horrified, but rather, we both had a good laugh.

I also told her of my imprisonment and of the lad, Robert's murder. She was mortified with revulsion. I told her I wanted to go with Sir Drake, but more important, I had vowed to free the lads in Swansea and asked if I could return there. She said she would see that justice would be served. We also talked about my future. She did want to keep me close and safe on the one hand, but she also knew no one could be kept safe now until the coming siege was over.

So as we talked, we agreed I could return to the streets of London and that in fact she might have little covert missions to do for her. She wanted me to be able to come freely to her like a good Alley Cat. Her personal ladies-in-waiting and page would know and have a place for me when I visited the palace. Nothing fanciful like the royal chambers, and that was just fine. She told me she expected me to behave as a gentleman with them. And most important, I could go with Drake if I wanted to. I was now beyond being a favorite. That was different. She wanted me to be one of her after-hours people, a confidant, even a friend. I was overwhelmed and still am to this day. I stayed with her ladies and the page that night and they treated me as one of their own. I was not the first stray orphan that had this honor either.

Captain Robert took me to our new residence he had rented. I had so many clothes now, we had to take a carriage. I was told the clothes were mine. I couldn't possibly use half of them, so I eventually gave one to the Theatre for a costume and sold or traded some for plainer clothes. Our rooms were like the ones I envied when I was alone on the streets a few months earlier. They even had a balcony that I didn't have to climb up from the ground to reach. There was even a writing desk where I could keep quill, ink and papers.

I went back to the Theatre and did some scribing on Shakespeare's next play. Writing is constant rewriting. Many a poet has said the first draft is shit. I would do a new copy for William eliminating all the scratch outs and corrections, and then redo that page again the next day with more changes. Now it's easy with your magic keyboard scribes to change words and sentences let alone print a copy. I had to rewritt this very parographe several time's. I'm amazed at what your times have done to the English language. Admittedly, it's been like trying to learn a foreign one for me. Your use of bloody comas is the worst. At least I don't feel too bad butchering it more while writing this. But most important, I will always capitalize "Queen" out of respect for her. And so, that's that, actually. Try punctuating that last sentence, Shakespeare couldn't.

I eventually ventured across the river to Southwark with Captain Robert. I was still watching for Jack. I still didn't see him, but we did go down to the tavern. The bartender was still there and happy to see me. He had been a little concerned that I just vanished one day, but that wasn't unusual if you were in the tavern business. I continued to buy Robert dinner whenever I could get away with it. He had been given an allowance for my expenses and we were both content to live modestly. I also stared over the graveyard but did not venture in to visit Sir Reynolds. Robert no doubt figured out this was my previous summer's home.

We did go to Westminster Abbey and I saw the tombs of Henry V and Henry VII. Henry the VI was missing. They had been lying dead for a very long time, I thought. It occurred to me that most people are dead a lot longer than they were alive. We took Communion and Robert understood why I would, even though I was Catholic.

"Someday I'll take you to a Catholic Church," I told him, and he knew I meant when we were at peace.

I did finally see Jack. He didn't recognize me in my peacock clothes. He was scared at the sight of the soldier with me. I had to coax him like a cat that knows you but is too scared to come out. He stared at me in disbelief when he recognized me.

He looked dreadful. He tried to whisper to me, "Topcliffe's been looking for you!"

"I know, I found him first," I replied. "I know you're hungry so I'm going to get you the best dinner ever. But first we're going to get you some better clothes that don't stink." Now he was really confused. But just like a cat you are about to feed, he followed us.

I introduced him to Captain Robert. "This is the lad, Jack, that taught me how to be a thief. Couldn't have made it without him."

"Pleased to meet you, and glad you did," Robert said, as Jack looked totally bewildered on my confessing it. "He's told me a great deal about you, including his telling of how he gave you pennies off the eyes of a plague's corpse." I had embellished that story a bit.

We did get him some clothes, shoes, a nice coat and fed him. I gave him a couple shillings and some loose pence. He said he had to work the streets by himself now that Wilson was gone. He said the new "proprietor" was always rough on him and didn't want him in his area. Captain Robert offered to take care of that problem if he wanted. I found out where I could find him in case there was some work for him. I also told him he could leave a message at the Theatre if he ever needed help.

He actually did go to the Theatre to see if he could get some work. It ended up being rather awkward. When Shakespeare first arrived in London, Jack had picked his pockets. William recognized him. Jack told James and Ellen Burbage he was my friend. They remembered me telling them about Jack. They remembered I too had picked pockets. They did give him work and he eventually started to learn to read and write. He got the nickname of "Presto's Friend."

Part 2 – The Cabin Boy

Word finally came that I was to meet Drake at Plymouth to join him on his ship "Revenge." I had word her Majesty wanted to see me before I left. She had told me she would send for me when she wanted a visit from her Alley Cat. She also indicated I could come on my own if I ever needed to see her. I was now to visit in the coming evening. Her page had told me where to come and whom to see at Whitehall to get in privately. I took a water taxi to the "Privy Bridge," which was a private landing at Whitehall for her Majesty and her guests.

Once again, she already had her "mask" removed. She wanted to wish me well and warned me not to get killed or she would be very upset with me. We talked about the mood of the city. Many nobles and merchants that could afford to had sent their families to live in the country. The common people just had to stay and work and hope to keep their families safe. Yes, they were afraid, but London did have confidence in their Queen.

She had sent for me because she wanted to give me something. She gave me two ornate boxes and said, "Before you leave, I wanted to give you this to replace something taken from you. I didn't know which one of these you would prefer, so I thought I'd let you choose."

I opened the first box and there was a beautiful rosary in it. It was made with pearls and small emeralds in silver settings along with a fine silver crucifix. It was the finest I had ever seen. She pointed to the second box before I could say anything and motioned for me to open it. I opened it and started to cry. It was a plain wooden rosary with well-crafted small wood beads and crucifix. It was like the one from Father McNee.

"I had it made special for you," is all she said with a kind and happy smile and then added, "Please use it to pray for us, pray for all of us."

I was overwhelmed and thanked her as I slipped it over my head and around my neck. She knew I would choose this one. She had given me a letter stating she had given it to me in service of my Queen in case anyone questioned my wearing it. A rosary was not the safest thing to be caught with in England, especially with the Spanish Catholic siege that was soon to come.

Captain Robert would take me to Plymouth by horse, which would be a long trip. First, he had to get me a horse. He had his own large stallion that I had met almost a year ago. I needed a smaller horse and a mare would be best. Mares were far faster in addition to being smaller. The Muslims had used them effectively during the Crusades against the Christian's heavier-armor-laden stallions. Interestingly, the English were about to use the same strategy using faster lighter ships against the slower-heavily-armed Spanish ones.

Mares with light riders were also used to quickly dispatch messages. They had become far more valuable now. Robert simply rented me one from Walter van Hertz's Rental Horse, a Dutch business. Yeah, I'm pulling your leg on that one. It was actually van Avis, which was far more *enterprising* with *thrifty* pricing. I have no idea where he got my horse. She was gray with a white diamond on her forehead. We fit together very well. Robert called her "Molly" for fun, after the girl in Gloucester,

I think Captain Robert had a bit of a soft spot for Molly. He had known her for some time. She had come from a merchant's family but had refused to be wed in an arranged marriage. That put her out on the street. She was quite intelligent and had even learned to read. That was highly unusual for a common girl. She was not your "Yes Sir," type of girl. Robert enjoyed her company, not just for a little physical intimacy, but more for her charm and wit.

Robert was to be wed once long before he knew Molly. This too was an arranged marriage. He barely knew the girl, and she too had fallen in love with another. She was found in a compromised position and the marriage contract was nullified. Robert was actually relieved. He wanted to be a soldier and he didn't think it would be fair to the girl if he only rarely could be with her and not be able take care of her.

At the same time, he got his opportunity to become a soldier when there was a rebellion in the North. It was led by the Earl of Northumberland who wanted to see Catholic Mary Queen of Scots replace Protestant Queen Elizabeth. The Earl ended losing his head over it. It also resulted in Queen Mary being tucked away in various English castles for about eighteen years until she had her head lopped off after one too many conspiracies.

So Robert went off to war in 1570. He was about the same age as the young Earl of Essex had been when he recently went to war in the Netherlands. Robert had fought gallantly, not only for his Queen, but also his fellow soldiers. Topcliffe had fought ferociously in this short rebellion also.

Robert was well educated and had a keen mind. These valuable talents, however, eventually placed him in the position of investigating dishonest magistrates and recovering taxes due his Queen. In reality, this was far more important than spilling blood on the battlefield because there had to be gold to spill blood. This was not the career Robert had sought, especially now with the pending invasion from Spain. He was, in fact, quite grateful that Walsingham had arranged for him to be in the Queen's Personal Guard. He hoped someday he would serve her Majesty in person, and did not mind that his first assignment was to keep an eye on an alley cat. We had become friends and I enjoyed traveling with him and learning from him.

I had to learn how to ride properly. The first trick was to get used to the motion of the horse and go with it. You did not want to be bouncing down while the horse was bouncing up. This would cause considerable discomfort especially at a gallop. I quickly learned that trick, as my voice was still finishing changing and I decided it would be better not to sing like a castrato.

It was well over a 200-mile ride from London, but it was still quicker by land than arranging a ship. Fortunately, we arrived a day early and I had time to recover. It was good to walk about again, and I was able to see the port and part of the immense navy that would be part of the coming battle. Drake was back in port resupplying.

The admiral and captains I had met earlier in London had gathered to plan strategy and divide into commands. This would normally be the time to depart for raiding the Spanish ports, even as far as the Americas. Drake had tried to convince the Queen, and Lord Admiral Howard, to give him fifty ships to attack the Armada in Lisbon. He wanted to bring the fight once again to Spain, rather than letting them bring the fight to England. Hawkins was in agreement with this plan. The counter argument was it was critical to have all the ships close to England to protect her from attack. Her Majesty and Howard did not agree to Drake's plan, but he would continue trying with letters from Plymouth. By now there was little doubt Parma's army was preparing to attack across the sea from the Dutch coast. Walsingham had his spy network busy trying to determine how soon the Armada would be fitted, and the size of their army. The feeling was the Armada would not be ready to depart till sometime in May. It was already mid-April.

The day had finally come for me to step aboard the Revenge. I parted with Captain Robert and I thought he would be returning to London. He was, in fact, being sent on another mission by Walsingham. He boarded a different ship with his horse. I was welcomed aboard the Revenge by Lieutenant Jonas Bodenham, whom I had met at Drake's party. Word had gotten around about the stray cat that was coming aboard from those I had met at the party. I did feel welcome.

The Revenge was a "race-built" Galleon design ship. She had a 250-man crew. It was smaller than this class of Spanish ships, but faster and far more deadly. It had one lower deck with cannons. Above that was the exterior main deck in the middle with cannons and the main mast. Then there were two upper decks with cannons. The front one was the forecastle deck with one mast. The rear was the quarterdeck also with one mast. There were also cannons below this deck at the level of the main deck including two cannons out the back. On top of the very rear of the ship was the poop deck with a small mast. That is where the captain commands the ship. It is not where you take a poop. The word poop, in this case, is of French origin. Figures.

The captain's cabin is at the rear of the ship. It had an exterior balcony around it called the captain's gallery. This was kind of like an open-end observation car at the rear of a train during your past golden age of steam. This is the cabin I would be staying in with Drake himself. Here I would learn navigation. There aren't any crossroads or mileposts in the sea. I had to learn about latitude and longitude and we didn't have GPS witchcraft to do it with. The main purpose of a cabin boy is education. I had pored over maps and charts in the library at Whitehall, so already I knew most the coastline on both sides of the sea and channels.

Drake's ship, the Revenge, was named for a reason, *revenge*. The Spanish had gotten a head start plundering the New World and found gold and silver throughout the Central and South Americas. They also wanted it all for themselves and forbid trading with other countries. Hawkins and Drake had established illegal but generally peaceful trading with these "New Spain" American ports over twenty years earlier.

Unfortunately, the storm winds of Fate battered their six ships, and they limped into San Juan de Ulua (Veracruz). A Spanish treasure fleet also soon arrived. Negotiations were made and they agreed to let the English fleet make their repairs and leave, but it was trap. The Spanish attacked and destroyed Hawkins trade fleet killing, capturing, and enslaving most of the English seaman. Hawkins and Drake's ships were the only two to barely escape.

Thereafter, Hawkins, Drake and other privateers started attacking and plundering Spanish treasure ships and ports. This brought wealth to the crown. Hawkins busied himself building the English fleet with modern ships that would now fight the Armada. This fight was personal on both sides.

I should note with shame and sadness, I had a total lack of understanding and compassion at the time regarding slavery. The original business that Hawkins and Drake were in, before they basically became pirates, was the slave trade. They would collect slaves from West Africa and take them to the new Spanish and Portuguese colonies. There they would sell them to the plantation owners for gold and silver. Slavery was legal in Spain, her colonies and many other countries. Slavery was not acceptable in England. The Elizabethan court had ruled, "That England was too pure an air for a slave to breathe in." England, however, was indifferent to making money off them. The Romans, of course, and many other ancient civilizations, had their economies based on slaves. History is full of slavery.

I had been sold illegally as a slave, so I was sensitive to its injustice. I was against someone being made a slave "illegally." At the same time, I wasn't thinking about the "legal" ones. I had envisioned the legal slaves like everyone else of my time, that they were savages from Africa and now the New World. It was even generally the concept they weren't necessarily God's creatures or even human. We were taught that God had made them inferior to serve us. I had never seen a slave yet and hadn't given it much consideration at age fourteen. I still hadn't learned there was no such thing as a legal slave, and they are as much as God's creatures as I.

It was a cruel time. It was a time of wars, prejudice, slavery, greed, religious intolerance, stupidity, and starving homeless orphans. *Nothing at all, like it is now in your modern times.* But still there was good. Most the time, people were decent. Most the time people helped one another. Heroes were still heroes even if they could be just as much of a villain during different times or parts of their lives. There is good and bad in all of us. Drake is my friend, and I will always stand up for him.

Drake welcomed me and soon we were off to form up his fleet. Herding ships was like herding cats. I have no idea how Drake or Hawkins could do it, but these were the best captains in the world as the Spanish were about to learn. Lord Howard would be joining us in May. Then the three would have a privateer fleet of a dozen ships with Vice Admiral Drake commanding the Revenge, Rear Admiral Hawkins the Victory, and Lord Admiral Howard the Ark Royal. Raleigh had commissioned the Ark to be built, but basically had to sell it to the Crown for IOU's against debts he owed them. The English navy would have almost 200 ships including these dozen privateer ones. Part of the fleet was in the North Sea to guard London. They actually had more ships than the Armada. There would only be around sixty at Plymouth though, to meet the Armada.

The Spanish would have 130 ships to start with, including much larger and more heavily gunned ones. In fact, the Spanish had twice the firepower of the English fleet. They had a new Commander, the Duke of Medina Sidonia. King Phillip had appointed him when the commander and architect of the Armada, the legendary Marquis of Santa Cruz, died this February. This would have been like the English losing Drake, or in more modern times, the Allies losing Eisenhower before the equivalent opposite direction D-day invasion. Most of this was known, even on the streets of London, because the Spanish had published it in leaflets!

The Duke of Sidonia was an important obedient and efficient aristocrat. He was just the administrator the King wanted. He begged the King not to give him this command pointing out he had no naval experience and physically got seasick. Phillip wanted someone he could trust to follow his invasion orders and plans, so Sidonia relented and took charge of the Armada.

Drake had promised I could fire a cannon. Firing a cannon was easy. Aiming it was the problem. There was little adjustment that could be done with the gun. It was the ship that had to be aimed. Drake, or "El Draque" the Dragon, as the Spaniards called him, was a genius at this. The gun crews had to know when the ship was about to be in position and be ready to fire. The captain had to know when the guns were ready, and the communication was the sea and timing. All this had to be done repeatedly on a rolling sea with a moving target. A target that possibly had twice as many guns trying to blow you out of the water and board you. The English fleet had no intent on letting the Spanish grapple, board and have a fight on board between soldiers. No, the English would come in a line one after another and bombard the Spanish fleet, circle back, and repeat it like a pack of wolves.

Drake assigned me to the man who commanded the cannon fire. Everyone just called him "Gunner." One of the tricks being tested to gain cannon range, was to bring the ship in fast at an angle from let's say the port side to position for a broadside volley. Just as our ship came into range at this angle, we would turn hard starboard, which would raise the port side cannons so their volley could be fired with more elevation. This would give them a better range. If timed perfectly, the maximum rise would occur as the ships were parallel for the broadside. The hard starboard would also quickly get the ship out of range as it continued turning away at an angle. There was a downside though. As the port side rose to increase the cannon elevation, it also raised the tender belly of the hull and would be the same time the enemy would want to fire.

We would practice this maneuver chasing another ship towing a target launch, and only fire one cannon. He had to make sure we didn't actually hit the chase ship. He offered extra beer portions for anyone who hit the launch. The firing would give the rest of the cannon crews the feel of the precision timing and the range. Gunner was teaching me the art and would eventually let me light one off. He would do this with each gun crew. You also had to consider the slight delay of lighting the charge. And all of this further hinged on the wind for maneuvering.

"Holy shite!" is all I said as I jumpéd when I heard the first cannon Gunner fired. Everyone laughed. It was loud and everyone had stuffed wads in their ears. When I finally fired my turn, I again jumped and yelled, "Holy shite!" My timing was true though and I didn't even hit our chase ship! After that everyone was yelling "Holy shite!" as they fired. Drake just shook his head.

Another thing that made Drake shake his head was my black tightly fitting shirt with pockets of sawdust sewn in. Yes, I had actually talked Alexander into having it made. I told him I didn't need any more clothes made, and I'd be outgrowing them anyway. The Queen had ordered some nice clothes made for me, but I don't think she meant to keep churning them out.

I tried out the first attempt in what I had dubbed Phillip's tub at Whitehall. It was difficult to submerge my head wearing it, but I didn't know if the pockets of sawdust would keep my body afloat. Whitehall had fountain like pools inside. The nobles would use them in summer to cool down. There were also outside ponds with fountains used for cooling, but it was too early in the year for them to be in operation. The Romans had brought the baths to England over a thousand years ago, but Whitehall's pools were used more for cooling. After all, bathing wasn't all that popular, but nobles always liked finding exclusive activities.

So I used an inside one to test my mad idea, which is generally what anyone thought I was when I hopped into the shallow pool. It did indeed work somewhat, it would help keep me afloat enough to rest and not drown quickly. I had Alexander add more bands of sawdust to it. I also had tight fitting black pants or trews, which is no doubt where the word trousers came from. I never had tested this final version.

So there I was about to make a fool out of myself jumping in when the maneuvers dropped anchor for a bit. I could float and paddle about successfully. My nickname of Alley Cat had followed me, so there was a bit of laughing that I must be a cat who was afraid of water. It wasn't the water I feared. It was the drowning bit.

We returned to Plymouth in mid-May. Lord Howard was coming to join the fleet and make Sir Francis Drake Vice Admiral of the fleet. On May 23rd, Drake's Revenge raised the Vice Admiral flag. I was proud to be aboard to see it. Drake, Hawkins and now

Howard still wanted to take the fight to Spain. They wanted to attack the Armada before it could even leave Lisbon. They waited for permission from the Queen, but it didn't come. She wanted to keep them close. They continued readying the fleet for the coming battle. The Armada had put to sea on May 19th.

Lord Howard also received worrisome news. The day the Armada weighed anchor, there was the beginning of an attempt to overthrow the King of France, Henry III. Fortunately, he had escaped from Paris. Henry III was a Catholic King, but he had arranged a peace from their religious war, with tolerance for Protestants. He had no love for Spain. Now the French Catholic League, led by Henry I, Duke of Guise, was raising a rebellion. Some of the same fanatics that had caused the Saint Bartholomew Massacre were part of this league. This would make France an ally of Spain. The last thing England needed now was not knowing which way France was going to flip, as the Armada prepared to sail.

I had been to sea out of Plymouth several times for almost two months now. I learned all the positions for firing the cannons. I was also given a long dagger to carry like a sword and taught some defensive moves. The rest of the men also practiced fighting with swords. I realized I would be so dead if I had to fight with my "kid's sword." Fortunately, Drake was planning on blowing any Spanish ship out of the water before it would be close enough to board us.

I then had my heart broken. I was not to be on the ships to fight the Armada by order of the Queen. She decided to keep me safe on land. I argued, but to no avail. It was the Queen's orders. So I tried to talk Drake into at least letting me help with the rowboat fleet starting at the Lizard, at the tip of England. It wouldn't be disobeying her Majesty. Besides, I didn't really have a practical way to get back to London.

When her Majesty invited me for dinner on my birthday, I had commented that I was willing to take a rowboat and throw rocks at the Armada if I had to. Oddly enough, there was a rowboat fleet. There were small boats along the southwestern tip that went to sea to watch and be able to signal if they saw the Armada. At best, the Armada might be sighted fifteen miles out from the coast. If small boats were sent out a few miles, their line of sight would increase that distance. They would need to have something to signal the shore with, especially after dark. Several towed another small boat that could be set on fire, or even blown up.

There were new beacon towers built all along the coast that branched out and would be lit at the first sighting of the Armada. They were built the same way the Romans had set up signaling. The English had also adopted it long ago to warn of Viking invaders. The first one would be lit so the next one would see its fire by night or smoke by day and then light theirs and so on. The signal could be relayed to warn London within several hours. The southwestern most tip of England was the Lizard of Cornwall. Its beacons went to Plymouth first, where the fleet is located. It might take only an hour to send the signal there.

You would think the Armada would hug the French coast, but Spain thought they had the most powerful navy in the world. They would also know the English fleet, and Drake, were waiting at Plymouth for them. After all, they had their own spy network. The Spaniards arrogantly thought they could smash the English fleet, and finally rid themselves of El Draque and his pirates.

Drake ultimately relented and sent me to the tip of the Cornish coast. He wrote me a letter saying I was to help with the boats. I was sent with men that were to report back to Howard as to how effective these boats might be along with other land-based preparations. The boats, like other forms of lookouts, were placed along the coast up to Plymouth so the Lord Admiral's fleet would not be taken by surprise. With a letter from Drake himself, I of course, made it sound like I was to command a boat. I would work the one at the Lizard.

Part 3 – Justice

When Captain Robert boarded a ship in Plymouth after delivering me to Drake, he did not return to London. He was assigned two soldiers to join him on a mission from Lord Walsingham. The ship was bound for Wales. He was to bring justice to the lads in Swansea. He had papers under the signature of her Majesty stating the accusations I had made as indisputable testimony. He had the power as a Captain in the Queen's Personal Guard to take whatever legal action and judgment he deemed necessary to bring justice. He was also to find my Bible. I, of course, wasn't there, so I am telling the story as I understand it.

Robert and his two men had brought their horses with them and they all would be returning to London when this business was finished. Robert would finally be in the fight protecting London and his Queen. He stopped in Neath first to notify the local magistrate of his authority in this matter and to have two of their soldiers placed at his disposal.

He now headed to the Lord Stevens' coal dig with his now, four soldiers. His soldiers announced his arrival at the "Big House" and instructed that Master Powell meet him. Robert was ushered inside, and the servant was sent for Powell.

When Powell arrived, Robert introduced himself. "I am Captain Robert Barrington of Her Majesty's Personal Guard. I am here at her request. Where can we talk privately?"

"I am humbly at your service and will help you any way I can. My meeting room is this way, Captain Barrington," Powell said nervously with a bow. They went to the next room and Robert dismissed his men to attend the horses. Powell's servant offered them food and drink.

"Yes, that would be fine, and for my men also," Robert told the servant as Powell beckoned him to be seated.

"How may I help you Captain?" Powell asked as Robert sat down at the head of a long table.

"Her Majesty and Lord Walsingham have sent me here to inquire about an indentured Irish boy who arrived here last spring. We need to know every detail about him. When he got here, what became of him, along with all documents or notes you may have. We are particularly interested in a Protestant Bible he carried with him and what became of it. The boy's name is Presto. Tell me everything you remember," Robert instructed.

"Yes, I do remember the boy you mention. He was brought here like others for crimes of being a thief. Ireland is overrun with orphan vermin, so they send some to us in hopes of making Protestants of them and to have them work off their sentence here," Powell answered.

"How did he arrive and in whose company?"

"He came on a ship from Dublin with a Master Barnett. He usually has the task of bringing them."

"Were there any more of these Catholic criminals here with which he might have had contact?" Robert asked, making it sound like he supported the process. This was a tactic he used when he was doing his tax audits. He would be sympathetic with the one he was questioning without them even realizing they were confirming more areas he could interrogate them about.

"Yes, there were several boys he would have been sent to work with."

"Now tell me about the stolen Bible the boy had with him," Robert said, making it sound like he thought I had stolen it.

"Yes, he had a Bible hidden in his effects. He claimed it was his, but of course, we knew he was lying."

This confirmed the Bible that I, Presto, claimed had been the single item of Fate that led to even this very moment, was real. Robert and Walsingham and her Majesty never had any doubt, but Powell's admission corroborated it.

Robert had a flash of contempt toward Powell which he subdued and continued, "Where is this Bible now? Her Majesty desires it and you better pray to God nothing has happened to it."

Powell looked frightened and stumbled to reply, "I, I turned it over to Lord Stevens of course, Captain Barrington, My Lord." Robert wasn't a Lord, but there was no need to correct him.

"Excellent, I will send my soldiers to retrieve it and have Lord Stevens brought here. I have a letter from Her Majesty ordering its return. You will give my men a note stating you gave the Bible to your Lord. For both your sakes, I hope he has taken good care of it. And now, where do you have the boy?"

"He's dead, Sir, My Lord Captain. He tried to escape and drowned," Powell answered now with all the color draining out of him.

"When and how?"

"It wasn't more than a month after he got here. He robbed us and snuck out during the gale that hit us."

"How do you know he drowned? Did you retrieve his body?" Robert asked obviously knowing the answer.

"Well no, Captain Barrington, we never found his body. He ran away during the storm just when we needed him the most. He went back to Swansea and robbed and vandalized a shop. We found some of his effects there, along with some down by the docks. We figured the sea surge got him. Saved us the bother," Powell said without any remorse.

Robert sat and marveled how well my ruse had worked. "That is why I will need to talk to any other lads or workers who came in contact with him. Who managed him as I'll need to talk to them also?"

"That would be Master Crowley. He oversees the men I employ and these filthy-Irish convicts."

"Send for him, I will want him to assemble these thieves as I will question them first. In the meantime, I assume you keep a journal registering where they came from and when they arrived. I want to see it." Robert of course, knew of this journal my name was written in. "There may be other names of criminals he might have known previously. How many do you have, and are they the same ones as when Presto was here?

"There are five, and I believe there are still three from when he was here," he replied.

"Have any escaped or left since Presto tried to escape?"

"No, none have ever escaped. One more died since this Presto was here," he replied without concern.

"How?"

"Winter influenza, we lose most of them then. Master Barnett usually replenishes them in spring. In fact the new ones only just arrived. We're still breaking them in."

With that the servant brought some wine and light food as it was mid-morning well before the lunch meal. Powell sent him to bring his journal and then bring Crowley. While waiting he wrote the note to Lord Stevens as requested and one of Robert's soldiers was sent to deliver it. Powell supplied an escort that Stevens would know. Robert left them instructions that Lord Stevens was to wait to see him in this room *with* the Bible.

While waiting for Crowley, Robert looked at the journal. Powell had opened the book to the page my name was on. He saw the date I arrived and the date I died with the clause "drowned escaping." He saw there were two more names below mine and they must be the ones Barnett had recently brought. He would send an arrest warrant for him later as he had the name of the ship. In fact it was often the same ship.

As he studied the previous pages, he found the name of the lad that had died in winter. It was Liam. No last name, and some of the other boy's names were barely legible. There was a column listed as 'Crime' and all the entries showed 'Thief.' As he studied further back, he found Thomas's name. Apparently, he was still alive which was a relief and meant he had an eyewitness. As he continued going back slowly and deliberately, Powell sat nervously. Finally Barrington saw, the lad, Robert's name and noted the death day was three days before mine. It showed "fell escaping." Robert's heart sunk as he went back to the beginning and saw there were about twenty names total with death dates going back to about the time of the end of the second Munster rebellion. They all showed 'illness' or 'injury.' That was the extent of their obituary.

Robert finally asked, "I see there was another one of these criminals who tried escaping three days before Presto. Tell me of the events surrounding this escape."

He fell and cracked his empty skull open when we were tracking him down. Served him right, he was always rebellious." Powell answered coldly.

Crowley arrived and entered asking, "You wished to see me, Sir?" He looked at Captain Robert and knew he was a man of authority.

"Yes, this is Captain Barrington. He is here on Her Majesty's business regarding that thief, Presto, we had here last spring. It appears that Bible he had stolen I told you about is of some importance," Powell replied.

"Yes, I remember him, insolent and useless vermin. Drowned himself, deserved it too," Crowley sneered.

"Pity you didn't find his body though it would have made matters so much easier. The issue of the Bible is not to be discussed with others. Do I make myself clear?" Robert said sternly.

They both nodded.

"Crowkley is it? I wish you to assemble the Irish convicts for me to question. How do you keep them under control? I expect them to be kept in obedient and respectful order. Do you understand?" Robert asked.

"It's Crowley, My Lord. I will assemble them outside. They're too filthy to bring in here. I have two dogs that keep them in order."

"Good, bring the dogs too."

Robert closed the journal, not to return, but to take with him. The sound of barking and growling indicated the lads had been assembled. Robert had his remaining three soldiers join him and gave one of them the journal.

Master Powell introduced Robert the way he was instructed. "This is Captain Robert Barrington of Her Majesty's Personal Guard. He has some questions he wishes to ask you."

"Gramercy, Master Powell," Robert said as he turned to the boys. "As he said I have just a few questions. I expect you to tell me the truth. I represent the Queen and lying to me is the same as lying to Her Majesty. You may speak freely." He paused to make sure all understood his words. "First I want to talk to those who were here when a lad by the name of Presto was here. Step forward." He waited as the boys looked amongst themselves frightened and he repeated firmly, "Step forward!"

Three of the boys stepped forward. Robert looked at each one of them trying to size up which one looked the bravest or leader as he wanted to start with him first. "What is your name? Come here," and pointed to one of the lads and then the ground in front of him.
\
"Thomas, My Lord," and he advanced to stand in front of the Captain and his men. The dogs started to growl.

"Very good," Robert said as Thomas approached. "Silence those dogs," he ordered. Crowley gave a pull on their leash and the dogs immediately obeyed. "I see you have them well trained."

267

"Yes, My Lord. They do exactly as I tell them," Crowley grinned.

"I'm sure they do. Now Thomas, I saw in Master Powell's journal you were indentured here because you are a thief. Are you a thief, Thomas?"

No, My Lord, none of us are thieves. We were all abducted and sold here as slaves!" Thomas asserted.

"The boy lies!" Crowley shouted as the dogs started barking and growling again.

"I am talking to the boy now and do not like being interrupted. You will all have a chance to be interrogated. I've told you before to silence those dogs," Robert demanded.

Crowley again pulled the dogs back and finally answered, "Yes My Lord," as Robert waited for his reply.

"Now I want to ask you, Thomas, about another boy who was here at the same time as Presto. His name was Robert. Do you remember him, Thomas?"

"Of course, I do, My Lord," Thomas replied indignantly.

"It seems they both tried to escape just a couple days apart. Did they know each before, Thomas?"

"None of us knew Presto. Nor did we know each other until we were brought here, My Lord."

"Do you have any idea why either one of them would have tried to escape, Thomas?"

"You mean aside from being made slaves and being beaten and abused and made to eat garbage and starved, My Lord? No, I can't think of a single reason other than the ditch they throw our bodies in when they've killed us, My Lord of the Queen's Guard!" Thomas shouted as he stood tall shaking.

"Insolent peasant, how dare you speak to the Queen's Captain with these lies!" Crowley shouted as the dogs again growled.

"Crowkley, I informed you before, I was talking to the lad and you would have your turn later. I also told you to keep those dogs silent unless I decide I need them. Do you understand?" Robert asked with a surreal calmness.

"Yes, My Lord," as he again pulled the dogs back.

Robert turned back to Thomas. "Boy, I want you to tell me exactly what you know first of Robert's escape and what happened to him. Consider the fact you are talking to the Queen and must tell the truth. Just as you would tell the truth to one of those priest's you confess to. I will know the truth. Do you understand?" Robert asked again in a surreal tone.

Thomas nodded, shaking as he spoke. "Crowley beat Robert mercilessly like he does me now. I don't care anymore. If you want the truth, I'll give it to you. When Robert escaped from him, he knew he wouldn't survive. He wanted it over. Crowley murdered him. He let the dogs loose on him and they tore him apart. Then he brought Robert back here and had the dogs tear him apart again in front of us where we stand. Do you want to see the ditch where what's left of him is buried along with the rest of us? Do you? DO YOU?" Thomas cried out.

The dogs again started barking, snapping and growling has they pulled to advance. "How dare you lie and accuse me of anything. You Irish-Catholic-vermin, you have no rights, your word is *NOTHING!*" Crowley screamed.

"SILENCE!" Captain Robert yelled and drew his sword laying its blade on his own shoulder as he paced forward. "No one make a sound, including the dogs. Does everyone understand?" Robert circled by Crowley and the dogs, then the boys, then to Powell and finally back to Thomas. "It seems the boy has accused you of murder, Master Crowkley, so now it is your turn to tell me what happened to Robert and then Presto."

Agitated, Crowley answered, "The boy lies. Robert ran away and fell and broke his neck while we tracked him. There was nothing we could do for him. Master Powell was here, he saw him."

"And did your dogs tear the boy apart, Master Crowkley?"

"Of course not, the boy has gone too far with his lies."

"You're the liar!" Thomas screamed.

"Silence!" Robert again ordered as the dogs started up again and Crowley again held them back.

And the lad, Presto?" Robert continued.

"He ran away during the gale and went looting and then he drowned, serves him right the useless bastard," Crowley spat.

Thomas was shaking trying to hold back his anger and terror and tears. Robert continued pacing with his sword. "It seems someone is lying to me, to Her Majesty."

"The boy's word can not be taken over ours. He's a criminal," Powell now stated breaking the silence.

Robert stopped and spoke quietly face to face with Thomas. "I'll admit you're a brave lad, as stubborn as you Irish come. Now can you be brave a little longer? I want you to trust me, to trust *Presto*." He continued staring into the boy's eyes that now had a puzzled look. "Stand perfectly still and answer my question bravely one more time." Then he nodded slightly to the boy.

"Bring up the dogs," Robert ordered. Crowley brought the growling dogs up directly in front of Captain Robert and Thomas and held their leash tight. Crowley had the look of absolute loathing in his eyes.

Robert placed his blade gently on top of Thomas's shoulder. "I am going to give you one more chance, Thomas, to repeat your charge. Did these dogs tear the boy, Robert, apart?"

There was absolute silence, as the boy took a deep breath. "Yes, Crowley had his dogs kill Robert and then tear what was left of him apart in front me and Presto, all of us."

With that Captain Robert raised his blade ready to strike. Thomas closed his eyes as the dogs started barking and pulling on their leash. It was over in mere seconds. Robert swung his blade hard and true and took the head off the first dog who didn't even yelp. He swung a second time and the second dog fell silent.

"NO!" Crowley screamed, "NO! Not my dogs!"

By then, Captain Robert had brought his blade back up and while still holding it smashed his fist into Crowley's face. His lips and nose exploded as he fell back over his dead dogs. Thomas opened his eyes and stared dumbfounded at the sight. Powell and the other boys stood stunned and frozen in place.

Captain Robert now spoke calmly as he wiped the blood off his sword. "The lad Thomas has told the truth. There is another witness who has testified Robert was killed by these dogs under Crowley's direction. The testimony also states Crowley had them tear Robert's remains apart here where we now stand. This witness' testimony is beyond reproach by the order of Her Majesty."

"But there was no one else here, there were only the boys. There can't be any other witness," Powell now protested in disbelief.

Robert turned and faced Thomas with Powell looking on. "Oh, but there *IS*. There was another witness here who managed to escape and went through hell and back and made it to London vowing he would seek justice. The witness' name is Presto!"

"Presto's alive?" Thomas asked bewildered.

"But he's dead," Powell proclaimed.

"No, Presto is quite alive. And I am here as the sword of justice by the order of the Queen."

"But he's a common thief. He's a Catholic peasant from Ireland and he stole Her Majesty's Bible. His word is dirt. His word can not be accepted over ours," Powell declared.

"Oh, you wish to challenge Her Majesty's authority? Would you like me to add treason to the charges to be leveled against *you*?" Robert said with chilling clarity.

Powell suddenly realized that he was at serious risk. "No, My Lord," he answered humbly.

Thomas was still standing frozen on the spot, still not believing what was occurring. Robert motioned to him to rejoin the other lads. As he walked slowly and then ran back to them, their excitement was growing. Robert then proclaimed, "With the full authority of Her Majesty, I am here to free these lads from this unlawful slavery. They will all be compensated by Lord Stevens for their confinement. For now, they will be housed, fed and clothed. They will then be educated, taught a trade of their choice and sent to wherever they wish."

The lads of Swansea couldn't believe their ears and erupted into cheers. They jeered at Crowley and Powell. Robert let them sling vile insults at them. Crowley and Powell dared not speak. Crowley was still holding his mouth and probably couldn't speak anyway. Finally, Robert told the lads to settle down.

Robert then continued as he turned to Crowley and spoke with contempt. "Stand up! You will be charged with murder along with other vile acts. Before you are hauled away though, you have a task to perform." With that, Robert took the journal back from his soldier and shook it in Crowley's face. "You are going to dig up every lad in the ditch and lay their bones out respectfully name by name. There will be coffins made for each of them and they will be given a proper Christian burial. *Do You Understand?"*

Crowley slowly stood defiantly and trying to speak, sputtered, "And if I refuse to dig up that vermin? We'll see what Lord Stevens has to say."

"He will be here shortly, and I might well throw him in irons. And as to you, how would you like to be taken to London and have a traitor's execution? By, let's say Richard Topcliffe. I'm sure he could squeeze you in," Robert said coldly and then turned to one of the soldiers. "Guard help this vermin Crowkley find a shovel and make sure you get some hard work out of him. You can reward him with a drink of water or punish him as you see fit."

Robert turned to the raggedy lads and said, "All of you look starved and cold. Master Powell, you are to have a healthy meal prepared for the boys *inside*. I think the room we met in will be a nice place. I and my men will join them. Your servant is to find new clothes for all of them. Shoes too. Do you understand?"

Powell was dazed by the turn of events. "We can't let them in the house, they're filthy, and Lord Stevens is coming."

"You're right, you shall set a plate for Lord Stevens too and he can join us. I'm sure the boys won't mind. I wonder if they've met before. Good way for Stevens to see what all the stink is about," Robert said with animated sarcasm. "Show the boys inside. Now!"

Mortified, Powell led the jovial boys to the meeting room and told his servant of Robert's demands. Robert told the boys to sit and the servant brought something to drink. They started to ask questions as to how Presto escaped and why the Queen was helping them and if this was all true. Were they truly free? Before Robert could even begin to answer, Lord Stevens arrived.

"What the hell is going on? Why is this filth in my dining room? Who is responsible for this?" Lord Stevens bellowed as he was escorted inside.

"You must be Lord Stevens. Please sit, we have some catching up to do," Captain Robert said cordially and pointed to one of the seats next to the boys.

"Did you bring Her Majesty's Bible?" He asked his soldier who had escorted Stevens.

"Yes, Sir! Captain," Robert's soldier answered. He advanced, taking it carefully out of a protective leather sheath, and placed it on the table in front of him.

Robert, ignoring whatever Stevens was protesting about, carefully opened the book to page 173. I, Presto, had mentioned that I had written my name in the Bible when I first learned to write it. I signed it on the page that was the date of my birthday. That is March 17, Saint Patrick's Day of course, which would be written 17-3.

Captain Robert looked up with a sigh of relief and joy that he *had* the Bible. By now Lord Stevens was scolding the boys and ordering them to leave. He demanded Powell come in and straighten this all out. The boys were carrying on talking without any respect or formality.

In a clear and commanding voice, Robert ordered, "SILENCE!"

They all stopped and looked to Captain Robert. "That includes you too Lord Stevens." Stevens stared aghast.

Robert quickly continued, "I would like to thank you, Lord Stevens for bringing Her Majesty's Bible and keeping it safe. Her Majesty and Lord Walsingham, who sent me here to retrieve it, will be most pleased. They also sent me here to investigate your illegal indenturing of these Irish lads along with twenty or so more your man Crowley is digging out of the ditch for proper Christian burial. Her Majesty and Lord Walsingham will be very displeased. Crowley is under arrest for murder. I have not compiled the list of charges against your other man Powell, who also represents you."

Now it was Lord Stevens who sat silent not knowing his status. He had never been talked to this way, let alone ordered to be silent. He had been given the letter written by Walsingham with her Majesty's seal ordering him to comply with Captain Barrington's authority in finding the Bible. He also realized Captain Robert had been sent to investigate these slavery allegations that were his ultimate responsibility.

Still, he was a lord and certainly the Queen would consider this a trivial matter. He was clever enough though to know it was a bad idea to fall out of favor with her. He was a viscount, the lowest noble to be called a lord. His title was primarily due to this land he was attempting to build into a thriving coal trade. He had no significant titles and was not known by the Royal Court in London. He decided it would be best to be courteous to the Captain.

"I am glad to serve the Queen and had no idea it was stolen from Her Majesty. I am honored it was I who found this Bible and protected it for Her Majesty. But why are these filthy vermin in *my* dining room?" Stevens asked calmly, but with assertion in his voice.

Captain Robert replied, "Lord Stevens, you are responsible for stealing this Bible. It was taken from one of the lads who was abducted and sold to your coalfield as a slave. The boy's name is Presto. Do you remember him? He came here about a year ago."

"Yes, I remember him. He robbed us and tried to escape during the gale that almost took down this building. He's the one who stole the Bible. He drowned," Stevens replied as the boys started to laugh.

"No, he didn't," Thomas said laughing along with the other boys, "No, he didn't!"

"Settle down boys," and they fell silent as Robert spoke again.

"You seem to have the wrong impression Lord Stevens. First, the boy Presto is alive and escaped to London. I recently accompanied him when I delivered him to Sir Francis Drake, who is now his guardian. Second, the Bible taken from him was his own. Her Majesty has sent me to find it so she can return it to him, *personally*."

The expressions on Lord Stevens's face, let alone the boys, were so far beyond stunned that my keyboard scribe has looked high and low without finding the right word.

"I'm sorry, we had no idea he was of noble birth. I will investigate how this injustice occurred. I will send apologies to Lord Presto," Lord Stevens said humbly.

"You are looking at how this injustice occurred. He was abducted just like these boys whose faces you are looking into now. Presto is an Irish orphan, as common as the land he's from without any prior status. He is nothing more than an Alley Cat who escaped and scrounged his way to London and then bravely saved Her Majesty's life," Robert proudly said. "Now you are going to pay these five lads for their suffering and all the past one's suffering. You are going to see to their education, food, shelter and from now on, their every need. You are going to pay for the proper burial of the lads who didn't survive and were thrown in a ditch. It would be wise for you to whole-heartedly support this endeavor. It might help you in my report to Her Majesty."

And so, Lord Stevens took that moment to throw his two men under the carriage. He claimed he knew nothing about the lads being bought as slaves, and said he thought they were indeed criminals. The fact there were no documents releasing them from any jurisdiction to him, and he clearly knew when each died, made him more than willing to support the survivors. Robert found a nice place on Stevens' personal estate to intern the ones that Crowley was digging up. Their markers all disappeared during Cromwell's Puritan takeover. Their names are long since forgotten like so many orphans from all the wars through the centuries.

Crowley and Powell were imprisoned at Neath waiting trial which was not a priority with the Armada and the battles that lay ahead. Robert could have easily ordered Crowley executed, but saw the poetic justice of having him rot in prison and be treated the way the Irish lads of Swansea had been. Robert returned with his two men to London with the Bible. Captain Robert presented it to her Majesty personally, which would be the first time he was received by her. It was his arrival with the Bible that made her decide to pull me from Drake's Revenge. It seemed this Tyndale Bible had once again changed my Fate and placed me on the shores of the Lizard of Cornwall to watch history pass me by.

Part 4 – Holiday

I was on holiday. As the world was about to sail by into madness, I was on holiday. I had never been on holiday before. The Cornish coast was magnificent. It had bluffs overlooking the coast filled with coves and beaches. There were indeed lizards scrambling across the rocky areas. I'd never seen lizards before in Ireland. I'd never heard of St. Patrick driving them out along with the snakes, but then I hadn't spent time on the Irish coast either. Maybe Ireland has lizards too? I do not know the history of this name "Lizard of Cornwall." I assumed it was because of the lizards, but the locals said it came from an eventual mispronunciation of some old Cornish name.

My duty was to help with the small boats on the lookout for the Armada. Drake had sent me with a letter and expense money to live on. I was billeted in a small inn on the coast. I had a single room with a cot, chair, small table, oil lamp and a pot. Not the type used for cooking either. It was not at all as grand as Whitehall, but much nicer than the graveyard. My duty simply ended up being to go out on the small coastal watch rowboat at the tip of the Lizard.

There were already men of authority in charge, including Captain Thomas Flemyng. Captain Flemyng had a fast pinnace, the Golden Hind, that he patrolled the coast with all the way to Plymouth from an isle south of the Lizard. A pinnace is a small fast sailboat. They were being used for communicating and transferring supplies and passengers between the ships, and between land. Yes, the name is easily mispronounced just like my Dumas name and was the source of many a tavern joke. I remember there was a particularly good one with a duck, but it eludes me. With that thought, good luck to anyone who reads this tale out loud.

There was a small watch boat roughly corresponding to each warning beacon or tower along the coast. Ours was painted black without a sail to help conceal it on the sea. When we had enough, we had a crew of six oarsmen, a helmsman to steer, and a lookout to lookout. I was normally the lookout but took turns at each post. Our crew was normally old men and boys a little older than me. The rest of the area's men were either in the service of her Majesty, or out to sea fishing, which was an important livelihood. We also had a small black boat in tow with pitch-soaked burlap to set on fire and a small charge of gunpowder to make a more visible fireball, smoke and loud explosion. We would go out so our signal could still be seen from the coast.

I gave an earnest effort to this task, even though no one seriously expected the Spanish Armada to be so stupid that they would appear off the beginning of the coast of England. How arrogant could they be to announce, "We're here, come get us," and give Lord Howard time to ready his fleet? The Channel was around a hundred miles wide at this point. Why eliminate the element of surprise? I hadn't considered the wind direction might just play a part. So I was a teenager on holiday with a summer job. It was like summer break from school, not that I ever went to one.

It was now late June and the summer had begun. I usually took the night watch so I could enjoy the sunshine of the day. If the weather was too rough, we didn't go out because the Armada would be laying anchor somewhere anyway. The Spanish had already learned herding, let alone advancing 130 ships in a storm, was a really bad idea. They had left Lisbon in May with fanfare but had been scattered by storms and they stopped in Corunna at the very northwest corner of Spain. Much of their food and water was contaminated, so they had to resupply. A handful of English ships weren't helping either, as they were busy trying to harass them and pick off strays. As far as we knew, the Armada was still trying to get their act together. It had been a month already and they still hadn't sailed!

So I was enjoying the sun, for I might as well. I was still burning that I couldn't be along side my hero Drake on the Revenge, but there was nothing I could do about it. I had gotten burned to a crisp with a sunburn earlier on the Revenge as the weather warmed up and the crew was mostly shirtless. When I did the same, the sunburn on my Irish skin kept me in the cabin for several days. I used the time productively to study charts and maps.

I was bashful at first to take off my shirt because of the marks from my lashes that still stood out pinkish red. The crew was somewhat surprised seeing them. Flogging was a typical punishment on a ship for discipline, and some men bore similar older white scars. They had never seen it on someone as young as a cabin boy. Flogging was done with a cat o' nine tails which had nine knotted tails. It could tear a back up mercilessly. For the punishment of a boy, however, there was a reduced cat that only had five smooth tails.

This whip had the humiliating name of "boys' pussy." It was administered to the boy's bare bottom while he bent over a cannon barrel. This was known as "kissing the gunner's daughter." You can now better understand some of my concerns when I was supposedly going off to become a cabin boy. That was little more than a year ago, and I was no longer worried about such things. These practices were perfectly normal back then and continued for the next several hundred years. Ironically, some of the expressions from then still haunt your modern times. "Letting the cat out of the bag," or "Not enough room to throw a cat," or "Pussy whipped," may not mean what you thought. I suppose that might have been a little creepy, but I'm telling it like it is.

This is not a fairy tale, though fairies can be very vicious, and you best not cross them either.

As to my explanation of my whipping scars, I simply said with a humorous grin, "My Irish stubbornness sometimes pisses people off." Besides, warriors liked sharing their tales and showing off their battle scars. I never did bring up their source, Topcliffe.

I also was wearing my wooden rosary her Majesty had given me. This initially shocked Drake's crew, as it would be the last thing you would expect someone to wear on his ship. I told them her Majesty had given it to me to pray for us all. Drake actually hated and mistrusted Catholics. But he now appreciated there were some of us that wanted our Catholic Church to reform, and the only way to do that was to defeat the Spanish. We had to free the world and all religions, including Catholic, from its grip. He knew I was fighting ultimately for peace between our religions, but that wasn't going to be today.

So with my nice seaman's tan, I had found a beach that was great for a daytime swim. That is why I preferred doing the cooler evening watch. I had become a good swimmer thanks to eating regular, building my strength and having grown a bit. I'd got used to the taste of seawater too. The first time I tasted it was when I was hurling over the rail on the ship to Swansea. It didn't really add that good of a seasoning to the flavor already in my mouth. Sometimes some of the lads from our watch boat could sneak away from their chores and join in on a swim. Some girls would sneak out and watch us too. They were also impressed with my scars.

I also had found that my horse was still in Plymouth being used by messengers. I received permission to take her when Howard's men brought me down to inspect the land lookouts. I had become a good rider. I would take the horse out on rides to see the coast and sights. My privates and Molly had quickly learned to get along on my first day's ride out of London. In fact, Captain Robert had given my horse her name, Molly, during that initial learning period of discomfort. I wondered just really what went on with their Molly that night in Gloucester, especially remembering all the strange screeches. I still had so much to learn I thought, and I wasn't too sure I wanted to learn about that. Then again ...

So it was now July and still no word of the Armada. It was getting maddening. For one thing there would be little communication. The Armada would likely sail well past us and we wouldn't know until the beacon tower's warning would reach us down here. Then all we'd know is that it was sighted. We wouldn't know of the battles, or who was winning. News would have to come by rider or boat and London might well fall long before we knew. Then what? Who knows what retribution the Spanish would take? And here I was stuck at the end of the world.

I refused to consider making any kind of plan should the Spanish be victorious. The reason was simple. I didn't have too. Drake was going to win, period. In the meantime, Drake, Hawkins and Howard, did finally get permission to attack the Armada at Corunna. They left the first week of July with favorable winds from the northeast. They turned right around and came back a few days later when the wind reversed and sent them back to Plymouth. The wind that was now favorable for the Armada to follow.

So the first week of July passed and then the second. I was doing more of the daytime watches now because our crew was short during the day as the old men and lads had other work to do. I still wore my sawdust laden black clothing that was miserably hot in the July sun. At least I could cool down in the ocean once we got out far enough. We did some fishing and of course brought food, water and beer with us. I also always brought a rock along, just in case we met up with the Armada.

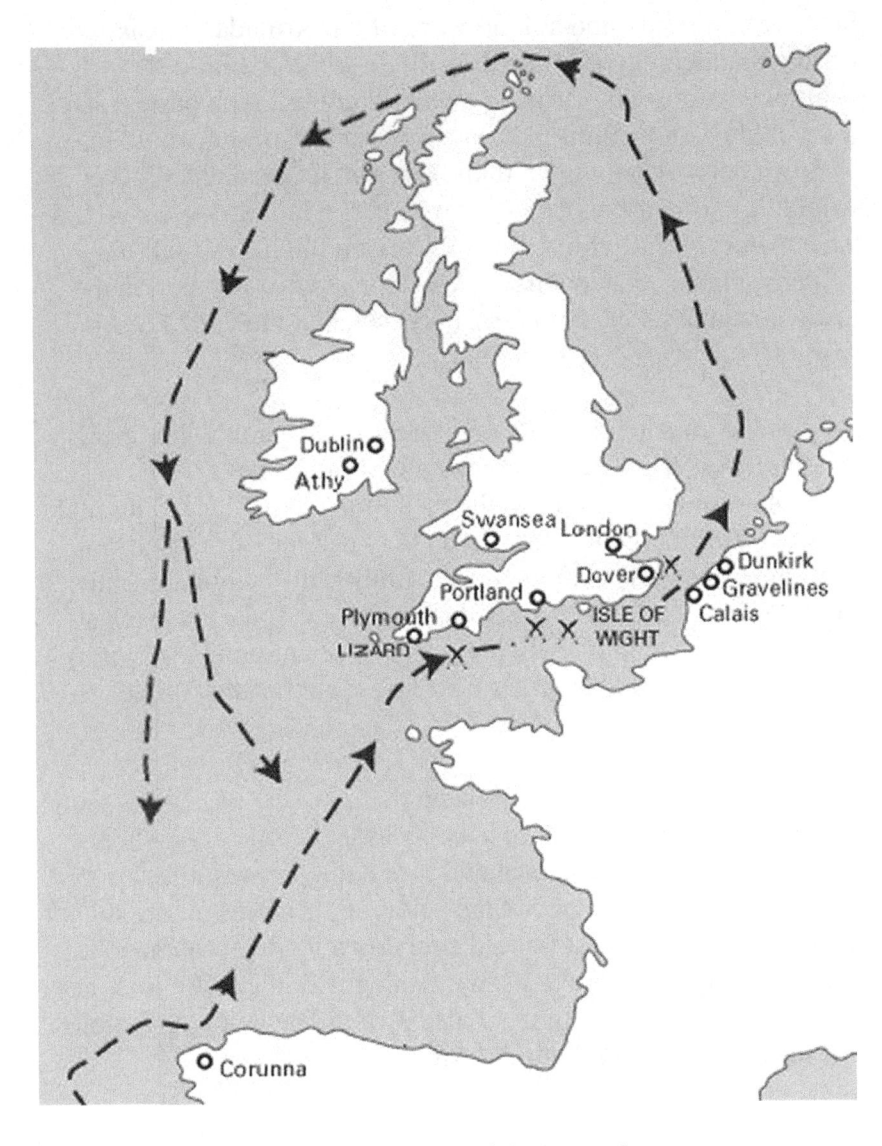

Route of the Spanish Armada

Revenge

Armada Sighting

Chapter 7 – The Armada

Part 1 – The Sighting

It was now Friday, July 19th, 1588. Still no word of the Armada, but it had to be on the move, somewhere. We boarded our little boat at dawn and rowed out. We were two men short and debated whether we should bring our little fireboat with. We were going out further now figuring we would have a better chance of seeing the Armada. If we did, we could row toward land and set off our signal. The fireboat was open at the bow, with a match cord wick going to the flammable pitch material in the middle. This part was covered with a pitch-laden tarp. There was another match cord that went from there to the rear of the boat into a small keg of gunpowder, also under the tarp. We obviously couldn't test it.

The day slowly passed, and it was now midafternoon. Our shore was barely a distant sight to the north. The channel actually runs west to east till almost Dover where it finally starts bending north. We were watching far to the west to the open sea for the approach of the Armada and to the south toward France. We weren't exactly paying any attention toward our own almost invisible coast.

One of the lads, Jonathan asked, "What's that?"

"What's what?" I replied, "Where?" as I turned and looked to the south and west.

"No, not that way," and then pointed to the northwest. "There."

Sure enough, way to west but to the north of us toward our coast was a speck coming up over the top of the horizon. We stared in awe as it started to take form. It was a sail. Now we did occasionally see ships go by. There was still some traffic coming from and going to Plymouth. We also would see fishing boats, but today we were completely alone. The afternoon sun to the west was our reference to navigate. If it had been cloudy, we wouldn't have gone out this far in case we lost sight of land.

Then we saw a second speck take form, this one was about half the distance between the first sail and us. Two ships? The second speck also grew into a sail. As it did another one popped up just south of the first one. As we stared at this surreal sight, still a fourth one popped up just to the north of the second ship we saw.

"Ooh shite," I breathed, "If those aren't ours, Fate is finally upon us!"

It was like an army of spiders advancing. The sails of the ships were popping up and filling their way in toward the center from either side. By now we could see red crosses on their sails. They were Spanish! We now saw masses of ships and they were all between the coast and our boat. We had to turn about and row north as fast as we could before they were upon us and cut us off. We turned and rowed, but they were gaining on us. We also steered a little on an angle to the east to try to run ahead of them. The fireboat was slowing us down. At the rate of their advance, we were going to be caught in the middle.

It was time to light the fireboat and hope we were close enough to shore for it to be heard. Hopefully, the coast would be watching and see our signal and the Armada. Our signal would also be seen by the Spaniards, though. It was time for me to dive in and get back to light her up. As the other men and lads were stronger than me for rowing, it was obvious that was my task. I wasn't doing a whole lot of good as the fifth oar anyway, unless we were trying to add a little east to our angle.

So over the side I went, and a few feet back was the fireboat. I climbed on board and ducked down in the front to get the fire supply's tinderbox. There was a length of match cord to ignite in it, with a flint and striker. I would need to strike a spark to this match cord and use it to light the cord around the flammable pitch in the center. Once lit, I would quickly get back to our boat and cast the fireboat off.

They rowed on. We still had more than half of the way to clear the north pincher of their arc. I lit the tinderbox's match cord. Then I lit the match cord going to the pitch and got ready to get back to our boat. The pitch didn't take. It only smoldered. I tried lighting it with my length match cord, but it still just went out. I was determined to light this damn thing. We hadn't been dragging it around these past weeks just to abandon it. But I realized we wouldn't make it to shore unless we cut the fireboat free.

"Get to shore as fast as you can and warn them," I screamed as I tried to cut the rope tied to my bow. "Tell Drake I went to throw a rock and blow up the Armada to slow it down!"

They yelled, "What are you doing?"

"The bloody thing won't light. Get clear, I'll get the fire going if it's the last thing I do!" I yelled back.

They all yelled, "No, get back here, you can still get back!"

But it was too late. I had managed to pry the towrope's loop free with the boat's short, hooked knife. They started to slow their rowing. "Go!" I yelled. "You've got to get by them and send the warning. I'll swim back later." So they looked back forlornly and started rowing with all their might. I did a final bow and sat down adrift without a paddle as the Armada closed. "Shite, I forgot my rock!"

So as I sat there adrift without a plan, I realized I had just done several really, really, stupid things. Aside from forgetting my rock, I hadn't grabbed any water. "Water, water, everywhere, but not a drop to drink." See, I finally said that right. If I was left adrift, I was going to die of thirst, a most miserable death. Of course, when I finally lit this bloody thing up, I was going to blow myself up anyway. The Queen is going to be really pissed off at Drake, I thought.

"Well Alley Cat, looks like this is finally number nine," I said aloud.

I decided I might as well go out with a bang. I would wait till I drifted into one of their ships and light mine. It was actually my only chance. I would dive overboard and hope to get clear of the blast. Then I could swim and somehow catch one of their ships as it passed. There were a bunch of them. I would likely be captured, but who knows how Fate was going to play this one out. What could possibly go wrong?

I cut my length of match cord into shorter pieces. The knife was ridiculously dull. I cut off some of the pitch-soaked tarp. I placed it with one of the short pieces of match cord into the rest of the fire material. Hopefully, that will do it. I watched as my little crew's boat cleared the Armada's north arc, quite handsomely without me in tow. They had made it. It would still take time for them to get back to shore and then find someone to get the warning out to light the first beacon. I was just hiding under the black tarp bobbing along waiting for my prey. I kept peering out, as the ships lumbered ever closer. There was now one bearing down on me. So with a couple of Hail Marys, I tried to light the wick going to the pitch again. Nothing.

"Come on! Light damn it!" I said out loud in the middle of my prayers. "Oops, sorry, didn't mean to curse," I breathed, realizing I would probably be meeting Saint Peter any minute. I was truly hoping it would be Father McNee and maybe The Patrick. My boat bounced off the ship's side. I could hear exclamations from their crew, but they took no action. So I drifted on.

I decided to just light the damn thing any way I could whether I was next to a ship or not. I tried again, but still nothing. I climbed back under the tarp to the rear and found the gunpowder. I brought the keg forward and pulled the match cord wick out of it and poured some of the gunpowder onto one side of the pitch. Then I stuffed the keg under it on the other side. I wrapped the remaining match cord around the pitch. If I lit the gunpowder on one side of the wadding with the pitch it should finally catch on fire. If it did, I might have time to dive overboard before the keg exploded. I would wait until I bumped into the next ship.

A large galleon ship was bearing down on me. In fact, it looked like it was going to cut my boat in half. I again took my remaining burning match cord out of the tinderbox and then lit the gunpowder. This time fire sprang to life. I dove over the side. Bump. My little boat crashed into the port bow of the ship. I desperately tried to swim to the starboard side. As the ship lumbered past, I tried to reach anything I could on its side. There was nothing to grab. Then there was a thunderous explosion and the ship rocked toward me.

"Holy Shite!" I exclaimed as I remembered I was still praying. Miraculously, I managed to grasp some wooden maintenance footings on the hull at the rear and was able to pull myself on. I was then able to climb up and hide by the rudder.

I could hear excited voices and hoped I hadn't been seen. There was smoke bellowing from the deck above that had the smell of pitch. I realized I had just attacked a galleon ship of the Spanish Armada. "Boy, are they going to be pissed!" I breathed aloud. Then I added, "I'm not a ghost yet either, so that must have been only number eight." I looked up and saw the captain's cabin. Its windows were open overhead to let the summer air in. This ship didn't have a balcony around it like Drake's.

Well, I was getting thirsty, so this might be a good time to see if there was anything to drink. I also had to get out of sight before other ships spotted me. I was able to climb up remembering how I used to on the dwellings of London that did have balconies. I stopped by the open window and didn't hear anyone. I peered in and no one was inside. The captain was no doubt on deck putting out the fire. I flung myself inside and ran to the cabin door. I secured it with its bar. The captain's cabin is the most secure part of the ship. It was the safest place to barricade if under attack or mutiny. Then I looked around. It was time to think as fast as a dream again. I saw a leather pouch of water or wine, didn't matter, and grabbed it. I saw a chart on the table and grabbed it too, stuffing it down my shirt.

The only weapon I had was the hook knife with a wooden handle I used to cut the match cord. I had slipped it into my shirt earlier. Now it had slid down to my pants. This was a real good time to make an adjustment. Now what? This probably wasn't the best ship to try to hide out on, so I might as well set it on fire and dry off a bit. I looked at the captain's bed and drapes. Lots of things to burn. There were lamps filled with oil. I doused his mattress and the cabin walls. One lamp was already lit with a closed shade around it. I waited a moment, opened it, and then threw it on the pyre I had made. The flames took and climbed up the walls and drapes. Then there was loud banging at the door.

"Time to go," I said to myself. I hadn't really thought of this consciously, but I knew it was the same way I came in. Setting the captain's bed and cabin on fire along with more of his ship, probably would not improve my welcome if I were caught. As I started to climb back out the window, men were climbing down from above.

I yelled "Fuego!" and dove overboard as the fire or fuego chased me out the window. All the men saw as I flung myself out the window was a boy in black disappearing into the sea. I hit the water flat and it almost knocked me out, but at least it didn't rip my sawdust shirt off.

I floated dazed and looked like I was dead as the ship labored onward. No one fired a shot as they had no idea what I was as I bobbed away. I saw smoke coming out of the back of the ship, but the front fire seemed to be out. They no doubt thought the English were setting traps in the channel that would explode. As I started to dog paddle, I took inventory. I had the pouch and thank God it had water, so I took a small drink. I would have to ration it. I also still had the knife. It was a good thing I had repositioned it or I might be singing soprano.

As the ship sailed on, I looked to the north. I could see the coast. I could also see wisps of smoke coming up all along the way every so often heading to the east. *The beacon torches had been lit!* Their signal was on their way to Plymouth, London, and all of England! I didn't know if they had heard my explosion and seen the smoke first, or if our little watch boat had safely made it back already. Our little boat had in fact made it back. Ultimately it was Captain Thomas Flemyng that took his pinnace, the Golden Hind to Plymouth and reported the Armada's sighting. Now all I had to do was find another ship without being seen and board it.

Yah, I think this was back to be number nine as I swam in the infinite sea.

I was surrounded by the immense Armada. It was in a half moon shape with the heaviest war ships around the edges and leading the middle. No doubt the meaty ships of cargo, supplies and soldiers were those surrounding me now. They kept coming toward me. They seemed to be moving slower now, possibly because of the unexplained explosion. They also must have seen the smoke signals and figured out what they were. The sun was getting lower and made the sea glare. I saw something bobbing in the water. It almost looked like a small barrel or keg like the one my gunpowder had been in. I swam to it and held onto it. I could wrap my arms around it, and it gave me good cover.

"Many thanks Lady Fate, in case I haven't had time to mention it," I said to the sea.

Now I just waited for a ship. And there were still plenty of them. The ones in the center were one after another, but I realized even they would soon run out. The bright reflection and glare on the water also helped hide me. Fortunately, the lookouts were looking for English ships, not drowning alley cats. A large Spanish galleon finally was heading straight for me. I abandoned my barrel to swim to the ship. I tried to claw my way along the side hoping there would be something I could grab by the time I reached the rear. This was it, nine coming up! I didn't see ships behind it as the remaining ones formed another arc far to either side.

It really wasn't all that hard. There were lots of things to grab mostly for maintenance if repairs had to be made. There was even a small ledge along the bottom at the end. I was able to pull myself up and work my way to the rudder. There were two rear gun ports above just like on the Revenge. There was quite an overhang above it with several decks of cabins. Fancy, but no balcony. I could climb up to get to the gun ports. I peered in to find nobody was manning them. I climbed in and quickly found a place to hide. The mechanism that controlled the top of the rudder was a good hiding place. The ship looked like it was just built. The timber had that "new boat smell."

I had seen the name of the ship as it passed and caught enough of it to recognize some of its words. The name was "Nuestra Senora del Rosario." I knew the last part meant "Lady of the Rosary," or Mother Mary. I was saying Hail Marys which is a Catholic prayer as I was trying to save my life once again. Saint Patrick, Saint Bridget of Kildare, and of course Father McNee, were also on my short list to pray to. How strange I thought, the men on this ship were all probably saying the same prayer to Mother Mary.

"Hail Mary, full of grace, the Lord is with thee. Blessed art thou among women and blessed is the fruit of thy womb, Jesus. Holy Mary, Mother of God, pray for us sinners now and at the hour of our death, amen."

We were all praying for one common thing, to come back home. I didn't think it right to pray for my enemy's death though. That just seemed like blasphemy. It also occurred to me that for Elizabeth to win, thousands of their prayers would have to go unanswered. And mine was just one more lone prayer in a sea of thousands. So we sailed onward, and I rested like a scared cat with one eye open, praying.

Part 2 – First Engagement

When the signal and word reached Plymouth, legend has it that Drake was playing a game of bowls, which is kind of similar to bowling outdoors on the grass. He reportedly was to have said, "We still have time enough to finish our game and beat the Spaniards too." I don't know if he actually said that as I wasn't there, but it sounds like something he would do. He probably won, too!

The English fleet had one small problem, the tide and wind were against them and they would have to wait to sail out. They also had to quickly organize these almost sixty ships which were in port resupplying. I, of course, had no idea what was going on. We must have turned a slight bit to stay away from the coast because the cloudy sun no longer shined straight into the rear gun ports. We sailed on slowly till almost sunset and then dropped anchor as a storm came in.

We had stopped! The Armada would not have anchored if we were going into battle. I had sailed enough on the Revenge to figure how far we might have gone by now at this rate. We were still at least a day well west of the port of Plymouth. I knew part of Elizabeth's fleet would be there but didn't know if Drake was at sea or at port.

I could hear the men on the ship moving all around. This small two-gun deck was below the cribbing that held up the pulleys that swung the rudder's till. There were strong bulkheads that closed in this area. The galley or kitchen was probably above it. The captain's cabin was another level higher than the galley. Below me, no doubt was the magazine. This would be the number one target in case Drake dropped in to say hello. I sat there and considered how Lady Fate had such a humorous sense of irony, that she might well have Drake be the one to blow me up. Wouldn't that suck?

Why had we stopped? This made no sense. There was a storm, but we had sailed through far worse with Drake while I was on board the Revenge. I dared not peek out the gun port to see if I could tell anything. I had found a good hiding place. I was hiding like a cat up by one of the rudder pulleys on the starboard side. A soldier had come in earlier and looked out of one of the gun ports around sunset, probably to just get some air. The lower decks could be miserable with heat and humidity. He stayed for a while until another soldier joined him and they talked and laughed a bit. A third man stuck his head in and yelled at them and they left. As the evening set in, more men would come and go.

It got darker and darker, thank God, and it appeared there were not going to be any lights lit inside. At least the Spanish weren't so arrogant to light up their fleet. I might be safe till dawn. I heard a boat on the main deck being launched. I knew that sound from being on the Revenge. There are sounds unique to sailing ships just like you now have the distinct sounds of trains and planes. I love the sound of the rumble of a train, especially when they had steam. The sounds of these great sailing ships have long since passed.

Later, I heard the launch boat return and hauled back up on deck. I didn't know I had ended up on the flagship of squadron leader, Teniente General Don Pedro de Valdes. The 130-ship Armada was divided into ten squadrons. This was the Andalusia squadron. The fleet had stopped for a war council meeting with the squadron leaders and Commander Sidonia. The English Plymouth fleet was in terrible peril. They were trapped by high tide and the wind was against them to maneuver. If the Armada decided to attack Plymouth, they would discover the English fleet's plight. The Armada might destroy them in port if they came in with the tide. Fortunately, Sidonia decided to stick to the plan, which was to load Parma's army on his ships and take them to the Thames to attack London by land.

In the meantime, Howard was having his own war council. The first thing Elizabeth's fleet had to do is get out of Plymouth before they were trapped. The fleet would have to be towed out. Through the long night, ship-by-ship, they were brought out to sea by long lines of rowboats. The next key was to flank around the entire Armada and get behind them, so Howard had the wind at his fleet's back. This advantage was known as having the weather gage for attacking. The Armada would have to turn to engage them and fight into the wind.

The English fleet would have to tack against the wind to get around the Spanish. A sail ship cannot move forward against the wind. It can, however, "tack" the wind by shifting its sails back and forth in such a way that it can zigzag forward. To do this maneuver and get around the Armada with a fleet of ships, would be miraculous.

So the first evening I spent hiding in the rafters. The night was sultry. Men started drifting into the rear gun port deck to sleep. Between the sounds of the sea, the noise of the rudder mechanism, talking, snoring, farting, whizzing out the gun ports or into a bucket, I didn't have to worry about any sound I would make. After they finally seemed to sleep, I was able to take some sips of water and at least whiz down the wall. I mentioned earlier the ship had that new boat smell. I was referring to the wood. Aside from that it stunk like hell, so my wee-wee wouldn't matter. I also knew I wouldn't be eating for a long time, but I had gone days without food on the streets of London. I dared not sleep for fear they might find me. I was exhausted though and kept fighting to stay awake as the ship rocked back and forth.

I looked around in the dark. No one was stirring. I decided to hop down and see if there were better places in the ship to hide. And I was also just curious. I warily crouched down and moved with stealth, hugging the walls. I met another battle worn cat along the way and we hissed at each other. I stood my ground and then defiantly passed it. I wasn't looking for a fight, but I wasn't going to run either. He followed me until I snuck by other men and went down into the holds. I might find something to eat after all.

One man saw me as I tried to slip by him. He said something in Spanish, but I only recognized the word "gato," as he reached out to stroke me. I hastened my trot. I could hear rats too, lots of them, too many of them. I remembered the other battle worn cat I had seen and knew all too well what it was like to go into battle with a rat. I decided maybe I should go back to the gun port before I got totally lost or injured. I had seen enough. There were supplies and weapons everywhere, which was great for moving around while staying hidden. There were also men everywhere trying to find someplace to lie down and sleep. Those that saw me did not take offensive action. At least these Catholics weren't killing us as mediums or familiars of witches anymore, as they had centuries ago.

I made it back to my perch above the rear gun port and hid. Then nothing. Nothing happened. The men started stirring, got up, or were chased out in the morning. I realized I must have fallen asleep after all. The Armada was again lumbering slowly on and was headed east with the same southwest wind blowing it. All the men finally left. I snuck down to the gun ports and refilled my pouch from a barrel of water and took a long drink. I looked out and saw nothing but Spanish ships around me. I was in awe at the magnitude and terror of the sight. A soldier came in and I froze looking out the gun port. He started talking and I started retching out the back. I put my hand up behind me waving him back. He just laughed and left. I shot back up to my hiding place and stayed put.

Where was Drake? When was the battle to begin? I was trapped and I knew what a cat felt like in a cage. I had nothing to do, so I took out my hook knife. I started to cut at the rope holding the pulley to the hull that had the steering cable running through it. It had almost no effect, as the blade was worn, and the tip had long snapped off. Still, I just kept cutting to keep busy. If I managed to cut the pulley free, the ship would have no steering. The day passed. The sea got rough and there was rain. Men came and went. I kept cutting with seemingly no progress.

I thought of what I had seen on the ship during the night as a P`uca (Pooka). My Prince Enros could become a shape-shifting P`uca as a cat. I know because I had seen it in his dreams. I also wondered if my P`uca might have taken a poop, as I no longer had the need. Fortunately, I had no recollection of any of that bit, but I did have a rather odd taste on the tip my tongue in the morning. I drank more water. We sailed on. Still nothing. Where is our fleet? Did they forget about the Armada? Were we even up to Plymouth yet?

Finally it was evening again. It was much the same routine as the night before. We again stopped. I was giddy and exhausted. I was cramped and aching from hiding. Once again, the men found places to lie down and try to sleep. I feared falling asleep and being caught. I kept nodding off and fought to stay awake. Then, once again I remember exploring the ship.

This time I remember seeing the lower gun decks and their huge cannons. They weren't the same as our cannons. First their gun carriages were larger with only one pair of huge wheels rather than four small wheels like ours. I thought the two guns where I was hiding odd, but it seemed all their cannons were like this. How on earth did they pull them back far enough to swing them to load them? There were also supplies stored all around them in the way. I again thought it was best to return to my perch.

Then I woke with a start. There were noises again with the men stirring as the sun first announced the beginning of July 21st. Well, actually it was July 31st since I was on a Spanish boat. I realized I again must have gotten some sleep undetected. I hoped the men would leave soon. I hoped there would be a battle soon. It was the only hope of getting back to one of my own ships. Where were they?

I got my wish. The men left and I was alone again. I had to move, so I again snuck down for water and then sprang back up to my perch behind the bulkhead wall. Well, I didn't spring, I could barely move I was so cramped up. So I went back to whittling on the rope holding the pulley to the hull. Shortly after, men rushed back in and I froze thinking they had seen me earlier. They looked out the rear gun ports exclaiming things in Spanish I didn't understand. It occurred to me I should have tried to learn a little more Spanish rather than swimming and riding on holiday. I didn't actually think I would ever meet any of the enemy, just maybe fire a cannon at them. Besides, I doubted there were many Spanish teachers on the Lizard.

They also loaded both guns! They did not do it as efficiently as my gun crew! They were looking out the back excited, so that meant our fleet was behind them and we would have the advantage of the weather gage. I assumed the English fleet had come out of Plymouth after the Armada had passed. But we weren't up to Plymouth yet. Howard and Drake's ships had, in fact, somehow miraculously tacked the wind and flanked behind them through the night! And now our fleet had the advantage of the wind at their backs to attack. My pulley was getting rather active, as the ship was doing more steering movements now rather than just trudging along.

After what seemed like an eternity, I finally heard the first cannon shot. It must have been midmorning by now. Shortly after, another one fired but not from the same place. My pulley immediately started singing and I could feel our ship turn. I could hear excited voices all around me on the ship. I waited and wondered why there weren't any more shots. Was the first an act of chivalry throwing down the gauntlet from Howard's fleet? The second one was likely a signal from the Spaniards to turn and form up for battle. Then all hell broke loose. I heard multiple broadsides being fired. We had only fired one cannon at a time for practice on the Revenge. A broadside was deafening.

Broadside after broadside and multiple cannon fire continued on and on. The smell of smoke and gunpowder filled the sea. I had no idea who was winning. I had no idea how many were dying. Our ship was making vague maneuvers, but we weren't engaging. We weren't firing. The men by the rear guns had left. I was alone again. Though this ship certainly had many guns, it must have been held back to protect the transports in the center. Men would come and go, and I dared not climb down to look as the day raged on.

It was already afternoon and I did finally sneak down because I just had to have a look see. I made sure my rosary was outside my shirt. I peered out the gun ports. There were lots of Spanish ships, but the battle was in front of us. I didn't see any of our ships. I thought I might dive overboard to escape, but there was nothing to escape to. I looked out the gun port while leaning over the huge, loaded cannon. It would be like shooting geese in a barrel. I saw their tinderbox with the match cord. It was smoldering inside. I picked it up and was ready to prime and fire when I stopped. I looked at the match cord and looked up.

What would happen if I were able to burn through the heavy rope cable securing the pulley to rip it free? The cables running through it from the ship's steering wheel above would lose control. The rudder would go limp. They wouldn't be able to control the ship from crashing into all the other ships surrounding it. I decided there was no time to dilly-dally. I managed to cut a small length of their match cord off from the burning end. I scrambled back up to my steering pulley and held the burning end of the match cord to the rope cable and frayed ends I had been cutting earlier. They smoldered and I started cutting again as the rope started to burn. The embers eventually went out, but I had made incredible progress. No one would notice the smell of the smoke I made either.

The battle raged all around me out of my sight. I could tell we had changed course several times. There were some extremely close cannon shots now, and I couldn't tell if we were firing, or being fired at. I cut and cut harder and harder while I used the match cord to help burn the cable. I considered going down and grabbing some gunpowder, but men were scurrying in and out looking out the gun portholes. It was getting cloudy out and I wondered if that was strictly from the cannon smoke, or if the weather was changing. The ship was starting to roll more so it must have been both.

The rope cable holding the pulley was near through. It was cutting more easily now as it was stretching apart. I didn't want it to snap while there were soldiers below me, so I would wait till I was alone again and try another frantic attempt. I had already decided if I succeeded, I would jump down and dive out the gun portal on my side. They would figure out it had been cut and finding me at the same time would not be pleasant. I was waiting for a soldier to leave. I thought if the rope finally snapped, the pulley might fly by and hit him in the head. Or if it at least distracted him, I might make it to the gun port. The only weapon I had was the dull hook knife. Then I flinched as I heard one massive explosion and thought a ship must have blown up. I hoped it was an English cannonball that had found its mark. Then I considered it could be us next time.

'Leave, just leave,' I prayed. And then he quickly did. I cut as hard as I could and held the last of the burning match to it.

Twang, Wumph. My keyboard scribe couldn't find any better words either, let alone how to spell them. Probably could throw in some clunks, too.

Twang, Wumph, as the rope snapped, and the pulley crashed its way across the gun galley. I froze there stunned for a second realizing it had worked! "GO!" I yelled to myself as I leaped down from behind the bulkhead. I hadn't hit the deck before the ship swung to starboard throwing me down as I landed. I picked myself up and crawled out through the gun port and dived overboard. I hit the water and tried to swim to the back of the ship. It was slowly rotating away from me as I tried to grab onto something and look for a better place to hide in this immense sea.

Then there was a loud crash followed by the sound of splintering wood. The Rosario had collided into the side of another ship. They twisted around and groaned with the sound of timbers snapping and splintering. The sudden stop allowed me to grab the back of the ship and try to work my way to its side. The two ships tore apart and the Rosario slowly floundered away from the Armada. The front bowsprit, that holds the front sail over the bow, had been torn off on impact. It wrapped around the front starboard side of the ship. Pieces of the bowsprit's sail were dragging along with ropes and rigging still clinging to the ship.

I let go of the end and let the ship's front rotate to me. I slipped into the pile of dragging rigging and sail, unnoticed amongst all the debris that was floating in the sea. The sea was also getting rougher, but this debris from the collision offered excellent cover. As I clung to the wreckage, Rosario's crew was desperately trying to secure the front mast from breaking. All its forward rigging was ripped away when the front bowsprit was torn off, and this had damaged the front mast. Now the rigging behind it from the main mast pulled back on it. The wind was blowing into it too. There was no way to control the ship's heading, so all the sails had to be lowered and secured. The anchor would be all they had to try to hold her.

The ship was like an angry hornet's nest of activities with orders being shouted. More soldiers had come on deck too, not wanting to be below in case the Rosario was attacked or went down. This was a much larger ship than Drake's Revenge and I was astonished how many men were on board. There were far more than Drake's, and we had a crew of 250 (plus me). The sea was getting rougher and I was being buffeted about holding on for dear life. The rigging was a lifesaver, but at the same time it could pull me under.

Then we hit another ship and the front mast finally gave way. It crashed back into the main mast damaging it too. I was slowly watching the ship die. Two Spanish patache-type ships approached. These are small ships with two sails good for fast maneuvering. They have shallow drafts. They make excellent communication boats. The Dutch use similar boats they call "flyboats," but theirs are used as combat ships. The English call their similar ships the already mentioned pinnaces, though they could include smaller single mast ones too. One of the pataches shouted across to the Rosario, and after a while left.

A huge galleon came up and tried to get a rescue line over to the Rosario, though the sea was too rough. They managed, but then the line broke. I could hear the exchange between the two ships, but of course, I couldn't understand any of it in Spanish. Though I didn't know it, the ship was the San Martin, the very flagship of the Duke Sidonia himself. It gave up and left. After a bit more, the other small ship left after having had some men transferred to it on the other side. Fortunately, the rigging I was clinging to was keeping the visiting ships generally on the opposite side.

While all these activities were occurring and the small ship assisting left, I realized the battle had stopped. The cannon fire had ceased. The sea was getting rougher and the sun would soon be going down. We were adrift and alone. As I watched this drama and realized how much damage I had done, I had my own drama occurring. I was starting to drown. I barely had strength to hold on anymore. I had tucked my rosary back in my shirt so I wouldn't lose it. Now my shirt had been ripped open and most of the sawdust was gone. My water pouch had ripped free a long time ago. I was constantly spitting out seawater each time I got dunked. I decided my only chance was to try to climb on top of what was left of the front dragging sail. I'd best plan for a surrender.

With great difficulty I managed to climb up on the "yard" timber where the bow's sail was still partially attached. This timber and the rigging made a bit of a raft which I had been clinging to from underneath. Exhausted, I laid on it and held on. I made sure the chart I had taken was-well hidden in my pants. I looked about at the Rosario and toward the Armada. It was moving on the horizon, and likely our ships were following it. I realized the Armada had sailed away and abandoned us. 'Guess this was number nine after all,' I thought. About that time, the men on board started shouting and pointing at me. 'Great, maybe I can get rescued by a sinking ship,' I told myself.

Part 3 – Rescued

So I tried to sit up and start waving frantically and yelling the few words I had learned in Spanish along with the same in English. "Ayuda, ayuda, help! Catholic, I'm Catholic. Cabin boy, grumete. Help, Ayuda!" I kept yelling and waving. "Irish!" I threw that in too.

They motioned to me to try to climb up closer on the dragging rigging and someone threw out a rope. They yelled something in Spanish and made gestures like I was to tie it around me. I was able to grab it and secured it to myself. They motioned for me to come toward them, so I got up close to the hull as they pulled in the slack. If I fell back into the sea, the rigging might crush me between it and the hull. They signaled me to jump across closer, so I leaped toward them. They pulled up on the rope and I bounced off the hull as they pulled me up onto the main deck.

"Gracias, gracias. Agua, agua por favor," I gasped thanking them and asking for water. The decks were crowded even though the main mast might come crashing down. A soldier gave me a cup of water and I drank. I gagged at first drinking it too fast. I drank more slowly the second time he offered it to me. It had a different taste and I didn't know if that was because I still had the taste of seawater I had been constantly spitting out, or if it was because it came from Spain.

A priest worked his way through the men around me and asked me with a Spanish accent, "Are you English?"

"No father, I'm Irish, an indentured cabin boy, a grumete," I answered not knowing how much English the father knew. I had spent the last two days figuring out what I was going to claim, or lie about, if I was caught.

"How did you get here, what ship were you on and what happened to it?" the priest now inquired.

"The captain threw me overboard. He hated me because I'm Catholic and Irish. You can see how he's whipped me," I replied as I started spinning my tale and pointed to my scars from Topcliffe below my rosary.

"What ship, who was the captain, why did he throw you overboard?" the priest now asked in rapid succession.

"The Dreadnought, it was Captain Beeston. He threw me overboard because I cheered a Spanish ship for blasting us good. I grabbed some timbers and have been floating ever since. I floated into your wreckage and was able to pull myself up. Many thanks for saving me. Gracias. Are we going to die? Is your ship sinking?" I asked. I had met Captain George Beeston at Drake's party and knew of his ship. He's a fine a gentleman as can be. He ended up being knighted for his action against the Armada.

"No, boy, we're not going to sink, God is with us. What is your name? My name is Father Diego."

"Robert, Robert Doyle, Father, I'm from near Smerwick in Munster, Ireland." I knew the priest would know that village. It is where the Spanish and Vatican forces lost the battle and surrendered during the second Munster rebellion before they were all massacred by Raleigh.

He cursed the English and as he did, I realized that I should be cursing those English forces that had brought so much death to Ireland too. I also realized all these men were probably going to die because of my hand. I also knew I was going to join them in the ever-blackening sea. The sun had set, and the darkness buffeted the ship like the ocean around us. What had I done? But then I remembered we were at war and I had chosen my side. What did I think was supposed to happen? And here this priest and the soldiers were helping me. I was too exhausted to feel anything. I just wanted to stop thinking.

I tried to stand just to see if I still could. About then, some commands came down and the priest asked if I was able to walk. It seemed their captain wanted to see me. We went up on the quarterdeck behind us where he was overlooking the attempts to secure the main mast. He had a short conversation with the priest no doubt finding out what I had said. I doubted I was much of a priority.

Then to my surprise, the priest introduced their commander to me, "This is General Don Pedro de Valdes, the squadron commander. He welcomes you."

I was stunned, and even more so when the General addressed me in English, "I understand you have been abandoned in the sea. It seems we both have that in common. You must need drink and food. The priest will take you to my quarters and see to your needs. I will speak with you at a later time."

"Many thanks. Gracias General, you are most kind," I replied not knowing the proper way to address him especially since I didn't catch half his name. "Gracias."

He then gave instructions to Father Diego and I was escorted to his cabin. His quarters were quite lavish and there was a cabin boy that set about taking care of my needs at the direction of Diego. He was about my size and found some plain dry clothes for me. I was taken to a small quarter with a bunk. I changed trying to keep the map hidden in my wet pants. I was exhausted, but equally hungry and was grateful for food, water and even wine. Well, at least I'm going to drown in style I thought, and I couldn't believe my luck.

Father Diego came in and told me the priests on board were holding Masses, taking Confessions, and offering Communion. He was to see to my needs and ensure I received the same. The last Catholic services I had been at were the ones I had done before Father McNee went to his rest. I was grateful, especially since we were all likely to drown. The Confession was a double-edge sword though. I might be responsible for the deaths of these hundreds, but this might not be a good time to mention that to the commander's priest.

I fully appreciated the phrase, "The devil's in the details," as I gave summary of sins in my Confession. I mentioned that I had lied, but not what those lies were. I said I was fighting in a war and I might cause the death of others, without mentioning that meant everyone on this ship. I had long since prayed for forgiveness for the thieving and other things I had to do to survive alone on the streets of London and saw no reason to bring them up again. I felt peace in my heart, so I was grateful to receive Communion.

Father Diego told me to rest. I was immediately out like a light as I was so exhausted. I slept deep and only woke when I heard two cannon blasts from the Rosario. It took a moment to figure out where I was, and I decided that it must be part of some strange dream and promptly fell back to sleep. I would learn later the blasts I had heard were in response to a small ship firing off muskets. They had requested the Rosario to surrender. Needless to say, they didn't stick around after they were answered with cannon shot.

I was sitting at a desk in a comfortably cluttered study. There was a brown tabby cat sitting on my lap. I realized I was recording an account of the battles with the Armada. I didn't have quill or pen though. Instead, there was a flat instrument that had rows of buttons on it. Each button had a letter, number or symbol. I didn't recognize all the symbols. I was also looking at a window's glass plate in front of me that covered the parchment I was recording the story on. If the buttons were played on the instrument, letters, and hence words, appeared on the covered parchment. It was wondrous, but its magic didn't seem a surprise to me.

There was also an object the size of a mouse that could be used to magically transform my parchment into a painting. Some of them were even moving paintings. As I looked around further, I saw scattered sheets of paper that had printing on them. There was another device that had more completed printed sheets in it. I surmised it must be some kind of printing press. There was also a model of a boat. It was the Revenge, sitting on top of it, but it wasn't painted correctly.

I started to read what I had written. I was telling about being rescued by the Rosario and was finally getting some much-needed rest. I was somehow writing an account of what was happening to me with these magical devices. Actually, I must have been rewriting it because there was much more beyond this page. I was about to start reading what was to happen next when I woke up.

In that brief moment as I woke, I remembered this strange dream before it faded into reality. I had been brought out of my sleep because the general wanted to see me. I stretched, shook off my dream, and was escorted on deck. The ship was still adrift and the glow on the horizon indicated there was a new day approaching. There were only a handful of men on the decks hidden from sight. There were also ships approaching.

"The English are coming," General Don Pedro calmly said. "I hope you received good rest and found our food acceptable."

"Yes, gracias General," I answered and without thinking added, "Will there be a battle?" Don Pedro de Valdes did not answer. He just studied what was coming while deep in thought.

I watched as they came closer and grew more recognizable. The ships were tacking against the wind, zigzagging back and forth coming back from the east. The general was right. They were English. No Spanish ship could sail like that! As their shape took more form, my heart began to soar. One shape was growing into the Revenge! The general's face was already ashen with resolve to save his ship, to save his men that had been abandoned by their own Armada. His lower gun ports were closed to prevent the sea from coming in. The next few moments were going to be critical. Did they know that was Drake coming for them? Was there going to be a battle? Were we going to be blown out of the water? Would the Rosario surrender? Would the Spanish soldiers try to overwhelm the Revenge? I had no idea what I should do, and because of that I decided I should let the adults sort this one out. After all, this wasn't the first time Drake had captured a ship.

The Revenge came along side with its gun ports open ready for a broadside. A voice boomed across the sea between us. "I am Francis Drake, and my matches are burning!"

Voices quaked in terror, "El Draque!" The name rolled like waves from the hidden men's mouths in a hushed fear except for General Don Pedro. He almost had a proud look on his face. I didn't know if that was a good sign or a bad one.

General Don Pedro de Valdes started giving orders. I did hear the word "render," which was another of the few Spanish words I had bothered to learn. The ships hailed back and forth as I watched from the deck. A flag of truce was raised, and the general went across in his deck's launch boat to the Revenge to negotiate. I could see Don Pedro and Drake talking. I held my breath. After a while, Don Pedro walked alone to the rail and stood for a while looking out over the vast sea. He returned to Drake and cheers rang out from the decks of the Revenge. He had surrendered!

I recognized Lieutenant Jonas Bodenham on the deck of the Revenge. He was the man who had welcomed me on board there almost three months ago. I started waving and yelled to him, "Presto, Presto!" and he looked toward me. "What took you so long?" I exclaimed.

I could see him look across to me with an astonished gesture. "Presto? You're supposed to be dead!"

"Sorry, but I am part cat remember," I replied and then added, "Though I think I've burned up ten lives by now."

"Don't go away, we'll make arrangements to get you," Bodenham yelled back.

"I don't really have any place else to go." I said as waves of shock overwhelming me. It was over! And I started to cry.

There were many activities that followed. The Rosario's launch boat returned with soldiers to start securing the ship. There would be hostages sent back over in it as further guarantee of their surrender. I was also to be sent over in the next trip. I was shaking now as I stepped down into the small boat that would take me from the Rosario. I needed help getting out as I stepped onto the deck of the Revenge. It was like a surreal dream. Jonas Bodenham separated me from the hostages and welcomed me.

He took me straight to Drake. "Alley Cat Presto, ninth class, at your service, Sir!" I greeted with a grin.

"You really are alive. I didn't believe what I was hearing. We had received a message that you drowned or blew yourself up with the warning boat. Wherever did you come from? Are you hurt?" Drake exclaimed as he greeted me.

"I came from Ireland, I thought you knew that." I answered still grinning. "Oh, you mean *now*. That's a bit of a story. I finally got the bloody warning signal to light as it bumped into one of their ships. I dove overboard and got away before she blew. I managed to get to the back of that ship and snuck on board. I climbed up into the captain's cabin and started a bit of a fire. Oh, and I stole a chart. It's hidden in my pants in one of the servant's quarters in General Don Pedro's cabin. He was kind to let me rest there after they rescued me."

I took a breath and continued, "Anyway, I didn't want to get caught on that first ship, so I jumped back overboard and drifted awhile in my sawdust shirt and a wooden keg Fate had sent me. I was able to grab hold and climb in the rear gun ports on this ship.

I've been hiding on it for two days now by the starboard rudder steering pulley. Took me till last afternoon to cut it loose with a dull knife and finally a match. You should have seen it fly! I dived out through the rear gun portal as the ship crashed and tore its front end off. I hung onto its debris till last night and then finally asked for their help. They were quite kind, though they didn't know what I had done. I met General Don Pedro and he had me taken to his quarters and fed me. Then, I finally slept till I was brought on deck and saw your ship coming!"

"You cut the rudder pulley loose," Drake repeated in disbelief.

"Aye, what else was I to do while hiding? Tell me about the battle. I heard it all day. I pray we didn't lose any ships. How many lost on both sides? Did we stop the Armada?"

"Slow down," Drake answered. "We did some damage. We didn't lose a single ship, but unfortunately, neither did they. This is the only ship we have captured all day. It is the flagship of the Andalusia Squadron," Drake paused and then added, "A dull knife and match you say? But are you injured? I'll see that you get anything you need in my cabin. I have quite a bit to take care of. You go rest up, that's an order!"

"Aye, aye Captain. And many thanks! You don't know how happy I am to see you. You are going to give them quarter, aren't you?" I asked remembering Smerwick. "Their men did help save me."

"Well, I really don't have the time to massacre them and I'd prefer to have more surrender without a fight. We need to learn as much as we can from this ship and see what is in her hold. Don Pedro will be quite valuable too. He will be staying in my cabin, so you'll have to entertain him till I get through."

"*Me?* But I don't know what I should say or do," I responded with alarm.

"Come now, you've had dinner with the Queen. You're clever, you'll think of something. Who else on board do you think knows what Alexander taught you? Just make him feel comfortable. I want to have a friendly relationship with him and find out as much as I can." Drake said with an encouraging grin and then hastily added, "I wouldn't mention the bit about wrecking his ship though."

With that I headed to Drake's cabin. I had never been more excited. Don Pedro had already been escorted there by Lieutenant Bodenham. Bodenham was glad to see me. He wanted to work with Drake on securing the Rosario. He didn't want to have the honor of watching the general. Don Pedro was a man of honor and was obliged to behave as a guest, and I would be his host.

Bodenham introduced me, "General Don Pedro, this is Master Presto, Sir Drake's assistant. He will see to your needs as best he can on a warship. I'm afraid we don't have quite the same comforts as your ship."

"Gracias Lieutenant. *At least you have sails*," Don Pedro answered. "I have met this lad, but I thought you were from a different ship?" he said as he looked at me puzzled.

"I will be happy to explain that to you General, but may I get anything for you first? Some ale, a morning meal possibly? Dawn has brought us a new day, and I've found it is good to take advantage of it when she is quiet. You must be exhausted as I was when you rescued me," I said, trying to move the conversation to gratitude and service rather than the lies I had first told. His English was quite remarkable, by the way. He thanked me and asked for something simple. The lieutenant left and made arranged to have ale, biscuits and cheese brought up.

After he left, I went into a chest that had finer porcelain plates and crystal for drinks I knew were for guests visiting on board. I set a place and I poured him some water. He asked if Drake was joining him. I told him I suspected Sir Drake would be occupied with securing his ship and everyone's safety for quite some time.

Don Pedro then beckoned me to join him. "I am confused as to how you ended up in the sea?" as he drank the water I had poured.

"Ah, English water. Please sit, you must be thirsty and hungry too. Tell me how you came to my ship."

"General," I began, "I'm afraid I must apologize for some things I told Father Diego that were not truthful. You saved my life and you and your crew were most kind. First there are truths that I did tell. I am Catholic. I am Irish, probably a product of the rebellions in Munster. I was given to a retired priest, Father McNee, when I was about one year of age. He raised and educated me and gave me my name, Presto, when I was baptized. He was not without humor and didn't know what to call me, so he picked Presto, because suddenly I was there. Everyone thinks it's my nickname, just like Sir Drake's is El Draque or The Dragon. I actually do have a nickname, it is Alley Cat, but that is another story. I simply make up a normal name for myself when I need to. It is less complicated and why I lied to Father Diego."

"I see, so you are an orphan of war then. Were you indentured into Sir Drake's navy?" Don Pedro asked.

"No General, it's far more complicated. I was to learn a trade on the sea after Father McNee passed on. I was to start as a cabin boy, of course, but it was all treachery from which I escaped. That is why I have the scars I bear. Sir Drake heard of my forlorn state and bold escape and took me in to continue my education. When I was drowning at sea I came upon your ship. I wasn't sure what would happen to me if I said I am part of El Draque's crew. I apologize for telling Father Diego that another English ship had thrown me overboard. Otherwise, I was afraid I might be thrown back overboard, and the sea around me was so terribly black."

"I think I understand your position, but I don't understand how you ended up in the sea. Does Sir Drake know you are still Catholic? I don't wish to say something inadvertently," the general said.

"Gracias General, but yes, Sir Drake knows I am Catholic," I replied as I took my rosary from inside my shirt and hung it out proudly. "As to being in the sea, I was ultimately trying to get to Sir Drake's ship to join him. The little boat I was traveling in was in rough waters and I ended up in the sea adrift and alone. I thought I would drown as no one could get to me. Fate sent me a barrel though to grab. The sea was filled with many things from the battle I could use to stay afloat, your ship being the largest. I again must thank you for taking me in and your hospitality, and again apologize for not being totally truthful." I had sincerely spoken the truth just then. I had however, like confession, carefully left out all the important details.

"You are indeed lucky to have survived, God has obviously been watching over you. I am happy I could be of help in his plan. He has a plan for all of us." Don Pedro said.

As the coming battles loomed ahead, it occurred to me what God's ultimate plan is for all of us. He is, eventually, going to kill us. I could have done without that epiphany. At least I think that's the correct word. My keyboard scribe's help is merely, "You wrote it, you're on your own. And you best not want to piss off the Big Man."

Our meager breakfast arrived, we said grace and ate. I suggested the clearly exhausted general rest. There was a clean full-sized bunk I usually used when I was on board. Drake's bed was a mess so I suggested the general get some rest in the clean one until I knew what arrangements would be made for his stay. I told him I would report back to Sir Drake and then return with any news as to his ship and men. He thanked me and exhausted, quickly found rest. There was a soldier stationed outside the cabin, so I told him the general was resting and I went to find Drake.

Drake had a busy morning. The Rosario had to be secured. It was literally a gold mine. It was carrying 50,000 ducats of gold to pay Parma's army. More important, it was carrying gunpowder, lots of gunpowder and shot. The first battle had used a major portion of the English ships' powder. Replenishing it was more important right now to stop the Armada than the gold found on board. The Rosario would be towed to Tor Bay in Devon west of Plymouth by the ship Roebuck. The Roebuck was with Drake's Revenge when he approached the Rosario. The captured 397-

man crew (which did include several officer's wives) were imprisoned at the Old Barn at Torre Abbey. This ancient stone barn is known as the haunted Spanish Barn to your day.

Word had got out that I was on the Rosario for two days and the crew was happy their Alley Cat had found his way back. After a day of battle the Rosario was the only ship taken. Drake's Revenge was the lead signal ship the previous night, following the Armada as it headed east. It was known the Rosario was left adrift. Drake put out his lantern and headed off to find her. Unfortunately, the English ships following the Revenge lost formation and had scattered through the night. Soon the Revenge would be ready to clip along again to find and rejoin its fleet.

I went up to watch the activities on the poop deck. Drake came up later and he told me the tales of battle that I could hear, but not see. He told me how Admiral Howard had tacked the wind and got around the Armada on the side open to the sea and attacked the heavily armed galleons on the southern defensive arc. Drake had eleven ships on the coastal side of the arc and attacked their north side. The strategy of blasting by, literally, in a single line formation had worked well. Their galleons were only able to fire a single broadside at the first ship, while taking a barrage of fire from the rest sweeping past. Problem was, they still hadn't got in close enough to do heavy damage or slow the Armada down. They had however, damaged Vice Admiral Martinez de Recalde's flagship the San Juan.

Drake had explored the Rosario and gained valuable intelligence. Aristocrats commanded Spanish ships with bureaucrats as advisors. The crews were composed of seamen who were below the rank of the soldiers. There were also many priests that held mandatory services daily. The soldiers were not adept at reloading their guns. The logistics of the cannon's materials was poor. There were not enough trained men to reload and fire them efficiently. The ship's crew was trained to grapple and board their enemy, and then fight a land war on deck. Much of this was generally known by the English, but to see into its actual shortcomings was of value.

The Rosario had not repaired the pulley I had cut loose, and the rudder had jammed so hard to starboard its hinges were damaged. The steering cables could not pull the rudder to port from the ship's wheel. So its till was tied to keep it straight when it was towed. Drake still couldn't believe the damage I had done with a match and knife. He also found the waterlogged map I had taken of interest. It was of the Flemish coast showing the sand bars and depths. This meant the first ship I had boarded was more interested in that coast than the English Channel they had just entered. If the Armada were going to try to take an English port, they wouldn't be studying a map of the hazards off the Netherlands' coast. This further supported Walsingham's intelligence that the Armada was headed to pick up Parma's army.

I found out later the explosion I heard was a Spanish ship that wasn't even engaged in the battle at the time. It ended up being the San Salvador. The magazine had exploded in the rear. We would learn the blast killed almost 200 men. The Armada rescued the rest of the crew but eventually set the San Salvador adrift with all the burned bodies and remaining injured men that could not be transported. The English fleet was able to eventually capture it and it still carried desperately needed gunpowder and shot in its front hold. In fact, between it and the Rosario, Howard's ships had captured about as much gunpowder as used in the first day's battle.

Drake sent me back to the general and told me to learn as much as I could. Don Pedro rested for a while and we spent the remaining afternoon talking. I told him his ship had been safely secured and was being towed to port by the honorable captain of the Roebuck.

He was vocally upset his ship had been abandoned by his commander, the Duke of Sidonia. He blamed his cousin Diego Flores de Valdez, who was the Duke's primary advisor on the San Martin. There was apparently bad blood between the cousins over the family's estate. He went into details about how the Armada had been grouped tightly partially due to his cousin's advice. This had contributed to two ships steering into him. I simply listened with sympathetic interest.

Don Pedro also was concerned about my soul and pointed out the papal bull ordered that I was to denounce the Queen or risk damnation. He did not understand why an Irish Catholic would fight against the Spanish.

"We will free you Irish from the boot of the English," he declared.

Now it was time for me to be delicate, as I wanted him to understand and trust me. I decided to respond truthfully. "My Lord General, the Irish do not wish to replace an English monarch with a Spanish one. The Irish will someday have their freedom from the English. I fear we would never have the strength to free ourselves from the Spanish. Like the English, you keep what you take. As to my soul, I am fighting for Sir Drake and our ship. He is my honorable friend and mentor. The papal bull does not say that as a Catholic, I can't fight against a Catholic country, whether France or Spain, to defend my own land. England is now my country and I'll get back to find freedom for Ireland later." I realized I had actually just spoken treason, and I wasn't doing it just for a show.

Though he didn't agree with my explanation, he did not hold it against me. I told him I was glad he and Sir Drake had reached an honorable agreement that avoided bloodshed. He said he had chased other ships away through the night and had stood ready to fight should the English try to take his ship. He might not be able to maneuver, but he was an armed floating fortress. The primary goal of ships fighting was to take them, not sink them. The English would have to use the Spanish strategy of boarding the ship and taking it by force. This would mean the English ships would have to endure broadsides to get close enough to grapple and then fight Don Pedro's well-trained army on board. The English would have to pay dearly to accomplish this and it would have taken some of their ships out of position for future battles. The only reason he surrendered was because it was to the Knight Sir Francis Drake.

We had finally gotten underway. It was a beautiful day for sailing. It was a day without battle. We found our fleet had regrouped and was now giving chase to the Armada headed east. There are historians that say Drake's departure from the fleet and going on a treasure hunt jeopardized defeating the Armada. First off, they are forgetting Fate always offers opportunities that in the end, if followed, determine the outcome. Most battles are not determined by brilliance, but usually unforeseen luck, or who screws up the most, which the Spanish were doing quite well. Nothing had been gained after a day's battle. Nothing would be gained again if it were repeated the next day. The English fleet regrouped and got some gunpowder resupplied thanks to Drake and the Spanish. We also had a day to recover from battle, not that there was any time for rest. For those armchair historians, I have two words, "Bite Me!" You weren't there! Besides, I preferred not drowning and becoming a ghost again.

Part 4 – Portland Bill

We caught up with our fleet and the Armada headed toward Portland Bill on the coast. We would prepare for another battle the next day on Tuesday the 23rd. On the night of the 22nd, the wind died, and the sea became calm. Drake had taken Don Pedro to the Ark Royal to report to Lord Howard and plan their next strategy. Howard was concerned the Armada might try to take an English port. They had passed by Tor Bay without taking action. This was much to his relief since he was one of three ships that could defend it when they passed.

The previous night had little moon over a misty sea. When Drake left formation, Lord Howard caught up to a stern lantern that he followed through the night. He assumed it was Drake's. As the sun came up, about the same time Drake would have been approaching the Rosario, Howard realized he had been following the Armada's stern lantern. He had three ships against their roughly 125. Howard's fleet was scattered to the west of him just on the horizon. Oops, *awkward!*

Howard turned about and tacked back toward his fleet. Oddly, the Spanish did not come after him though they clearly saw him. The Spaniards would have to try to give chase by tacking the wind too, but they would be no match for Howard's fast and skilled Ark Royal. The Spaniards did have four galleasses that had oars in addition to sails that could have given chase effectively. However, Lord Admirals were supposed to fight each other, and the Duke of Sidonia must have wanted to keep that honor for himself.

So that morning the fleets lined up thusly. The Armada was passing Tor Bay. Howard was immediately behind. His fleet was scattered behind that. Drake was with the Rosario and would have to sail hard all day to catch up. And lastly, the Roebuck would tow the Rosario with 396 prisoners to Tor Bay.

Interestingly, when Howard wrote his reports weeks later, he mentioned he had stared down the Armada with only three ships. He seemed quite proud. Howard also knew all his captains were basically like independent cats. In the end, this was the one thing the Spanish could not overcome. In the Spanish fleet, Sidonia sent a message by pataches or pinnaces, to all of his ships after the first battle. Any captain who did not remain in formation would be hanged, immediately. The Spanish Armada was not Spanish. It was a coalition of many Catholic countries, all mostly under the boot of Phillip. These ships included Spanish, Portuguese and Italian ones from Naples, Venice, Genoa and Sicily.

Howard was concerned there might be a chance the Armada would try to take Portland Bill the next day. He had an even greater concern the Armada might try to take the Island of Wight beyond that, the following day. That would give them a safe harbor in its bay, the Solent, until it was ready to meet up with Parma's army on the Flemish coast. It would be the last English harbor he could use.

I was pacing like a cat in a cage as I pondered going into battle for the first time. I waited for Drake's return from the Ark that night. Since I had been trained in all positions to fire the cannons, I expected that I would be used there. Drake had second thoughts.

He told me, "Her Majesty will skin me if I get you killed a second time. We already sent dispatches to Walsingham earlier. We had included you were killed trying to warn us of sighting the Armada."

"And where is safe?" I replied. "Where is there a place on a ship going into battle that is safe from a cannonball that Fate has inscribed your name? I spent two days on the Rosario hiding from the battle. I'm not doing that again."

"You'll do as I say," Drake said sternly. "I'll lock you in the hold if need be. The wind has stopped. When it picks up, it will probably come in from the northeast and the Armada will have the weather gage. We will be fighting into the wind. They will have the advantage."

"And you will need everyone to work the sails to fight them. You've trained me for the gun crew. I *am* part of your crew. You're not going to lock me up and you know it. Let me do my duty. Let me work the gun crews on the quarterdeck. I'll be right under your eye. If I fail in my duties, you can order me below."

Drake looked at me as he remembered how many times he had been in battle and his first one. He knew I had to fight, but also realized I hated to have to fight. "Alright, but don't try to do some heroic stupid thing. Just do your duty and follow orders."

"Aye, aye, Sir. I won't let your crew down and many thanks, Sir. Shake?" I said as I extended my hand.

Captains give orders, they don't shake hands to acknowledge them. He stared at my hand and finally gave it one shake while he shook his head. "Don't forget to keep your dagger at your side. Now get some rest, that's an order. Besides, your pacing is driving me mad."

The wind did return by morning and Drake was right, it was against us. The Armada galleons could turn on us this time and have the wind to their back to attack. The only good thing about it was that the Armada's relentless eastward progress was now sailing into the wind, and that made it impossible for them to advance up the channel.

We were off Portland Bill as we readied for battle. They were coming to us. The Spanish galleons on the crescent's horns were turning to take up offensive positions. The initial battle involved Howard's fleet on the coastal side. This was the only time the Spaniards had the advantage of the wind. Shots were fired, but nothing was really accomplished. Even with the wind, the Armada was unable to get close enough to grapple and board. Then late in the morning, the wind turned around and we could finally position for a healthy attack.

Drake was on the seaward side this time. This was opposite of the first battle near Plymouth. I was on the quarterdeck with our cannons loaded. *The Spanish cannons were loaded too.* The galleon we were about to engage was huge. It may have been the Armada's Vice Admiral's ship, The San Juan. It had far more firepower. We closed on each other waiting to fire. My heart froze in my chest as I tried to prepare for the first full broadside to be fired. I flinched from the roar of our cannons when we fired ours first. Now we were a heartbeat away from the Spanish lighting theirs.

I stared motionless waiting for that moment, but then I remembered I had a duty to perform. Our cannon had fired and recoiled back. It had been pulled back further so it could be shifted slightly to make room for the ram. One of my gun crew, Peter, rammed the wet swab down to clean the barrel and put out any burning embers before I was to load the pouch of gunpowder. Failure to put out all burning embers would result in a really bad hair day. I placed my charge into the muzzle while Peter flipped his ram around and shoved the gunpowder down the barrel. As soon as his ram was out, the cannon ball was added and rammed down with some wadding to keep it from rolling back out.

Then the gun was turned back and run out the gun port by the brute strength of the rest of the gun crew on the ropes and pulleys. The charge was punctured and primed while the gun was aimed and finally a burning match cord held in a linstock stick ignited it.

The linstock kept you more than an arm's length away when lighting the charge. You better be in the clear when it fires because the heavy gun is going to recoil back against its ropes and smash you like a bug if you're in the way.

There was no time to watch the Spanish galleon fire its first broadside or see where their cannon balls roared. Their broadside fired just as I was waiting to load the gunpowder pouch into the muzzle. I flinched again as I held the pouch of gunpowder in my hands, knowing what one spark would do. I continued with the next task of readying the cannon ball. It was also my responsibility to make sure I closed the magazine box tight after I removed each gunpowder charge to load. I was taught that you generally only forget once. I don't know where the enemy's broadside went. There were so many new noises, I didn't know if we were hit or not. I didn't know if we hit them. I heard men yelling, but not screaming in pain.

And then we were upon another ship and we fired just as they fired. Drake was leading the charge, of course. We constantly fired and reloaded, fired and reloaded. Then there might be a reprieve as we maneuvered and danced with an enemy ship to get in position to do it all over again. The roar of all the ships around us firing was horrific. Our shot and powder had to be restocked too. This was normally one of the jobs of the youngest seaman like me. On the other hand a stronger soldier not adept at seamanship or firing a gun could carry far more.

This game of tag went on all day. During the reprieves as we repositioned for the next attacks, I could look over the rail to see what damage was being done. I looked at our ship and didn't see any serious damage. In fact I didn't see much of any damage on any of the ships around us whether enemy or not. Late in the afternoon, Admiral Howard tried to position the fleet in a battle line for a final assault, but then decided not to follow through. We had not scattered the Armada and we had done little damage now with two days of engagements. It was time to try a new strategy. The day's battle was done.

I smelled like gunpowder and was blacked with soot. My hands and face were sore from burns and abrasions. Not bad really compared to being smashed by our cannon or hit by a cannon ball. I was exhausted. We were all grateful to clean up a little though salt water was a real eye opener. I was hungry but almost too exhausted to eat. At least I had the cabin in which to rest. There are some advantages to being a cabin boy though I was more officially an alley cat.

I hadn't really had time to watch Drake during the battle. I was too busy with the cannon and he was busy commanding the crew's actions. He came through the decks after the battle and spoke with each crewmember telling each of us that we had fought well. When he came to me, I hadn't cleaned up yet. He smiled and extended his hand to shake. I put out mine and he simply said, "Well done Presto, *well done.*"

Part 5 – Isle of Wight

We all knew there would be another battle the next day. We all knew we hadn't stopped the Armada despite our best efforts. The next battle was far more ominous and critical. It would be for the Isle of Wight. Drake left for another council of war with Admiral Howard and other captains. They had decided to try a nighttime attack to break up the Armada's formation. Nighttime attacks were basically unheard of. Problem was the wind died down and both fleets just floated about with the sea in a slow easterly direction.

In the morning, Drake had the seaward side of the Armada while Howard had the coast. The wind finally came up for a couple hours for a brief battle. A Spanish galleon, the Gran Grifon straggled behind on the seaward side of the Armada. Drake went after it and he and his fleet gave it several broadsides before the San Juan and several other galleons joined the fight. I was once again working the quarterdeck cannons. This time the Armada's cannonballs were hitting us. Halfway through the battle, as I was loading our shot, a ball exploded the top rail above my head. It showered me, and the rest of our cannon crew, with chards and splinters of wood.

Fortunately, no one was hurt other than some minor cuts. All I know, is it scared me enough that I wouldn't need to go pee again for the rest of the battle. This was a newer type of fear. I had been in peril many times before and, of course, was in utter terror each time. That fear was different because I was still in control of actions that would affect the outcome. I could think at the speed of a dream, and thanks to Fate, prevail. Here, I had no control. I couldn't think my way out of what was to come. Now it was strictly up to Fate with no paths to choose from.

It was a very hot battle. The Spanish Gran Grifon was taking severe damage. Now for the first time I heard men not just yelling but screaming. It was the screams of the banshee. The Gran Grifon was finally rescued and towed by the Spaniard's galleasses ships. The Armada had four of this type of ship. It was the first time I had seen one up close, too close. It was like a heavily armed galleon, but it had huge oars like a Viking ship so it could maneuver without the wind. Galley slaves did the rowing. Sadly, as we fired shot into them, we might be killing English slaves, just like the ones that would have been captured from Hawkins and Drake's fleet at Veracruz twenty years earlier. Not that any of them would have survived till now.

As I fired my cannon at the galleass, I had an epiphany regarding slaves. I realized, as an awakening, that those slaves in the galleasses, whether English or from Africa, were not "legal" slaves. There is no such thing as a legal slave. I also now knew they all had souls. I could feel them and hear their cries. I now understood every man, woman and child, and probably cat, had a soul. But I had no time to think of souls, I had a duty with my cannon.

This time Drake was getting in a lot closer and we took a hit to the yard timbers holding the lower sail to the main mast. As it crashed down close to me and the quarterdeck, any notion the Revenge was immortal passed. The damage seriously cut down on our maneuverability. Fortunately, that was about the time the wind again went calm and the battle basically came to an end. Perfect for a ship of 250 men to make repairs. You don't sail around the world without knowing how to fix your boat. I watched and learned but was glad I didn't have to do any of the climbing for repairs. The Armada Vice Admiral's San Juan had taken far more severe damage on the first day's battle. It had been repaired and was firing at us the following day at Portland.

Howard's fleet had now grown to over a hundred ships as more joined from ports up and down the coast. There was also another fleet based out of London under Captain Henry Seymour guarding Dover and the entrance to the North Sea. Admiral Howard had sent out small ships up and down the coast to request gunpowder and shot to continue the fight. The Privy Council in London had also sent dispatches to those ports that had been cleared by the Armada. They wanted them to send their powder to defend London. Though they probably hadn't received London's dispatches, the ports sent everything they could muster to Howard.

It was also time for a new strategy, so Howard once again called for a war council. With over 100 ships now, he decided to break his ships into four, about equal size fleets. That way each could work independently to take opportune advantages to break up the Armada or assist each other. He made two new Rear Admirals. John Hawkins would be one commanding from the Victory. Martin Frobisher would be the other commanding from the Triumph.

Martin Frobisher was of the same mantel as Drake and Hawkins. He had sailed with both. He had started as a cabin boy on ventures to West Africa. Later, he would do privateering in the Narrow Sea, or as you now call it, the English Channel. Eventually he would captain unsuccessful ventures to the New World to find the Northwest Passage to the Pacific Ocean. Unfortunately, luck was rarely with him. His ventures had not brought him wealth like Drake and Hawkins. He was an excellent, bold captain though, and now in the service of the Queen. He had fought gallantly during the previous battles. Did I mention he was a bit of a hot head too?

The four fleets were lined up to fight in the following way, assuming the wind would ever come back. Frobisher would have his fleet on the southern coastal side of the Isle of Wight. Howard and Hawkins would take the center behind the Armada. Drake would again take up position on the seaward side furthest to the south. In the calm of the night, the Spanish and English ships had all drifted east past the west entrance or narrows to the channel between the isle and the mainland.

We were all just south of the Isle of Wight come morning. Now all we needed was the wind for battle. The strong tide was also critical. In the morning it would flow into the east end of the bay and would be the only time the Armada could enter with the tide. If they did, they could easily take the Isle of Wight that had limited defenses against such a huge force. They would then have the safe harbor of the Solent, while waiting until they heard from Parma. I never did understand how they planned to get out of the bay with the English fleet blocking it. On the other hand, the Spanish would have a 20,000-man army on English soil and what if they decided to use them to take a hike to London? I figured the grownups knew what chess game they were playing.

There would essentially be three separate major battles occurring. I only witnessed the one on the seaward side with Drake's fleet. I would learn of the other battles the next morning. Each admiral would write his own account. I'll try to tell it to you in the order it happened, though the events overlapped.

The first action or smoke I saw was from the center behind the Armada. There was still no wind and we were drifting toward the east inlet with the tide's current. Once again there were Spanish stragglers that had fallen behind. In this case there were two. Hawkins went after them by using rowboats to drag him into position to attack. It might seem to be a lack of chivalry to attack loners, but there is a simple strategy. The Spaniards will respond by sending their ships for relief disrupting the formation. This will bring ships to battle and bring on a melee like we had done the day before. That's why we were there, after all. And a melee it became. The Spanish sent their galleasses in and Lord Howard brought in some of his ships by rowboat too. The Spanish probably got the worst of it again.

In the meantime, Frobisher's fleet was between the isle's coast and the left side of the Armada. There was no wind, and again it was the current that was moving everyone along. The current was faster along the shore, so Frobisher's group had caught up and was alongside rather than behind the Armada. This gave Frobisher the ability to move forward faster as if he did have the wind while the Spanish could do little more than drift. A battle ensued and Sidonia's San Martin was in the fray. The galleasses were busy with Hawkins and Howard so they couldn't help.

The wind came up a bit and now the Spanish fleet could maneuver to put up an effective fight. They bore down on the English fleet that now pulled back before they were cut off. Unfortunately, Frobisher's ship, the Triumph was too far ahead and did get cut off. The Triumph was one of the English navy's largest ship, comparable to the Sidonia's San Martin, Recalde's San Juan, or even Don Pedro's Rosario. It was a slower ship and now Sidonia was sending ships to catch it and grapple and board it. He might finally capture an English vessel, and largest one at that.

Frobisher put out his rowboats to keep him ahead of the oncoming onslaught. Other launches from shore and ships, seeing his peril, added in. Almost a dozen finally joined in with every back and muscle doing their all. Finally the wind increased with a slight change of direction and Frobisher was free to maneuver out of the Spaniard's way.

In the meantime, Howard seeing what was happening to his left fleet sent in ships to assist. Now they had wind to flank around the left crescent and squeeze the Armada away from the inlet. This shifted more Armada ships around. Recaldes's San Juan came over from the seaward side just about the time Drake was coming up to attack the extreme right tip of the crescent's defensive position with his gun's blazing. Hawkins in the meantime was nipping at their center. This caused more shifting of the Armada's fleet.

When the wind had finally picked up, Drake was able to come in and start his attack at the tip of the crescent. I was once again working the quarterdeck cannons. The first galleon was easily out gunned, and we were hitting it, but it was doing little to us. The firing was as intense as the previous battles, and no, I was not getting used to it. You never get used to it. The galleon knew it was out gunned and slithered into the arc to let a larger one take the lead in the fight.

It was broadside after deafening broadside as our fleet fought and shoved the rear part of the arc inward while splintering its side formation. All of us were getting in closer and closer to fire. This was much closer than each previous battle. The net effect was that Drake was squeezing the Armada to the north. The rest of our fleet was squeezing it to the south, keeping it from entering the bay. And we were all headed straight to the Owers. The Owers is a group of jagged rock formations both under and above the sea. The Spaniards would literally be destroyed within the hour if they didn't turn one way or the other. The wind was also shifting more from the west. The Armada would have to essentially make a U-turn and sail west to duck back into the Solent. Not possible, even with the tide in their favor.

Closer and closer we came to the Owers as the battle raged on. I, of course, had no idea where I was other than next to my cannon. Drake knew though and pressed on. Unfortunately, the Spanish had charts and pilots who knew where they were too. Sidonia fired a signal cannon and the entire Armada made a southwest turn and headed out to open sea. It was over. The Spanish were not stopping by for lunch at Wight, and they sailed on to meet their cursed Parma. Good thing too, we were running out of shot.

We had prevented the Armada from stepping foot on English soil. This was cause for celebration. We hadn't stopped them, but by the time the Armada reached Calais to try to figure out how they would pick up Parma's Army and where, we would be almost 200 ships strong. We would be joined by Henry Seymour's London fleet. So we did celebrate the next morning.

It was a beautiful Friday morning. The wind was at its usual from the southwest. This was perfect sailing weather for the Armada and us heading to the end of the Narrow Sea and destiny. It was about two days away at the Armada's lumbering rate. We were desperately trying to get resupplied by ships coming from our coast. The Spanish had no way to resupply theirs. Drake had me join him in our launch boat, and we headed to Lord Howard's Ark Royal. Several of the captains were going to be knighted by Howard, and I was going to be able to watch! Don Pedro would be there too, and he had continued to be most talkative. He still didn't know the hand I had played with his ship, and it was going to be left unsaid. Seems all my deeds were being left hushed up, but I didn't mind. As long as her Majesty or Walsingham or Drake knew, I was proud enough.

The ceremony was held on the Ark's quarterdeck as the crew looked on from the rest of the ship. Other ships were also brought in close to observe. I was one of the guests to witness the knighting with Sir Drake on the quarterdeck. He said, "Someday, I have no doubt you will be recognized and be knighted yourself."

The first to be knighted was Rear Admiral John Hawkins from the Victory. The rest followed one by one, though I don't remember in what order. Of course, Rear Admiral Martin Frobisher from the Triumph was one. Thomas Howard from the Lion was another and is related to the Lord Admiral. George Beeston from the Dreadnought was also knighted, and the one I met at Drake's party. There was also Lord Edward Sheffield from the White Bear and Roger Townshend, whose ship I do not know. All had fought gallantly just as Vice Admiral Drake and Lord Admiral Howard. I couldn't believe I was standing in their midst. Some of these knights were not nobles or lords, they were common. Sir Francis Drake and Sir Martin Frobisher started as cabin boys! As in my Ode to a Knight, it didn't matter. It was the deeds and the resolve. So I returned with Sir Drake to the Revenge and we sailed onward.

Part 6 – Hellburners

Welcome to Calais, France. It was part of England just prior to Elizabeth becoming Queen, but that's another story. It was Saturday afternoon and the Spanish fleet dropped anchor. It took only two days to reach Calais with the wind from the southwest after the Battle of the Isle of Wight. Our fleet mostly just followed, occasionally biting at their heels just to remind them we were still there. We had a productive trip meeting up with pinnaces from along the coast to resupply us. The Armada took up their usual crescent defensive formation and now faced toward the cliffs of Dover just across the channel.

We arrived and dropped anchor in Wissant Bay just short of the Armada which meant we kept the weather gage. Admiral Seymour's fleet from the North Sea tacked west against the wind and soon joined us. We were now five fleets with almost 200 ships strong. The channel is only about twenty-one miles wide and was a bit crowded with the enemy fleets just out of gunshot range of each other. I had never seen as many ships. I don't think anyone had.

"Now what?" I asked Drake.

"Well, I suppose we're going to blow the shite out of them, and send them all back to hell," Drake calmly replied. "I can get you back to London if you want. We sent a note with a dispatch once we had found you but haven't received any instructions."

I looked out over the immense number of ships all around the sea waiting for battle. "No. I think Fate has dealt the cards. I might as well see the hand through," I replied.

"I knew that," is all he said.

There was another concern. No one knew if France was still neutral. Their King Henry III was basically a hostage under the control of Henry of Guise in Blois, France waiting for word of the Armada's victory. France was close to becoming a surrogate of

Spain. Catholic King Henry III had brought peace to France after their religious wars by allowing the Protestants the right to worship. Spain and the Vatican could not accept this. Don Bernardino de Mendoza, the Spanish Ambassador to France, had orchestrated the coup. It was timed for the Armada's departure.

Mendoza had been Spain's ambassador (and spy) to England until the year 1584. He was expelled for being involved in the Throckmorton Plot to overthrow Queen Elizabeth and replace her with Mary Queen of Scots. Do not confuse this plot with the unrelated Babington Plot two years later that cost Mary Queen of Scots her head. Now Mendoza was involved in a plot to overthrow the French King. Yeh, these guys do get around. He was already sending dispatches to the Vatican reporting of a great Spanish victory. The Pope had promised Spain one million ducats when the Spanish landed in England.

So this final battle wouldn't just determine Protestant England's Fate, it would determine Catholic France's too. Spain would have the New World, Portugal, the Holy Roman Empire including the Netherlands, France and England. They would also control the Vatican through all these countries's Cardinals. You may have noticed I left out Ireland, even though it is predominantly Catholic. As I mentioned earlier, we weren't likely to trade one country's monarch for another. Of course, we probably wouldn't have much choice.

There are few days in history that determine the Fate of humanity. If England loses, there will never be English colonies in the Americas of the North. That would mean there would be no rebellion 200 years later to overthrow English tyranny that would replace Spanish tyranny. The world as you know it, would be different. *You probably won't exist.* There would still be many wars, even World Wars, but they would not be same wars you know. In the end, maybe it wouldn't make any difference for humanity.

Parma was just up the coast less than thirty miles away at Dunkirk, and finally in contact with Sidonia. Now he had to organize his army for a mad dash out of the canals across the sandbars of the Flemish coast. He had to reach the Armada in deep waters when Sidonia could get the Armada in position. There were a few wee problems with this grand carefully planned scheme. The Dutch rebels controlled the shallow waters of the coast between Parma's army and the deep waters with their "Flyboats." The Spanish or English fleet drafts were too deep to enter these waters. A fleet of Dutch flyboats under Lieutenant Admiral Justinus of Nassua, were lying in wait, ready. Phillip II and Parma did not have a fleet of armed shallow draft ships to defend against Justin. A bit of an oversight to the grand plan, don't you think?

It would be like one of those horror nature moving painting shows you can watch. You know, the one that shows some newborn critters making a mad dash across the sands to the sea, before they are devoured by predators. Why would you even watch such a thing? Parma would pack his army into barges as tight as in a slave ship. They would be in battle armor with weapons. They would not be a ninety-pound-boy, trying to stay afloat with sawdust sewn into his shirt. They would all drown.

So now, before the battle begins, we have all the chess pieces in play that will determine whether you will ever be born. Of course, I had no idea what was going on as I looked out over the sea. And essentially, neither did anyone else. Admiral Howard did not know if the Dutch fleet were in position, and if he could even count on Admiral Justin to help. Howard had five fleets with Admirals including himself. Each would pretty much fight this brawl as they saw fit. Sidonia and Parma had no idea how they were going to coordinate transferring the army, which wasn't completely ready. Elizabeth, William Cecil, Francis Walsingham, and a host of others, were frantically preparing defenses along the Thames, pretty much in a state of mayhem. And all I knew is that I had to go pee.

"Come on, get in the launch," Drake told me. It was Sunday morning.

"Where am I going?" I asked, confused.

"You're coming with me to Howard's ship for a council of war," he answered. "You might as well watch. You're a scribe and somebody will need to write down the story of this coming battle someday. It won't be me, and I know you can tell a better tale."

So we went on board the Ark, and I watched them make a plan. Drake was first to bring up fire ships, though they were all probably thinking the same. Even the Spaniards expected it. Problem was, no one had prepared any ships in advance. The first plan was to send to Dover for ships and combustibles to prepare. Sir Henry Palmer, from the London fleet, was sent to make and supervise arrangements.

Drake had done the math though. It would take too long to wait for the Dover plan. The tide would be perfect tonight. There was no time to wait. He offered one of his ships, the Thomas, to immediately turn into a fire ship. Hawkins followed with one of his own, and soon there were eight ships offered.

The captains got busy preparing the ships as a fiery present for the Spaniards. They stuffed them with anything to make them blaze. They would go in with their full sails on fire. The ship's stores and water barrels were mostly removed, but the cannons were left. They were double-shotted, so they would go off randomly and explode as they got hot enough. It was a hectic day and night of ingenuity. But by midnight, as a perfect breeze blew in with the tide, we were ready!

The Spanish feared what was coming. Fire is the worst thing on a wooden ship. Everything on a ship is flammable, from the wood, to the sails, to the men. The ships are also loaded with gunpowder. Drake and I had only discussed the dangers of drowning, and maybe being eaten at sea if the lifeboat didn't get rescued soon enough. Being burned to death or blown up had not been discussed. Sidonia had his pinnaces in position to intercept and tow any burning ships from the path of the Armada. Sidonia had left instructions that the ships were to maintain order and only temporarily move out of the way if a burning ship bore down on them. There was one catch, Hellburners.

The world's first weapons of mass destruction were introduced at the siege of Antwerp three years earlier. Parma had laid siege to the rebel capitol. He had cleverly built a platoon bridge of ships across the inlet leading to Antwerp. The bridge was fortified on either side with forts. It cut off any form of trade or relief. The Dutch fleet had tried to destroy this bridge, even using fire ships. Parma had pinnaces to grapple and tow any fire ships away. Any damage done to his bridge blockade, was quickly repaired.

With the aid of Queen Elizabeth, the Dutch built two "Hellebranders." They were designed and built by an Itallian, Federigo Giambelli. They were not built as fire ships. They were built as time bombs. One of them used a clock driven fuse and its bomb chamber was encased in brick, rock and even tombstones sealed in lead. It was innocently hidden in a wave of fire ships that the Dutch rebels sent into the platoon bridge. Most of the fire ships were caught, boarded and had their fires put out. This Hellburner drifted gently into the bridge where it met the west shore. It was even boarded to put out the deck fires on piles of wood camouflaging the weapon within.

The explosion was heard over fifty miles away as all hell broke loose! The fort blockhouse on shore disappeared with its garrison. A portion of the bridge with all its soldiers vanished. About 800 men were instantly killed. Most of them were vaporized but body parts were found more than a mile away. Parma was thrown to the ground and his page, standing next to him, was killed by the concussion. Everyone on board the Spanish Armada knew of the Hellburners. *And the Spanish knew Giambelli was in London!*

So at midnight, our eight ships were set ablaze and piloted in a perfect line across, into the Armada. Their pinnaces managed to grab two of them, and tow them off. As the remaining six sailed into the heart of the Armada, their overheating cannons started to explode. The ships sails were ablaze, and the sea was being showered in sparks, flames, and explosions. As I watched, I thought this is what it would be like to be attacked by fire breathing dragons. Everyone on the Spanish ships must have thought the same, and that El Draque was coming for them!

Part 7 – The Battle of Gravelines

Once again, we were in the dark. We didn't know what had actually happened. There was the initial blaze from our fire ships and fireworks from their cannons. There was no great fire that lit up the shores of Calais afterwards. Only the dawn's early light would tell.

It was Monday, July 29th, and the dawn did come and slowly lit up the horizon. One could slowly make out a scattering of sails to the north, and they hadn't been there the day before. As the light grew, one could see something missing to the east toward Calais. The Armada was gone! One could see wisps of smoke from the shore. These were probably the smoldering skeletal remains of burning ships. Whose ships was unknown from this range. Eight would have to be our own fire ships. How many Spanish ships had we burned?

The only Spanish ship left at Calais was one of the four cursed galleass driven by ores and sail. It had apparently been damaged when the Spanish fleet panicked and did everything they could to get away from the fire-breathing dragons bearing down on them. It was a complete route! They ran away in utter terror of the hellburners, not that there were any. They managed to scatter so fast that not even one caught on fire.

Up toward the north, the rising sun told what was to come. Five Spanish galleons stood their ground in the open sea ahead of their scattered fleet. Five galleons stood against the entire English fleet. One was Sidonia's flagship, the San Martin. Another was Vice Admiral Recalde's San Juan. Howard trumpeted the call to battle. It was time to attack the Spaniards before they could reform their cursed defensive arc. Vice Admiral Drake was to lead the charge with his fleet. We would head straight for Sidonia's San Martin.

The Spanish had started with 130 ships. Five got lost along the way from Corona. One blew up during the first battle and you already know the story of the Rosario. The English fleet, despite five engagements, had not sunk a single ship. The English fleet was now almost 200 strong. Fortunately, no English ships had been lost either, other than the eight fire ships voluntarily destroyed. The battle that was about to occur, however, did not involve all of these 300 plus ships.

The Spanish Armada, as huge as it was, only had a portion of ships for fighting. All their fighting ships had soldiers on them for warfare. They manned the guns rather than the seaman. The galleons were built for fighting and they probably had at least twenty-five of them. They had the four heavily armed galleasses, too. These were effective cursed ships. They each had twenty-eight ores on each side providing power in addition to sails. The Armada also had maybe another thirty well-armed carracks. These ships carried far more stores and supplies and were a century older technology of the galleons. The Rosario, which had only been built the year before, was built to this older design. The Armada also had over thirty of the patches, or pinnaces, for communication and transporting supplies between ships. There were also two hospital ships. The rest of the fleet was pretty much for hauling the bulk of men and supplies.

The sizes of the fighting ships varied, just as did the English. For a comparison, Drake's Revenge was a little less than 500 tons. The San Martin, San Juan, and Rosario were around 1,100 tons. Most of the galleons and carracks ranged starting around 400 tons up to the 1,100 tons for the largest. They also carried seamen and soldiers. The largest had around 150 seaman and 300 soldiers. They all had a full complement of priests.

The English fleet also had around twenty-five galleons. These did most the fighting. They ranged in size starting closer to 250 tons and went up to the 1,000-ton range. Most were more in the range of Drake's Revenge. The rest of the fleet were armed merchant vessels mostly under 250 tons and the pinnaces under 150 tons. Yes, I'm doing a lot of rounding. And I'm basing both the Spanish and English numbers on what armchair historians compiled long after those who fought had turned to dust (or seaweed.) Actually, much was known of the Spanish Armada at the time, even on the streets of London. The Spanish had boastfully published lists of their squadrons, including many of their ships and commanders. All I know is there were a hell of a lot of boats of all sizes.

The accounts of this historic battle are surprisingly lax. No one could watch the whole action from above to make an accurate report. That is, except for our Lord, and he was probably busy keeping track of incoming souls. Like the previous battles, most accounts were written from the perspective of individual captains or seamen writing about just what small portion they had seen, same as I'm doing now. Most of a full day's battle was summarized in a mere page and this would be written long afterwards. The Spanish wrote far more complete reports but were based on their own ships and rarely knew who was actually shooting at them. The English wrote very little at all.

So my story of Drake's Revenge is also probably less than a page. I was again with the cannons on the quarterdeck. The Revenge began the charge and we headed straight for Sidonia's San Martin with the rest Drake's fleet following.

I knew we were going to get close, because Drake told me, "Keep your arms and head inside the boat!" Not that I was planning on doing otherwise.

I didn't know how close, until I saw the San Martin's growing forecastle looming above us as our forward port guns fired. You know you're close when the enemy ship is casting a shadow on you! We fired our broadside and quarterdeck guns as they fired their broadside. Our cannon balls ripped through them and once again I heard the cry of the banshee. Their cannonballs also tore through us in an explosion of wood splinters, dust and smoke.

I let out a "Holy shite!" as I again remembered I was praying, just like I had in all the other battles. We reloaded and sailed on as the rest of our fleet came in close and continued firing broadsides. The San Martin didn't have a chance to reload in that short of time, so they were hit hard.

We moved on as Drake headed for the scattered Armada ahead. Now that their fleet's formation was finally broken up, Drake no doubt wanted to keep it that way. We sailed into them firing right through their fleet. We were firing from both sides and again closer than the previous battles. Their fire was not as lethal as that first broadside from the San Martin. We ran through and got beyond the north edge of their fleet. The coast line now bent to the north rather than the east. We were off the coast of Gravelines, a small sea village about halfway between Calais and Dunkirk. Drake was looking for something. He was looking to see if Parma was coming out with his army in barges to finally link up with the Armada while Sidonia held the English fleet off to the south.

The sea to the north was a beautiful site. There was nothing there! No Parma. He either had not come out, or Justin and his Dutch flyboats were making one of those horror nature shows out of Parma's barges. So we tacked back south and started blowing more shit up. After a while, I was almost in a daze. Load the cannon, fire. Load the cannon, fire. Keep your head and arms inside the boat. Pray the next cannon ball that hits the ship doesn't shatter the timber next to you and tare you to pieces. Pray there won't be screams from the men on this ship. Just pray that it comes to an end. You could hear the battle to the south. There was smoke and thunder and the screams of the banshee everywhere.

And then there was the sea and the weather. The sea got rougher. There were rainsqualls that came up. I was getting seasick. I thought I had gotten over that back in April. April, when I was all excited about going to sea with Drake. April, just before those beautiful weeks on the beaches of the Lizard. I could be there now. After all, I was right. Drake and Howard and all the rest were going to win. I could tell right now the Armada had been stopped. Now all I, we, had to do is live to tell about it.

In the afternoon, our firing was slowing down, as we were starting to run low on shot. The battle had raged most the day. Despite our efforts to keep the Armada from regrouping, they had gotten back into some kind of a formation with Sidonia's steadfast group. As the battle raged around us, time stood still for just a moment. We had just let loose a shot. There was a loud explosion and I was thrown back. Everything started turning white. I felt like I was floating, but not in the sea. I remembered talking to Father McNee and The Patrick too, but I couldn't remember when.

I was back in the cluttered study. I was writing the story about the Armada battles again with the help of the brown tabby cat on my lap. I had written many more pages since the last time I remembered being here. I was writing about the battle of Gravelines. I was starting to write about the morning's battles. Frobisher's fleet had followed ours to engage the San Martin. Frobisher had turned round and attacked with his fleet like a pack of wolves. Hawkin's fleet followed and did the same. Seymour's fleet also joined in. Galleons and carracks from the scattered Armada to the north eventually rejoined Sidonia and Recalde's five ships. A gruesome battle followed the rest of the day. Howard eventually joined in that battle too.

At the beginning of the day's battles, Howard had gone to Calais to destroy a cursed galleass, the San Lorenzo. It had been damaged during the Armada's previous night's flight. It was a peculiar battle, not to make light of it. As the four English squadrons went off to fight the San Martin and his four most stalwart ships, Howard headed to the San Lorenzo. It was lumbering along the coast like some giant multi-legged insect. On seeing Howard's approach, the Lorenzo moved in too close to shore and ran aground. It tilted up on an angle on the seaward side.

It was too shallow for Howard's ships to follow, and one other ship, the Margaret and John, also managed to run aground. The only way to take the Lorenzo was to board her with men in longboats. A heated musket battle followed and probably cost more English lives than any other battle in the fight with the Armada. The Ark Royal's Lieutenant Amyas Preston, who led the attack, was gravely wounded. I had just met him on the Ark Friday, during the knighting ceremony. The battle abruptly ended when a musket shot killed the Lorenzo's Capitano, Hugo de Moncada. Ironically, it was Moncada that had requested

Sidonia's permission to attack Howard when the Ark had been following the wrong lantern.

The Ark's crew, along with the crew of the ship Margaret and John, boarded and attacked the remaining Spanish. The luckier survivors abandoned the ship on the shore side. Howard's crew then went about looting the ship. The Privy Council and Her Majesty expected ships to be captured and their treasures taken. They actually did find a payroll of 20,000 ducats. The governor of Calais, Monsieur De Gourdan, sent emissaries to inform Howard's men that the ship and its guns belonged to the governor, but they were welcome to the spoils. Unfortunately, Howard's men tried to rob the French messengers too, and that didn't go over very well. Calais Castle opened fired with their cannons as a warning, and the English withdrew.

Howard then headed to join his other fleets that were in a heated battle with the San Martin. The San Martin, and the couple dozen galleons and carracks that eventually joined her, were mercilessly bombarded. The carnage of their soldiers and seaman was gruesome. The battle raged on as it headed toward the sandbars or shoals of Dunkirk. The wind and sea were taking the tattered Spanish fleet into them, and their ultimate destruction. Then apparently, they had their prayers answered, and the wind changed direction away from the coast. The Armada limped out to the deeper waters of the North Sea. Howard called off the attack because the English were basically out of gunpowder and shot and followed them up the North Sea.

In the end, it was a miracle the San Martin could still stay afloat. The Armada fighting ships were in pieces. Blood flowed out of their listing ports. The Maria Juan went down. The San Mateo and San Felipe were so close to sinking, that they purposely ran aground on sandbars. They were captured by Justin's Dutch flyboats. The Spanish records admitted to a thousand dead and as many wounded. The English casualties amounted to around a hundred, not many at all, unless you happened to be one of them.

Part 8 – The North Sea

The first sense to return is hearing. I heard a howling in my ears, but I couldn't decide which side was louder. It drowned out any other sounds if there were any. The next sense was that I could feel the howling rolling back and forth like the sea in my aching head. I felt nausea, and I felt dizzy. I did not want to tempt the next sense of sight. I didn't know if I wanted to stay or not. The next sense to waken was smell, and all I smelled was burnt. The burnt smell of smoke and gunpowder and hair. Then there was taste, but the only taste was that of dry. Slowly, thought and hence memory, was also slowly returning.

I remembered I was finishing writing a tale. I had written it a long, long, time ago. I didn't remember if this was still part of that tale, and whether I was still writing it now. The howling of the banshees in my head was still there, but I realized I could hear other sounds. They were the sound of the sea and the wind and the rain. The howling I heard was from in my mind. I still dared not open my eyes.

Then I heard a cabin door open. I was hoping it was Father McNee coming for me. I heard a familiar voice.

"Are you still alive?" the voice said.

'I don't know,' I answered to myself. I guess it was time to open my eyes and find out. The sense of sight was the most glorious thing. Though everything was still hazy, I could see the light filtering through the cabin windows. A lamp was starting to glow brighter and brighter. And in it, I saw the familiar face of Francis Drake.

"What happened?" I replied, as I spoke for the first time.

He raised me up a little. "Here, drink this. It's beer. I think you need one." He held the cup to my mouth, and I tried to drink. I swallowed, and I felt that I still had a body attached to my aching head. I tried moving.

"Easy, easy. How do you feel?" Drake asked. "Do you remember getting knocked out? You were delirious when you came to or dreaming the strangest dreams."

I felt the back of my head. I could feel a long tender gash. I slowly sat up. "How did I get knocked out? All I remember was being with our cannon."

"We're not sure. It's as if the cannon ball you had just fired hit one coming in. Knocked the entire gun crew down," Drake said.

"How bad were they hurt?" I asked with pleading eyes, as I started to swing my feet over the side.

"Singed everyone's hair like you. They're all right after a little stitching. The rest of our crew did remarkably well. When you got knocked over, you must have hit your head hard."

As I tried to sit up, I realized something was wrong. "What happened to my bunk?"

"Oh, that. Right after Peter put you in here, a cannon ball came whizzing through the wall and took out the bottom of your bunk. You can see the hole through the side. Peter says it lifted the bunk straight up, and then it crashed down. He thought it took a couple of his toes off." Drake said as he pointed at the wall. "You were both lucky."

I could see splinters blasted across the cabin. "How long was I out?"

"Peter picked you up from your canon right after he was able to get back up himself. He was afraid you were dead, and he brought you right here to my cabin. He thought our cannon misfired or blew up at first. He had just laid you down when a cannon ball came knocking. That's when he said you came to and started talking like you were somewhere else. What do you remember?" Drake asked.

"I'm not sure yet. It all still seems a dream. I dreamed we won. I dreamed Sidonia's ship was near sunk. I dreamed Lord Howard captured one of those cursed galleasses. I dreamed the battle's over, and the wind has blown us all past Parma's army."

"I don't know how you could know that unless you've been talking to ghosts," Drake replied with concern. "You should write it all down sometime. The last cannon ball that whizzed through my cabin was one of the last shots fired. Then we had a blinding rain squall."

"There are many ghosts and banshees out today. I think I have already written it down with the help of a cat. That's what I've been dreaming, anyway," I said. He looked at me with a very puzzled expression. I drank the rest of the beer as he offered me a biscuit. He had already been banging it against the side of the table to knock any insects out of it for me.

"How is the ship? Do we have serious damage? I heard that first broadside hit below deck. Is our hull holding?" I now asked with concern, though I just naturally assumed we weren't sinking.

"We took a lot of shot, but not one through our hull. Odd, considering we took many hits at the same range, and we were blowing holes in theirs. Our main mast is riddled good, but it's of fine Irish oak." Drake answered. I then remembered how many ancient Irish oak forests had been cut down building English ships, and how so many of the fay or fairies had lost their homes.

"Get some rest. I just wanted to look in on you. I'll have the physician check on you again as soon as he can."

"No, I've had my rest. I'm all right now. I want to go up on deck if I may, Sir. I need to feel the life of the sea and the wind. I need to clear my head of a few banshees too." And with that he helped me out onto the quarterdeck. I stood by my cannon looking out over the rolling ocean. The rain was now a soothing mist. The sea and wind around me were alive. It was in control. We were only along for the ride.

Howard had sent dispatches with the ever-faithful pinnaces to Walsingham, Cecil, and Elizabeth. If they sent him more shot and gunpowder, he could finally destroy the Armada. He also desperately needed fresh victuals and water for his crews. Now he was just following the Spaniards with nothing more than a bluff. He couldn't attack or defend against them. The Armada could still return if the wind came round, and they could still try to link up with Parma. The danger wasn't over yet.

Lord William Cecil, the Lord High Treasurer, had to find the funds to pay for the war. He and Walsingham were coordinating the incoming information and planning at Whitehall. They would report to her Majesty at St. James Palace, which is little further west of Whitehall in London. The news that the Armada had been kept from meeting Parma was, of course, a relief. The word that the Armada had been heavily damaged with many casualties was also welcomed news.

There was a sinister problem though. Howard had only taken two ships and maybe sunk up to a half a dozen after six engagements. He wasn't fighting a traditional naval war with battles on board between soldiers. He had only lost about 100 men. Normally there were much higher losses in such battles. That was expected. The pay for the crews was based on these cold expectations. Men are expected to be killed in battle.

Now Howard wanted more victuals, gunpowder and shot. The defenses for London and the Thames were mustering men of arms from throughout the kingdom. They would be disbanded the moment the danger was passed. All of these costs had to be paid for. As I had pointed out earlier, the war was going to be paid for in blood and gold. I hadn't realized at the time that gold was the dearer.

We sailed through that first night after Gravelines following the Armada, but more to the seaward side. I have no idea whose lantern we were following. The sea was rougher than I was used to. I heard one of their ships lagged behind crippled. It had tried to surrender but went down before there was a chance. Tuesday morning saw us near the Flemish Zeeland Banks and islands. We were still to the seaward side of the Armada. The wind was from the southwest, so it was blowing all of us up and toward the deadly shore. Then the Spaniards did something surprising. As beaten as they were, they stopped to turn and offered to fight.

"Are they mad?" I exclaimed. I had hoped not to fire my cannon today. Then I remembered we were almost out of shot. But there was no reason to fight. The Armada was about to be destroyed anyway. The Zeeland Banks had more shallow sandbars than Dunkirk. The wind would blow them right onto the shoals, and even if we weren't there, they couldn't escape.

We just sailed on and watched for their final destruction. They had wanted to die fighting. Every one of their ships had charts and knew what Fate awaited them. Then the wind suddenly shifted from the southwest to from the southeast. Their sails filled just in time to inch them away from the shoals and back toward deep water. Once again, they had been saved by the wind. It was a miracle, and I thought that our Lord must not be taking sides. He was just being kind and answering so many of their desperate prayers.

So we followed. The sea stayed rough and there was another council of war in the evening. Drake was agitated when he returned. It seems him and Frobisher had got into quite a quarrel. I didn't have the details, but all of these captains were a breed of independent cats. They didn't always see eye to eye. So we sailed on through the night and next day following. Some of the commanders of the privately owned ships in the English navy started slipping away, feeling the work was done. We sent more pinnaces out for supplies and to London with messages. Is anyone there, does anybody care???

The next day, Thursday, was the beginning of a new month. Another council of war meeting was held. This time, Frobisher was not included. I suppose that would indicate he had not been the winner of a quarrel with Drake. The meeting determined two items. First, Howard would send Lord Seymore and his fleet to return and guard the Thames. This was in case Parma tried to come out on his own and the Dutch weren't there to stop him. Lord Seymour was apparently furious, because he wanted to stay with the rest of Howard's fleets, in case there was another fight with the Spaniards. The other agreement was that Howard and the rest would follow the Armada as far as Scotland. Howard would put into the inlet of the Firth of Forth to try to resupply and then return home. Howard drafted a document to the Queen and the Privy Council stating this decision and had it signed by his admirals and captains present. These included Drake and Hawkins.

The next afternoon, we waved good-bye to the Spanish Armada as the wind continued to blow them northward. We did not wish them a safe voyage. We arrived in the majestic Firth of Forth. Just up the inlet was Edinburgh Castle where James VI, the King of Scotland was born. He was now twenty-two years old. He was only one when he became King, and his mother, Mary Queen of Scots, resigned. He never saw her again. She had been executed just two winters ago. King James had been raised as a Protestant. I wondered if I would ever meet him.

Part 9 – Tilbury

We put our bow into the wind to head home. Heavy storms came up the last couple days and I basically stayed in the cabin. I had gotten over being seasick, but not in this weather. Drake was going to put the Revenge in at Harwich, knowing his main mast would need replacing. It would be time for us to part. He said I was welcome to join him on future voyages if I were interested, provided her Majesty would allow. Since I was still a bit green from the recent weather, I think he suspected I had my fill of the sea. I wasn't sure myself. I doubted a life on the sea was for me, just as I had thought when I was offered a cabin boy position in Ireland,

He gave me various papers to get me back to London. He gave me a draft for a monthly allowance and introductions to some that might help my future. These introductions included having me visit and even stay where he was sending Don Pedro de Valdez.

Drake told me the general rather liked me. He also said he would like me to look in on him to make sure he was well. After all, Don Pedro would be worth over a thousand pounds in ransom. Doing a little spying on him could be useful too since he would be doing the same to us. Most important, he gave me a letter to personally deliver to her Majesty. He did not want it seen by the pence pinchers as he, of course, wanted to spend money. He wanted to take the war to Spain before they could recover and bring the war back to England. *He wanted to build an English Armada.*

We had not received any instructions regarding me after the dispatch was sent that I had been found. We did not know if I was to return to Captain Barrington, or where I was to go. Once again, I had no idea what my future was, but that was nothing new. With the area preparing for siege, security was heightened and wondering around looking like a lost alley cat would not get me to London. Drake had found me clothes that made me look more like a ship's officer, rather than a Spanish cabin boy. Those clothes were shot, anyway. I had my dagger to wear too. I was even given a hat, which blew off into the sea my first hour wearing it. We arrived in Harwich on Thursday, August 8th. From there I had papers to get me to St. James Palace with Drake's message for the Queen.

On the same day, Queen Elizabeth left St. James Palace. Her royal barge took her from London and onto meet her troops at Tilbury. She was preceded by barges with silver trumpets blowing, announcing her passing. She was followed by a flotilla of barges with lords and nobles and gentry. Most were dressed in full military peacock attire. With her in the royal barge were two of her favorites that certainly bear mentioning. One was the young Earl of Essex, Robert Devereux, Master of Horse. He was the same I met at Drake's party and told me not to be surprised if her Majesty invited me to visit as an after-hour's Alley Cat.

The other was the Earl of Leicester, Robert Dudley. He had become Master of Horse when Queen Elizabeth first became Queen. They were childhood friends and history does allege they had quite an affair. They were already older, and in their twenties at that time. I wouldn't know, as I certainly wouldn't ask the Virgin Queen about such matters. He was one of her principle suitors and would have become King of England if they had wed. There were many lords against this union, especially since he happened to be married. The only one who could grant him a divorce, was the Queen herself. That would be a bit awkward.

Of course, it ended in a tragedy, and not a wise choice for Shakespeare to use for a play. Robert Dudley's wife, Amy Robsart, died "accidentally." She fell down the stairs in the manner where she was staying. That house was conveniently vacant on that fateful evening. She broke her neck, yet her headdress was not disturbed. A formal hearing was held, and it was ruled accidental. There were conspiracy theories that Dudley had arranged it so he would be free to marry the Queen. There were also theories that William Cecil or others, had arranged it to ruin Dudley and prevent a betrothal to her Majesty. And then there was the theory that Elizabeth had it done herself.

In any event, the affair gradually simmered down, but Dudley always remained in her Majesty's heart. He eventually became the 1st Earl of Leicester and had recently been in the Netherlands trying to help lead the alliance with the Dutch rebels. That had not gone so well. Leicester was now the Lieutenant and Captain General of the Queen's Army defending London. He was in charge of her defenses and organizing the army at the fort at Tilbury. Tilbury is on the north side of the Thames close to where the river joins the inlet from the North Sea. It is maybe only twenty-five miles from London.

As word came that the Armada had sailed north over a week earlier, Leicester suggested the Queen review her troops at Tilbury. A fortnight earlier, he was in a complete panic because the countrymen called to arms were only slowly arriving from the surrounding regions. They were disorganized and somewhat in chaos. The fort had not been fortified and supplies were not in place. He had done a remarkable job in such a short time, because that's what he was good at, organizing and command. Now that things were in order and the army probably wasn't needed anyway, there was a perfect opportunity for a military spectacle. It would be one of the greatest political appearances and speeches of her Majesty's reign.

When the Queen arrived at Tilbury, she requested to see her army. Despite the constant fear of assassination attempts, she would inspect her fellow countrymen without an armed escort. An Earl, carrying the Sword of State, preceded her. Following him, were two pages in white velvet. One carried her silver armor helmet while the other led her white horse. On either side rode her two favorite Earls. One was Earl of Essex, Robert Devereux, Master of the Horse, and the other, of course, was Earl of Leicester, Robert Dudley, Lieutenant and Captain General of the Queen's Army. Following them was the Master of the Tilbury Camp, Sir John Norris. He was a soldier and another favorite of the Queen. That was her entire escort, two boys, three horses, and four men.

The Queen rode a white horse. She was in white velvet wearing a silver armor breastplate. She rode with her small escort throughout the entire camp so all could see her pass. The encampment was supposed to be a force of 25,000 men to fight Parma's army. At least that was the claim to all her countrymen and especially Spain. Historically, no one seems to know for sure, and some say it was only about 6,000 men. The army was dazzled, and their morale soared. Her Majesty loved every moment of it too. So much that she decided to do it again the next day.

In the meantime, I was on shore at Harwich. I presented my papers and, with Drake's name on them, was given a horse. Horses were as important as the army and the navy. The "Master of Horse" may not seem like that big of a title, but it was as important as Lord Admiral or Lieutenant and Captain General. The Queen's Master of Horse was in charge of all the Crown's horses across the kingdom. Every horse had to be accounted for, fed, stabled, and transported to where they were needed. There was an army of quill pushers that knew exactly where my horse Molly was down at the Lizard, and a record of when Captain Robert received her for me last April. Every lord with a stable also had a Master of Horse.

My plan was to get to London as quickly as possible and stop in at the Theatre first. That was where I had left my belongings and most of my twenty-five pounds. It would be on the way since I would be coming from the northeast. I didn't know where to find Captain Robert, or Walsingham, or anyone else for that matter. I figured I could clean up and put on one of the peacock attire her Majesty gave me. Then once presentable, I would head to St. James Palace to see her Majesty and deliver Drake's letter.

I would ride with the next messengers heading to London with dispatches. It was at least seventy miles, but I wouldn't have to worry about getting lost. We left in the afternoon and laid over at an inn about a third of the way. Word had quickly spread that her Majesty had gone to Tilbury to visit her army. No one knew how long she would be there. I wasn't likely to be able to get to the Tilbury Fort the next day since I didn't even know exactly where it was. I decided to stick with my plan and head to London. It was the longest, hardest ride I had ever done. Fortunately for the horses, the messenger escorting me arranged for fresh horses about half way. I always regretted not being able to see my Queen at her finest hour.

The Queen had spent the night at a manor house a few miles away. She returned to Tilbury Friday morning the 9th. Her Captain General Leicester had arranged a marching review, cavalry tournaments, and dining with her captains. She also spoke the words of a speech she had written. These words gave heart, ultimately to her entire kingdom. Though I did not hear them, with these words, she raised the hopes of her people.

"My loving people, we have been persuaded by some that are careful for our safety, to take heed how we commit ourselves to armed multitudes, for fear of treachery. But I assure you, I do not desire to live to distrust my faithful and loving people. Let tyrants fear. I have always so behaved myself that, under God, I have placed my chiefest strength and safeguard in loyal hearts and good will of my subjects; and therefore I am come amongst you as you see, at this time, not for recreation and disport, but being resolved, in the midst and heat of the battle, to live or die amongst you all, and to lay down for my God and for my kingdom and for

my people, my honour and my blood, even in the dust. I know I have the body of a weak and feeble woman, but I have the heart and stomach of a King, and of a King of England too, and think foul scorn that Parma or Spain, or any prince of Europe should dare to invade the borders of my realm; to which, rather than any dishonour shall grow by me, I myself will take up arms, I myself will be your general, judge, and rewarder of every one of your virtues in the field. I know already for your forwardness you deserve rewards and crowns; and we do assure you, in the word of a prince, they shall be duly paid you."

In the evening, she had returned to St. James Palace. That same Friday I continued riding to London and arrived at the Theatre by dusk. There was no play that night. There had been much excitement throughout London regarding the Queen's journey to Tilbury. I felt excitement as I walked up to the Theatre's door, I had entered through so many months ago.

Smiling, I knocked. Ellen Burbage answered and screamed as she almost fainted back. Not exactly the welcome I was expecting.

"Presto! You're supposed to be dead! Are you a ghost?" she exclaimed. Her scream must have been heard by James because I could hear him rumbling down the stairs.

"I'm a cat, remember, I have many lives. You obviously heard of the first dispatch that thought I was killed. I am sorry you didn't hear of the second message that I had been rescued. By Drake himself, I might add," I answered with a bit of a grin.

By then, James had arrived. "Presto! But, but I thought..." and he drifted off without finishing. By now Ellen was hugging me over and over.

"Captain Robert came to tell us when they had word you were killed," Ellen explained. "Then we received a letter from him that they had found your body and were sending it home. Her Majesty is planning a funeral for you when they receive it, or you, or when... She's having a head stone made up. But you're alive!"

"What?" I now exclaimed. "The dispatch was supposed to say they had found me and would send me back to London as soon as it was practical…" And I drifted off wondering if they had not included the one key word, "*Alive*."

I had told the Queen I hoped for a stone that said I wasn't an "Arshole" when my time had come. Did they interpret the dispatch that Drake was sending me home for that, rather than a burial at sea? He was there when I had said those words. By now, James was hugging me too, and we were all starting to laugh. I found out Captain Robert was still in the Queen's Personal Guard and in attendance at St. James Palace. They had received his letter from there.

They offered me some food and drink. I told them part of the stories of my adventures. The kitty, Hope, had already found me, and I don't think she was going to let me leave again, ever. I decided I should get cleaned up the best I could and head to St. James to see if Captain Robert was there, and if her Majesty had returned. I also knew they had a stable there so my horse could be taken care of properly after the hard day's ride. We had found some food and water for her though.

I asked if I could return if the Queen or Robert weren't at the Palace, and of course, they wanted me to come back if I could. With that, I headed for the Palace. It was already dark when I arrived. I presented my papers to the guards and asked if Captain Barrington was there and if the Queen had returned. She had just recently arrived, and Robert was there also. I requested they send for him, as I had a dispatch from Sir Drake to personally deliver to her Majesty. I instructed them not to tell anyone my name.

Captain Robert came down the walk most the way without recognizing me standing in my naval uniform with my pouch.

Then he slowed his approach and exclaimed, "Presto?" Then he quickened his pace and shouted "Presto!"

I bowed and let out a "Meow" and then added beaming, "Yeah, I know, I'm dead. Been there, done it, back again! Didn't you get the second dispatch? And how are you?" Then I stood there with that lovable kitten look.

We both started laughing and hugging. Then remembered we were men, stopped, and started all over again, anyway. "But I don't understand. The second dispatch said they were sending you back to us. The Queen thinks you're dead. She was quite taken when she heard you were killed," Robert replied rather excited. "How, what happened? You're alive!"

By now the other guards were totally confused but simply let us go on babbling since we weren't making sense anyway. I gave Robert the quick Veni, Vidi, Vici version of my adventures. "I forgot my rock. I tried to blow up an Armada ship. I went swimming. I broke an Armada ship. I went swimming again. Drake rescued me. I shot a cannon. And I fell off the bloody horse just before I got here. Yeah, forget about that last bit. Oh, I almost forgot being blown out of my shoes, and having my bunk blown out from under me. And I have a private letter from Sir Drake to deliver to our Queen." That's all a bit paraphrased.

"I'm taking you to the Queen right now. She's already had one of the best days. This will make it the absolute best," Robert said.

"I hope she doesn't faint and think I'm a ghost" I said.

"She's the Queen, you should have seen her today. No, she won't faint. She's no feeble woman! She's our Queen!" he exclaimed.

My horse was taken to the stables. Captain Robert led me through the palace. As we headed to her Majesty's chamber, he told me how on the day before, she had worked her way through her army like a true knight. No, like a King! Then he told me of how she inspired all with her words today. He greeted the other guards at her door and was announced. I had already surrendered my dagger. I stood at the door until he summoned me as I heard him speak to the Queen.

"Your Majesty, Lord Burghley," he began. "I apologize for disturbing you. Your Majesty, I have a messenger with a private letter addressed to you from Sir Drake. The messenger has ridden hard from Harwich, to bring you this dispatch and personally deliver it."

"Do you know if this man is true and is surely from Sir Francis?" she replied.

"I know he is true, with my life, Your Majesty," Robert answered.

"Then let him enter."

He signaled a guard to bring me forward. With a beaming grin, I strutted in like a cat with its tail held high. As I approached, her Majesty stood abruptly, as she recognized me.

She then literally ran to me saying, "Presto, Presto! My Alley Cat!" and met me halfway. Before I even had a chance to bow, she grabbed and hugged me. Her guest, who had been sitting at the table with her, rose with alarm.

"Presto, you're alive! We had a dispatch that they had found you and were returning you to us for a proper funeral. I am already having your stone made!" she exclaimed.

"Your Majesty," I replied, and finally bowed awkwardly, as she had finally released me. "The dispatch was to have said Sir Drake had rescued me and would return me to London when possible."

"But we had been told you drowned trying to signal us the Armada was sighted. How did you survive?" she asked. Then added, "Here, come sit. Do you need food, drink, what can we get you?" And with that we turned and went toward her table as her guest was just starting to come toward us.

"Oh, Spirit. I would like to introduce you to Sir Presto. He's the lad, my Alley Cat, you've heard so much of," she said.

Then she introduced Spirit to me. "Presto, this is Lord William Cecil, 1st Baron of Burghley. You have met his son, Robert."

"My Lord, I am indeed honored to meet you. And I was amazed at the wonderful collection of books you have in your library," I said with a bow.

"Yes, I have heard much of you. I understand you even wrote something in one of my rarest books." Lord Burghley replied.

"Spirit, you should give him that book as a reward for his service," her Majesty said, with an almost mischievous grin.

Burghley's face dropped briefly before I quickly replied, "Oh no, Your Majesty. That book belongs in a collector's hands. I had my time in the book's history, now it is Lord Burghley's. I do hope he reads the words of my Ode that I wrote in it so long ago." With that, his face relaxed.

She returned to her chair and we sat. She also beckoned Captain Robert to join us. Her page produced crystal goblets for some rather fine wine. She wanted the details of my adventure, but we also remembered that I had a dispatch from Drake.

Lord Burghley said, "Drake no doubt wants more funds from us."

"My Lord, you have to spend gold to spill blood. You also have to spend gold to save blood." I replied, and suddenly realized I was speaking to the Lord Treasurer.

"You know of the contents to which my Dragon writes me?" her Majesty asked.

"I was in his cabin as he wrote it. Or tried to write it as the sea was a bit rough. So I know of his thoughts and concerns, Your Majesty." I answered.

I then presented Drake's dispatch. "Your Majesty, I beg that you give full consideration to Sir Drake's words. Some of them are of an urgent matter regarding the plight of our crews who gallantly served you in the battles. They need victuals and water. Disease has already broken out on at least one ship. They need your help.

There are also words that need longer reflection. I would recommend that those will need more time to consider."

She broke Drake's seal and looked at the introduction. "You are correct, my Alley Cat. I will need time to give careful thought to Francis's words. I will set them aside until tomorrow. Now I just want to hear your tale before I retire. You shall stay at the palace tonight. I believe you enjoyed having tea with me, so we shall arrange that again for tomorrow. Captain Barrington, you will attend also. And now my Presto, tell me your tale."

I then told her my tale, the tale you have already read that I have previously set down into words. I told her of lighting the fireboat signal and ending up on the Rosario. I told her of Don Pedro and being rescued by Drake on the Revenge. I told her of being on the cannon crew through the battles of Portland and the Isle of Wight. I told her of Drake offering one of his own ships for the fire ships. I told her of the scene of the burning ships being piloted into the Armada, and finally having it scatter in terror. Then I told her of the Battle of Gravelines, and how our cannons and brave men won the victory. I must admit, it was a better performance than I ever did with the tales I would tell on the street corners of London.

It was finally time to part, as you might remember she had a rather busy, though excellent day. Her page found me quarters for the night, and I departed. She had Captain Robert stay behind as I left. I was concerned that if we were to have tea the next day, the clothes I had were getting a bit ripe from the previous couple day's ride. I had not changed at the Theatre, after all. I also didn't know when we were to meet. My questions were quickly answered in the morning when her Majesty's page presented me with fresh clothes and told me he would take me for tea in the early afternoon. He also brought breakfast. He had been my servant during the night.

The page brought me to her Majesty's chamber, and Captain Robert was already seated with her. The table already had tea and treats including that wonderful cocoa cake. There was also a nicely carved box sitting on the table. I noticed her Majesty and

Captain Robert both had a strange grin on their face they were trying to hide.

We had our tea and treats, and I told more tales of each battle. I told of all their stories, giving credit to each gallant crew and commander. After all, I just hid behind a cannon most the time. They were the ones that really fought the battle.

As we had our cocoa treat, her Majesty said, "Presto, I have something for you." And she slid the box toward me.

I didn't know what to say other than, "Your Majesty, you've been so kind already. You don't have to spoil me more."

I slowly opened the box and removed a book. I stared at it in disbelief. I opened it to page 173 and started to cry. It was my Bible.

Both her Majesty and Captain Robert just smiled proudly as I just kept repeating, "Gramercy, gramercy, so many thanks, so many thanks."

I eventually recovered to start asking questions, "But how did you get it, what became of the other lads?" I asked. Then, with pleading eyes I asked the most important question, "Did they survive?"

Captain Robert answered, "Her Majesty sent me to Swansea after we parted in Plymouth. Justice has been served. The lads have been freed and are receiving care. Thomas is alive and as brave as you. Sadly, a Liam died of the winter illness."

"I remember Liam, he was always the quiet one," I said, thinking that wasn't much of a memorial.

Robert then told his tale of his trip to Swansea, that he had arrested Powell and Crowley, and killed the two cursed dogs. He also said Lord Stevens had agreed to see to the surviving boy's education and future, for the rest of their lives. The lads had already returned to Munster and had a solicitor to insure their care. I was ecstatic. Barnett had also been found and the illegal trade of Irish orphans had been stopped. Well, at least this illegal group of them.

I thanked her Majesty and Captain Robert numerous times more, probably to the point that they wanted me to stop. Captain Robert remained part of the Queen's Personal Guard. He would be protecting her. I had enough of an allowance from Drake to find a place to rent. I wanted to go back to the Theatre and the Burbages, after all, they were really the only ones I knew. Yes, I had probably met the most important men in all of England, but of them, it was only Drake that I could probably call a friend. He would be off to sea, of course, and I didn't think I belonged there.

I hoped I could continue being an after-hours Alley Cat, and still visit her Majesty. I also did want to see Walsingham and Robert Cecil again, and even the young Earl, Robert Devereux. They might have some use or work for me. I might be able to become a real knight someday. The Queen had called me "Sir Presto" when she introduced me to Lord Burghley. Had she planned to knight me when I was dead? If I were a knight, I would go to Wales to visit "The Girl." I had not forgotten her. I will never forget her. I knew she was probably betrothed by now. I would just have to wait for another lifetime and leave it to Fate.

But Ellen and James Burbage had become more like family. Aside from Robert Barrington, they were really the only ones I could share how much having Father McNee's Bible back, meant to me. I enjoyed the playhouse. I enjoyed the words. I enjoyed the writing. I enjoyed the players and the poets. And I enjoyed writing this tale for you!

Spanish Armada

Sir Francis Drake by Marcus Gheeraerts

Epilogue – Drake is Dead

I understand a tale is supposed to have an epilogue. As this is the first tale I'm finally setting down in writing, I still am learning your norms. As you now know, I never was much on following rules. This tale is near its end because my past is still my future. I don't know the rest of my history much beyond this part of my tale. I only have a glimpse of my future in my dreams. I know what is written in history while I am writing in your time, but I don't know that history in my time, because it hasn't happened yet. Your time is not my future or my past. It's just a dream. It's all very complicated when you're a ghost, especially if you're an Irish one. As I first introduced my story to you, I wrote that I, Presto, am a ghost. And I wrote that I am writing my story from my time in your time. I meant that literally. Now that I've confused you with that bit, I can finish this next bit.

The next few months were filled with tragedies for humanity. The aftermath of a battle is always the worst. I am looking back on those months now from late that December getting ready for Christmas. I do not know what my future will be from there. My past months since stepping on shore at Harwich have been decent. I had come home whole. My worst injury to heal was probably from falling off the bloody horse just before I reached St. James. In my horse's defense, we had ridden hard all day and she just wanted some rest. The bump on my head and new bruise on my ass quickly healed. The wounds to my mind and soul will take longer.

The year before I only had bad choices to choose from to survive, and some of them tore my soul apart. This past year I also had to choose my path, and I had chosen to fight in a war. Granted, it wasn't for glory. It was to save lives in London. But at the same time, I knew it would cost enemy lives. I could not get the cries from wounded men, howling across the sea, out of my head. These were not the cries of seagulls or banshees. There were also the prisoners off the Rosario who were already dying. Suddenly, a small English port had almost four hundred men, along with women and boys, who needed food. They were the enemy who had come to kill us. Who was going to pay gold to feed them?

I always said it comes down to the math. I now saw, with crystal grim clarity, why Raleigh had been ordered to massacre the soldiers who had surrendered at Smerwick. They would starve or die of disease anyway. The only ones who would survive would be the officers, or aristocrats, who were exchanged for ransom. The Spanish had an alternative to slaughtering the common soldiers when the logistics were possible. That was to make them slaves.

I had played my part in war and it was over, at least for now. So once again, it was time to find work and let time pass to heal those thoughts of war. The Queen agreed I could go back to the Theatre and find work. James Burbage had given me shelter and food for pay, but he was a bit stingy with coin. With the allowance from Drake I could afford rent and food, but I really needed to find someone to actually pay me a wage for my labor. Walsingham might have some work for me. After all, I am a good scribe.

I had returned my horse at St James, so I was on foot. It was strange to just walk the streets of London again. It felt good. I went back to the Burbage's that afternoon with my returned Bible happy and content. I was glad to be home, for this had indeed become a home for me. I shared my relief and joy of having the only thing left of Father McNee returned. They shared my joy, as I knew they would. I also arranged for them to keep my Bible safe, just as they had kept my other belongings when I had left for Plymouth. We had a nice meal. I told them that I had an allowance from Drake, and I could afford a room to rent. I told them I would like to do some work for them, but I would likely be doing work for her Majesty, also.

They were going to give me their own room to sleep in that night, but I insisted I wanted to sleep under the balcony stairs just like the previous Christmas. I told them I needed to sleep there to put some ghosts to rest. They understood. They could tell I had changed. I wasn't a boy anymore, but I did snuggle with the cat, Hope, that night.

The next morning, I headed out hunting for a room and checked where Captain Robert and I had stayed previously. They were just evicting someone who had the very same rooms. I could have it the following afternoon. I spent the rest of the day just walking around London. I wondered if I could find Jack again. James had told me how Jack had come to them, and about the now humorous tale of his earlier encounter with Shakespeare. They told me he was trying to learn to read. He usually came by to see if there was any work when they had a new play. Shakespeare was going to be acting in their next play. It was written by another poet, though.

I finally headed back to the Theatre. I was also listening for any news of the Armada. Then I heard that Drake had been killed. I couldn't believe it. How was it possible? Where and when? The Armada couldn't have come back. Was it a storm? Did he get yellow fever like what was breaking out on some of the other ships? I anxiously tried to get more information. I had been fortunate, I hadn't lost anyone close in the battles. Now I knew what it must feel like for the thousands of English and Spanish wives and mothers and fathers, who waited for word of whether their husband or sons were going to return.

It wasn't like I could wonder into Whitehall looking for Walsingham to find out. I didn't know exactly where he was, or if he had word yet I was alive. I'm sure he had a good laugh when he did. There was only one person I could ask. The Queen. She had said I could come after hours if I needed to see her. So, after a frantic day getting different stories off the street, I went to St. James Palace to see if she would see me.

The imminent stress of the invasion had passed, and she was soon going to get away for a hunting trip. That evening, like so many others, she was just trying to get the weight of the last weeks out of her mind. She did welcome me, though it was rather late. She already had her mask off and saw that I was almost frantic with tears.

She immediately set my fears to rest. Drake wasn't dead or captured. The Spanish, French or Vatican didn't know what had happened. The last they knew was that there was a battle at Gravelines and everyone sailed off into the sunset. They didn't know who had won, or where they went, or if they were coming back. Rumors of all kinds worked their way first to Paris, where Spain's Ambassador Mendoza, the architect of the French coup, sent dispatches to Phillip II and the Vatican. He reported of any news of Spanish victories, true or not. Paris was Catholic, and celebration services were to be held as soon as Parma's army set foot on English soil.

The stories he passed on included Drake's demise, destruction of the English fleet and even the invasion of England. The stories were printed in Paris leaflets. Pope Sixtus V was already being squeezed for the first 1,000,000 ducats for Spain. It would be a couple of months before the true grim aftermath would be known. It was a total tragedy on both sides.

For the Spanish, the winds of Fate never gave them a chance to turn back. Their course was set. They would proceed around the top of Scotland and then the west coast of Ireland the long way home. They did not know these coasts. They had little food or water. Their damaged ships were held together by twine. They had cut their anchors in their panic to get away from the Hellburners. They had nothing to hold their ships against the storms. And, as the English put it, "a Protestant Wind" blew them to destruction with the worst weather imaginable.

Ship after ship crashed into the rocky shores or just went down with the storms. Those who made it to shore where massacred just like Smerwick. No beheading this time, mostly musket and sword. There were claims the wild barbaric Irish did much of these massacres to rob them. But let's face it, who had the muskets and swords? In the meantime, disease and famine were more than keeping up. Sometime in October, when no more ships were coming home to Spain, the full magnitude of the defeat sunk in. Only about half the Armada's fleet made it home. The battles had cost around 1,000 casualties and about the same wounded. The total losses by the time the last ship of the Armada entered a Spanish harbor was over 20,000. More would die on shore. Vice Admiral Recalde died four days after safely bringing his battered ship, San Juan and crew, home. Sidonia returned to his orange groves and never saw his King again. Don Pedro's cousin, who had told Sidonia to abandon the Rosario, was thrown in prison.

The English did not fare any better. They had not lost a ship other than the ones burned as fire ships. They only had about 100 battle casualties. Yet in the coming next couple months, at least 5,000 died. The ships were held out to sea for the possible return of the Armada. They were not resupplied with victuals, fresh water, or beer. The ships were kept commissioned. Many were kept in port while men died. Disease had already broken out before the first ship had even made it to Harwich.

Despite the cries of Howard and Drake and Hawkins, the plight of the fleet was abandoned by London. The Privy Council and Burghley, the Lord Treasurer, wanted to know why the English fleet had not boarded and captured more ships. And Gold. Though the Armada had been stopped, the English fleet was not given a hero's welcome. Howard, Drake, Hawkins and other officers set up a relief fund for the surviving seaman out of their own pockets. I would not learn of these tragedies until later in the year.

I went back to the Burbages the morning after my evening visit with her Majesty. I was greatly relieved that Drake was, of course, alive. There would be a play the following week and rehearsal would soon begin. The Theatre would soon be transformed into the mayhem I had relished what seemed another lifetime ago. I was looking forward to seeing Shakespeare again. I asked if there was anything I could do to help before I set out to move into my rented rooms. James gave me the play to read in case he needed help later with the writing. I then had company before I left.

A messenger arrived looking for me with a dispatch from Whitehall. It was from Walsingham. He wanted to see me at the Gatehouse the following noon. He was going to send Captain Robert to take me there. The Gatehouse was not exactly the place I would normally go to on my own and simply knock on the door. But I wasn't concerned. I had survived Topcliffe before and now the Spaniards. With luck, maybe Walsingham will have some work for me that pays.

The next day Captain Robert came for me. I had gone back to the Theatre in the morning after settling into my rented rooms the evening before. It felt strange being able to afford my very own place to stay. I was dressed in the officer's clothes Drake had found for me along with my kid's sword. Robert rode up with his horse and brought the one I had from Harwich. We headed for the Gatehouse.

As we rode, Captain Robert said messengers were sent from St. James with dispatches and would then return with ones from Whitehall. He said one messenger had told him of telling Walsingham that the Queen's Alley Cat had returned. He said it was quite amusing. Walsingham was actually with Topcliffe at the time getting a report on possible Catholic rebellions. There had been the fear the very signal lights that announced the Armada's sighting would be the call to arms for a Catholic uprising. As it was, there was no rebellion. It appears I was right, most English Catholics feared King Phillip II far more than Queen Elizabeth.

At first, Walsingham thought the messenger was referring to my remains. Topcliffe also knew my nickname, and gleefully offered to find a ditch and some lye to cover me.

The messenger clarified his dispatch, "My Lord, you must misunderstand. Her Majesty's Alley Cat visited her last night after riding in from Harwich."

"Who exactly do you mean?" Walsingham asked confused. "What Alley Cat?"

"They said you would understand. Her Majesty has only one Alley Cat, my Lord," the messenger had answered.

The messenger said Walsingham started laughing, while apparently Topcliffe knocked something over.

We were escorted by the Gatehouse's Captain of the Guard, to the very same room and table I had met Topcliffe at in March. Captain Robert was armed, of course, and I wore my dagger. Walsingham was already there and rose to greet us and just shook his head in disbelief.

"It appears you do have nine lives," he said smiling. "You might consider conserving some of them."

"I'll not argue that point, My Lord," I replied with a grin. Then with all sincerity, I added, "I want to give you so many thanks for sending Captain Robert to save the lads in Swansea and find my Bible. You don't know how much it means to me."

"Well, that is the least we could do for the loyal services you have done for our Queen. You can send word to the lads through their solicitor in Munster who takes care of their affairs. They will be happy to hear you are not a ghost again."

We had the informalities of some rather fine wine and cheese. I again told the story of my adventures and was getting better at it each time. Some would find my tale beyond belief, but Walsingham knew Fate tended to make my adventures unbelievable.

Francis Walsingham had summoned me because he wanted to have a more candid written report on the battles with the Armada. The dispatches he had received had too many disconnected pieces. He thought I might give him a clearer picture. Walsingham said he would likely find other work for me too. I told him about the false reports that I heard were spreading. That led to the idea of a task to sort all the news coming in, and what lies the Spanish were telling. I would not be the only one assigned to this task.

He left to attend to other business at the Gatehouse that was clearly none of my business. He left me with Captain Robert at the table, and I set about writing a chronicle of the events. A little later, the Captain of the Guard returned, followed by none other than Topcliffe.

Topcliffe's face was livid as he saw and approached me. "What is that doing in here?" he asked with cold malice in his heart.

Guess he's still holding a grudge I thought as I answered in my sweetest Irish brogue, "The same thing you're likely doing. I am here in the service of Her Majesty and Lord Walsingham. I assume that is why you're here too? May I offer you some wine or cheese?" I stood as I gestured to the wine and Robert also rose.

"This time you will not trick or escape me," Topcliffe said angrily as he placed his hand on the top of his sword's hilt.

Captain Robert stepped forward pulling his much heavier sword halfway out of its scabbard. "There will be no threats directed at Master Presto. You best remove your hand from your sword." The other captain froze.

"You dare threaten me? I am Sir Richard Topcliffe. I am the Queen's chief interrogator. How dare you raise your sword against me!"

"And I am Captain Barrington of the Queen's Personal Guard. Anyone who threatens this lad commits treason in the eyes of Her Majesty. I will cut down anyone who threatens him harm. Do you understand, Sir Topcliffe?" Robert replied forcefully.

I quickly interrupted as I looked directly at Topcliffe, "Let us remember we all serve Her Majesty and are on the same side to defeat the Spaniards. You and I will no doubt be archenemies for life. But we will have to make truce between us in order to serve our Queen." I paused and then calmly continued. "You're not going to be able to kill me unless you want your head taken off. And that will not do the Queen we both serve any good. So thank you Captain Robert for clearing things up for Sir Richard, but your sword will not be needed. May I suggest we all toast our Queen with this exceptionally fine wine? And celebrate our victory over the Armada that I am now writing my report on for Lord Walsingham."

Topcliffe and Robert's eyes remained locked as Topcliffe withdrew his hand and Robert gently slid his sword back in place. I retrieved two more cups from the fireplace mantle and poured four cups from the bottle we had shared earlier with Walsingham. I directed the cups toward both captains and Topcliffe. "Now that we have an understanding, may I propose we now toast our Majesty," I said eloquently as I picked up my cup.

Topcliffe couldn't very well refuse a toast to her Majesty. He and the captains picked up their cups and raised them. Topcliffe then added, "And death to all Catholic traitors."

"And Protestant traitors too," I quickly added as we drank the toast.

"Some time we should talk privately Sir Richard," I said diplomatically. "I know that secrets are always of interest to you. There are secrets you are not aware of that we share. We have both done harm to each other, but I think the ledger is balanced. It would not be the first time adversaries put their differences behind for the good of their Queen." I had spoken these words in the hopes Topcliffe could control his hatred, especially when we had the misfortune to breathe the same air in a room together.

Before he could answer, Walsingham returned and saw our four cups and empty wine bottle. "Ah, I see you're all playing nice. No heads on the floor, good. Very good. Richard, I was hoping you would be here and know you are not to even think about harming the Queen's Alley Cat," Walsingham said looking at Topcliffe.

"And Presto, I know you have quite a tongue, but there is a time when you need to show respect. We all serve our Queen. Do I make myself clear?" Walsingham asked as he looked at both of us.

"Yes, my Lord. You know I am here to serve Our Majesty and to defeat the Spaniards. And you know why. Gramercy," I replied.

Topcliffe gave a slight bow to Lord Walsingham, "As you wish, and if I may, I have work to do for *Her* Majesty." He again gave a courteous bow and left.

I went back to writing my report. The tension in the air cleared and Captain Robert and I had a bit of a laugh once we were alone. He would return to his duty to protect his Queen. I would work at the Gatehouse when they received dispatches that were newly translated papers to review and summarize. I also worked at the Theatre. I was supposed to receive pay for my work, but for some reason, it never came. Oh well, the allowance from Drake did come as a regular draft. He said I was due something for being the first on board the Rosario. He had made arrangements through his friend, the Earl of Essex, to use his solicitor Sir Francis Bacon. I could hear Fate laughing at the irony of having Bacon working for me.

It would soon be the Queen's birthday. There would be big celebrations while few would know what horrors were occurring on our ships at sea. I didn't expect to be invited to any of these parties with the lords and nobles, nor did I have gold to find a gift. The best her Alley Cat could possibly do, would be a dead mouse, maybe in an ornate box. She would see the humor in that, but I decided best not to.

I decided the best present I could give would be my words. I would write a letter again thanking her for her kindness to me, that I thought she was the grandest of all Queens and wish her my best. But there was grief for the Queen. Her beloved "Eyes," the Earl of Leicester, Robert Dudley, died in early September. This was just a couple days before her fifty-fifth birthday. She did not come out her chambers for days and did not want to see anyone. There were no celebrations.

I certainly didn't know what to say or do. I felt I wouldn't belong there now anyway. So I wrote a second letter expressing my sympathy. It wasn't as good as my birthday greeting, and I didn't know if I should send either of them. I worked at the Gatehouse going through and sorting all the reports coming in on the Armada and our fleet. I organized what we knew was true and what was being written that were lies. Much of the lies were at the hand of Mendoza. I became horrified as other reports of what was happening to our seaman also became grimly clear. I was empty inside. How could we have stood back and let our own men die? Her Majesty was still grieving over her Leicester, and I don't think she understood or believed what was really happening. It was already too late for those who had perished.

It was now December. I would spend Christmas again with Ellen and James Burbage. Her Majesty would spend hers at Richmond Palace. She was again our strong Queen, but still privately mourning. I did not know when I would see her again. My last late-night visit, begging her for news of Drake, might have been the last opportunity. I suppose time will tell with the coming year. I hope to eventually visit Drake and also Don Pedro.

There was one event in December worth mentioning. You'll remember I had related the Spanish Ambassador Mendoza and the French Duke Henry of Guise were busy overthrowing the French King Henry III. They had him under their control at the Chateau de Blois. He had somehow managed to flee from Paris the night of the coup, and found refuge in Blois, France. The Duke, however, was slowly forcing the French King to agree to Spain's and the Pope's will. The Duke had become Lieutenant General and, in effect, was in charge of the country. They also wanted to change the King's heir from his Protestant cousin, Henry IV. Spain and Pope Sixtus V were arranging for Cardinal Charles de Bourbon to become the next King. All they had left to do was to get the King to remove Henry IV from the line of succession.

Well, it appears the young King Henry III wasn't quite as impotent as they all thought. On our December 13th, the King arranged a meeting with the Duke of Guise in the council room where his brother, Cardinal Louis of Guise, was already waiting. The King cleverly maneuvered the Duke for a private meeting first. They met in a private room next to the King's bedchamber without the Duke's personal guards.

It was like a scene out of Shakespeare's yet to be written Julius Caesar. The King's royal guards were waiting for Guise with their knives. They stabbed him as the King calmly watched. His brother, Cardinal Louis, was executed later that day. So much for Phillip II and Mendoza's plot. The news had reached us within days. It pays to be one of the first to review foreign news at the Gatehouse. Well, I haven't actually been paid yet.

It is now a clear crisp December eve. It has been a good day ending with a fine meal with friends. I know my tale is finally done because I've not yet lived tomorrow. I've not found any reference to me in your modern times, so I know not what happens to me next. Apparently, I will not become Principle Secretary. I am back in my room with a warm hearth and a warm kitty on my lap I named Tiger after a most noble cat. Of course, a stray from the streets outside my window has claimed me for his own. He sleeps on my lap now as my guardian angel. I have been writing these final words the old-fashioned way, with a quill. I have set it down happy in the thought I am finally finished. I know not if my spirit is actually writing this tale with your magical devices a long, long, time from now. Only you will know by reading it. I am ready for sleep and sweet dreams, and the days of unknown adventures that lay ahead.

I stare at those last words I wrote with quill so long ago on this glowing parchment behind the glass. It is late, and I feel my kitty, Rose, on my lap. She is telling me it is time for rest. I am happy with these final words too, especially since my keyboard scribe has been kind tonight. I look forward to the dreams that lie ahead and the coming times with "The Girl" who has long been with me and this kitty.

I have closed my eyes in both times to sleep. I have dreamed parts of many dreams in both times. I see that I am alone, and I have grown old. I see by a long-burned candle, that I am in a prison. I recognize this prison and know exactly why I am here. It is almost dawn as I can see an ever so slight glow wrapping around the windows. The unstoppable morning of my execution has come to bring me sunlight.

I am in Dublin Castle. The charge is treason once again, though that makes little matter. I have been fighting a rebellion both with and against English soldiers for years. Aye, it's a bit complicated. I fight for our King, Charles II, against the cruelty and treason of the curse of Cromwell. One of his captains has long hunted me all this time and has finally won. Took him bloody well long enough. He has done something rather clever though. He has never been able to prove treason and he doesn't want to make me a heroic martyr. That would matter little, there are so many these days that no one can keep count. Instead of sending me to the block to be chopped up for treason, he has worked out a different charge with the Viceroy of Ireland. He has convinced the Viceroy to burn me at the stake for practicing witchcraft. Being a Catholic and a warlock will be my crime.

They know it's not true, but it will make for such a grander spectacle. Funny thing is, it's maybe not totally false. I have long had dreams of my Druid Prince Enros. He had inherited the "sight" of his Nephilim ancestors. He knew how and when his Nephilim spirit would leave him. He was taught to love our Savior by The Patrick himself. But he was also taught a few secrets by a Druid Wizard. I have read of tales of this wizard, wrongly named Merlin, in romantic stories of old. Tales I read as a boy in Father McNee's library. Someday, I should finish writing the tales of my own Prince Enros for all to read.

I have even confessed to practicing magic. I had to. It wasn't due to a threat of torture. I've been tortured before. I'm too old to be tortured now. The captain knows my bones wouldn't take it, and I even taunted him to try. No, as you can already tell, he is far more evil and cursed than that. There was a boy, Ayden, a common thief, in the cell next to mine. Like me, he is also an orphan. He is about the same age as the boy in London who now sleeps and is dreaming this very same dream. The cursed captain gave me a simple choice. One way or the other, he's going to take me to the stake. He threatened to have the boy in the cell join me as an accomplice, unless I confessed to practicing witchcraft. Or he could let the boy, Ayden, go free. My choice. He has taken the boy away with him.

Oh well, I know the end. Now it is time to finally play out this dream as the sun's glow slowly burns another night away. It is time to see what is really *beyond the veil*. This dream, is the one that first haunted me as a terrified boy in a stormy graveyard long ago. I dreamt it before I ever met the Queen, or Drake, or all the others. Deep down, I have always known it will end this way. But I have outsmarted my enemy in one, well, two ways.

First, I sent him on a fool's errand to find a stash of useless rusty guns hidden in a dried up well. The cursed captain, who so wants to delight in my screams, will not return in time. Second, the guards are my friends. As a Knight, even though I am condemned, I do have some privileges. At least I convinced them of that. They have been kind enough to give me two kegs of strong ale to enjoy my last night. I have already put half a one away, and now am going to quickly down the rest. By the time I get to the stake, I won't be feeling a thing. I might as well try to go out with a bang. Already I'm starting to giggle. Maybe I can just blow the flames out. It might even rain. I am actually grateful for one more grand adventure. Beats waiting for my bones to wither.

"Meow."

"Oh, hello. Have you come to see me off? I can only give you one more pet. You're such a special kitty. Have you been my faithful P'uca all this time? Let me now gaze again into your knowing green eyes. I think I hear the guards stirring and it will soon be time to go. Will you stay close so I can be in your eyes at the end? Don't be sad. I'm kind of looking forward to once again seeing all the past ghosts of my life. I know what heaven brings too. There are so many books and theories and ideas of what heaven is like, but it's really so very simple. It is just one fateful word. It is the word our Savior tried to teach us above all others - *Kindness*."

So with that word of "*Kindness*," I close the glowing parchment I have written my words upon. The glass window now glows with the artwork I have made for the cover of this tale. I look deeply into my ghost's haunting green eyes as they stare back out at me, and now, *You*.

Presto, the Queen's Alley Cat, is now available as an audiobook performance on Audible Books.

I hope you will enjoy my next adventures in:
Ghosts of Presto.

Acknowledgements

Those who helped the tale be told:

Presto — Ghost

Gary Baloun — Ghost Writer

Sherry Baloun — Loving Muse and "The Girl"

Millie — Spirit Kitty Muse and Guardian Angel

Rose — Kitty Muse and Keyboard Warmer

Paisley Rose — Scottish Muse and Fine Author

Patricia Coughlin — Irish Muse and the Finest Grammar Editor

Jennifer Vivian — Scottish Muse with a drop of Irish blood

Linda Barrington — Excellent Grammar Instructor

Finian Schwarz — Finest Talented Audio Book Performer

Books:

The Armada, by Garrett Mattingly, 1959.
The finest and most accurate book written on the Spanish Armada!

Literary adventure tales preformed on moving paintings:

Sir Francis Drake, Eistree Studios, England, 1961-1962
Terence Morgan as Sir Francis Drake, my hero!
Michael Crawford as John, the Cabin Boy. He also can sing a pretty good tune.

The Scarecrow of Romney Marsh, Walt Disney Productions, 1963
Patrick McGoohan masterfully as Dr. Syn. Vicar by day, smuggler by night.

Fighting Prince of Donegal, Walt Disney Productions, 1966
Elizabethan Ireland seeking her freedom.

Will, TNT, 2017
Lukas Rolfe, talented actor as Will's Presto. Well done!

Harry Potter by J. K. Rowling, Warner Brothers 2001 - 2011
A tale worth telling, a tale well told, especially if read by Jim Dale.

Flash Gordon, Universal Studios, 1936
Buster Crabbe as Flash Gordon. If Francis Drake had a Rocket Ship …

Zorro, Walt Disney Productions, 1957 – 1959

The Addam's Family, Filmways Inc, 1964 – 1966
For a bit of grim humor.

The Munsters, MCA Television, 1964 – 1966
For a bit of silly humor.

Jojo Rabbit, Taika Waititi, 2019
Roman Griffin Davis, talented actor as Jojo. Incredible tale of mirth and tears.

Plays:

The Tragedy of Julius Caesar, William Shakespeare

Love's Labour's Lost, William Shakespeare
"Veni, Vidi, Vici."

Hamlet, William Shakespeare
"To be, or not to be."

Richard III, William Shakespeare's Prince Edward:
"But come, my Lord; and with a heavy heart, thinking of them, go I unto the Tower."

Presto's P'uca

Made in the USA
Monee, IL
03 January 2023